# GIRL UNKNOWN

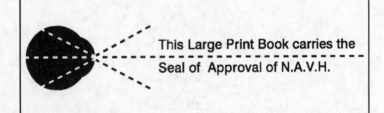

This Large Print Book carries the
Seal of Approval of N.A.V.H.

# GIRL UNKNOWN

## KAREN PERRY

**THORNDIKE PRESS**
A part of Gale, a Cengage Company

Farmington Hills, Mich • San Francisco • New York • Waterville, Maine
Meriden, Conn • Mason, Ohio • Chicago

Copyright © 2018 by Karen Perry.
Thorndike Press, a part of Gale, a Cengage Company.

**ALL RIGHTS RESERVED**
Thorndike Press® Large Print Thriller.
This is a work of fiction. All of the characters, organizations, and events portrayed in this novel either are products of the author's imagination or are used fictitiously.
The text of this Large Print edition is unabridged.
Other aspects of the book may vary from the original edition.
Set in 16 pt. Plantin.

**LIBRARY OF CONGRESS CIP DATA ON FILE.**
**CATALOGUING IN PUBLICATION FOR THIS BOOK**
**IS AVAILABLE FROM THE LIBRARY OF CONGRESS**

ISBN-13: 978-1-4328-4917-7 (hardcover)

Published in 2018 by arrangement with Henry Holt and Company

Printed in the United States of America
1 2 3 4 5 6 7 22 21 20 19 18

# GIRL UNKNOWN

# PROLOGUE

The water is cold but there is a promise of heat in the early morning air. It will not be long before sunlight reaches the garden. Insects buzz and rustle in the undergrowth, the scent of lavender drifts from pots on the terrace. Drips roll from the edge of the diving board, making lazy plopping sounds as they meet the rocking surface of the pool.

A seagull landing on the wall casts a beady eye downward into the water, scouting for food, or maybe just curious. The drips from the diving board slow.

The bird surveys the garden, the squat silent house beyond, shadows on the terrace. It raises a wing and with its yellow beak jabs at its feathers, rearranging them. It straightens up, folds back its wing.

Something in the water rolls — or rather someone. [The watchful seagull blinks.] The water darkens. A figure submerged, a face tilted, the mouth open but no shining thread of bubbles.

That sound — the *drip-drip* of blood hitting the slick surface of the pool before moving slowly through the blue-green water, mingling until it disappears.

# PART 1

# CHAPTER 1
## DAVID

I should, I suppose, go back to the beginning — to the first time we met. The first time she spoke to me, to be precise, for I had seen her before — spotted her among the first-year faces staring out at me from the lecture hall. It was hard not to notice her, not with that hair. A great glow of it, radiantly blond in long loose curls like a soft release of breath. In the dimness of Theater L, it caught the light and reflected it back, golden and iridescent. I noticed the hair and the bright moon-shaped face beneath, and I thought: *new penny.* Then my mind turned back to my slides.

There is an energy on campus during those first weeks of the new semester that is like nothing else. The air is charged with the frisson of possibility. A cheerful busyness takes hold, giving a new life and sheen to every faded surface, every jaded room. Even the most hardened staff veterans have a spring in their step for that first month, and there is a sense of hopefulness that's infectious. Once the madness of Freshers' Week has worn off, and the pace of lectures and tutorials has been set, a briskness falls onto campus like a flurry of autumnal leaves. It zips through the corridors and stairwells, hurries across the wide-open spaces where the students gather to talk and drink coffee. I felt it too — the beat of possibility, the urge to get a head start on the year. After seventeen years working at this university, I was still not immune to the buoyant lift of first-term energy.

It was a couple of weeks into the semester when she approached me. I had just given my Thursday morning lecture on modern Irish history and the students were filing out from behind their desks, a buzz of conversation rising as they climbed the steps to the exit. I was closing my laptop and putting away my notes, silently calculating whether I had enough time to go to the common room for a coffee, when I felt someone's presence and looked up. She was standing across from me, holding her folder against her chest, her face half hidden behind the long golden strands of her hair.

"Dr. Connolly," she said, and immediately I caught the hint of a Belfast accent.

"Yes?"

"I was wondering if I could talk to you?"

I slid the laptop into my bag, fixed the strap over my shoulder, and noticed a kind of wariness hovering behind the big round eyes. She was fair-skinned and had a scrubbed-clean look about her unlike so many of the female students who come to class layered in makeup, a miasma of chemical smells surrounding them. This girl was different — there was a freshness and a simplicity to her appearance that set her apart and made her appear terribly young.

"Of course," I said briskly. "I have a meeting in a few minutes, but you can walk with me, if you like."

"Oh. No, that's okay."

Disappointment, a faltering expression that piqued my interest.

"Perhaps some other time," she said.

"My office hours are on Fridays between three and five. You're welcome to drop in. If that doesn't suit, you can always e-mail to arrange an appointment."

"Thank you," she said politely. "I'll do that."

We walked together up the steps to the exit, not speaking, an awkwardness between us.

"Well, good-bye then," I said, checking

my watch and ducking into the drift of students heading toward the stairs.

By the time I reached my meeting, I had forgotten her. Funny, recalling it now. Such a momentous thing, our first meeting. Since then, I've come to look at that moment as the point in which my life split — like a page folded over and creased down the middle so everything fell into before or after.

My office is on the third floor of the Arts Block. It's covered with book-filled shelves and framed prints: the 1916 Proclamation, prints of two William Orpen sketches from the trenches in World War I, a framed and faded photograph of my grandfather with others from the Royal Dragoon Guards, and finally a cartoon from the *New Yorker* featuring two academics squabbling — the last, a gift from my wife. There's also a family photograph of the four of us hiking the Hell Fire Club in the Dublin Mountains that I had taken with my phone last summer: Holly's hair is wind-tossed, Robbie is grinning, and Caroline's eyes are watering — we look happy, individually and as a family, my arms circling us all in a messy embrace, the city and suburbs, this campus and office, a distant blur in the background.

The closest thing I can see of that outside world and the most appealing feature of the office is the window that takes up the entire southern wall and looks out onto the courtyard at the heart of the building. A small copse of birch trees grows there, and throughout the year I like to look out onto the changing colors of the leaves and watch the passage of the seasons.

I've spent my entire adult life — apart from three years working for my PhD at Queen's University, Belfast — on this campus. I've loved every minute of it and I considered myself lucky to be here, gradually moving up the ranks from adjunct to associate professor, and I love the interaction with students at lecture and seminar level. I love the curious and inquisitive minds I meet, the irascible and sometimes irreverent arrogance of the students' interrogations of the past. I'll admit I was ambitious, and I've had to work hard. It's not like things came easy for me, not like others who seem to have a natural flair for reading the past. My work was painstaking, but it brought its pleasures.

Even so, she arrived at a special moment of opportunity in my career. My old teacher and the head of our department, Professor Alan Longley, was due for retirement in two years' time. He had hinted strongly on more than one occasion that his position could be mine — if I played my cards right, so to speak. Of course, head of department would mean more work, but I was ready for the extra responsibility and willing to accept the challenge. Such was my life: the happy construction of work I had built around me, until last autumn, that is.

Back then, during those weeks in September, as the light changed and the air took on the first chill, I knew next to nothing about her. Not even her name. I don't think I thought about her again until that Friday afternoon when I held my student hours. The first of them began trickling in shortly after three — a second-year student wanting to discuss his essay, a final-year student already nervous about the prospects of graduation, another considering a master's. One by one they came, and I found I began to search for *her* among them, each time expecting to see her bright moon-shaped face appearing around my door.

In my office, there is a low coffee table and two small armchairs I brought from home and this is where I conducted my meetings with students. I don't like the power imbalance when I sit and stare at them from behind the desk. I kept the door open throughout these meetings, with both male and female students alike. You see, years ago, when I was a junior lecturer, a colleague was badly stung by an accusation from a female undergrad who claimed he had molested her in his office. I remember at the time being shocked; he was such a weedy guy with an unattractive habit of sniffing continuously while concentrating on a point. Strange though it may sound, I couldn't imagine him having any sexual desires. Most academics are normal people, leading their lives in the manner of any professional person. Some, however, are cloistered, ill-equipped to cope beyond the protective confines of the university. That was Bill, a hardworking historian, but naive, it has to be said. Not an unkind man, and quite gentle really, and the accusation hit him like a rocket. Overnight, he became this wild-eyed loon, determined to proclaim his innocence, often at the most inopportune moments — in school meetings, in the staff room over coffee, once at an Open Day. The claims were investigated by the disciplinary board and deemed to be unfounded. Bill was exonerated. The student graduated and left. Bill continued with his work, but a change had come over him. He no longer came for coffee with the rest of us, and he avoided all social interaction with students. It was no surprise when, a year later, he announced he had taken up a position at a university abroad. I've no idea where he is now, though I think of him from time to time, whenever some other scandal erupts on campus or when I feel the weight of some female student's gaze a little too heavily upon me.

Something about the way she had looked at me that day, the way her voice had faltered, made me think of Bill. I was curious, but wary too. The doe-eyed ones, the ones who look young and innocent, they are the ones you have to be careful of. Not the savvy girls with their Ugg boots and fake tan — they can hold their own and have little interest in pursuing a man like me. I'm forty-four years old, the father of two children. I eat well and I exercise regularly. Most days I cycle to work, three times a week I swim. I try to take care of myself, you could say. Now, I'm not the best-looking man in the world, but I'm not the worst. I'm just shy of six feet with dark hair, brown eyes, and sallow skin. My dad said we had Spanish blood flowing through our veins: "From the sailors on the Armada, shipwrecked off the West of Ireland all those years ago." I don't know if that's true or not. But after what happened to Bill, I have to presume it's not beyond the realm of possibility that an impressionable young student might develop a crush. But I've been married seventeen years, and I was aware how costly a stupid mistake could be. Besides, I had too much to lose.

I suppose that's what flickered across my mind the first time we spoke. Her reluctance to walk and talk with me — as if the weight of whatever she wanted to discuss required privacy, silence, the full focus of my attention.

That Friday, I fully expected her to come to my office. She didn't. I have to admit I was disappointed. There was no explanation — not that I needed or expected one. Nor was there an e-mail seeking an appointment. The following week, I did see her again in my lectures, her eyes fixed on the notebook in front of her, but when the hour was up, she filed out of the theater with the other students.

The matter went clean out of my head, and would, I'm sure, have been forgotten about in time. I was busier than ever, juggling my lectures and research along with various other work commitments, not to mention all the administration I had to do. I would also be talking to various media outlets about the 1916 centenary celebrations in the coming months. Caroline had started a new job. Between us we shared the school drop-offs as well as the kids' after-school activities. Life was full. I was busier than ever. I was happy. I know that now.

Then, one afternoon, in October, returning to my office from a school meeting, I found her sitting on the floor next to my door. Knees drawn up, hands clutching her ankles. As soon as she saw me, she got to her feet and pulled at her clothing.

"Can I help you?" I asked, my hand searching in my pocket for the key.

"Sorry. I should have made an appointment."

"You're here now." I opened the door. "Come in."

I went to my desk, placed my bag on it. The room was chilly. I walked to the radiator and ran my fingers along its top. The girl went to close the door.

"No, you can leave it open," I said.

She gave me a slightly startled glance like she wished she'd never come.

"Let's sit, and you can tell me what's on your mind."

I took one of the armchairs, but she just stood fiddling with the zipper on her sweater. She was small and thin, bony wrists emerging from the cuffs of her sleeves, which had been picked and unraveled. Nervous fingers constantly moving.

"What's your name?"

"Zoe," she said quietly. "Zoe Harte."

"Well, Zoe. How can I help you?" I asked while tidying a bunch of journals at my desk.

Her hands became still and in a voice that came out clear as a bell, she said, "I think you might be my father."

# CHAPTER 2
## DAVID

Students come through my door every day of the workweek. Some of them have ordinary questions, course-related queries. Others are in trouble. They want your help. They may not even know what's wrong. And then again others *are* trouble. Over the years, I have had my fair share of problem cases. They have ranged from benign to complex. But none of them was like this. None of them spelled trouble so clearly and lucidly, or announced the problem with such a candid, if sheepish, clarity.

"I don't understand," I said.

"Can I close the door?"

"No, I don't think that's a good idea." I gestured for her to sit down in the chair opposite.

"I know it's probably a shock," she said, taking a seat and putting her bag down by her feet.

"A shock?" I said. More of an intrusion,

or a preposterous allegation, than anything else. I inspected my itinerary for the day. It was full: one meeting followed by another. The module review committee was going to be particularly taxing. I also needed to get to the library to talk to Laurence about the oral histories he was sourcing for me from the British Library.

"Well, yes . . . I've come in here out of the blue and revealed to you that I am your daughter."

"Sorry, I'm still struggling to follow. Why is it you think I might be your father?" I said.

Her expression didn't change. Shy, meek even, as if she were here against her will. "I've been thinking about how to put it so it wouldn't come out as bluntly," she said, leaning forward slightly. "It doesn't seem to matter which way I turn the phrases over. You are my father," she coughed awkwardly into her sleeve. "I thought it would be better to tell it to you straight rather than dancing around it, if that makes sense?"

The planes of her face were smooth. It was an open face, an honest one. Her eyes were green, wide and clear. Her hair fell over her face occasionally and she had to push it back every so often — a kind of tic, I supposed.

"Actually, it's a relief to tell you," she said, giving me a watery smile. "You've no idea. I've tossed this around for ages: sitting in your lectures, knowing all the time you're my father and that you had no idea. It got so I couldn't bear it. I felt like I had to tell you."

Her voice, though tentative and soft, had the earthy guttural of the North in it — and because of all the reading and research I was doing recently, I thought about those American soldiers during World War II stationed in the various towns of Northern Ireland — Coleraine, Ballycastle, Portstewart — and their unwritten legacy: the ones who left behind sons and daughters they may never have known about, while others were sought out later in life by their offspring. I had always thought this a joyful, if complicated, legacy — an ancillary tributary to the river of the past — an enriching one even.

Still, I became annoyed at the vagaries of my own mind and the distraction the girl had brought about to my day: her prank, the articulations of an unsound mind — whatever it was.

I took my notebook into my hands, drew myself up from the chair, and walked to my desk. I felt the short fuse of my temper fizzle.

24

"Again, what makes you think that I'm your father?"

The smile fell from her face. She reached into her bag for a tissue. I could tell she was struggling to maintain her composure. Perhaps I had been too curt. I had after all a duty of care to her as a student. She was young, lost; it must have been very difficult for her to pluck up the courage, however misguided it was, to come in to talk to me.

"Listen," I said, "you're clearly upset. And believe me, it's not the first time I've had a student here in tears. University life can be daunting. People struggle. But there is help out there if you ask for it. Let me give you the number of someone in student services who can help."

I went behind my desk and wrote the number on a Post-it. Claire O'Rourke, a counselor on campus, was an old friend. As I wrote out her number, I wondered briefly what Claire would make of the girl's claims.

Ripping the page off the pad, I went to hand it to her but she didn't reach out for the note, she didn't look at it at all.

I returned to my desk.

"If you don't want the number, that's your call," I said. The situation had grown tiresome. I had work to do. "I'm trying to offer you help, but I can't force you to take it."

I tapped the space bar on my keyboard, stirring the computer to life. The monitor brightened and the image of Robbie and Holly dissolved before me.

"My mother's name was Linda," the girl said. My hand released its hold of the mouse. "Linda Barry," she added.

Linda Barry? Hearing her name seemed to prod an unhealed wound inside my unconscious mind. I felt like I was dreaming or as if time was playing tricks. My mouth dried up a little.

"Linda Barry?" Just like that I was transported to another time, another place, as if her name were a password to the past — to my past, to a younger, more feckless, and passionate young man and to the time that went with it. The password took me to pain too. I felt winded, and all at once on guard.

I looked at the girl for any signs of resemblance. The figure of another student appeared in the doorway.

"Dr. Connolly?"

"Not now," I said testily. "I'm in the middle of something." I switched off the monitor. "Come back later . . ."

"A little over a year ago, she told me about you," the girl said, her voice barely a whisper.

"She told you about me?"

"She thought I needed to know," the girl said, pulling at the strands of her sleeve.

I could tell she was waiting for me to say something while the possibility of what she revealed began to ghost its way through my mind.

"She told me when she was a student at Queen's University, you were her course tutor," she said. "She told me how you had become friends, and how, for a while, you were lovers."

It felt wrong — listening to a student discussing me and Linda, describing us as *lovers.* Could it be true? Did Linda have a child?

I thought about that weekend we spent in Donegal before we split up. Three days in a remote part of the countryside. It had felt like I was shrugging off my previous life: the years of study, the immersion in academia receding from memory, like waking from a long dream. Beneath the surface, there had lingered the knowledge of a parting. Soon, I would be returning to Dublin to take up a position in the university from which I had graduated three years before. The life I had lived in Belfast, at Queen's University, would draw to a close. And this relationship, this love affair — I had no idea how much it meant to me — it too would be put to rest. We both knew it, although neither one of us had said so.

The girl held a hand to her lips and I saw there in the rounded shape of her face a resemblance. A simplicity that could have been plain were it not for the liveliness of her eyes — Linda's eyes, or were they? I couldn't be completely sure.

"I don't see how . . ." I began.

"She said your affair was brief. Afterward, she went abroad to do a master's degree. That's when she discovered she was pregnant."

I had, by then, completed my PhD and returned to Dublin. I had met Caroline again and our relationship — broken for those three years in Belfast — had resumed. After Linda, after the swirling highs and lows, I felt ready for something solid, stable, and dependable. "But she never told me."

What a relief it had been to climb into marriage, to feel the solid structure of it form around me. But with this girl in my office, I was again at sea. The roar of waves in my ears drowning out much of what she was telling me. I kept thinking of Linda with a baby, *my* baby. How could she not have told me? How could she have gone through all of that alone?

"This must be difficult," she said, regaining her composure. "It's got to be a lot to take in."

With a slim frame, all wrists and knees, jeans clinging to thin legs, heavy oxblood-red boots, there was something vulnerable about her: even if she had just lobbed her little grenade and set me reeling.

"Yes, you could say that."

"I know," she said, an uneasy smile spreading across her face. "But you have to know that I don't want anything from you."

"You don't?"

"Nothing!" she said, laughing nervously. "It's just I thought you should know."

"And that's all? There's nothing else?" I asked.

She started to pick again at her frayed cuffs.

"Just to talk, I suppose."

"To talk?"

She squirmed, grew sullen. The shield of hair had fallen over her face again. She made no effort to push it back. Quietly, from behind it, she said:

"I just wanted to get to know you a little."

It was a reasonable request, I supposed.

"Did Linda put you up to this?" I asked. "Does she know you've come to see me?"

In retrospect, I see how foolish I was — how ridiculous I must have sounded — to think an old girlfriend had spent the last eighteen years hatching a plan to bring about my undoing.

"My mother's dead."

Dead? Said so matter-of-factly. The first time I kissed Linda it was because she had dared me to. "Go on," she had said as I walked her home from an evening guest lecture. "You know you want to." I had played dumb, but all the time, I was stepping closer to her, and she was stepping closer to me, until her hands gripped the pockets of my coat and my hands found their way to her waist. It was not a lingering kiss. She had pulled away, and I had felt I had been on the brink of making a terrible mistake, though unsure whether the mistake was to follow her or to let her slip away.

How strange and unreal it is to hear of an old lover who has passed away. To think the time you shared is no longer a common memory between you, no longer a testimony subject to agreement and dissent, no longer a space of contested but cherished moments — like the rising smoke from a bonfire on a Halloween night in Belfast. Gone — like the fading autumn light at sunset. Such a death is like a sudden pull in the heart, a brief awakening, and the realization that the lost lover's life had continued all that time you were apart.

"I'm so sorry," I said to the girl. "What happened?"

"Ovarian cancer. It's just coming up to a year."

Now this timing made some sort of sense: a young woman whose mother has recently died seeks some kind of replacement to make up for the loss. It's possible. Psychologists might call it transference, and stranger things have been known to happen, certainly, on this campus. But I was curious.

"And when did Linda tell you about me?" I asked.

She pushed back her hair.

"It was toward the end."

"Is that why you came to this university?"

She blushed, squirmed in her chair.

"I dunno. Maybe. I've always liked history, and with Mam gone, I just wanted to get away, you know? Start over somewhere new."

Whatever about the truth of her claim, I couldn't help but admire her a little, the curious tilt of her chin, the bravery in her optimism.

A sudden rap on the open door startled her. She stood up quickly. Another student appeared in the doorway.

"Dr. Connolly."

"Just a moment," I said.

The girl was already fixing the strap of her satchel over one shoulder. "I should go," she said.

Awkwardly, beneath the gaze of the other student, we said good-bye to each other. I turned back into the room, went to the window, and waited for the young man to sit. Below in the courtyard, staff and students sat at tables among the birch trees; the noise of their conversation rose into a barely audible hum. Shadows moved overhead, the day darkened. The student behind me cleared his throat.

"Would you mind waiting?" I said, making for the door. "I'll just be a moment."

She was at the stairwell by the time I caught up. Hair falling over her shoulders, strolling away. I called to her and she turned. A door opened and a flurry of students came streaming out, passing us in a noisy group.

"I wanted to ask you," I said, "have you told anyone else? Any of your friends? Anyone in the class?"

"No," she said.

"Can I ask that you don't? Please. Not yet, not until I've had some time to take this all in."

"Don't worry," she said, her voice flat and

unreadable. In her eyes, there was a flash of pity. I felt a nudge of something too: shame perhaps. However foolish, I still believed I could contain whatever it was that had been released.

"I won't say a thing," she said slipping into the stream of students passing, leaving me there, sweat on my palms, holding on to the rail, conscious that I was about to be swept up by something beyond my control.

# CHAPTER 3
## CAROLINE

I can remember when it began.

One afternoon in early autumn, I had been called away from the office unexpectedly because of David's mother, Ellen. There had been an incident.

I was just settling her with her tea tray and the TV on, when my cellphone rang, David's number appearing on the screen.

"Caroline?"

"I was just going to call you."

"Why?" he asked. "Has something happened?"

Something in his voice: a scratch of irritation or a wrinkle of concern.

"Who is it?" Ellen asked, her voice quavering with nerves.

"It's David." I turned up the volume of the TV, then pulled the door closed gently behind me.

In the hallway, I sat down on the stairs and felt the carpet rough at the back of my legs, a musty smell rising from it.

"Your mum," I told him. "She went wandering again."

"Oh Christ."

"She's fine —"

"What happened?"

I told him about the phone call I'd received. Ellen's neighbor, Marion, had phoned, sounding breathy and rushed: *You told me to call if ever something happened.* I listened as she told me how she had found Ellen in Tesco crying in the Frozen Food section, not knowing where she was or how she would get home. It was not the first such occurrence.

"I've settled her now," I told him. "I gave her some beans on toast."

"Should I come over?"

Ellen was just beginning to get over her shakiness. The last thing she needed was to relive it for her son.

"Leave it until the weekend. Give her a chance to recover."

"Okay," he said. Then, "Caroline?"

"Yes?"

He hesitated. "Nothing. It can wait."

But it was there in his voice, a note I couldn't identify.

I knew it at once: something had happened.

■ ■ ■ ■

She came into our lives, into our home, at an awkward time for me, a time I think of now as being filled with nerves and self-doubt. I had, after a fifteen-year hiatus, returned to work at the advertising agency I had left when Robbie was born. Everything about that office felt changed, like foreign territory I had visited once but of that visit I retained no memory. Nothing was familiar.

The decision to give up my career in order to raise my children was not something I regretted even though it had been a strain at times: the boredom, the loneliness. There was a deep need within me to create for my children a warm and loving environment where there would always be someone making sure they did their homework, putting dinner on the table, checking on them when they were in bed at night. I did it gladly. My only continuing contact with the agency was a calendar arriving every year at Christmas, each month headed with a sleek image of a car or an alcoholic drink or whatever product they were being paid to push. When the calendar arrived and I read all the names signed on the inside flap, I confess I felt a pang, a twinge of something close to envy.

36

Fleeting, but I was aware of it nonetheless — a seam of uncertainty or regret that could be tapped into whenever I was reminded of what I had given up. When I met Peter by chance and he mentioned one of the girls in the office was taking maternity leave for ten months, the idea took hold. My children were old enough. I had time on my hands. Although I had been out of the game for so long, I felt the pull of it, the undertow of a distant longing. I hadn't counted on Zoe. I hadn't even known she existed.

That evening, after I'd left Ellen, I drove home through heavy traffic, the image of my elderly mother-in-law crying next to cabinets full of fish sticks and frozen peas still alive in my mind. Opening my front door, I heard noise from the living room, movement upstairs. I kicked off my shoes in the hall, pausing briefly to enjoy the relief. Having hung up my coat, I went into the living room.

Robbie was sitting on the couch with his legs tucked up under him. On the telly a woman was sobbing in front of a studio audience, the man beside her mortified.

"Hello, sweetheart," I said. "Sorry I'm so late."

"Hey Mum," he answered.

"I was at Nan's," I told him, although he hadn't sought an explanation for my absence. "Where's your dad?"

"Upstairs."

He was still wearing his school uniform and, after shooting a quick smile in my direction, went back to staring avidly at the screen, the room dark apart from the light cast by the flickering images. The studio audience hissed and booed, the presenter advancing through them smugly. Robbie shifted under my gaze and I caught a glimpse of an empty potato chip bag stuffed down the side of the couch beside him.

"You didn't eat a whole bag, did you?"

He smiled again and pulled a face.

"Sorry, I was hungry."

"Robbie . . ."

"Sorry!" he said again, still smiling. At fifteen, he was at an awkward transitional stage, trapped in the hormonal no-man's-land between child and adult. At moments like this, when his roguish grin surfaced, he was my little boy again. I let it go.

Climbing the stairs, I could hear music coming from Holly's room — some tinny pop — and beneath it, the sweet faltering accompaniment of my daughter's voice. I stepped past her room and, opening our bedroom door softly, I saw David stretched

38

out on the bed, eyes closed, a glass of wine in one hand resting upon his chest. I stood over him watching, his handsome face serious, even in repose, lines from laughter and concentration hardening into permanence. He stirred a little.

"You'll spill that."

His eyes shot open and he sat up quickly. I reached forward and rescued the glass from his hands, put it to my lips and drank.

"I didn't hear you come in," he said, blinking and running a hand across his face.

The wine warmed the back of my throat. I set the glass down on the nightstand and sat on the bed beside him. He lay back, locking his hands behind his neck, and I felt a brief and surprising nudge of desire. I could lie down on the bed next to him and with the dinner drying out in the oven we could slip off our clothes and forget the troubles of the day for a while. It seemed so risqué, the thought of sex at this hour of the evening with the children in the house, the TV on downstairs. I put my hand on his shirt front, traced a line down to his belt. This kind of spontaneity still felt unnatural in the wake of what had happened between us. His eyes closed and he shifted under my touch, tacitly agreeing to my unspoken suggestion.

Holly's bedroom door opened, her footfall in the hall outside. My hand paused and David opened his eyes.

"What do you think?" I asked.

He sat up and swung his feet onto the floor. The moment had passed. He reached for his wineglass on the nightstand and said: "Come on. Let's go and eat."

In the kitchen, he flicked on the radio while I got the lettuce from the fridge. A talk show was on, the presenter's voice with her forensic questioning filling the space between us as she took some politician to task over the failed attempt to legislate for abortion in the case of fatal fetal abnormality. A year or so before, we had undertaken a large renovation of our home. Besides an attic conversion, a large extension had been built onto the kitchen, the additional space allowing room for a sofa and a stove as well as a large dining table and a kitchen island. The work had been costly and we couldn't have afforded it were it not for a small inheritance from my parents who had passed away some years prior to that. A loan from the credit union helped with the funds needed.

It was David's habit on evenings when he was tired after work to throw himself on the sofa, the two of us chatting while I prepared the dinner. On this particular evening, however, he leaned against the counter, while I rinsed the salad leaves in the sink, and he asked me about Ellen. I was tired but answered his questions, and he took it all in, his arms folded. Something needed to be done about her deteriorating state of mind, and we batted ideas back and forth, although we were reluctant to get into it.

There was something else I needed to tell him. I was weighing up whether to say it now or wait until the kids had gone to bed. David seemed distracted and I had the beginnings of a headache. I asked him to pour me a glass of wine while I spun the salad. When he went to call the others for dinner I decided just to say it, to get it over with quickly before the kids came into the room.

"There was an e-mail from the school," I said, taking down the plates and spreading them along the worktop. "Robbie's parent-teacher meeting is next Tuesday. Are you free?"

He put the empty bottle into the crate by the door.

"Next Tuesday?"

"Yes, in the afternoon."

I took the lasagna from the oven, placed it

41

on the trivet, and began separating it into segments. He was standing next to me, waiting to take the plates to the table.

"Can't you go?" he asked.

"It wouldn't be for long. Just an hour or so. You can take those ones."

I nodded at the first two plates, and he picked them up but didn't move away. I could feel him waiting for something more from me. I put food on the other plates, then opened the oven and returned the dish to keep it warm.

"Caroline —"

"Please. It's just one afternoon."

"It's not that. You know it's not."

I could feel the color coming to my cheeks. I picked up the other plates and waited for him to let me pass.

"It's been a year." His voice was soft but firm.

On the radio, the presenter was affecting a heavy sigh, the one she used to signal the end of an interview. The kitchen door opened.

"Please don't make me," I said. I stepped past him. I put the plates down hard on the table.

Over dinner, Holly talked about a school trip to the Burren that was planned for the end of October. Cheerfully animated, she spoke of caves and calcium deposits, limestone and the area's varying plant life. Robbie lolled in his chair, one elbow on the table, picking at his food. David was quiet. The children, no doubt, put it down to work. We used to joke about it — the kids and I. "Dad's gone over to the dark side," we would say whenever he became distracted and vague. His silence that evening seemed heavier than usual and I attributed it to the parent-teacher meeting. I knew he was thinking of what had happened the year before, the whole awkward business at the school rearing its ugly head again. To combat his silence, I recounted the drama of my afternoon, the phone call at work, the confused state I'd found Ellen in.

"First thing tomorrow, I'm calling Dr. Burke," I announced.

"Poor Nan," Holly said, drinking her water, her eyes behind their glasses perplexed.

"She'll be fine," David said, the firmness in his voice a kind of warning.

He was put out over the school thing, and I supposed he was entitled to feel resentful, but still. I had spent all afternoon taking care of his mother.

"Are you going to eat any of that?" I asked Robbie.

He seemed tired, pressing his fork against the raft of pasta hardening on his plate.

"I'm not hungry."

David dropped his cutlery onto his plate with a clatter, making us all look up.

"Maybe if you hadn't shoved a whole bag of fucking Doritos down your throat, you'd be able to eat," he snapped.

Robbie's mouth opened as if he were about to say something, but no words came out.

"David, please," I said sharply.

He stared at me across the table.

My husband is a sulker, not an exploder. He wears me down with his stubborn silences. We had made a point of not arguing in front of the children — even when our marriage was under strain. We held our fights in private, and we maintained a strained sense of civility whenever the kids were around. The quality of his discomfort this time was different from before. I realized that it wasn't about the school at all.

"Let's just eat," he said.

Addressing his plate again, he speared some pasta with his fork. We had forgotten about the salad still sitting next to the sink, but neither of us made a move to go get it. The jingle of the drive-time show was playing on the radio, its cheerful beat pounding through the speakers; we sat together without talking until the meal was done.

Whenever I try to remember how it all started, I don't think of the morning I found out, or the first time I saw the haze of yellow hair, her feline stare. I think of David that evening, the coiled rope of tension within him, the shiftiness of his irritation. I didn't know it was because of her — Zoe. I didn't know she existed. But that was when I first felt her shadow falling over me. The first time I felt the ripples of a new presence within my home, like a dye entering water, already changing its chemistry.

# CHAPTER 4
## DAVID

I woke up the next morning to the thought: she is dead.

Linda is dead.

It wasn't grief I felt. How could it be? She hadn't been in my life for a long time. But there was a sadness, and a shock that left me feeling out of sorts, on edge. I got up, threw water on my face, shaved, showered, and pulled myself together as best I could. Over breakfast, the world resolidified around me. Robbie and Holly were absorbed in their cereals while Caroline got their lunches ready. I finished breakfast quickly, leaned in to Caroline to say goodbye, and felt the warmth of her kiss on my mouth. I told myself: everything is going to be all right.

I pedaled away from the house, my lungs filling with air, flew past the traffic while trying to convince myself that even if Linda had passed away, what this girl had suggested was some kind of joke, an elaborate student prank. A student's life is full of madcap behavior; stunts and dares. Somebody had simply put the girl up to it. That's why there was no reason to tell my wife what the girl had said. Why get into a difficult conversation with Caroline over something that would ultimately turn out to be a hoax.

On campus, I spent the first hour going through my in-box. What struck me initially was the amount of noncollege work I had taken on: media commitments, interviews, op-ed pieces, book reviews, as well as board and committee duty. I replied to as many e-mails as possible before rushing to a tutorial with my third years, followed by coffee, then seminars until one. My first-year lecture was after lunch and as the time approached, I grew twitchy. My palms became sweaty, the coffee in my stomach churned. I told myself to stop being paranoid and walked into the theater, down the steps, swung my bag onto the bench, and hooked my laptop to the projector. When I raised my face to the students, my heart was beating high and light. A hush came over the auditorium. As I talked, I scanned the room for her but drew a blank. Twice, late-comers interrupted. I looked to the swinging door only to find it wasn't her. During the last few minutes, I opened up the lecture to questions: it was another chance to search for her hidden among the sea of faces. By the time the lecture ended I was sure of it: she wasn't there.

After that, I put her out of my mind. I had more pressing concerns, chief among them my mother's failing health. A colleague whose parents had died in the past year had remarked to me at the time how it was astonishing the speed at which an elderly person's health can deteriorate. I was reminded of that conversation when I thought about my poor mum and how rapidly she had gone from a vibrant, independent, mentally agile person to this bewildered old lady, frightened and confused by the change coming over her. Despite Caroline's suggestion that I give Mum a few days to recover before visiting her, I found that I couldn't wait. Concern made me impatient, and more than once that week I spent my lunch hour cycling to my mother's home to sit with her, holding her hand, and tentatively open the difficult conversation about the possible next steps to ensure her safety and well-being. I had given some thought to having her move in with us, but I knew Caroline would be against the idea — she had recently returned to work, things were busy enough with the kids' after-school activities, and Robbie had exams this year. Instead, I began researching the availability and costs involved in arranging for home help, as well as exploring some sheltered accommodation options, unsure of which route would be more suitable or necessary.

Preoccupied as I was with my mother, not to mention my heavy workload, I managed to banish Zoe and her preposterous claims from my thoughts. It was not until Friday, toward the end of a meeting with my most promising PhD student, Niki Agsten, and her co-supervisor, Dr. Anne Burke, that my mind returned to Zoe. Niki's subject was the study of the role of women during the Great War. At the meeting, she was telling us about something she had stumbled upon during the course of her recent research.

"It was in the court records," she said. "I was going through the year 1918, when I came across this."

Anne and I listened while Niki read out a statement from a witness detailing an account of a woman giving birth and subsequently taking the life of her newborn baby.

"It's strange," Niki said, "but since I read the account in the court files I can't stop

49

thinking about her. She tried to strangle her own baby with a sock. When that didn't work, she tried crushing it beneath the weight of a window frame. What was it that made the woman believe that letting her baby live would be so much worse than having to live with its death on her conscience?"

Anne made some answer but I was lost to the conversation, my mind tumbling back through my own history. An image came to me of Linda sitting hunched in a bathroom, her cheeks flushed with heat, the test in her hand, a line on a stick. My imagination ran riot. I thought about the panic she might have felt, the loneliness. I wondered too why she had never told me? That is, if what the girl had said to me was true, which I still did not know. And if it was true, what might it mean to my relationship with Caroline, to the challenges already facing our marriage, not to mention how it might affect our children? Too many what-ifs crowded my mind, and too many unanswerables made it impossible for me to concentrate.

"David?" Anne was waiting for an answer.

"Sorry?"

"Next Thursday — are we agreed?"

"Yes," I said. "Yes, of course."

They left. And I thought about how I had buried the girl's words, transformed them in my mind into a joke, reduced what she had said into a student spoof or the workings of an unsound mind. It occurred to me that there was something desperate in the way I was trying to blot those words out. Blot *her* out.

I went to my desk, stirred my computer to life, and clicked on to the Internet. It didn't take long to find it. Still I was surprised. DNA testing seemed so foreign, a product of a more litigious society than Ireland, but there it was in black and white — a company in Dublin that carried out paternity tests with a 99 percent accuracy assurance, discretion guaranteed.

What did I need? A swab from the inner cheek was best, but there were other sources: a hair (with follicle, preferably), a toothbrush. I must have spent twenty minutes trying out the various methods in my mind for proving — or disproving — the girl's claims to my paternity, all the ways I had of capturing her DNA.

I considered carefully how to bring the matter up with Zoe. I thought about asking her permission, telling her I needed to get the paternity test done — but every time I included her in the discussion, my imagination tangled the possible outcomes into something messy and complicated. The etiquette involved in seeking another person's consent to test their genetic material was beyond me. The minutes ticked past. My thoughts grew more confused: a sudden flash of how crazy this situation was made me close down the DNA page. I told myself to get a grip. When Alan put his head around the door and asked if I'd join him in the common room for a coffee, I was more than relieved.

Alan has been my friend and mentor since I was an undergrad. A wise old soul with a gruff exterior, it was he who had offered me my first post-doctoral position after Queen's University, Belfast. I owe him a lot and feel a firm affection for the guy, despite our differences. He's an old-school historian, baffled sometimes by my approach to history. My adventures in the media irk him in particular. That afternoon, as we strolled to the common room, he took a pop at my latest article.

"The Sports supplement!" he said. "What are you doing writing about sports?"

I laughed. "You don't think sport is relevant to history? What about the 1933 Olympics?"

"Come on. He's hardly Jesse Owens, is he?"

"Can you think of a more controversial

figure in Irish sport?"

"I just don't see why you're wasting your time mixing it with the polemicists . . ."

"Go on say it. You think it's drivel."

"I was going to say journalism."

"You were not."

He laughed.

"Sport, the arts, popular culture, all of it informs the national consciousness," I said. "It makes us who we are as a nation. All of it is history in the making."

We picked up our coffees and sat. Alan was smiling at what I had said. I could tell he was not in the mood for argumentative banter today. "I'm supposed to go to this conference in East Anglia next month," he said, leaning forward and examining his cup. "To give a talk . . . I was wondering if you would go in my stead."

"Really?"

"It would be good for you," he replied. "And your CV."

How often was it said to me that if I did a favor for someone, it would advance my career at a later date? I didn't mind standing in for Alan, but it wasn't like him to duck out of a commitment unless the reason was serious.

"Sure, Alan. I'll go, but is everything all right?"

"I've been doing some thinking," he said seriously. "My health is not good — a problem with my heart. They tell me I should have surgery, but I don't know if I want that. At my age . . ."

"You're only sixty-two."

"Well, exactly. That's my point. I want to live a little while I still have time. So I've decided to take early retirement."

"Early retirement?"

"What? Did you think I'd be here forever?"

"Yes," I said.

A kind of sadness was pulling at me. I have never been very good at endings or good-byes.

"This time, I really do mean it," he said.

He didn't need to spell out the rest for me. If Alan left, there would be a position for a new professor. This was my chance. I couldn't help feeling a spark of excitement. The way he suggested my filling in for him just now, it almost felt like favoritism. His kindness had always, it seemed, extended beyond a professional duty.

The possibility of the professorship stayed with me all the way back to the office, my mind brimming with ideas, rushing on to a few months ahead, the interview board, the presentations. I began making a mental tally of the papers I hoped to publish that year, including the book I was finishing, wondering how my research outputs would compare to those of the other candidates. The idea was so consuming that I almost didn't notice the slip of paper on the ground as I opened the door to my office. Shutting it behind me, the paper fluttered in the draft. I leaned down to pick it up and read the words quickly.

My excitement vanished. The lead weight dropped back into my heart.

The note was short, written in an elegant hand — signed with a flourish, her name a slash across the page.

Meet me this evening? Madigans, after work. Say 6:30 p.m. Zoe.

I took the note, folded it, and placed it carefully in my wallet.

Friday evening, and there was a sense of expectancy in the air; the collective relief that the end of the week had arrived presented itself in a frenetic busyness on the roads and pavements. The wind had whipped up and I pedaled slowly to Donnybrook. Traffic was thick, people hurrying to get away from the working week, their desks, bosses, and obligations.

By the time I got there, the pub was heaving: office workers, students, mechanics from the nearby bus depot — all of their voices blending together in a dense cloud of talk. I found her sitting on her own at the back, a bottle of beer in front of her. One elbow on the table, her head was resting on her cupped hand, her face blank as she fiddled with her phone. For just a moment, before she saw me, she looked so young, so harmless. I couldn't help but feel sorry for her.

"You came," she said, smiling, getting to her feet.

"Zoe," I said.

"I saved you a seat." She gestured to a stool. "I'm so glad you're here. I wasn't sure you'd come. Let me get you a drink."

"No," I said.

"Please. It's the least I can do."

"I'll get my own," I said, catching one of the bar staff's attention and ordering a pint and another bottle for Zoe.

She leaned on the table, one hand wrapped around her beer, her face open and smiling. About us, voices rose, shouts of laughter; brass instruments played boisterous ragtime through hidden speakers. We almost had to shout to be heard.

"I had no idea this place would be so busy," she said. "I'd have picked some place quieter."

The truth was, I felt protected by the noise and the clamor of people. Somehow, I didn't want to be cloistered in some quiet booth with a student, a stranger. Who knew who might see?

"I just thought that as it's close enough to college, it would be convenient."

Our drinks arrived and before the glass had reached my mouth, she was raising her bottle.

"Cheers."

*Sláinte,*" I said, with a strange premonition of how I might take Robbie for his first drink, to a dark pub, where a father and son could bond. Instead, I was with a girl I barely knew.

"I wanted to apologize," she began, "for the other day. Taking you unawares like that. It was unfair. I'm really sorry," she said, small creases appearing at the sides of her eyes.

She wore a plain red sweater, and I wondered briefly whether those big army boots were still on her feet. "You're not mocking me, Zoe, are you?"

"God, no!" Her eyes became round. "I just think we got off on the wrong footing."

"What you're saying about me, about being your father, it's very serious."

"I know, I know." She looked down at the table, shaking her head. I drank deeply. I had prepared something to say, but I wanted to get it right. However, she spoke next. "I want you to know that you don't need to be afraid . . ."

"Afraid?" I said.

"Of me," she uttered in a small voice. "I mean it. I don't want to hurt you. I don't want to get you into any trouble."

"What sort of trouble could you get me into? I haven't done anything wrong."

"No, I know. I didn't mean that you had. I meant that I don't want to make things difficult for you with the university or with your wife."

"My wife?"

"Yes," she said. "Have you told her about me?"

It had been nearly a week. Not a long time in the large scale of things, but it had been a painstaking week of concealment and circumspection. All that time I had been keeping it from Caroline, telling myself I was protecting her, but what I was really doing was protecting myself. I hated keeping secrets. In fact, as a couple, I thought, we were done with all that. The past had taught me one thing — secrets will come out, and by keeping them there are always repercussions, but I had ignored my own hard-learned lesson. Not telling Caroline seemed a big mistake.

"I haven't told her about you, no," I admitted. "Not yet. Not until I'm sure . . ."

"Until you are sure?" she queried.

"You can't blame me. It's a shock, and I still have to establish the veracity . . ."

". . . establish the veracity," she said under her breath, reaching for her bag. For an instant I thought she was going to leave. Instead, she rooted in the tartan canvas satchel until she found a white paper bag with the logo of a pharmacy printed on it.

"Listen," she said, her tone becoming reasonable, almost businesslike. "After I left your office the other day, I began thinking about what it must have been like for you, having me waltz in there with my big news, and what a shock it must have been. You had every right to be skeptical. I mean, that's a reasonable response. So then I thought, well, why not just get a DNA test done?"

"Yes," I said quickly, somewhat taken aback at the ease with which she suggested it. All this time I had been agonizing over the ways to delicately suggest the same, not expecting her to come out with it, so calm and matter-of-fact.

"I've found a company who'll do it for me. All I need is a sample from you." She rummaged in the paper bag, taking out a specimen jar and a small plastic bag containing three or four Q-tips. Confronted by these items, I found myself growing deeply uncomfortable as the practicalities of the test presented themselves.

"A swab from your inner cheek will do," she said, watching me with her steady gaze, no hint of nerves or awkwardness at what she was suggesting.

"What, here?" I asked. "Right now?"

"Why not?" she asked. "Just a quick scrape along the inside of your cheek and that's it." Her eyes were unblinking as she watched me struggling with indecision. "Unless you prefer to go to the Gents and do it there."

It was a ridiculous dilemma — retreating to the privacy of the men's toilet seemed squalid and risked making me appear prudish in her eyes, or conducting the test here beneath her gaze in this most public space? I decided upon the latter, hastily rubbing at the slick private surfaces of my mouth, then popping the Q-tip into the jar and returning it to her outstretched hand. The episode was brief but there was something sordid about it. Getting the DNA tested — it had been what I wanted — but this somehow felt wrong. The way she had taken control of the situation, watching me retrieving my sample and handing it over to her. Maybe it was a generational difference, but I felt like she had gained the upper hand and I was already in over my depth.

"I'll send it off tomorrow," she told me as she wrote my name and the date on the jar's label. "It only takes two weeks."

"Right."

My phone rang. It was Caroline. I hadn't told her I was going out. I'd have to say I was working late or taking the visiting professor out for a drink.

Zoe said: "Take it if you need to. I don't mind."

I did not relish the prospect of having to lie to Caroline, particularly in front of Zoe.

"That's all right," I said and ignored the ringing phone.

She had her satchel on her knees and was putting the specimen jar carefully away.

"Oh, and I also have these," she said, taking out a tatty envelope and spilling the contents onto the table. "I thought I should show them to you."

I picked her birth certificate up and

61

looked at it. The date of birth read March 3, 1995. My eyes sought out the details of paternity, but there was nothing conclusive. The certificate simply read: *Father Unknown.* The document didn't prove anything, but before I could remark upon it, she tapped her fingertips on a strip of photographs, the only other item to have fallen from the envelope.

"Recognize these?"

She slid them closer to me and I leaned forward to look.

"They were taken in May 1994," she added. "If you look at the back, you'll see Linda's handwriting."

Four square photographs from a booth in a train station. My youthful face beaming back at me. A set of different poses — two students goofing around. I sported a beard that year — strange to see it now. It wasn't just the beard that was different — my eyes seemed wider, my whole face more open. There was humor and fun there and for a second I was back in that booth, Linda on my knee, my arms feeling her body tremble with laughter as she half-turned to me, her face against mine, telling me to be serious now. How she held me close, our smiles captured as the flash startled us, hanging on to each other, it seemed, for dear life.

"I do remember . . . it's just that it's difficult for me," I said, hardly daring to touch the photographs.

I wanted to say something else. I wanted to say something firm and reassuring. But the words wouldn't come. I would only end up sounding like the uptight academic I did not want to be, a supercilious father figure.

My phone rang again, startling me. Caroline's face flashed on the screen.

"I have to go."

"Oh," she said, and I could see her disappointment.

I put on my coat, checking to make sure I had my wallet, my phone. The photographs remained on the table between us, and Zoe made no effort to remove them. Instead, she seemed to be holding back, as if there was some further business we needed to conduct.

"David," she said as I got to my feet. "About the test . . ."

"Yes?"

She glanced up at me, an embarrassed smile on her face. For the first time since suggesting it, she appeared nervous and unsure.

"The thing is," she began, "it's kind of expensive."

Another embarrassed smile, her eyebrows

raised, she gave me a meaningful look.

"Oh," I said, the penny dropping. "You want me to pay for it."

"Only half," she countered quickly. "We could split it. That would be fair, don't you think?"

I shrugged. "Yes. Of course." I wanted to appear reasonable but again I felt tripped up by my ignorance, my total lack of experience in such matters. I took out my wallet.

"It's a hundred and eighty," she said apologetically. "Ninety each."

"I only have a fifty on me."

"That's okay. You can give me the rest another time."

I held out the note and she took it, saying something about how she would reimburse me should the test come back negative. I hardly heard her, my attention snagged by a woman at the next table glancing in our direction. This was all so public — the swab, the specimen jar, and now the money. I felt like I had entered into a transaction that was both public and shameful. I stuffed my wallet back into my pocket.

"Well, good-bye, Zoe."

She made to get up and I sensed her intention toward some kind of farewell embrace. But I had no desire to entertain such a thing and turned away quickly, heading out the door without looking back. I had compromised myself enough for one evening.

# CHAPTER 5
## CAROLINE

I'm not the first person whose marriage has been rocked by an affair. Every day millions of people all over the world are unfaithful to their loved ones. I don't know why I was so surprised when it happened to me. But one of the things I learned during the crisis is that people can find different paths back to each other. Not every journey is the same. For me, the only way to deal with all that hurt and anger and resentment was to seek counseling. Talking things out, examining my life and some of the choices I had made, helped me come to terms with what had happened. David was supportive of this therapy, although when I suggested that we attend some sessions together, he balked at the idea. I'm not saying he didn't make an effort to mend things between us, but his response was different from mine. I needed to talk it through, to pick over the past in order to understand what had happened.

David's response was to buy a new kitchen. For a man who has made a career out of examining and understanding the past, his reluctance to plow through the history of our marriage in order to fix it was baffling to me. I'm not saying I didn't recognize the love underlying the renovation project. It was just another example of how, after twenty-odd years of being together, there are times when my husband still seems unknowable.

The crisis in our marriage happened quickly — a lightning bolt — but resolved itself slowly, seeping away like water finding a drain. I have learned that there are several steps — significant markers — along the path to reconciliation. The first time you have sex after the betrayal has been discovered (for us, it was four months later). The first time you share a joke, laughing together in a way that feels unencumbered by all the wrangling and negotiations surrounding your decision to stay together. The first time he comes home from work and leans in to kiss you hello in a way that feels meaningful rather than dutiful. Slowly, the different elements of your life together are reasserted, carefully put back in place. At times it feels difficult, awkward, even fake, like you're just playing at being married to each other. At

other times the pieces fit into place naturally, giving you hope.

When Zoe came into our lives a year had
passed since the affair. Even though we were
well on our way to patching things up, that
fissure in our marriage was still there. I
wonder now if that fault line hadn't existed,
would things have been different? If our
marriage had been stronger, would we have
been able to resist her?

Most of our friends don't know about the
affair. Chris and Susannah were the only
ones we told, but I'm sure others must have
wondered, because for a whole year we
slipped off the circuit. It was easier to avoid
other people than to present a united front.
We turned down invitations to dinner, to
drinks, to the theater, e-mailing apologies
for not showing up at Christmas parties,
fortieth birthdays, housewarmings. Neither
did we issue any invitations of our own,
which must have seemed unusual — before
it happened, we regularly entertained at
home. We used the house renovation as an
excuse, but really it was because neither of
us felt able to go through the choreographed
dance of host and hostess when we were
still, to an extent, tiptoeing around each
other.

On that particular Friday evening — the

Friday I'm remembering — it was the first time we had invited friends round since our marriage had unraveled. I had invited Peter, my boss, an amiable man, and his wife, Anna, whom I didn't know very well. Chris and Susannah completed the party.

That evening the rain was coming down in sheets, streaking the windows, the umbrella stand in the hall filling up as everyone arrived. David was late. The guests were in the living room and I was fixing drinks in the kitchen, when he came in and began stripping off his rain gear.

"Sorry, I got held up at work," he told me, bundling his stuff into a sodden mass and coming toward me, kissing me hello. "Sarah had her orals today, and the visiting professor stayed on."

"Have you been drinking?" I could smell the beer on his breath.

"A quick one in the common room."

I snapped open a can of tonic and began pouring it into the gin.

"I had to take the man for a drink — out of courtesy, Caroline. He'd come over from England to do the orals as a favor."

"I tried calling you."

"Did you? I must have had the phone on silent."

He moved past me to the sink, filled a

glass with water, and gulped it down.

"You forgot, didn't you?"

He put the empty glass on the draining board. "I'll run upstairs and change."

For a Friday evening supper, I had decided to go for something fairly casual — mussels in white wine to start, then lamb chops and a fennel salad with some crusty bread. A cheese board, and then for dessert, toasted brioche with figs and pistachio ice cream.

Throughout the meal the conversation pitched and rolled between various topics: the water charges, local politics, gossip about a shared acquaintance whose prurient misdeeds had recently made headlines. David, having recovered from his lateness — or perhaps in a bid to make amends — was lively and animated, steering the conversation, never allowing it to flag. Repartee sparked back and forth between him and Chris, with Peter joining in from time to time. It was, on the whole, a very male-dominated discourse. Anna seemed the type of person who was more interested in listening and agreeing, laughing in all the right places rather than adding much by way of her own opinion. Susannah was unusually quiet. Chris is always the heart of the party — mocking, grandiose — and when things are good between them, Susannah is his perfect partner, taking his cues, matching his quips with barbs of her own softened by the tongue-in-cheek manner of her delivery. They are the perfect dinner guests — funny, engaging, interesting. But that evening, from the tightness in Susannah's face, the way her eyes narrowed over her glass as she looked at him, I knew it wasn't going to be like that. At first it was just casual sniping, nothing major, but gradually over the course of the meal as she emptied her wineglass and then emptied it again, she seemed to withdraw into a troubled silence.

After the coffee was finished, over whiskey and port, talk turned to a recent case where photographs of schoolgirls in Northern Ireland had ended up on a voyeuristic website regularly trawled by pedophiles. Anna's niece was one of the girls whose image had been stolen.

"I mean, it's shocking," she told us. "A fifteen-year-old girl, having her image abused in that manner."

"What was the photo of," Chris said, "if you don't mind me asking?"

"Of nothing! Girls playing around, messing. It was innocent stuff."

"Hmm."

Chris looked skeptical, and I saw a flare of color appear at Anna's throat.

"Why? What are you saying?"

"Well," he said, shrugging. "Teenage girls messing around? It may seem innocent to you, but let's be completely honest here. A lot of girls have shed their innocence by the time they're fifteen. You see them hanging around in packs — they are well aware of their power —"

"Their power?"

"Yes! They understand inherently the power they wield over boys and men. What they possess — youthful bodies, burgeoning sexuality — it's highly potent stuff. My God, you just have to look at how they're dressed to see how they flaunt it. And why shouldn't they?"

"It's one thing for a girl to wear a miniskirt on O'Connell Street," Anna countered, "but it's quite another for some pervert to steal her photograph and put it up on his grubby little website for all his friends to letch over."

"Do you know what annoys me?" Chris said, leaning forward with a new intensity. "It's these people who take photographs of themselves with their smartphones and post them on Facebook or whatever, send them to their friends, and then whine when someone else views them —"

"Hang on a minute." Anna sat up a little straighter.

"I mean it's the same with these celebrities and their nude pics. For Christ's sake, who could be stupid enough to post those shots of themselves and then be shocked when they enter the public realm?"

"It's hardly the same thing," Peter said reasonably.

"No, just listen to me," Chris continued, warming now to his subject. "Caroline, does Holly have a smartphone?"

"Yes, but we monitor her use of it," I hastened to add. "She understands we can access her phone at any time, read her texts, her IMs, her Facebook posts, everything."

"Okay. And does she ever use her phone to take pictures?"

"Of course, but they're very innocent. She's eleven, for God's sake! And she doesn't post them online — she's not allowed to put pictures up on any social networking sites."

"Not now, maybe. But how long are you going to be able to police it for?"

"For as long as we pay her phone bill," David interjected, grinning and taking a slug of whiskey.

"What if she's staying at a friend's house?" Chris went on. "That happens still, right?"

"Yes," I agreed, cautiously, not liking where he was going with this.

"A slumber party with a group of girls. Giddiness sets in. The tone of the conversation changes, they start talking about boys they fancy. Someone takes out a smartphone. Pictures are taken. One of them — one whose parents aren't as vigilant — posts them on Facebook. And next thing you know, you've got a picture of your daughter in her nightie doing the rounds of the Internet."

"Christ," David said, shaking his head.

"So what are you saying? That it's inevitable?" I asked.

He reached for the whiskey bottle. "Maybe it is."

"My niece wasn't pictured in her nightie," Anna added. "I'd just like to make that clear."

"There was flesh shown in those pictures," Chris countered.

"That doesn't mean they were having a pillow fight in their underwear!"

"Now there's a thought," Chris said, winking at Peter.

Peter stiffened. I looked at Chris. How much had he had to drink? It had been a few months since I'd seen him and there was a new fleshiness to him, shadows around his eyes that suggested ill health or unhappiness. He was a bit of a shambles, what with the weight he'd put on, the doughy pallor of his complexion. He had always possessed a kind of louche charm, relaxed good looks, and a face enlivened by humor, but in the half-light thrown by the lamps and the candles, he looked a bit washed-up, bedraggled, lost.

"I think you're making too much of this," David told him, adopting a friendly, reasoned approach. "The photos were probably of girls in their hockey gear, or something equally innocent. The fact is these trolls and sickos trawling those websites will corrupt even the most innocent image into something titillating, but it's a perversion in their own minds, not anything these girls are projecting."

Chris laughed, a honk of disbelief. "Oh, come on, Dave!" he said, slamming one hand on the table, still playful, although a hardness had entered his voice, his eye. "Can you hear yourself?"

"What?"

"You make it sound like they're all angels! You, of all people, should know about the scheming ways of teenage girls!"

David paused, just briefly, his glass halfway to his mouth. "What the hell is that supposed to mean?"

But something had entered that pause. A

shiver of uncertainty. A cool doubt I had felt of late.

Chris was off now explaining how David, as a university lecturer, must rub shoulders every day with teenage girls, harlots, as he described them, calling into his office, batting their eyelids at him in a bid to up their grades or be excused from a tutorial or whatever. Good-natured banter, I suppose, but most of it flew straight past me. I couldn't stop looking at David. The change was so subtle that only a wife would have noticed. The flush of color in his cheeks from the drink had faded away, most of the blood leaving his face. His lips had thinned slightly, and a new sharpness had entered his eyes. He seemed wary, shaken even. And it came to me then: my husband was keeping something from me.

How long did the moment last, I wonder? The opening out of that realization within me, everything falling into place: his recent behavior, the silences, the sudden snapping, the forgetfulness. I had put it down to the pressures of work, the consuming nature of his passion for history. Now I saw it was something else. I knew all the signs of concealment — we had been here before. The heat of sudden anger flared within me. I wasn't afraid — not then. That would come later, when I knew her, when I felt the insidious creep of her presence through our lives. What I felt more than anything was shock.

I don't know what Chris said next — I missed it in the storm of my own private feeling — but whatever it was, it made Susannah snap.

"Oh, my God," she said, the disgust in her voice hauling me out of my reverie. "Do you even listen to yourself? Have you any notion at all of how sad and creepy you come across?"

"It's called honesty, my dear," Chris replied, his voice elevated. "Something you wouldn't recognize in your line of work."

Susannah is a corporate lawyer, openly acknowledged as the real breadwinner of the two. Chris, who worked for a newspaper in a subeditorial role that matched his whimsical nature, liked to refer to himself as a kept man, often joking how work for him was like a hobby. There were no such jokes that night.

Turning to Peter and Anna, who seemed increasingly uncomfortable, he explained, "Oh I know she looks like a woman, but Susannah is actually a shark."

Susannah is a striking-looking woman with strong dark features and a sharp angular haircut. On that occasion, her features appeared even more pronounced than usual, lipstick in a deep plum color, her mouth a grim slash in her face.

"Listening to you talk of teenage girls in such a manner? You're just another drunken letch," she said. "God, when I hear you say these things, it makes me so fucking thankful we never had children."

His eyes grew small. "We never had children because I didn't want them. Any child I had with you might be born with a dorsal fin and several rows of teeth."

There was a moment of silence like a held breath before Susannah stood up suddenly. Her chair swung backward and Peter had to grab it before it fell. Without saying a word, she left the room.

Chris broke the silence.

"Oops," he said, and tried to laugh, but it came out as a gasp.

"Are you all right?" David asked.

Chris picked up the dessert spoon from his plate, turned it over, put it back. In the hall, the front door slammed.

"One of us should go after her," I said.

Still looking at his plate, Chris said, "Be my guest."

The rain had stopped, water pooling in dips in the paving.

I could see Susannah striding down the street and shouted for her to stop, but her footfall didn't slow and I had to run to catch up with her.

"Please come back," I said when I reached her.

She kept walking, holding her coat closed with one hand, her handbag clenched in the other. There was something terrible in her balled-up anger, her refusal to speak until she reached the corner where our avenue meets the main road.

"I'm so sorry, Caro," she said. "We've ruined your evening, haven't we?"

Her eyes flicked past me to a taxi slowing as it neared and she stepped out onto the road with her hand held aloft.

"Please don't do this," I said, but her mind was made up.

The taxi drove away and through its rear window, I saw the sharp silhouette of her haircut; I knew that what had happened between them could not be undone.

Peter and Anna were at the front door when I reached the house, already in their coats, full of smiles and words of thanks for a lovely evening, then hastily departing. There was no sign of David. They hurried away into the night, and I closed the door on the darkness. In the kitchen, Chris had his head in his hands, and David was pouring him another whiskey.

"Chris is staying with us tonight," he told me.

Normally, I am the one to offer comfort, to know the right words to say.

"I'll go make up his room," I said.

As I closed the door, I saw them clink glasses, a solemnity in the gesture rather than any measure of cheer.

An idea had gotten its claws into me — the notion that David might be having an affair. A dalliance with a colleague or some postdoctoral student. Some silly girl looking for excitement with an older man, the thoughtless facilitator of his midlife crisis. We might have been able to weather the storm of such a crisis, but what was to come — the slow erosion caused by her destructive presence — proved far worse, a dark cavity that would open up and suck each one of us in.

# CHAPTER 6
## DAVID

I was rinsing wineglasses from the night before, dog-tired and hungover. Chris had just left. Daydreaming by the kitchen sink — a memory came to me of Linda wearing a shirt of mine, her legs and feet bare on the hard tiles of that kitchen floor in our Donegal cottage. Those same feet, the night before, had pressed into the small of my back, the soft balls of her heels. I thought back to how I traced a finger over her temple, along the sloping curve of her cheek, and told her it was all going to be okay. I drew her close enough to feel her body against mine, to feel caught in the green haze of her stare. I kissed her, felt the tenderness of her lips against mine. A sense of certainty had come over me — the sure knowledge that we were safe, that no harm could come to us. Twenty-four years old, my whole life ahead of me.

"Who is Zoe?"

Disturbed from my daydream, I turned and saw Caroline. In her hand was a piece of paper.

"I found this in your wallet."

It was the note Zoe had slipped beneath my office door, the one asking me to meet her in Madigans.

"Why were you looking in my wallet?"

"It fell out. I was doing the laundry."

I put the dish towel that was slung across my shoulder on the draining board and took a deep breath. "Close the door," I said. "We need to talk."

She did as I asked and the chatter from the television in the next room became an indistinct hum. I gazed out into the garden where everything for a moment appeared to be moving in slow motion — the russet leaves falling from the trees, and above them a dense body of clouds rippling by in waves. In the distance, there was the dull sound of a car starting. Caroline waited, a tense look on her face.

"Do you remember me telling you about Linda Barry?"

"Yes?"

"Zoe is her daughter."

"Her daughter?" she repeated.

I pulled at my earlobe. "She's also one of my students. There's no easy way to say this. . . . She thinks I might be her father."

Caroline put the note down on the table, but she kept her eyes on me.

"What?"

"I know. It was a shock to me too."

"Is it true?"

"She seems to think it is. Linda had told her about me. She had her birth certificate with her."

Caroline pulled out a chair and sat at the table.

"A birth certificate?" she said.

Her resolute calm and steady nerve disarmed me. It would not have been unreasonable for her to raise her voice or to display some outrage. Instead there was a steely implacable propriety. I shouldn't have been surprised. Caroline had always demonstrated an inner resolve.

"It didn't actually name me as father . . ."

"Then how can you be sure she's your daughter?"

"I can't, not categorically. But there is a resemblance to Linda, I suppose, and the dates match up. She had some photographs . . ."

"Photographs?"

"Of myself and Linda."

Caroline looked about her as if to reassure herself, to check that she was where she thought she was: the kitchen with its stereo on the countertop, the glass fruit bowl, the children's assorted books and computer games, the black-and-white framed pictures of us as a family on the far wall. I thought she might reach out and touch something — the need in her appeared so real.

"And where is Linda now?" she asked evenly.

"She's dead," I said, and it sounded like a vindication, though I hadn't meant it to. Caroline's eyes widened.

I took the chair opposite her and went on to tell what I knew of Linda's passing.

She reached for a napkin from the holder on the table. "When did this happen? When did this girl come and see you?" she asked.

"I found out at the start of the week."

"The start of the week? Why didn't you say something?" She became a little more worked up, annoyed now by the delay in my telling her. "Why did you wait to tell me?"

"To be honest, I needed more time."

"More time?"

"It was a shock to have her walk into my office and make that claim. I needed time to think it through before telling you." I remained calm, pragmatic. "I wasn't trying to keep it from you."

"You should have told me right away," Caroline said.

"I wanted to get things clear in my head."

"And are they?"

What was in my head was an image of the whitewash of water whipped up by the wind on the beach in Holywood, breaking relentlessly wave after wave against the shore, where Linda and I had once stood hand in hand.

"I don't know," I said. "The girl makes a convincing case." I meant Zoe, but I was thinking of how Linda and I had tripped our way down Botanic Avenue on those evenings on our way to the pub or a poetry reading at Oxfam.

"But how can you be sure?" Caroline asked.

"We're getting a test done."

"What? Like a paternity test?" she asked, with a nervous laugh.

"Why not?" I answered.

She folded the cloth napkin, pressed it flat with her palm for an iron. "How do you even go about such a test?" she asked.

"It's relatively straightforward," I said, explaining how to retrieve samples and send them off to a lab. My voice enunciated these words with cool clarity, but I was thinking back to the scene in the pub, how sordid and underhand it all felt — handing over the money.

"I can't believe it," she said. "It seems so unreal. A DNA test?"

"It's the twenty-first century, Caroline. People get their DNA tested all the time."

"On TV, maybe. Or in America. But this is Ireland. Do you know one single person who's done a paternity test? Even a friend of a friend?"

I knew what she meant. Despite the rapid progress of recent years and the sweeping modernization across Irish life, some things remained stubbornly untouched. Our nation was, in some respects, still repressed. Divorce was relatively uncommon. Women needed to leave the State to terminate a pregnancy. Baptism was a stamp required to secure a school place. DNA testing seemed reserved for the sphere of criminal investigations, not for private citizens seeking personal information.

"When are you going to arrange all this?" Caroline asked.

"It's already done."

"What? You've sent it off already?"

"The results should come back within two weeks." I was fudging the issue of which one of us had sent the samples. Somehow I knew Caroline wouldn't be happy at the thought of the matter resting in Zoe's hands.

She was looking at me strangely, a wary examining look.

"Did you have any clue?" she asked. "Any inkling this might be possible?"

"No."

"You never suspected?"

"Never." As I watched for her reaction, I noticed something else, something within me, a disbelief at my own words because, to put it quite simply, they were not true. *I did suspect.* But it was a buried, unconscious suspicion. Ever since that weekend in Donegal, the seed of possibility had stayed with me. Had we been careful? Linda had asked me back then. Careful: up until then, we had always been careful. In fact, care was what had defined our relationship. We had to be both careful and circumspect. Nobody knew we were together. Nobody knew we were even lovers. She was my student, after all.

"It's hard to believe . . ." Caroline said bringing me back to the present. "What will you do if it's true? What will we do if she really is your daughter?"

"If she is, she is. It doesn't have to change everything; it doesn't have to disrupt the lives we have. We'll adjust, get to know her, try to make room for her in our lives."

"As simply as all that?"

I said, "Why not?"

"Have you thought how this might affect Robbie and Holly if it's true?" she said. "If they find out that they have a half sister?"

I had thought about it. I was worried about how they might react. There had been enough disruption in their lives, and God knows I didn't want to see them hurt. "We'll manage, but first let's get through this next step."

Caroline considered what I had said, and asked, "What is she like?"

"She's young . . . bright, a little shy. She has all the gaucheness of a teenager and at the same time enough nerve to walk into my office and introduce herself as my daughter . . . whether it ends up being true or not, I have to take it seriously."

Caroline listened, concentrating, trying to process it all.

"So when did this take place?" She gestured to the note discarded on the table — *Madigans . . . 6:30 p.m.*

"Yesterday. I met her at the pub before the dinner party."

"You told me you were taking a visiting professor out for a drink."

"Well, I didn't. I met Zoe."

"Why didn't tell you me? Why did you

have to lie?"

"We had guests in the next room. Do you really think that was the time for me to bring this up with you?"

"I just wish you could have been honest with me."

"And you are an expert on honesty now?" I snapped. Caroline looked more disappointed than hurt. I apologized, but the awkwardness was back.

"All these years . . ." she said.

I wanted to say what a relief it was to tell her, but I didn't. The strange mix of emotions I was feeling — at once frightening and painful — stopped me.

Her fingers tapped the tabletop.

"All of this. It makes me uneasy."

I said nothing. What was the point? The wheels of whatever it was had been set in motion. Caroline held her hands to her face. She was deep in thought — weighing everything. I stood up and looked back to the sink, the wineglasses refracting the morning light. I thought of that morning in Donegal and just like that she was there like a ghostly presence in the background, my old flame — Linda. All these years . . . whenever I missed her, whenever I wondered what might have been, when I was with someone else, or when I was with my wife, she still seemed there, in the shadows. It had happened more than once, when I made love to Caroline, a feeling that in some strange way I was still making love to Linda.

"Promise me something," Caroline said. "Promise me you won't seek the girl out or spend any time with her that you don't need to. Not until we know for sure."

"She's one of my students. I'll see her during lectures."

"Can't you change that?"

"How?"

"I don't know. Get her to change class."

"It's a bit late in the semester for that," I said, before adding: "Besides, the class is compulsory. She can't drop it."

"Is it even allowed? Won't the college object when they find out what your relationship is to her?"

I shrugged. "It's not as uncommon as you'd think — a lecturer ending up with one of his or her kids in their class. There are rules, of course, like not being able to mark your child's exams or classwork." Caroline looked skeptical. "As soon as I know for sure that I am her father, I'll let the college know and we'll take it from there."

"All right," Caroline said unhappily. "But outside of lectures, will you promise me you'll keep your distance from her? Until these results come back?"

"I promise," I said.

The radio was playing in the background: a listener was complaining about the impending water charges. Another demonstration was being planned in town, he said, and as he did so, it occurred to me that within this house, within the confines of what we called our home, there was something of a real and indelible crisis going on, something that was going to disrupt our family unit irrevocably, but outside, beyond the boundaries of our home, life carried on — people were up in arms about water charges, about employment, about governance and corruption, but the very same people were going about their daily business. Life carried on — no matter what.

"What are you two talking about?" Holly said, standing in the doorway with her coat on. I don't know how long she had been standing there or how much she had heard.

"I'll be with you in two minutes," Caroline said before Holly walked out into the hall to wait for her.

"No contact with the girl," she said to me. "Not until we find out more."

"Agreed," I said.

She stood up stiffly as if the truce she had

made with me was an unsatisfactory one but one she had to accept whether she liked it or not.

# Chapter 7
## Caroline

My husband is not a vengeful man. Yet, that Saturday morning when he told me about this daughter — about Zoe — as I sat and listened to him talking of DNA tests and establishing parentage, one distinct notion kept rising to the surface: this was his way of getting his own back.

It was all so unsettling. Who was this girl? What did she want from us? I had no way of knowing how it would impact our lives. No idea to what extent she would want to become involved with our family. Would she expect to be treated in the same way as David treated Robbie and Holly? Would she expect us to provide for her? Pay her college tuition? Her rent?

"What about Robbie?" I had asked him. "What about Holly?"

"We'll manage," David said.

A feeble answer. Our children. How would they cope with the revelation of this new sister? Even after the news had sunk in and the shock had dissipated, how would they react to this person? Would they feel displaced? Resentful? Ashamed?

I said nothing of this to Holly as we drove out west of the city. Instead I allowed her to chatter on as she switched from one radio station to another, a happy buzz of excitement coming off her at the prospect of our shopping trip. Since turning eleven, she had developed a pressing desire to assert her own taste and I had promised to buy her new Ikea furniture for her bedroom. It was late morning by the time we had finished pushing through the showrooms and we were downstairs in the warehouse, both of us a little weary and looking forward to coffee and a scone, when it happened.

Holly had returned to the bed linen department, having changed her mind about the pattern she had chosen, so I was alone in the aisle, scanning the stacks of brown boxes for the one I wanted. Having found it at last, I pulled it out and hoisted it onto my shopping cart, and I was just straightening up when a woman came toward me and slammed her trolley into mine. Instinctively, I gripped the handle and looked at her. She was staring right at me, her eyes bright with fury. Before I could say anything, she slammed her trolley into mine a second time and I let out a cry. The force of the impact caused some of her items to clatter onto the concrete floor. I didn't move, the suddenness of the aggression, the sharp focus of it, shocking me into inaction. She was a woman of my own age wearing jeans and a gray turtleneck, dark hair drawn back into a ponytail. I knew who she was, having seen her occasionally at the school gates before the time of my indiscretion but not since. Now she was fixing me with an expression of such venom as if she wanted to push me with her trolley back against the shelves stacked high with boxed furniture and watch as it all came crashing down on my head. There was something electric about the snap of current passing between us. It lasted no more than a minute. Then she drew back from me and turned, half-walking half-running, struggling with the heavy trolley as she rounded the corner. The items that had slipped from her cart — a set of mixing bowls and some magazine files — remained on the floor where they had fallen.

Shaken by the encounter, I glanced around to see if anyone else had witnessed this strange assault, and there was Holly. She was holding a different set of bed linen under her arm. She came toward me, and — this is the part that really kills me — she put the package on top of the boxes, and, without looking at me, without uttering a word about what she had just witnessed, she said in a small flat voice: "I think that's everything." She pushed her glasses back up to the bridge of her nose and starting walking toward the checkout.

Holly has always been the more resilient of my children, even though she is the younger. She lacks the sensitivity of her older brother, which has worried me from his infancy. I suppose because she is the baby of the family I sometimes underestimate her strength of mind, her astuteness. But every now and then she surprises me with her maturity. Did she know this woman was Aidan's wife? Worse, did she know what I had done?

"Holly," I said in the car. "About what happened back there —"

"Please, Mum," she interrupted. "I don't want to talk about it."

Throughout the journey home we were silent, but I kept thinking of her reaction — the coolness of it. Was it possible she knew? It made me wonder at how much she had been exposed to, my daughter with her steady gaze, her father's cool demeanor.

Guilt stirred within me again. Apparently, it was never far away.

More than a year before Zoe came into our lives, I became involved with a man whose son went to school with Robbie. The word "affair" seems wrong — a false name for what occurred between us. You can't properly call it an affair if there was never full-on sex, can you? A fling, perhaps, although that makes it sound so throwaway, as if I'm the type of woman who whimsically forgets her marriage vows whenever the fancy takes her. I am not that type of person. His name was Aidan — *is* Aidan, for he hasn't died, he's just not in my life anymore; we met through the Parents' Committee. This "fling," for want of a better word, lasted for three, maybe four months. It was not love. It was never that. When it ended, Aidan and his wife took their son out of Robbie's school and the family moved to a different part of Dublin. David and I made the decision to keep Robbie where he was. In hindsight, I think that was a mistake.

I thought David had forgiven me but, in the aftermath of his revelation, I began to suspect he had been biding his time, waiting for the right moment, the right opportunity to present itself. Revenge had come in a way I'd never imagined: in the form of a teenage girl.

I didn't speak about revenge to him. How could I? There was a time when I could have spoken my mind to David about anything. I never used to be afraid of confrontation. But something had happened in the aftermath of my indiscretion — a change in the dynamic between us. It was true that he had taken me back without punishment or reproach. But ours was no longer a relaxed home. An undercurrent of tension ran through everything. Even though we never told the children what had happened, what I had done, it was impossible to shield them from the atmosphere that developed between us. They regarded me with cautious eyes as if anxious I might plunge them back into a time of uncertainty. David acted with the same calm exterior, the same cool-headed thinking I had known of him. We carried on. We got through it. But I had lost some of my power. It had slipped away, relinquished because of the debt I owed him for his forgiveness.

On that Saturday morning, we made an agreement, David and I. We would put the matter of Zoe to one side until we had definitive proof. For the two weeks it took to decode the strands of DNA, identify a pattern, an affinity between David's genes and Zoe's — or none — for those two weeks we would try to live our lives as best we could. Everything would continue as before — work, the children, the house, our relationships. Just for those two weeks.

Easier said than done.

For the first week there was a buzz in my brain, a low-grade headache. I put it down to poor sleep. I tried to kill it with paracetamol so I could focus on my job but the headache persisted. Going back to work for a company I had once been a part of was not the triumphant return I had secretly hoped it would be. It was disconcerting how far things had moved on in the past fifteen years, making the landscape almost entirely unrecognizable to me. I willed myself to become absorbed in the challenge. All the while, in the back of my head, there was this hum: *Zoe.*

I don't think I even recognized her as a person then. I saw her as a problem I didn't know how to solve. Work allowed me to drown out the sound of the hum in my brain. But in the evenings, after dinner, the kids occupied with homework or friends or TV, when David and I were alone together, the sound returned, amplified.

"What does she look like?" I asked.

It was night, and we were both lying awake in the dark. Somewhere down our street, a car alarm was going off.

His gaze moved from the window to the ceiling, and I felt him smoothing the duvet around him.

"Much like any other first-year student," he said, his voice flat.

"Come on, David. They can't all look the same. She must have some distinguishing feature."

"Her hair," he said then, and I found myself grow tense. "She has this shock of blond hair. Long springy curls — almost white, it's so blond."

"She doesn't sound like you."

"Linda's hair," he remarked.

Linda. Her name spoken in the darkness of our bedroom. I thought of her, all those years ago, and imagined David running his hands over those blond curls, knitting his fingers up in them, marveling at them, loving them. I conjured up the image myself and then I wished I hadn't.

"And boots," he said then.

"Boots?"

"She wears these boots — military-looking things. Doc Martens I suppose. Oxblood in color. They look enormous at the end of her skinny legs. She's such a little slip of a thing. Shy."

The way he said it, I couldn't help thinking he felt affection toward her.

He lay there, staring into the dark. Outside, the car alarm had stopped, and silence came into the room like a sudden intrusion. He turned over, flattening himself out in preparation for sleep.

But I didn't sleep. It was as though each of us — in separate and distinct ways — had been plunged back into the past. Fragments of old memories were coming back at unexpected moments. As David's breathing slowed, were his last waking thoughts of Linda? As for me, I found myself going back farther to another time. A decision made. The weight of its seriousness pressing on my young shoulders. *"You don't have to come with me,"* I had told him. *"I can go on my own."* Trying to sound brave while inside I was dying. Did he remember that conversation, my sleeping husband? Was any of this coming back to him too? Old ghosts awoke, stirred angrily into life by this girl, like a wasp's nest struck with a stick.

It was a flare in my brain — her golden hair. Everywhere I looked there were girls with blond hair, hanging loose down backs and over shoulders, swinging in ponytails, with flicked fringes. I found myself staring at teenage girls, calculating their ages, assessing their likeness to David, to Holly. She could have been any one of them.

I didn't intend to seek her out. But one morning, driving along Morehampton Road, running an errand for Peter, it occurred to me that if I kept on driving I would reach the UCD campus.

I rang the History Department office while driving, saying my niece was a first-year student of history; she had been visiting with me last night but had left her phone in my house. I had no way of getting in touch with her, I said, and wanted to drop it off at the university.

All I wanted was to get a look at her. I had no intention of approaching her. First Years had American history in Theater J that morning, I was told. All I needed was to see her. Once I had done so, my fear would subside, or if not my fear, then at least my curiosity.

The possibility of bumping into David, going from his office to a lecture, had crossed my mind. If I saw him, then I would make something up. Part of me wondered what his reaction would be. Students were already streaming out of lecture theaters as

I ran up the steps and into the Arts Building, the corridors and foyers momentarily clotted with young adults. When I got to Theater J and looked around at the empty seats, the vacant space awaiting the next influx, I felt a small stab of disappointment.

*What are you doing?* I asked myself. *Foolish woman.*

Outside the lecture hall, students were drifting sluggishly along like hungover cows. I felt conspicuous among them, dressed in a black trouser suit and kitten heels, my shoulder-length brown hair flicked out at the ends. I didn't look like a lecturer, let alone a student. I probably looked like an accountant or a management consultant on campus to give a presentation. I would call on David. Surprise him. Make a serious attempt to bridge the gap we both knew had opened up between us since his revelation. Pushing myself away from the wall, I looked toward the stairwell, and it was in the act of turning that I saw her.

Blond hair, just as he had said, luminous under the fluorescent strip lighting. Her face small and pale amid the haze of hair. A skinny girl and not very tall, but she held herself well, shoulders thrown back, a long straight neck, her bag slung over one shoulder — a casual, relaxed pose. And the boots he had mentioned, lending something firm and inflexible to her otherwise waiflike appearance.

She was standing by a marble and limestone sculpture known to generations of students as the Blob. I had wanted to catch a glimpse of her. Well, I had done that, yet I lingered. She didn't look remotely like either of my children. The lightness of her hair, the milky whiteness of her skin were at odds with the darker coloring that unified the four of us. I felt the doubt trickling in.

She broke away from her friend and walked through the thinning crowd of students, toward the exit. I watched her narrow back, her skinny legs, the careful manner of her walk — no slouching or dragging feet with this one. Reason told me to let her go, but impulse led me to follow her, and soon enough I was outside again, feeling the chill of the air, following her up the paved walkway toward the pond by the Engineering Building. All the time, I was trying to keep my distance, trying to walk as if I had a purpose other than stalking her.

She took a seat on an empty bench on the deck around the pond. As I neared, the sound of my heels on the deck rang out and I slowed my step. She was sitting with her eyes closed, her head tilted up to the sky, soaking up what little heat there was. Her pose was perfectly still, like a cat basking in the sun. I stopped, looked down at her, and slowly she opened her eyes. Green eyes, a little widely spaced, short dense lashes. They looked up at me in an assessing way, but she didn't say anything.

"You're Zoe," I said.

"Do I know you?"

Still so composed, so unfazed. A northern flavor to her voice.

"I'm Caroline," I said. "David's wife."

Her face cleared in recognition, eyes narrowing a fraction, then a slight flicker as she took me in, her interest piqued. She smiled, a slow lazy kind of smile and, it seemed to me, a little sly.

"So he told you."

A bristle of anger went through me. Of course he told me, I wanted to say. I'm his bloody wife.

"Do you mind if I sit?"

"Sure."

The bench felt cold against the backs of my legs. My gaze followed the curling path of a moorhen gliding through the reeds. That pond hadn't been there when I was a student. I could feel Zoe looking at me with that little smirk.

"You thought you'd come here and give me the once-over for yourself," she said.

A statement, not a question, and I could see how it was going to be between us. She had no notion of treading softly with me. Whatever charm she had reserved for David, it was clearly not going to be employed here.

"You can't blame me for being curious," I replied.

"True."

She turned her face to the sun, her shoulders thrown back, and closed her eyes again. I examined the planes of her face, looking for some trace of David, but there was nothing. She was completely unfamiliar to me. David's words ran through my head: *A little slip of a thing. Shy.* Was that really how he saw her? Some vulnerable waif? The unfazed stillness of her pose made her seem so sure of herself, so self-contained, nerveless where I was rigid and tense.

"What made you decide to seek him out now?"

"I don't know. I was always going to get in touch, wasn't I?"

"Why now, though? Why not before?"

"Now, before, later — what difference does it make?" She shrugged, then added: "I'm here in the college, after all. It seemed stupid to avoid it any longer."

"It's come as a shock," I said, "for David and for me."

"Hmm."

She said this in a ruminative, matter-of-fact way that infuriated me. There was no hint of her taking this seriously — it was all a game to her.

"I suppose I wanted to meet you so I could find out what your position is —"

"My position!" She laughed thinly, sounding insubstantial, lacking in conviction, although when she spoke the words were sharp and precise.

"Yes, your position. I wanted to see where you stood on this."

"You make me sound like a politician."

"Well . . ."

My voice faded. The truth was I didn't know what I wanted from her. Except, perhaps, for her to turn around and say it had all been a stupid joke, none of it was true. When I had made the decision to sit down next to her, I still thought if I just spoke to her — confronted her, I suppose — she would crumble, break down. There would be tears and an admission to a foolish spoof, some desperate grab for attention. But looking at this cat preening herself under the sun, it felt like I was the one close to a breakdown.

"Does David know you're here with me?"

I looked at her sharply.

"Yes," I said, the lie coming quickly to my mouth.

It was instinctive, the need to align myself with my husband in this girl's eyes. Something told me that if she knew the truth, then she could use it as ammunition.

"I see."

"He's my husband," I said. "I don't want him to get hurt."

She flicked back her hair, opened her eyes, leaned forward to pick up her bag, and got to her feet. Standing in front of me, she blocked the low-lying sun, her face in shadow, but still I could see her gazing down on me with those cold eyes. Without saying a word, she swung her bag over her shoulder and turned away.

"My position," I heard her say again, amusement in her voice.

Her laughter rang out as she walked back toward the Arts Block, and it stayed with me — the mocking ring of it. Sitting on the bench, I felt a shiver of nerves cross my shoulders. All those years spent thinking about Linda, wondering what she might have been like, trying to imagine her — now I felt as if I had finally met her. And I didn't like her. She unnerved me.

I told myself I was being ridiculous. Zoe was just a girl. A teenager. There had been no ghostly visitation. Yet I felt shaken from the meeting — unsettled.

Within my line of vision there was a bronze statue of two people reaching, leaping upward with arms outstretched, limbs entwined — a man and a woman — lean, youthful, athletic, their fingers splayed as if trying to catch the sun. I looked across at that piece of art in the wake of Zoe's departure and read within it energy, vitality, joy. It reverberated with optimism and boundless possibility, which made me feel a little sad because I couldn't feel any of those things, not then. That day, staring at those bronzed figures in the coolness of the October sunshine, I felt hollowed out, as if something had just been taken from me. She was a thief, come to steal from me all that I loved. I knew it then: I would have to guard myself against her.

When David got home from work that evening and I heard him in the hall, I stirred the spaghetti in the pot and felt a tightening beneath my ribs. From upstairs came the sounds of Robbie practicing his cello, a long, drawn-out note like a plea. David found me in the kitchen and asked, "Any news?"

I could have told him then. Instead, I lifted my face to receive his kiss, smiling right back at him.

"No. Not a thing."

# CHAPTER 8
# DAVID

As it happened, I kept my promise to Caroline. During those weeks I waited to hear news of the DNA test, I had no interaction with Zoe. I saw her once staring out at me from the sea of faces in Theater L, but only once. Her attendance at lectures was erratic and I could see from the tutorial sheets that her presence there was inconsistent too. It irritated me a little, this lackadaisical approach to her studies, and I had to remind myself that it was not my problem — not yet, anyway. Until her assertion was affirmed by hard science, I had to keep her at the same distance I kept any of my students.

My irritation was fleeting. I had other more pressing concerns. After consultations with GPs and geriatricians, I decided that the best option for my mother was to place her in a secure accommodation where she could be taken care of by experts. Her confusion was deepening; I was steeling myself for the day when I would arrive at her door and she would look at me with no recognition in her eyes. Anytime the phone rang in the house, I half-expected it to be news of another incident involving Mum wandering off, becoming lost again, and I grew increasingly anxious that some harm might come to her.

As luck would have it, I found a place for her in a facility at the foot of the Dublin Mountains, a place that came highly recommended by our GP. It wasn't cheap, but I was drawn to the warm, friendly environment and the emphasis they placed on family and togetherness. The last thing I wanted was for Mum to feel like she was being stuck in an institution, someplace cold and clinical.

On a weekday morning when I had no lectures, I cleared my diary and took Mum to visit the place where I hoped she would be happy. She was quiet, for the most part, silently taking in the place as the manager, a bright, friendly woman, brought us on a tour of the dining room and recreational hall as well as the other shared spaces, outlining in bright, positive language the social activities that took place here. Along the way, we were introduced to several residents as well as to members of the staff, and I felt my nerves begin to ebb away, reassured by the warmth and friendliness of those we met. It was not until we were led into the room that would be my mother's that I felt a dip in my optimism.

There was nothing wrong with the room. It was a good size, comfortable, airy, with a fine view of the mountains rolling down to Bohernabreena. The manager was explaining to Mum how she was to feel free to bring her own furniture and possessions, the bric-a-brac that had cluttered the rooms of my childhood, to make this room feel as much like home as possible. Mum had stepped toward the bed and was standing with one hand upon it, quietly contemplating it, when it occurred to me that the previous inhabitant had probably died in this room, in that very bed Mum was touching. And in all likelihood, my mother would die here too. A strange vertiginous thought. I felt like someone had punched me with it. I couldn't escape the feeling that by moving her into this room I was somehow hastening her doom.

"David," my mother said.

For weeks now her expressions had been vague, her eyes clouded with confusion. Her voice had grown thin and uncertain. But she was regarding me with a clarity and

113

force that took me by surprise. For an instant, her illness fell away. Her hand caught hold of my wrist, and she smiled a little.

"It will do just fine," she said, as if I were the one needing reassurance.

And it was like I was a child again, upset over some slight or intimidation that had happened at school, and the look she could give me, the warmth and firmness of her voice, the magical way it made the hurt diminish and fade.

The arrangements were made and after dropping Mum to her friend's house for the afternoon, I drove to campus, locking the car, and walked to the Newman Building, my lungs filling with the heavy autumn air.

There would be a slew of e-mail waiting for me, as well as course work to prepare, but before tackling any of it, I went to the common room for a coffee. After all that had happened that morning, I felt like I needed the jolt. Alan was there with another colleague of ours, John McCormack, the two of them sitting in the corner, sipping tea and chatting.

"Good morning, gentlemen," I said. "Setting the world to rights?"

"What else?" McCormack said.

He was four or five years younger than I was: prolific, brilliant, an international profile to be envious of. In history circles his books, *La Belle Époque* and *The Poets of the Russian Revolution,* were considered sexy, if anything in history can be considered such. Rather than academic publishers, he had commercial publishing deals. He had an agent, and his books were shortlisted for prizes where they competed with other non-historical titles. As a historian, he was a rising star.

"Join us," Alan said, and I sat. "John was just telling me about the conference in Birkbeck later this month."

"Will you make it?" McCormack asked.

I told them I hadn't planned on it this year. McCormack mentioned some of the presenters at the conference and how it was going to be a very full but fulfilling weekend. McCormack was, in many ways, everything I was not — we may both have been ambitious, but in different ways: he blazed trails where I dug ditches. I liked the dirty work, so to speak, and my pedagogic focus was, to the best of my abilities, student-focused, whereas I don't know how important McCormack considered the students in his overall plan — teaching to him was a necessary evil of the job, something that he was obliged to do in order to allow him to get on with what he really wanted, which was to write those critically acclaimed books. I had been asked the previous year to take on some of his teaching so that he had more time to focus on his research. I didn't mind. Neither did I begrudge McCormack his success — but I will admit to wondering about his professional integrity.

These are the kind of things I worried about at the time.

We talked more about the conference before Alan stood up. "I'm afraid I have a meeting. Duty calls," he said, bidding us farewell.

McCormack brought up the suggestion by the dean for a weeklong festival of teaching and learning. "For whose benefit?" he wanted to know.

"Our students could get a lot out of it," I said, but McCormack detailed how he thought it could only end up as more work, swamping us in greater administrative duties.

"By the way," he said in a confidential whisper, "I thought you might prefer it to come from someone you know rather than anyone else, but a colleague told me she saw you having a drink with one of the students. She did say it looked like a *com-*

*promisingly intimate encounter."*

"Who saw me?"

"It's not important who saw you, David, it's that you were seen."

My mind raced. Who had seen us? And what exactly had they seen? I thought of the swab scraping the inside of my mouth, handing the specimen jar to Zoe. This thought was chased by another — the fifty-euro note placed in her outstretched hand. I felt the heat rise in my cheeks.

"It's not what you think," I said, my voice lowered.

"It doesn't matter what I think."

"She only wanted some advice."

He smiled as if to say: that is what your office is for, not the pub.

"I suppose one needs to be careful these days," he said. "You know these things can spread if allowed to . . . escalate." He stood up, tapped his newspaper on the table. "I'd better go."

I tried not to let what McCormack had said bother me, but as I left the common room without the coffee I had come in for, I wondered again which colleague had seen me. It was frustrating, the thought of being gossiped about within the department. Did people have to worry about these kinds of things in other jobs? How might I have fared in what people call the real world? I used to balk at the description of the university as an ivory tower. The older I got, though, the more I wondered. I once heard a visiting poet say hello to Alan in one of the warren-like corridors in the Newman Building. "You're still here?" the poet had said warmly.

"I'm a *lifer,*" Alan had replied with a broad smile directed to me as if to say, "and so are you."

The thought of being institutionalized, even by a university, genuinely frightened me. It seemed that I spent more and more time in meetings than in researching my own books or, God forbid, teaching students.

I hurried to my office, pitching through the swinging doors and around the corner on the second floor, and there she was waiting for me. Leaning against the wall, the wires of a set of pink earphones trailing down her shoulders and into the phone she was holding, one foot tapping away to whatever she was listening to.

"Zoe," I said, a shot of panic going through my veins.

"Hello," she said too loudly, struggling to remove the earphones. "I wanted to ask you about the essay."

"Of course," I said, unlocking my office door. She followed me inside, and I asked her to sit down, making sure the door was still open. McCormack's words were running through my head. She sat down on one of the armchairs, swung her bag onto the floor by her feet. I perched on the edge of my desk, legs crossed at the ankles.

"What in particular did you want to discuss?"

"The essay. I'm sorry, but I didn't submit it in time."

"Oh," I said, a little annoyed. "Why not?"

"Well," she answered shyly, "I wasn't feeling well. And then the book I needed was not in the library. It wasn't on the shelves and it wasn't checked out. The staff had to put a search on it," she ended her excuses rather hopelessly.

"You should have come to me before the deadline."

"But I was ill . . ."

"Too ill to pick up the phone . . ."

She started to justify her non-submission, but I stopped her:

"It doesn't matter what you did or didn't do. I'm telling you what you should have done."

She looked at me for a second — the brusqueness in my tone giving her pause —

fixing me with a careful look.

"I'm sorry," she said cautiously.

"There are procedures. A form to fill out for mitigating circumstances."

"Mitigating circumstances?"

"This is far from ideal, Zoe . . ."

"I know."

The look on her face like she was regretting coming here and bringing this up. I was in no mood for it, not after all that had happened that day.

"Look, don't worry about it," I said, softening my tone. "I'll write a note to your tutor explaining. But you'll need to submit before the end of the week."

"Sure. Thanks."

I nodded my head in a gesture of dismissal and rounded my desk, reaching for the mouse to stir my computer back to life. The truth was I wanted her out of my office so that I could be alone with my thoughts, with my work. But she made no move to go, and I sensed there was something else.

"What is it?" I asked, somewhat irritably.

"I'm not sure I should show you," she answered, "given the mood you're in."

I stopped myself from snapping at her.

"Show me what?"

She leaned down and drew an envelope from her bag. Then rising from her chair, she crossed the floor to my desk and handed me the crisp documents that had been folded within. I understood instantly what they meant.

I took them from her hand, scanning the first page quickly before finding the results printed in bold capitals at the bottom. My heart gave a kick and I honestly couldn't tell if what I was feeling at that moment was relief or disappointment. The word POSITIVE seemed to pulse on the page.

"So now do you believe me?" The question was gently put but I felt prodded by it nonetheless. This letter — that one word — changed everything. The careful construction of my life was about to be altered.

"Of course." I flicked to the next page. This was the laboratory report giving an actual breakdown of the findings, detailing in scientific language and figures that I only partially understood, how they were able to determine the affinity between both sets of genes.

"Do you mind if I make a copy?" I asked.
"Sure."

It was a welcome excuse to turn my back on her, busying myself at the printer, trying to calm the churn of thoughts and emotions going through me. It was the oddest feeling — learning that I was a father again by way of a coldly phrased letter from some laboratory I had never heard of. I thought of the other moments in my life when fatherhood had come upon me — first with Robbie, an overpowering instant of fear and relief that he and his mother had come through a traumatic birthing experience; then with Holly, a moment of pure joy, looking on her tiny face and feeling nothing but love. And here I was again, forty-one years of age, standing in my office photocopying a letter observed by this young woman with her soft green eyes, her haze of blond hair, waiting for it to sink in that she was of my blood.

"Are you all right, David?" she asked, and I turned back to where she remained standing, at once surprised by her use of my Christian name as well as the tenderness in her voice.

"I'm fine."

"Do you mind me calling you that?"

"Of course not. Although perhaps not in front of your fellow students," I added, trying to keep my voice steady and authoritative. The truth was I had no idea what she should call me — certainly not Dad or Father. And how was I to refer to her now? As my daughter? It seemed too substantial a title given how tenuous the link between us felt.

I handed her back the original documents, which she shoved into the back pocket of her jeans. It showed a curious lack of regard for something so momentous. My own copies lay pristine and unfolded on the leather place mat of my desk. She stood, as if waiting for something from me.

"Well," she said, giving a quick, nervous laugh. "What now?"

"I suppose we need to take some time and let the news sink in. After that, we can have a talk about what the nature of our relationship might be."

How stiff and uncomfortable I sounded! Tripping over the word "relationship." For all the time I had had to think this thing through, I was as awkward and stilted as I had been the first day she came to me.

"Are you going to show the lab report to Caroline?" she asked.

"Caroline? My wife?"

"Yes."

"Yes, I suppose so," I replied, a little confused by her familiarity.

"Good," she said firmly. "Hopefully it will allay her fears."

"What are you talking about?"

I said this a little sharply, and she rocked on her feet, uncomfortable at the turn the conversation had taken. When she spoke again, her voice was softer, an air of apology hanging over her.

"It's just that she seemed put out by all of this . . . sort of angry, actually. Like she thought I was just making all this up to bother you."

"You've met Caroline?"

"Yes. When she was here on campus . . ."

"On campus?" I asked.

"On Tuesday. She said you knew."

I closed my eyes, rubbed them with my thumb and forefinger.

"You didn't know?" she asked innocently.

"No," I admitted.

Caroline had never said anything to me about coming to campus. But why wouldn't she? We had seen each other every day — it's not like we were ships in the night.

"It's been very busy at home," I said. I thought about Robbie's cello vibrating through the house, Holly's studious intro-version, the busy activity of family life. Outside, the sound of a drill rose and fell in intensity. Its bright hum seemed to fill the room. She stood there with her hands in her pockets, looking at me.

"I'm sorry, David. I thought you knew. The last thing I want is to make problems for you at home. Anyway, maybe she was just trying to warn me."

"Warn you?"

She took her hands from her pockets and turned to reach for her bag. She fixed the strap over her shoulder, an unhappy look about her like she was regretting ever opening her mouth about Caroline. I should, perhaps, have let her go, resolved to speak to my wife about it later in private.

But I said, "Wait, Zoe," then asked her to tell me what had happened, softening my voice in an attempt to calm her enough that she might trust me. She glanced at the door, which was still ajar, and I felt her pull toward it.

"Please," I said.

"It was after American history," she began, explaining how she had gone outside for some fresh air after the stuffiness of the lecture hall. "I was sitting at the pond by the Engineering Building when she came up to me. I don't even know how she knew it was me. I mean, I hadn't a clue who she was. It freaked me out a bit, the way she came up to me out of the blue and confronted me."

"Confronted you?"

"Maybe that's too strong a word to use. But, I dunno. . . . It felt sort of hostile."

She was trying to remain calm in her account, but her voice trembled.

"We talked for a bit. . . . I'm really sorry, David. She told me you knew."

I wasn't sure whether I should apologize or question the veracity of her claim. Either way I was dumbfounded by the idea of my wife acting surreptitiously, sneaking about campus without my knowing. "Did she tell you why she wanted to speak to you?"

"She asked me what it was I wanted from you, and how long I was going to chase after you, and when would I leave you alone?"

"What?"

"She asked me had I given any thought to the effect my claims had exerted on your other children. Had I given any thought to how it affected her?"

"Jesus."

"And she wanted to know had I considered the consequences of my actions and what I was going to demand."

"Demand?"

"Those were her words. I don't want anything. I'm not demanding anything. I never wanted to upset anyone, you or your wife, or your kids." She spoke clearly and calmly, but I could tell it was an effort for her. "She said she had come with your express agreement and . . ."

"And . . . ?"

"And she did not want to see you hurt . . .

as if I . . . as if I . . ."

The tears came. I came around my desk toward her, torn between sympathy and suspicion. Here we were again, thrown together — not in the crush of a pub, but alone, and, more worryingly, in my office — it was another compromisingly intimate encounter.

"It's just that I thought I had done everything . . . correctly." Zoe found a tissue in her pocket and dabbed her nose with it. "I thought I had approached the whole matter the right way."

"You have."

"I'm not doing this to hurt you."

"I know," I said, reaching out to touch her arm.

There was a swift and sudden knock on the door frame. I looked up. McCormack was standing there.

"Sorry, I can see you're busy," he said, gazing at Zoe and raising an eyebrow in surprise. "Perhaps you can ring me when you get a chance. Nothing urgent."

He smiled, left the door pointedly ajar while Zoe wiped her tears, blew her nose, and hitched the strap of her bag farther up her shoulder.

"I should go," she said. "I'm sorry to have sprung this on you . . . it didn't occur to me that you might not have known."

She walked out, and I was left again with the uncomfortable sense of being on the receiving end of an awkward revelation, something to remind me of how life could be so unpredictable and perplexing.

This time, I did not run after her. Instead I went to pick up the phone to ring McCormack but stopped. He could wait.

I sat down at my desk, the laboratory report and accompanying letter there in front of me. What would I tell Caroline? I would show her the report but not the letter. That was one thing I decided quite quickly. Zoe's name and address were printed on the letter but not on the report. There was no reason for Caroline to know that it had been Zoe — not me — who had taken the lead. I folded the report and tucked it into my inside pocket, then placed the letter carefully into a file and dropped it into the top drawer of my desk. And if this latest deceit on my part felt like a betrayal of Caroline's trust, well, I thought fleetingly, after her intimidation of Zoe, after her affair with Aidan, maybe she deserved it.

# CHAPTER 9
## CAROLINE

Before Zoe came along, David never talked of Linda. He would clam up anytime our conversation veered toward that corner of his past. I never met her but I would be lying if I claimed I never thought of her. Throughout our marriage, she was alive in some part of my imagination. Whenever I probed him about her, he grew sullen. He didn't love her, he said when pressed on the matter. It was never love, he maintained, and for a long time I believed him.

It was a lie though. He did love her — a fact I discovered on the occasion of my fortieth birthday. A weekend away at a farmhouse in Crookhaven, stunning views of the west Cork coastline — it should have been perfect. David and I, Chris and Susannah. "It's like Russian roulette, going away with those two," David had remarked on the way down, but he said it good-naturedly. We were both in high spirits, looking forward to the break, some time away from the kids.

Dinner in a lavish country house, a lot of wine, and one too many suggestive comments from Chris about the attractive young waitress — Susannah snapped, and they were off in their own whirl and tumble of conjugal battle, passion and principle tangling together in a barbed and nasty way. David and I glanced at each other across the swath of white tablecloth, unwilling to intervene but not wishing to bear witness either. The taxi journey back to our accommodation was icy and silent. Susannah went straight to bed, and I followed suit, leaving the two men downstairs with an open bottle of whiskey.

Sometime in the night, I heard their voices. The drink, rather than mellowing them, had made them garrulous — confessional. I got out of bed to use the bathroom and at the top of the stairs I stopped to listen.

"I don't know how you do it," David said, his voice sluggish and heavy with booze. "The constant bickering. The full-scale rows. Doesn't it exhaust you?"

"Completely."

"I don't get it. How do you put up with it?"

"Because I love her."

"Is that enough?" Disbelief crept into David's voice.

"Honestly, Dave, sometimes I think that it's over between us. God knows how many times I've resolved to leave her. But," Chris's voice softened, "it's always been Susannah. From the first time I set eyes on her. I can't not be married to her. She's the love of my life."

"Maybe sometimes you're better off not marrying the love of your life."

The way he said it, thoughtful and quiet, I knew it was a matter deeply personal to him, something he'd given thought to.

"Are you telling me you regret marrying Caroline?"

"I'm not talking about Caroline," he answered quickly, and I felt myself stiffen.

"Ah," Chris said as the penny dropped. "Linda."

Her name seemed to bloom in the air before me — a sudden burst of red — and I felt my hands grow cold. Understanding came quickly: how David must have talked of her to Chris, confided in him in a way that he had never confided in me. What intimacies had he spoken of? What admissions of love and regret had he made? That he had done this behind my back seemed a marked failure in our marriage. But worse — far, far worse — was the realization of how deeply lodged she was inside him. *The love of his life.*

"Do you ever hear from her?" Chris asked.

"No."

"Ever wonder where she is? Who she's with?"

"Sometimes. The odd time I'm reminded of her."

Chris went on, his voice more incisive. "Ever wonder how things might have turned out if you'd stayed together?"

The question chilled me. I found myself turning away from the possible answer.

David gave a hollow laugh.

"We'd be like you and Susannah — an endless series of fights and reconciliations. I wouldn't have the energy for it."

"But you'd have passion," Chris countered.

"Yes," David said, a tone of wistfulness coming into his voice. "We certainly had that."

"More than with Caroline?"

"Yes." The answer was immediate. He didn't even need to think about it. "Caroline is different. She's dependable, safe."

I'd heard enough. I had turned away, returned to the bedroom, wishing I had never left it. I slipped away to bed and when David came up sometime later, I held my body still, feigning sleep. He didn't try to touch me.

How to explain the quiet devastation caused by those words? Every time I remembered the wistfulness in his voice when he recalled his lost passion, something dark opened up inside me. Like the unfurling of a shadowy new fern. Had it all been a mistake? Our marriage, the life we had made together, our children? Everything I valued and loved, everything I had worked so hard for, I saw now it had all been built on a foundation of regret. He had given up his great love. With the cool detachment I knew him to be capable of, he had weighed up his options: passion and instability versus the safe warmth of marriage to me. No matter how hard I tried, I could not escape from the knowledge that I was not the love of his life. That title was claimed by a woman I had never met, a woman whose face I had seen once in a photograph I'd found hidden among his possessions.

That night in the cold darkness at the top of the stairs, overhearing the conversation, that was the moment when things began to unravel for me. Unhappiness swept in like the sudden arrival of autumn on a September day. I tried to rationalize it, telling myself David had been drunk when he'd said those words, he hadn't really meant them. But the truth of it niggled at me. I told myself to be satisfied with what I had: a good husband, wonderful children, a comfortable home. It was more than a lot of people had — an enviable life. But the rot had set in. My husband had no passion for me. In marrying me he had chosen to settle. A pinched, mean voice inside me whispered: *If you are not the love of his life, then what makes you so sure he is yours?* I had never thought of myself as a woman who would have an affair. But by the time I met Aidan something had changed. Like a stone dislodged deep inside me, I felt the structure of my being start to crumble.

After my affair ended, David and I went through a difficult patch for some time. Our bedroom, once a place of refuge and comfort — of love — became the arena for our hissed arguments, the to-ing and fro-ing of whispered accusations, of denial and blame. We tried to keep it from the children, remaining civil in front of them, a tight cordiality that seemed stilted and formal. Slowly, things got better. The atmosphere lightened. I still felt obligated to explain my absences, however innocent. I was careful of my behavior in front of David. I found that I censored my comments when speaking of other men — friends, colleagues. I tried to find happiness again within my marriage, within my home. With time, the stone that had been dislodged within me slipped back into place. Normality resumed. But then Zoe came along.

I thought about her constantly. At work, at home, in the evenings when I went out running, she was always there, shadowing my thoughts, clouding my emotions. I considered telling someone about her — confiding in a friend — but the only person I might have told was Susannah and she was locked inside her own conjugal disaster. Anytime I spoke to her on the phone, she sounded on the brink of tears. It was disconcerting, given how commanding she normally was. She had separated from Chris, finally moving out, and I felt I couldn't burden her with my own domestic turmoil. Instead, I kept it to myself.

"What is it, Mum?" Holly asked one evening over dinner, David and Robbie looking up from their plates. "Why do you keep staring at me?"

"I'm not."

"You are! Every time I look up, there you are, staring. It's freaking me out."

Scanning my daughter's face, interrogating it for traces of Zoe. Was there something in the slight flatness to her cheeks, the small nose, the wide, thin-lipped mouth revealing a straight row of small teeth?

An expression sprang up from childhood: *The cat can look at the queen.*

"Just eat your dinner," I said.

While we waited for the DNA test results, it seemed as if David and I were living within an unarticulated argument. We were cordial with each other but we took a measure of care when moving through our conversations, both of us cautious not to touch on the subject. We talked about the children, about work, exchanged words about shopping, cooking, household tasks. More than anything, we talked about Ellen. He seemed caught up in the minutiae of her move into the nursing home, familiarizing himself with her daily routine, having long, involved discussions with the staff over his mother's dietary requirements, her comfort, whether she was making friends. A role reversal was taking place — David acting as the overly concerned parent, Ellen the child in a new school. I understood that his fussiness and demands masked a deeper sadness, a cementing of knowledge that this move into the next stage of Ellen's life marked the beginning of a good-bye. Neither of us said anything about Zoe. Any thoughts or doubts I had I kept to myself, and if he had any misgivings, he didn't confide them in me. Then one evening, he arrived home from work, and I felt a change in him straightaway. When he came in from the garden, taking off his jacket as he closed the door behind him, I felt his muted anger in the way he seemed to shrink from my gaze.

"Glass of wine?" I asked, and he said sure, moving past me to hang his jacket from the hook on the door.

From the living room came a burst of laughter — Holly and two of her friends were watching the One Direction film. Beyond the window, the trees were dripping from a recent downpour, but it was warm in the kitchen, the mellow trumpet sounds of Kenny Durham coming through the speakers.

"Cheers," I said, and we clinked glasses. I sat down on the sofa and watched him lean back on a bar stool across from me, wondering what was pulling at him.

"You okay?" I asked, solicitous.

"Why didn't you tell me you met Zoe?"

he asked quietly.

My breath caught in my throat.

"I'm sorry. I should have told you. I'm not sure why I didn't."

He kept looking at me, a baffled expression clouding his face.

"I suppose I thought if I could just see her, just get a look at her —"

"How did you even find her?"

"I rang your department," I said, shame creeping up through me as I admitted it. It occurred to me that the methods I had employed, the way I had sneaked about, were like the actions of a suspicious wife trying to catch her husband in the act of adultery. If David saw the irony, he didn't say so. He was swiveling the bar stool slightly from side to side, the movement channeling some of his anger.

"Don't you think that's a bit creepy?" he asked. I had the sense that he was choosing his words. For all the care he took, I could hear the accusation behind them.

"You're right," I agreed, wanting to smooth things over, even though the need to talk it through was still there, the angry pulse of it running through everything. "I'm sorry. It was impulsive. I didn't think it through properly."

He drank from his glass, turned, and put

it on the counter behind him. I thought he was going to let the matter drop. But then he looked back at me and said, "Have you any idea how freaked out she was?"

A match striking tinder. The sudden spark, his concern for the girl, seeing how it overrode my apology, my discomfort. The anger I had been holding at bay came to life inside me. "How freaked out *she* was?"

"Yes. She was in a state when she came to my office today, in tears over what you had said to her —"

"What did I say? Tell me. What did I say to upset her?"

Still quietly, he went on. "She said you demanded to know what she wanted from me. She felt threatened, intimidated —"

"I didn't intimidate her. The way you talk of her, you'd swear she was this shrinking violet."

"She's just a kid."

"She's old enough to know how to manipulate," I snapped. "Clearly, she has you all figured out."

"Do you even hear yourself? Do you know how harsh you sound?"

"Well, what do you expect?"

He was making the bar stool swivel harder now, his anger growing.

"Come on, then," I said. "Tell me how

you think this should work. Should I just take it on the chin? Say: 'There, there, dear. Never mind about all this,' open my home and my heart to this girl — this stranger — without checking first to see if she's real, if what she says is true?"

The chair stilled and he said, "You should have told me first."

"I know. I know I should, and I've apologized for that."

"We agreed to wait, didn't we? Until the test results came back."

"Yes," I said, my voice cool and firm, "we did agree. And you also agreed that you wouldn't have anything to do with her outside of class — remember?"

"She came to my office. What was I supposed to do?"

"Tell her you were busy. Have her make an appointment."

"I couldn't. She was upset —"

"Oh, please. She sheds some crocodile tears and you cave."

"Don't be like that," he said.

"Like what?"

He thought for a moment, then alighted on the word.

"Hard."

I stood up and walked past him to the counter, threw the wine from my glass into the sink, a burgundy splash of it over the white surface.

"That wine tastes too sharp."

I turned on the tap and watched it sluicing down the drain, took the dishcloth and held it under the water, then flicked off the tap and wrung it out. I started to clean the spout, the taps, the area around the sink.

"Why are you angry with me?" he asked.

I wiped down the granite countertop.

"I haven't done anything to you," he went on. "I haven't been unfaithful."

He must have seen the way I stiffened, for he continued in a tone of irritation more than apology. "I didn't mean it like that. What I meant was it happened a long time ago, when I was free and single. I didn't screw Linda behind your back — we weren't together then. I never knew she was pregnant."

"Didn't you?"

"Of course not!" For the first time a note of real anger entered his voice.

"She never told me. I never knew there was a baby. Not until Zoe came into my office that day. None of this has happened to hurt you. It just happened, that's all."

He was so maddeningly rational. I had reached the end of the counter and pulled out the pestle and mortar. I saw a mark left on the counter. I went at it with the cloth, the perfect black circle it had made so stark against the natural veins running through the stone.

"I feel like you blame me for all this," he said, "and it's not my fault."

"I know it's not your fault."

"It was just a mistake."

"I know."

"You're going to rub a hole in the granite, the way you're going —"

I flung the cloth in the sink and said, "It's because of the baby."

"What baby?"

I turned and leaned back against the counter and gazed at him.

"Our baby. The one we didn't have."

It took a moment for his expression to clear and I saw, with a shock, that he had pushed that whole painful episode in our history out of his mind.

"Oh. That." His fingers went to the stem of his glass — there was still some wine in the bowl that he began to swirl in a slow, meditative way. "I hadn't forgotten. I just don't think about it anymore. It was so long ago."

I felt the counter behind me, the hard surface of it there to steady me. "She would have been twenty-one now," I said quietly.

"Or he."

He put his glass down, his brow creasing with a pained expression.

I waited where I was — I would not go to him — and after a moment, he got up off the bar stool, came over, and put his arms around me, pulling me into his embrace. I don't know how long we stood there, holding on to each other, and all the while I was trying to feel the warmth of his hug — the sincerity within it — but I kept thinking, *He's trying to silence me.*

He drew back, looked at me, our faces close to each other. "You okay?"

"Yes. I'm fine."

He held me there for another moment, then reached for the wine bottle and turned away.

"Is that it?" I asked.

"What?"

"Is that all you're going to say on the subject?"

He stood at the other side of the counter, filling his glass again, the look of forbearance on his face making me want to scream.

Patiently, he said, "It was a long time ago. I thought we'd put it behind us."

"You tell me about this girl — this daughter you fathered back when you were a student — and you never once think about our baby?"

My voice broke and I had to stop, feeling the rising commotion inside me.

I wanted to tell him that when I met Zoe — when I looked at her — all I could think of was the pregnancy I had terminated. After so many years of holding it at bay, never allowing it to cast its shadow over my life, here it was in front of me in the shape of that girl. All the memories of what had happened seemed stored up in her. I'd looked at her and felt myself being dragged back to a time when I was sick with fear and uncertainty, overwhelmed by the mistake we had made and the decision we'd had to face. Sitting alongside her in the sun, I'd felt as if I were back in the waiting room, a form attached to a clipboard on my knee, the deep pile of the carpet underfoot, the crisp-looking receptionist behind her wall of Perspex, and all the while my legs would not stop trembling. Twenty years old, in my final year at university, my whole life ahead of me. I had thought that once it was done, I would feel relief. And I did. But there was also the slow advance of dread crawling up from that empty place, the awkward rumblings of conscience.

"Anyway," I said, giving myself a shake as though to dispel this chill from the past.

"It's just nerves. All this waiting — it's making me jumpy."

He glanced up at me with a guarded expression.

"Once those test results come through, we can put this whole wretched business behind us."

I still remember the forced optimism with which I said those words.

"Caroline," he said slowly, and I saw at once how clearly I had been counting on it being false, her wild claim proven to be the troubled fantasy of an attention seeker. The long, awful time of not knowing was about to come to an end, and my throat grew dry and stiff.

"Tell me," I said.

He took a piece of paper from his pocket and held it out to me. And there it was in black and white. The absolute bitter truth: a positive match.

"I'm sorry," he said. "I know you hoped it would be different . . ."

I hardly heard him. I kept thinking back over the words he had used to defend himself. *It's not my fault.* Like a schoolboy pleading innocence. *It was a mistake.*

A mistake he had made twice.

That was what was so unforgivable. The very mistake we had made together — the baby we had accidentally started — he had repeated it with another woman. How maddeningly stupid of him. How unbelievably careless. For a man so self-controlled, composed, and careful almost to the point of coldness, it seemed wildly out of character. His Achilles' heel perhaps. Reckless with passion, he had fallen into the same trap a second time. Linda had kept her baby, though, and neither of us could have foreseen the consequences of her decision.

I held the document in my hands, my eyes sweeping over the columns of figures, the cold clinical terms. I thought of the strands of DNA they described and imagined them as threads escaping their spools. This paper announced it to me with certainty: Zoe was a thread running through the fabric of my family. In the same way my children were threads — even the child that was never born — all of them woven into a complex tapestry. Love, trust, fidelity — these were the strands that bound us together.

But families don't come apart because a thread has loosened. They break when it becomes sharp, brutal. It takes ripping and hacking to tear the tapestry apart.

# PART 2

# CHAPTER 10
## DAVID

It was nothing to be ashamed of. That was what I told myself at the time. This girl who had parachuted into my life out of nowhere was not an issue that needed to be covered up or explained away with a mixture of apology and discomfiture. If a mistake had been made, then it was the mistake of a younger man. What is youth without the odd indiscretion? The important thing, I reminded myself whenever I felt the doubt creeping in, was how I handled it now. It was a situation requiring calmness and maturity. I needed to be honest and up front, and offer no apologies, as there was nothing to apologize for.

Not everyone shared this view. Caroline, for one, shrank from the notion when I informed her I was going to tell the children.

"What?" she asked, clearly aghast.

"They have a right to know," I told her. "She is their half sister after all."

"At least take some time to think this through before we start telling people."

"You're talking as though it's the neighbors I'm proposing to tell. These are our children."

"Exactly. They're our children and we need to think about their welfare."

"I *am* thinking about their welfare. But Zoe is my daughter and they're going to find that out eventually."

"I just don't think we should be hasty. How are they going to feel when they find out?"

"They're not babies," I countered, irritation creeping in. "Robbie is fifteen, and Holly has always been older than her years. I think you're doing them a disservice suggesting they might not be able to handle it."

"It's not that," she answered calmly. "It's what they might think of you once they find out. That's what I'm concerned about."

"They'll take their cue from us. If we are calm about it, then they will react calmly."

"I'm not so sure."

"It doesn't have to be the end of the world. So I have another daughter. It's hardly Armageddon."

"Why do you keep doing that?" she asked quietly.

"Doing what?"

"That 'my daughter' thing."

"I don't know what —"

"You keep referring to her as your daughter."

"So?"

"Well, she's hardly that, is she? I mean she's a grown woman and the only involvement you've had in her life to date is having unprotected sex with her mother. It doesn't really constitute a parental relationship."

Her words stung, more so because of the truth at their heart. She had caught me out in my deliberate use of the term "my daughter" as if repeating it aloud could make me accustomed to the reality of it.

Even though I was openly dismissive of her concerns, when the time came to sit down with Robbie and Holly, Caroline looking on watchfully, I felt an inner trembling at what I was about to admit. In my mind, I had rehearsed my little speech over and over, explaining as gently as possible about a relationship I had had before they were born, the consequences of which were only beginning to play out, and even though the words spoken were as I had planned, they came out sounding colder and more matter-of-fact than I would have liked. And defensive.

"A half sister?" Robbie asked, with a

mixture of amusement and disbelief.

"Yes. Her name is Zoe. She's eighteen."

"What the fuck?" he had exclaimed, laughing to cover his shock.

"Robbie," Caroline said in partial admonishment but mostly to steady him.

"How come you never told us about her?" he asked me.

"Because I didn't know about her myself, not until a couple of weeks ago."

"You didn't know?"

"Her mother and I had lost touch."

"Who was her mother?" he asked.

"That doesn't matter." I was unhappy with where his line of questioning was going. "She was just someone I went out with for a little while. It's not important."

Immediately, I regretted that statement. For one thing, it seemed to suggest that I had been the type of person in my youth who slept around without any thought to the consequences — not the message I wanted to send my children. Also, I couldn't escape the feeling that Linda was somehow watching me, the breath of her spirit present in the room, witnessing my offhand dismissal of our love affair.

Caroline glanced out the window. Holly shifted a little on the couch.

"So what?" Robbie asked. "Do we get to

meet her?"

"Would you like to?"

Caroline, who had been silent throughout this exchange, interjected with a note of caution.

"I think we should all take some time to think things through, get used to the idea first."

"Why?" Robbie asked.

"This is a big change, love. We don't need to rush into anything."

"Your mum is right," I said, more for the sake of showing a mutual front than out of any real agreement. "If in a week or so you still want to meet her, then we can arrange something. Have her round for Sunday lunch. How about that?"

"Can we tell people?" he asked.

"It's not a secret," I assured him, but Caroline was leaning forward again with that circumspect look.

"I think it's best to keep it among ourselves," she said firmly. "For the time being." Here again our feelings diverged. While I believed that the sooner we made the news public, the sooner our situation would normalize, Caroline felt the need to contain it securely within the private confines of our home until she felt ready to face the world with it.

Robbie raised an eyebrow but he didn't object.

"We'll talk about this again," I said. "And if you have any questions . . . any time you want to discuss it . . . you just have to ask."

"Sure," he said.

"Okay, Hols?" I asked.

Holly said nothing, gave a noncommittal shrug. The whole time I was talking, she had sat there quietly, watchful, absorbing everything. Now her eyes flickered over me briefly — it was an assessing glance, the kind I had never received from her before. I saw at once that Caroline was right. This revelation I wanted so desperately to make normal had already altered our family bonds. Beneath my little girl's gaze, I felt myself changing, becoming a different kind of father from the one she had known and relied upon.

I was mulling all this over in a meeting with Alan later that week. We were discussing a funding bid to a government scheme attached to the Peace and Reconciliation Committee. Alan was supportive of the concept, agreeing to add his name to the proposal.

"Even if I won't be here to see it through," he said, referring to his intended retirement.

He was in good form that day, brisk and cheery, and once our business had been concluded, he capped his pen and flipped his notebook closed, expecting me to do the same.

"Actually, there's something else I wanted to speak to you about," I told him.

"Yes?"

"It concerns a student. One of my First Years. Her name is Zoe Barry."

I felt nervous about telling him. It was as if I were readying myself to own up to a transgression that had only just happened rather than something that had occurred almost twenty years ago.

"The thing is, Alan, it turns out that I am her father."

He put down the pen in his hand, realizing that our conversation was going to last longer than he had planned.

"It was when I was at Queen's University — I had a relationship with the girl's mother. I never knew she had a child. This all happened before I was married . . . I've only just discovered."

"Good Lord," Alan said.

"I wanted to let you know — let the department know. She's my student after all, and I didn't want there to be any" — I hunted about for the right word — "any misunderstanding."

"Right," he said, sounding slightly fazed by it all. His eyes flickered over my face and I wondered if he was making some kind of mental reassessment of me. A small bead of sweat rolled down my back.

"Have you mentioned this to anyone else in the department?"

"Not yet," I answered, wondering whether I should tell him what McCormack had said.

"Because she is one of your students, we will need to declare a conflict of interest when it comes to grading papers, assessments, exams . . . all the necessary protocols."

"Protocols?"

"Inform the registrar, the ethics committee, and let me see who else . . ."

"An ethics committee?"

"It will only have to be noted. Nothing to worry about . . ."

"What about confidentiality?"

"It's assumed."

He picked up his notebook and pen and got to his feet. At the door to his office, he gave me a few words of reassurance, making me feel even more like I had done something wrong. The way Alan put it, I had broken a moral code of the university, unwittingly or not.

I had confessed to Caroline, owned up to my kids, revealed all to the university, but where was the expiation of whatever guilt I had felt? When would I feel the burden of the past lifting? My wife's shock was one thing, my children's surprise another. I almost felt like I could deal with those twin pressures given time, but the university's insipid way of punishing me was more soul-destroying — all the paperwork to be filed, the ethics committee, the protocols and standards to be met — all that felt somehow like a figurative black mark against me — like ash on the forehead or a scarlet letter.

Not long after my revelation, Robbie came to me and expressed his wish to meet Zoe. While Holly appeared reluctant to learn anything about her half sister, Robbie had been peppering me with questions daily, mainly concerning what Zoe was like, although occasionally there were awkward inquiries about my relationship with her mother. I bridged Caroline's disapproval and arranged for Zoe to come for lunch one Sunday about a month after I had told my children of her existence.

The casual lull of a Sunday at home held a certain edge that day, a serration to the light of early afternoon and the energy that went with it. With Zoe's imminent arrival, I felt an air of nervous anticipation hanging in the rooms of the house.

When the doorbell rang, I called out that I would get it. Behind the frosted glass, there was the outline of a slight figure, hooded, waiting, expectant. I pulled open the door. She had been glancing back at the garden, surveying the clumped hydrangeas, the wine-red spread of acers, and as I drew the door back and said her name, she turned around and her eyes met mine. An uncanny tremor of déjà vu passed through me, and with it a fleeting memory of Linda on my doorstep on one of those feckless nights in Belfast, her voice emerging from the past: *You said I could drop by.* The answering kick of my heart.

"I hope I'm not late," Zoe said, smiling nervously. "I was in town and lost track of time."

"Not late at all." I stood back so she could enter.

Closing the door, I turned to find her looking around the walls of the hall, her eyes traveling upward. She was a little flushed. In her hands, there was a bottle of wine and a small bouquet of flowers. As if suddenly remembering them, she held both out to me and I took them and thanked her. For a moment, we simply stood there.

"Zoe, hello," Caroline said in a bright voice, coming out of the kitchen and wiping her hands on a tea towel.

She came forward and they shook hands, exchanging some pleasantries I didn't quite catch. I was still a little shaken from the sense of déjà vu; it felt as if I had asked not just Zoe into our lives but the shadowy aura of Linda too.

"I hope you're hungry," Caroline said, hanging Zoe's jacket in the hall and then ushering her into the kitchen. "David's been toiling over a hot stove all day."

"She's joking, by the way," I said, but the truth was I had gone to some lengths, preparing the dish, making an extra special effort. Earlier that morning, Holly had made a passing comment about how I was fussing.

"Goulash," I said.

"Something the soldiers ate in the trenches of one or another war, isn't that right?" Caroline jibed.

She gestured for Zoe to sit on one of the bar stools and started cutting the foil from the neck of a wine bottle.

"Red or white?" she asked Zoe.

"I'd prefer white, please."

If Caroline was feeling the strain, she hid it well. I noticed she had gone to some effort with her appearance that day — she was wearing a smart fitted dress and heels, diamond earrings winking from beneath her neatly curled hair. While there was no doubting her attractiveness, next to Zoe's casual beauty there seemed something overly formal and made-up about Caroline's efforts. She poured the wine into three glasses.

Jazz was playing on the stereo — easy listening, nothing to distract us from getting to know one another, but if everything did break down and go quiet we would not have to cringe in our own silences. Above the low melody, I could hear the rumble of footfall on the stairs. Robbie came in.

"Zoe, this is Robbie," I said by way of introduction. He held up his hand in a gesture only teenagers can pull off — a kind of salute.

All morning, the notes from his cello had filled the house. Not the beautiful sonorous sounds of performance but the harsher false starts of practice. Still there was something familiar and reassuring about them.

"Hi," Zoe said, a little apprehensively. She took a timid step back as if to fully take in her half brother.

Holly followed her brother but positioned herself behind one of the kitchen chairs before saying hello. She had been unusually withdrawn in the weeks since I had broken the news about her half sister, not her usual confident self. I felt a jab of uncertainty. All of us seemed unsure of how to negotiate the terms of these newly discovered relationships. In some respects, we reverted to the buttoned-up awkwardness of polite exchange that had marked a time after Caroline and I had patched things up post-affair, a time when we talked to each other in front of the kids with a forced civility, maintaining the pretense for their sakes that our marriage was solid.

That being said, Caroline remained resolute. She took command of the situation, enlisting Holly's help with putting out the food, instructing us all on where to sit.

"You have a beautiful home," Zoe offered politely, albeit with a wavering voice. Her eyes were casting around at the kitchen and the family room attached. Light flooded in through the glass doors and the skylight above. The weather was unusually fine for October.

Robbie asked Zoe where she lived, and he blushed a little when she answered.

"I rent a small flat in Rathmines. Just a

single room, really."

"What made you want to come to Dublin?" he asked.

She shrugged. "I've always liked it, since I was a child."

"Did you come down much?"

"I have cousins in Greystones, so sometimes we'd stop off in Dublin on the way to visiting them. Mam and I used to go shopping on Grafton Street."

I tried to picture it: Linda holding the hand of a little girl, gazing in the windows of Brown Thomas or Marks & Spencer. Dublin is a small city. Would it have been so far outside the bounds of possibility that I might have bumped into her? Would she have introduced me to her daughter if we had? Told me the truth, or tried to pretend Zoe wasn't mine? Would she have said anything at all?

"How are you finding UCD?" Caroline asked once we had started eating. I was afraid all the questions would make it feel like an interrogation to Zoe. She was obviously nervous enough as it was.

"I'm still finding my way a little," she said, smiling shyly. "But I'm enjoying it."

There were further questions about her lectures, about what clubs she had joined, the part-time job she had picked up in the

Students' Union shop. She answered them all patiently, and politely, even if there was a note of hesitancy in her voice, as if she did not trust herself completely to say what it was that she thought was expected of her. We were distracted by the food, passing bread, and dipping into the salad. To all appearances everything was going well, but beneath the small talk there was something else, a kind of undercurrent of suspicion so that no matter what Zoe was asked, what I heard was the subtextual riptide, the undercurrent of what was really meant: *Why are you here? What do you want?*

So it was a relief to hear her ask a question of her own and deflect some of the scrutiny. "Who plays the cello?" she asked.

She had finished eating, making a neat cross of her cutlery on the plate. The cello was leaning against the wall to the side of the sofa.

"That's mine," Robbie said.

"He's in the National Youth Orchestra," Caroline said proudly. "You should hear him play sometime."

"He thinks he's Yo-Yo Ma," Holly said quietly, a smirk on her face.

Robbie told her to shut up, and she pushed her glasses back up to the bridge of her nose. It was the first time she'd spoken since Zoe had entered the house.

"I love the cello," Zoe told him. "Can you play that Elgar piece?"

Robbie leaned his elbows on the table. "Not really. I'm trying to learn it, but it's like super hard."

"We played it at my mam's funeral — not a live performance, just on the stereo. Still — it was beautiful."

No one said anything. I had that groundless feeling at the thought of Linda dead in a box, the room swelling with the sounds of those melancholy strings.

"Sorry to hear about your mum," Robbie said.

"Thanks."

"It must have been shit," he remarked gently.

"It was," she said with some effort, "but I've been busy since it happened, moving down here and starting college."

"What about your family in Belfast?" Caroline asked.

Zoe brushed the hair from her eyes. "Well, there's just Gary — he's my stepfather."

"He must miss you."

"I don't think so."

"Oh?" I asked, surprised by the change in her manner. "Why not?"

"We don't really get on."

"You don't?"

She thought about it, no doubt aware of the weight of our stares.

"I dunno. We never kind of hit it off."

"When did he and your mother marry?" Caroline asked.

Zoe shifted in her chair: "When I was six." She picked up her fork and fiddled with it. After a moment's hesitation, she continued. "He was nice at first — always buying me sweets and toys and that. But after a while, he just got bored of me."

"That's awful," I said.

Caroline asked, "He and Linda had no children together?"

"No. I think Gary really wanted to have kids of his own, but when it didn't happen, he just grew despondent. Kind of jealous too."

"Jealous?" I asked.

"Of me and Mam. Our closeness. Especially toward the end, when she was sick."

"It must have been very difficult for you," Caroline offered, but I was more interested in this jealousy she had mentioned. Something she wasn't saying worried me: I didn't like the sound of this Gary bloke one bit.

"Your stepfather," I said, "do you hear much from him?"

She shook her head.

"I think he's glad to have me out from under his feet," she said, then almost as an afterthought: "I'm glad to be out from under his feet too."

"Really?" I asked.

"The way he used to go on sometimes, his temper . . ."

"His temper?"

The question startled Zoe, as if she hadn't realized she had spoken her thoughts aloud. "Maybe 'temper' isn't even the right word. It's more subtle than that. Oh, I don't know," she said, dismissing her words with a wave of the hand.

"Passive-aggressive?" I suggested.

She made a remark about how delicious the food had been. It was clear she didn't want to discuss the matter further.

Caroline got up to make the coffee while Robbie cleared the dishes. The topic was dropped, but I didn't forget it, even when the conversation returned to safer subjects: Zoe and Robbie discussing the various bands they were into, what films they liked, Holly answering to what her favorite subjects were in school. All seemingly normal chitchat, yet even with this congenial banter, there was a palpable tension running through the blood of the conversation. No wine, lighthearted chat, not even dessert, could dispel it. Or maybe that's just the way I saw it, because those words she had said about Gary's jealousy and temper stayed with me and made me feel a kind of protective zeal I had not expected to feel.

We finished our coffee, Robbie saying, "Can we go sit in the comfy chairs?" and everyone got to their feet.

Caroline, looking to clear the last of the table, was reaching across to take Zoe's coffee cup, and in the motion of reaching, her hand brushed against the stem of my wineglass. The glass, which I had recently refilled, toppled, sending out a splash of Burgundy, some of which hit Zoe's midriff, the rest spilling over her place mat, dripping onto her lap. Instantly, she got to her feet.

"Oh Christ!" Caroline declared. "I'm so sorry!"

"Here," I said, handing Zoe a napkin.

"It's fine," she said, dabbing at her T-shirt.

"God, I'm so clumsy," Caroline said. "Here, let me get you some club soda."

"It's all right, really," she said, laughing to show it was no big deal. Her cheeks had pinked with embarrassment, and she put the napkin back on the table.

"Do you want to borrow one of my T-shirts?" Caroline offered.

"Ah, no," she said good-naturedly, then gestured toward the door. "I'll just go to the bathroom, give it a bit of a scrub. That'll be enough."

She left the kitchen and I leaned down and picked up the napkin and began mopping up the spilled wine. Some of it had dripped onto the floor and I leaned down to clean it up.

"I can't believe I did that," Caroline said in a half-amused kind of way.

Her response annoyed me. It was almost as if she took some kind of pleasure in the act.

"Unfortunate," I commented.

"Shall I open another bottle?" she asked gaily, oblivious to my prickliness.

I stepped past her and threw the sodden napkin in the garbage. "Hardly worth it now, is it?"

"Oh God. You're not mad I spilled your wine, are you?" Her voice still held that slightly mocking tone.

"Her first time here . . . I don't want her to be put off by knocking wine all over her."

"It's not the end of the world. No point crying over spilled Burgundy."

Caroline's efforts of making light of the situation only caused me more agitation.

"Maybe I should check on her. Make sure

she's okay."

Caroline made a little noise of irritation at the back of her throat. "You stay here and finish tidying up," she instructed. "I'll go check on Zoe."

She disappeared out of the kitchen and Holly joined Robbie on the couch. The TV was on, and the two of them were absorbed. I continued with the cleanup until I heard footfalls on the stairs. Coming out into the hallway, I saw Zoe descending. When she caught sight of me, she smiled broadly.

"Thanks so much, David," she said, reaching the bottom step and taking her coat from where it was hanging on the newel post. "This has been really lovely."

"You're not going already?"

"Afraid so," she said cheerfully. "I've an essay to hand in tomorrow."

Caroline began coming slowly down the stairs.

"Let me give you a lift," I said, helping Zoe into her coat.

"I can walk home," she said, laughing at my offer. "I don't want to put you to any trouble."

"No trouble," I said, and she rewarded me with a grateful smile.

While Zoe turned to thank Caroline for the meal, I put my head around the door and told the kids that she was leaving. Robbie came out to say good-bye, but Holly remained on the couch. I decided not to make an issue of it.

"Sorry about the wine," I said, once we were alone in the car. "Caroline isn't normally that clumsy."

She told me not to worry about it, laughing it off.

I felt real affection for the strength she had shown: it was no mean feat to walk into another's family home and join the established rhythms of their life as seamlessly as she had.

"I know that can't have been easy," I said.

"It was really nice to meet everyone."

"I hope you didn't feel like we grilled you too much?"

"Not at all," she replied. "It was nice — getting to see another side to you."

"How do you mean?"

She shrugged, an air of slight embarrassment coming over her. "Outside of college, the private you, that's all. How you are with your family."

"Well, I hope you can get to know all of us better."

"I'd like that. Holly and Robbie are lovely. Robbie's so like you."

I nodded, wondering had she been hoping

to see traces of herself in his or Holly's face — some linking traits that marked them out as her siblings.

Neither of us spoke for a few minutes, the car filling with silence as I drove through Rathgar Village toward Rathmines. While the afternoon had passed off well, I felt a lingering sadness. It had started the moment she mentioned Linda's funeral. Briefly, I thought about how different our lives might have been had Linda made contact: a phone call, a letter — that's all it would have taken. What was so terrible about me that she felt like she could not get in touch?

We turned the corner into Rathmines, passed the neon shop-front signs blinking in the dark, the fast-food joints, the charity shop, the church with its copper dome. She directed me down a side street and the car turned onto a terrace of Georgian houses that had seen better days. I pulled the car up alongside the curb and she reached for the door handle.

"Can I ask you a question?" I began, tentatively. "Did Linda ever talk about me?"

She considered her answer carefully, as if she were remembering something difficult and painful. "Toward the end, when she was dying."

"But not before then? Not when you were growing up?"

"Not really." Zoe said reaching for the door handle, and I could sense her need to go. All the questions she had been asked that day — it must have been exhausting. Still, I wanted to keep her there, to find some kind of resolution to the problem that had been bothering me from the moment she came into my office and made her revelation: Why didn't Linda tell me?

"Well, there was one time," she said shyly, as if reluctant to divulge the information. "I must have been eight or nine. We were in Greystones with our cousins, and she took me on a special outing, as she called it, like it was something secret, just the two of us were to know about and no one else. She borrowed her cousin's car and drove up to Dublin, to Belfield. She took me onto campus. It was the first time I had ever been to a university."

"She took you to UCD?" I asked, confused.

"Yes."

"But why?"

"I don't know. We just sat there in the seating area near the Blob. I don't know how long we sat there — an hour, maybe. She told me someone she knew worked there — someone who had once been important to her. The whole time we were there, she kept looking around, as if she were waiting for someone. Then, it was as if she gave up. We went back to the car and drove away. She never said anything more about it."

I had the feeling that she was telling me this to make me feel better, but as I sat there, one hand still gripping the steering wheel, I felt an enormous sense of loss coming over me. The wasted opportunity, cruel fate — of all the hundreds, no thousands, of times I had walked past that very spot — had I only done so on that day — seen the face that had once been so familiar to me, so well loved, everything might have been different.

Perhaps she saw my reaction to her words. Awkwardness came into the car and she pulled the door handle, a chill air entering the space around us.

"If it helps at all," she said, one foot out of the car, "I could tell that she had never really forgotten you."

She stepped onto the pavement, pulled the collar of her coat up, and walked down the darkened roadway. I closed my eyes and breathed in the last traces of her presence. When I looked out onto the street again, all was quiet, orange pools of light shimmering in the darkness.

I started up the engine, pulled the car away, and above the white noise of the engine, emerging from the tangle of my thoughts, one phrase shone clear of all others — the thrill of them:

*I could tell she had never forgotten you.*

# CHAPTER 11
## CAROLINE

"I think it went well. Don't you?"

It was almost midnight. Hours had passed since he had dropped Zoe back to her flat, and David's voice retained its buoyancy, the same optimism that had imbued the whole afternoon.

"Yes. I suppose."

I was in bed already, reading my book, while he moved about the room, changing into his pajamas, getting out his clothes for the morning. There was an energy about him as if the day had bolstered his spirit, whereas, if anything, I felt drained by it all. I tried to concentrate on the words in front of me, but his jittery presence was a distraction. Putting down my book, I watched him fumbling around at the back of his wardrobe, looking for something he couldn't find.

"What are you doing?" I asked, a note of irritation coming into my voice.

175

"Looking for my climbing gear. Have you seen it?"

"David, you haven't climbed in years."

"I know. But I thought I'd go down to the Sports Center tomorrow, give the climbing wall a go."

"Why?"

"Why not?" he replied cheerfully, with no indication that he had picked up on my annoyance. "It's probably in the attic." He disappeared onto the landing.

For a few minutes, I sat fiddling with the page of my open book, listening to him overhead. Where had the sudden urge come from — to revisit a sport he had long forgotten about? Zoe, of course. I thought again of the two of them disappearing down the driveway into the evening. Ever since his return he had been upbeat, happy in a way that I hadn't seen for a long time.

"Find your gear?" I asked when he came back into the room.

"It's a bit dusty, but not beyond use."

He set about restoring order to his wardrobe.

"What was it like?" I asked. "Zoe's flat?"

"Oh. I don't know. I didn't go up."

"I thought you might have. You were gone a while."

"Was I? There was traffic."

"What's it like from the outside?"

"It's a quiet enough street — a terrace of brown-bricks in Rathmines, behind the swimming pool."

"The rent can't be cheap."

"A pokey room in a freezing attic. I don't think she can afford much else."

"I imagine it's all incense sticks and posters of Morrissey," I said, picking at the corner of my book.

"Her taste is a bit retro. What was it she told Robbie she likes? The Cure and Massive Attack. I mean, those were from back in our day."

"You make it sound like the Dark Ages," I said, the ice inside me beginning to thaw. The way he'd said it — *back in our day* — reminded me of our shared history, and the joy that lay within those memories, a joy that she couldn't touch. Putting aside my book, I pulled back the covers and moved across the mattress to where he was sitting, looped my arms around his neck, bringing my cheek alongside his. He reached up and grasped my wrist and I could feel his face against mine, smiling.

"I still remember you dancing around a bedsit to The Smiths," I murmured and he laughed.

"Me too," he added.

It was nice, the warmth between us — this sudden intimacy. After the day that had passed, it felt fortifying to have him back in my arms, his body against mine.

"I must dig out some of my old CDs," he said. "See if Zoe wants them."

One mention of her name and the mood between us evaporated. Where I was bathing in the warmth of an old memory, he was focusing on a future neither of us had bargained for. There was a frisson of excitement in his voice. Subtle enough but I caught it. I could tell how pleased he was with this daughter, taking pride in her originality, her desire to separate herself from the crowd. With the mention of her name it was as if, somehow, she had crept into our room.

"She's very beautiful," I said, tentatively.

It was true. She had the cool beauty of a glassy lake on a cold day — you wanted to stare at it, to take it all in, though you wouldn't want to touch it. A coldness that seemed biting. I said it to test him, I suppose. A childish need to hear him dismiss it or make some comparison. *Not as beautiful as Holly. Not as beautiful as you.*

"She's like her mother." His tone was matter-of-fact.

"You like her. Don't you?" I said. "I mean,

as a person."

He turned in my embrace so that he could face me, and I let my arms drop. He held on to my wrist, his thumb idly stroking the inside.

"There's something about her," he began cautiously. "I think it was brave of her, coming here today, meeting all of us. It must have been daunting."

"Daunting?"

"To her mind, we must seem this fully formed machine, this tight unit," he explained. "I'm sure she must have felt nervous."

I thought back to the moment just after Zoe had arrived and the introductions had been made. The way she had held out her hand to shake mine, giving me a shy smile, and said: *"I hope we can become good friends, Caroline."*

It was not what I had expected.

The smile was bright, but the handshake was weak. It was like trying to grip water. I couldn't dispel the sense that the words used had been carefully selected, well rehearsed. *I hope we can become good friends.* David looking on with a hopeful expression. There was something very adult in the phrasing, a hint of archness in her tone. Quite unlike that of any eighteen-year-old I had met. In advance of her visit, I had wondered if anything would be said about our conversation that day at the university, whether I should broach the subject with her, maybe even apologize. As soon as she spoke those words, I understood that they were her way of opening and closing the subject. It was, I felt, the most subtle of put-downs.

"I feel sorry for her," he said, rousing me from my private thoughts.

"Do you?"

"Listening to what she was saying about Linda dying. How lonely she must have been. And as for the stepfather. . . . He sounds like a piece of work."

"We're only hearing her side of the story, you know," I said, thinking of the way she had bowed her head and looked up at David with those big eyes. The coyness of it — the faux shyness, the manufactured vulnerability. How readily he accepted it, whereas with Robbie and Holly, he was impenetrable to their appeals for sympathy, often demanding proof to back up their complaints.

"What are you saying?"

"She's a teenager. They bend the truth to make it match their own view of the world."

"That's a little harsh."

"Haven't you said as much about Robbie

in the past?"

"That's different," he said, letting go of my hand.

"How is it different?"

"Because Robbie hasn't lost a parent."

I kept my anger in check, and said, "Okay. She's obviously grieving for Linda, but I'm sure Gary is too. People don't always communicate well when they're trying to cope with loss."

He looked down, took off his watch, and put it on the nightstand. Turning to get into bed, he said, not unkindly, "Shove up, there," and I scooched over to my side of the bed while he settled back against his pillow.

"The kids seemed to handle it well, don't you think?"

"Yes," I said carefully. I thought of Robbie's shy enthusiasm, the way Zoe seemed to draw him out with talk of music and film, shared cultural references. Holly had said little throughout the meal, and from the thinness of her mouth, the way her eyes caught mine, I could tell she was bothered by this other girl.

"Robbie was great," David continued. "They seemed to hit it off — him and Zoe. Did you notice?"

"Holly seemed quiet."

"Did you talk to her after Zoe left?"

"I tried to, but she was being cagey. You know Holly. She likes to process these things first."

"I suppose it's natural for her to feel put out. Until now she's been the only daughter."

*She's still* my *only daughter,* I thought, a surge of anger rising out of nowhere.

"You should tread carefully with her," I told him, a gentle warning. "She might be feeling displaced."

"I will. Thanks for today, love," he told me. "I know it hasn't been easy for you — all of this. It's early days, but I think it'll be okay. When she first walked into my office and dropped that bombshell, I was sure our lives were about to be turned upside down. But after today I feel heartened. Optimistic."

Now was the time to tell him, the opening I needed to voice my doubt, to express how I was unsure of the girl, wary. There was something about the way the situation was unfolding that was not right. I should have said it — I would have, but for the look in his eye when he turned to me.

"I think we could get through anything," he said, "you and me."

A quiet conviction in those words, which instantly summoned up the difficult work involved in mending the split between us. I felt the pressure of his grip and squeezed his hand in return.

He let go just long enough to turn out the lights, and he was back with me again, the two of us sliding under the covers. For a few moments everything else dissolved around us, the world narrowing to this room, this bed, this breath, this touch.

Afterward, he fell asleep with his arms around me. A short while later, I gently moved away, and he turned over and settled into a deeper sleep.

I stayed awake, listening to the noises of the house around me — the creaking of wind in the gables, the ticking of pipes deep in the recesses of the house, and the soft breathing of my husband. I thought about Zoe, her weak handshake, her behavior toward me. With the others, she was all warmth and charm and interest, but I got cold politeness. She hardly even looked at me, her eyes always sliding away from mine toward the others. Thinking, I realized the subtlety and slyness of it.

The spilled-wine incident had chilled me — her laughing refusals when I offered to lend her one of my T-shirts, the way she warmly shrugged off any apologies, making light of the matter. "It's not a problem," she had said of the burgundy splash across her T-shirt, like evidence of some act of violence, while she smiled and laughed, and then excused herself to use the bathroom. David mopped up the spilled wine while I cleared away the dishes. Together we set the room to rights. Zoe was in the bathroom for at least ten minutes and we both assumed she was rinsing the wine from her top.

"I'll go and check on her," I told him.

The cloakroom off the hall was empty, and as I climbed the stairs, I heard the sounds of running water coming from the bathroom. I knocked on the door and said her name.

"Come in," was the reply and I pushed the door open to find her leaning against the sink, attempting to wash out the stain from the T-shirt she was still wearing. It seemed an awkward task, and she didn't look up from it, her mouth set in a thin line of determination. As she wrung water from the hem, the T-shirt rose a little higher from her waist and I could see a band of pale flesh at her midriff, so thin she was almost concave.

"I just came to see if you needed help," I said. "Did you manage to get it out?"

"No."

"Perhaps some salt would help?"

She let go of her clothing and turned to me, her face a small pinched mask.

"It's fucking ruined," she said.

The words seemed to bounce off the cold surfaces of the room.

"Zoe, I —"

"Don't bother," she snapped, pushing past me, taking the stairs two at a time.

I remained in the bathroom, trying to make sense of what had just passed between us. The sudden ferocity of her words had taken me aback, the speed at which she had swung from warmth to hostility leaving me reeling.

There were voices in the hall and as I came down the stairs, I saw David helping her on with her coat.

"I can walk home," she was saying, laughter slipping easily between her words. "I don't want to put you to any trouble."

"No trouble," he answered, and she beamed back at him.

Then, seeing me on the stairs, she directed her smile at me, as if nothing had passed between us.

"Thank you so much for a lovely lunch, Caroline," she said warmly. "I really enjoyed it."

I must have mumbled some kind of good-bye, but for the life of me, I can't remember what. It was breathtaking, the way she turned on the charm in front of David, reserving cool hostility for the occasions she and I were alone together.

I could have said something to David — but what? That she had snapped at me? Told me her T-shirt was ruined? He would say I was reading too much into it, that I had misinterpreted her tone. To his mind, the whole time she was with us she had been polite, friendly — charming, even. He would think I was being unfair. Still, I regretted having let it pass with no mention at all.

I lay in bed listening to the patter of rain on the roof, the wind strengthening. Soon enough it was howling around the eaves, rain lashing against the windows. David stirred in his sleep but didn't wake. I lay there in the darkness, staring at the ceiling long after the storm was spent.

My unease after that first visit faded as the days passed. There was work, a dental checkup, the usual household obligations as well as visits to the nursing home where Ellen was settling in. Before I knew it, Sunday blew in and she was among us again — Zoe. I hadn't thought she would return so soon, but when David put it to her that she was welcome to join us, she apparently accepted eagerly.

Just like that, it became a pattern — a set piece that bookended the week. November passed, the weeks studded with these curious occasions. Curious, because although they became more relaxed as we got to know her, I still felt that there was something stagy about them.

Each week began to tilt toward Sunday, as if all the other days were treading water to make time pass. That day, those visits, took on a significance that made me feel uncomfortable. Come Sunday morning, a bounce and vigor would enter Robbie's step, and at the same time I could see a tightening in Holly's face. As for David, it used to be his Sunday treat to take himself off alone to our local pub for a quiet pint and to read the papers for an hour or two in the afternoon. After Zoe's arrival, that had stopped. Instead, he would drive to Rathmines to collect her, and after lunch he'd drop her back again, like some kind of shared custody arrangement after a marital separation. Only Zoe was not a child. And if David was in any way put out by this, he didn't show it. In fact, he appeared happy.

Another thing: those Sunday nights, after she had left, after we had all settled down to sleep, he would reach for me in the darkness, drawing me to him, fingers exploring the planes and declivities of my body, meandering lines traced over my skin. There was something different about our lovemaking then. It seemed to gain a new charge, a new intensity. I put it down to a release of tension. Sex on those occasions was rather like the sex had after a long and bruising argument — the sweet resolution of our bodies finding each other, the unspoken forgiveness in the dark. While there was something restorative about it, a small part of me was troubled. I worried that while for me it was a release of tension, for David it was something else.

I used to believe that when you embark on an affair, you lose interest in sex within your marriage. I have learned since that desire can be a blind grasping thing. In those months when I was seeing Aidan, I would often turn to my husband with the most ferocious passion, the desire within me like a little ball of electricity, charged and directionless and constantly seeking an outlet. When I made love to David it was with a blend of passion and guilt, desire and remorse, and afterward I had to resist the impulse to curl up under the sheet at the farthest side of the bed from him, my back turned so he couldn't see my shame.

On those nights after Zoe had left, when David reached for me in the darkness and I felt his intensity, it crossed my mind more than once that he was like a man in love.

# Chapter 12
## David

Timing is everything, isn't it? I sometimes wonder had Zoe come to me earlier, when she was still a child, when I had a chance to be a proper father to her, would things have worked out differently? The irony is when Zoe arrived in my life I actually thought the timing was right, fitting. My mother was dying. There had been no official prognosis, but I could see for myself the steep decline she had slipped into, the steady corrosion of her thoughts and memories, which brought about a corresponding weakening in her body. Within those short weeks, it was like witnessing a shrinkage in her, not just her brain growing porous but her body diminishing to a frightening degree. When I helped her into bed or out of the car, I noted with alarm the thinning of her limbs. I began to mentally prepare myself for what was imminent. While the sadness of my mother's decline was in my thoughts, I found some consolation in my growing relationship with Zoe. Her coming into my life at that time seemed a natural exchange — where one light was dimming, another had begun to glow.

She came to us every Sunday, and as the weeks progressed, I noticed with a touch of happiness how she grew relaxed, opening up a little more with each passing week. I felt a corresponding loosening within myself. At college, it remained awkward, and our dealings there retained a note of professional distance. But at home, I could be myself and so could she. As the days of the week passed, I would find myself looking forward to Sunday and to the ring at the door heralding her arrival.

I knew that Caroline wasn't happy about it. She had made some noises about Robbie and Holly feeling displaced but I couldn't help thinking that at the back of her words lay a petty meanness, a sort of jealousy over the time and attention I was giving to Zoe. Whenever we came close to discussing it, the conversation would teeter on the threshold of argument. Mostly we went around in circles avoiding anything too combustible. I promised to do something with just *our* kids, and did manage on a couple of occasions during those autumn months to spoil

Robbie and Holly. These events passed off peacefully enough, but I had the niggling feeling that such gestures toward Caroline and the kids were a kind of lame effort at ameliorating the disruption caused by introducing Zoe into their lives.

She didn't come to the house every Sunday. Sometimes, I took her to my local pub for lunch, just the two of us — partly as a sop to Caroline's mood, partly because I felt it important that we spend a little time alone in order to get to know each other better.

"How's the study coming along?" I asked one Sunday.

We were sitting in the corner booth, surrounded by wooden paneling adorned with tinsel, a rugby match on the TV above the bar, two lasagnas sitting in front of us.

"Okay, I guess." She took a forkful of food, spitting it out quickly, her tongue burned. "God, that's hot!"

She laughed, looking flushed and youthful.

"Here, take a drink." I pushed her bottle of lager toward her, drinking from my own pint while she raised the bottle to her lips.

"I can't wait for the exams to be over," she admitted. "Any hints you can give me about your paper?" she added, jokingly.

"Nice try," I said drily, enjoying her playfulness. "You know I won't be correcting your papers. Undue influence, and all that."

"Sure. I know."

I was relieved that she didn't query my admission: having to divulge the details of the protocols of an ethics committee was not something I wanted to get into. Besides, any mention of McCormack made me queasy; he had been given the task of grading a tranche of my papers, Zoe's included, and to reciprocate I had agreed to take a slew of his students' scripts. It had been an awkward moment but one Alan had dealt with in the Exam Board perfunctorily.

"You must be looking forward to Christmas?" I asked Zoe.

"A break yes, Christmas not as much."

"Bah, humbug," I joked, and she laughed.

"No, it's not that. It's just weird now, without Mam."

"Of course. I'm sorry, I wasn't thinking."

"That's okay," she said.

"What are your plans? Will Gary be expecting you?"

"Gary," she replied, disdain creeping into her voice. "Who knows what he's expecting."

Her jolly disposition faltered.

I'd been giving the idea some thought for a while, even though I hadn't discussed it yet with Caroline. The thought of Zoe spending Christmas in the chilly company of a stepfather who had little affection for her was troubling. I hadn't intended broaching the subject with her that day, but while it was on my mind, I decided what the hell.

"Maybe you don't have to go to Gary for Christmas," I ventured.

"How do you mean?"

"You could come to us."

"I couldn't, but thanks."

"Why not?"

She put down her knife and fork, and wiped her mouth with a napkin. I had the impression she was stalling.

"You should spend Christmas together, the four of you," she said quietly. "I'd feel I was intruding."

"Don't be ridiculous. We'd love to have you."

"Even Caroline?"

"Listen," I said. "Caroline will be fine. I'll square it with her."

She frowned down at her plate, half the food untouched.

"I don't know. She really doesn't like me. I don't want to cause any trouble for you — especially not at Christmas."

I could have tried explaining to Zoe that it wasn't personal, but she was so despondent that the words would have sounded hollow. I weighed the situation up in my mind — perhaps, in hindsight, I should have been more cautious — before saying, "When I told Caroline about you, back in October, it was difficult for her, but not for the reasons that you might think."

She was listening now, her despondency replaced by curiosity.

"She got pregnant, you see, when we were students. This was before I knew your mother."

I told her everything. About the pregnancy, the abortion, our subsequent breakup. She took it all in, unspeaking. Only when I was finished did she sit back. "Now it makes more sense."

"It's hard for Caroline, you see. She still feels regret about what happened. And when you came along . . ."

"I'm a painful reminder," she said, finishing my sentence. "Did you ever regret it?"

"No. No, I didn't. We were young. It happened. I never really think about it."

"Do you wish Linda had done the same?"

Her question shocked me. She held herself still as she waited for my answer.

"Of course not," I said.

Instinctively, I reached for her hand, held it there on the table. With a flash I thought of Linda that day in The Oarsman when I had told her about accepting a postdoctoral position in UCD. *"You're leaving Belfast?"* she had said, her voice small and shocked. It was the same day she had given her lecture on Walter Benjamin's angel of history. A doomed creature, she had called it: "It wants to make whole what has been destroyed." I thought about how Klee's painting *Angelus Novus* had been projected onto the wall of the lecture theater. How beautiful it was, how beautiful she was. I thought about how she had given me the exact same look as Zoe had just given me, her hand in mine, the same plunging feeling in my heart.

A cheer went up from the rugby supporters — Leinster had scored. I let go of Zoe's hand and we both sat back.

"Come to us for Christmas, Zoe."

She thought about it for a moment. Then smiling up at me, a bashful look on her face that couldn't disguise her pleasure, she said, "Okay, then, I will."

"What's this?" Caroline asked.

It was Christmas morning; Robbie and Holly were in the next room, still exploring their newly opened gifts while I was making coffee, readying myself for the Christmas lunch preparations. Caroline had arrived downstairs, festive in a red wrap dress and black heels, her hair loosely curled, and now she stood there, holding up the little silver box.

"A present for Zoe," I answered, adding sugar to my cup. "Coffee?"

"Please." She turned the box over in her hands. "Mind if I look?"

"Go ahead."

I poured her coffee while she prized open the lid and looked at the earrings. A pair of freshwater seed pearls, silver threads curling around them in the shape of looping petals. I had spied them in a jeweler's window in Powerscourt and thought at once of Linda, the one Christmas we had spent together — tinsel draped over the windows in her flat, a plastic Santa on the mantelpiece, looking at the earrings I had gifted her in the cup of her hand, saying, "You do it." How vivid the memory remained — my knuckles grazing the skin of her cheek, the whorl of her small ear against my hand, the feel of her soft fleshy lobe as I held my breath and pressed the sharp point into it. That moment seemed to me more intimate, more erotically charged, than the half hour we had previously spent tousling with each other under the sheets.

"They're lovely," Caroline said, her voice quiet and contemplative, betraying, I sensed, what might have been a touch of resentment. She closed the lid and returned the little box to the countertop, while I gave her her coffee, all the time hoping she wouldn't ask how much they had cost.

"What time did you tell her?" she asked.

"One."

I hadn't liked the thought of Zoe waking up on Christmas morning alone in her flat — especially when we were here at home together as a family — but it would have been a step too far to ask her to come first thing, too disruptive to the routines we had already established as a family over the years.

After coffee, the four of us walked around to attend Christmas Mass in our local church, then I left Caroline and the kids back at the house while I drove over to the nursing home. Mum seemed bright that morning, sprightlier than I had seen her of late, but the vagueness was still there as she glanced about her room as if trying to remember something she did not want to leave without. Whatever it was eluded her and I coaxed her gently into the car. Back at home, we settled her into an armchair close to the fire, and I left Holly chatting with her while I went to join Caroline in the kitchen.

She was wearing an apron over her dress, and there was a high color in her cheeks as her heels clacked over the kitchen floor.

"Can I help?" I asked.

"You do the spuds," she said briskly. "But first, be a love, and pour me a glass of wine. It will make tackling this goose a lot easier."

I plucked a bottle from the rack — a Margaux I had been saving — and poured her a glass. Without commenting, Caroline lifted the wine to her lips and drank. She let out a sigh and it felt like the tension between us was lifting, as if a temporary truce had been declared. My hope was that it would last beyond the day itself — that some kind of normality might return, a gentle remolding of our family to allow for the newest member. Glancing at the clock, I saw that it was half past twelve. Zoe would be here within the half hour. A tingle of nerves passed briefly over the back of my neck.

"We're on schedule," Caroline said, placing a hand into an oven glove.

Holly came in and set the table, and I sat for a while in the living room with my mother. *My Fair Lady* was on the TV and

Mum watched it with glazed eyes and a smile on her face. I kept glancing at my watch, growing a little agitated as it crept past one, and then toward two.

Caroline stuck her head around the door.

"Any sign of Zoe?"

"Not yet."

"Maybe try calling her? The goose will be ready soon."

I dialed her number and listened while it rang through to voice mail. I left a message, and then, just to be sure, sent a text as well, trying to word my message to appear casual.

Robbie came downstairs and announced he was starving.

"Is Zoe here yet?" he asked.

"Any minute," I said with an optimism I didn't feel.

In the kitchen, I asked Caroline if we could hold off for a little longer. She continued stirring the gravy but did not look happy.

I went upstairs and tried Zoe's number again. There was no answer. I considered driving around to her flat in Rathmines but, because I had already had a drink, I decided against it. Standing at my bedroom window, I craned my neck to see down the end of our road, searching for her blond hair above the hedgerows and gates.

By half past two, she still had not arrived.

"We'll have to start without her," Caroline said.

Reluctantly I agreed and we all sat down at the table and began tucking into the terrine that Caroline had made. A festive runner lay down the middle of the table, pillar candles lit, encircled by sprigs of holly and ivy. Christmas choral music came softly through the speakers. I knew that I was lucky. I was surrounded by my family, enjoying the spoils and privileges of hard work and a professional salary, sitting in our comfortable home. Yet, part of me was thinking about the dingy flat in Belfast, the plastic Santa, Linda and I eating with plates balanced on our knees, and it seemed to me, when I thought about it, how much happier I had felt then. I had been unburdened, my whole life still ahead of me, together with the joy of this new love that filled me up in a way that I couldn't measure. I ate the terrine, clearing my plate, feeling those thoughts go through me with a degree of discomfort and guilt.

We finished off the Margaux and I opened a Châteauneuf-du-Pape. After the goose, there was pudding, and we all agreed that we were too stuffed for a cheese board. Outside the window, the sky had darkened.

No one said it, but it was clear that Zoe wasn't coming.

"No word?" Caroline asked as we cleared away the dishes.

"No. I wonder what happened to her?"

"Maybe she went up to Belfast after all," she suggested, putting the detergent tablet in the dishwasher and flipping the door closed.

"You'd think she'd have rung," I said, thinking aloud. Caroline gave me a sidelong glance that seemed overladen with a wry weariness but didn't say anything. All day it had felt like she was giving off something — a kind of relief that Zoe had not turned up. It wasn't anything she said per se, just the relaxed relish she took in the day, without Zoe, as I perceived it.

"I just hope she's okay," I added, feeling prodded by anxiety. It was not like Zoe, no matter what Caroline was implying.

"I wouldn't worry," came her sharp reply. She wiped her hands briskly on the towel, then threw it on the counter with a flourish. "I'm sure she'll be in touch when she needs something."

As it happened, it was not Zoe who got in touch but someone else.

Christmas Day passed and I dropped my

mother back at the nursing home the following morning. Afterward, Caroline and I took the kids for a hike up around the Three Rock Mountain — a St. Stephen's Day tradition. I walked with my hand in my pocket, clutching my phone, waiting to feel it vibrate with an incoming call or text, something to explain Zoe's absence. I had left several messages, dropping any pretense of casualness as the time passed and there was no response from her.

Back home, I went straight through into the kitchen, putting on the kettle for tea, my hands and feet still numb from the bitter cold of the mountain air. I didn't hear the phone ringing in the hall. It was only when I heard Caroline's voice saying, "Is she all right? What happened?" and the rigor of her questions married to the polite but worried tone she was using alerted me to trouble. I stood in the kitchen doorway, watching her speaking into the phone, growing more anxious as she said, "Of course. I'll let him know immediately. He'll be over right away."

*My mother,* I thought.

But it was not my mother.

"It's Zoe," Caroline told me, her eyes fixed on my face, choosing her words carefully. "She's in hospital."

*"What?"*

"She's fine, David."

"What happened?"

Lowering her tone, so the children in the next room wouldn't hear, she said: "It seems she took an overdose."

Weakness came into my legs. The numbness left my extremities and I felt the stinging pain of pricking needles all over my feet and hands as the blood came rushing into them.

"She tried to kill herself?"

Caroline didn't answer that. Instead she told me which hospital and named the ward where Zoe was. I grabbed the keys from the hall table where I had left them and went back outside. My hands were trembling as I started the engine — it was still warm.

It's something no parent ever wishes to see — their child lying helpless in a hospital bed. Even though Zoe had been a stranger to me only months before, even though I had missed all the birthdays and Christmas mornings of her childhood, the first day at school, the hockey matches and end-of-year plays, as soon as I saw her lying there under the hospital blanket, tubes traveling into her veins, I felt a rush of protective love so strong that I had to stop and collect myself, lest all that emotion might break inside me and come flooding out.

She was lying on her side, a blanket covering her body. She was not fully awake — sedated, perhaps, or deep in a depression. A bruise blossomed on her hand where an IV had been inserted. I wanted to reach out and touch her, but I also did not want to disturb her.

As I was approaching the bed, her head turned. As soon as she saw me, the mask fell away, her face contorting with sudden tears that seemed to gust through her, savage and raw.

"Zoe," I said softly, pulling a chair up next to her.

She was trying to cover her face, hiding her brokenness from me, but the sobbing and shaking spoke of her fragility.

"I'm so sorry," she said, the words coming out liquid and halting, spoken between gulped breaths.

"Shhh," I whispered. "You don't need to apologize. I'm just glad you're all right."

She continued to cry but the sobbing had lost some of its raw edge, and while she was still upset, I could see she was calming. Passing my eyes over her, I saw how pale and gaunt she was, skeletal under that harsh lighting. All the color had been drained from her; even her hair looked drab and life-less. She was wearing a hospital gown, her bare arms emerging from the printed cotton. I was so used to seeing her swathed in baggy sweaters or long-sleeved T-shirts, the cuffs tugged down over her wrists and hands. With a shock, I saw the markings on the inside of her arms — a series of vicious little cuts like she'd been clawed by a cat, over and over. Some of the scrapes were fairly new, the scabs still present, while others had healed into fine pink lines, some almost faded completely. I saw these lines and felt emotion inflate within me, tears of shock and pity coming unexpectedly. I swallowed them away, taking her hand.

"What happened?" I asked gently.

"You must wish you'd never met me," she said hoarsely.

"Not at all. Quite the opposite."

It surprised me, how much I meant those words.

"Please tell me. I promise I won't judge. I just want to understand."

She turned over so that she was lying on her back staring up at the ceiling. Her face looked flatter, her eyes dulled. She had let go of my hand but still I sat close, leaning toward her, waiting.

"It just got to be too much," she began.

"Everything got on top of me. I felt like I was drowning."

I nodded encouragement. When she didn't go on, I prompted her. "Was it your studies? A lot of students struggle in the first year. It's very common."

"Yes," she agreed, but I could sense the tug of reluctance within her and knew there was something more.

"There's still plenty of time to catch up," I offered. "It's only the end of Semester One."

"Time," she said drily. The tears were gone now, and what remained was dry deflation. "That's part of the problem. I have no time."

I knew that she had a part-time job to help pay her rent, but as she detailed the jobs she had and the hours she needed to work in order to pay her bills, it became clear to me the burden under which she was struggling and how little time remained for her studies.

"What about Gary?" I asked, feeling somewhat awkward mentioning his name. "I had the impression that he was helping you out financially, paying for your fees at least?"

Even as I said the words, I felt fraudulent. Why did I expect this man I had never met to pay for her education?

"Gary has made it obvious that he wants nothing more to do with me."

She enunciated the words clearly, hardness entering her tone. There was a warning there to keep away, not to prod that sore too deeply. For now, I resolved to leave it be.

"How do you manage?" I asked. "With all these part-time jobs, you must barely have time to go to class, let alone study."

Honestly, and in a voice still scratched from the recent tubes down her throat, she described to me the various uppers and downers she used in order to get the work done, how she used medications to keep her awake through half the night when she needed to study, and then to induce rapid sleep when needed. It was depressing listening to it all, hearing the dry clack of her tongue against the roof of her mouth, her tiny frame dwarfed by the bed, the hospital cubicle, the austere reek of disinfectant in my nose.

"Well, that has to stop," I said, a fatherly instructive tone creeping into my voice. "You can't keep that up. Look at what it's doing to your body."

"I know."

"Zoe, something must have prompted you

to do this now," I said as gently as I could. "What was it?"

She tried to prop herself up but hardly had the strength to do that. Reaching for a bottle of water on the side table, she took a sip, then settled back against the pillow. She appeared sullen, a little ashamed, perhaps.

"It's stupid," she admitted. "I'm such a cliché. Trying to kill myself on Christmas Day. The Psych nurse they sent around to talk to me told me they get more suicide attempts at Christmas than any other time of the year."

"I suppose that makes sense. A lot of people find Christmas hard."

"Yeah. And without Mam, it's just . . ."

Her voice died away.

"What about us? We wanted you to come and have Christmas at the house. We were all expecting you. Robbie was really disappointed."

"You won't tell him, will you?" she asked quickly, panic entering her eye.

"Zoe —"

"Please? I couldn't bear it."

She started to cry again, and I put my hand on her arm to reassure her.

"It's okay, sweetheart," I said, the endearment slipping out, as easily as it would were Holly lying in the bed needing comfort.

She settled back, the fright going out of her eyes, but she remained uneasy.

"I've let you down," she stated.

"No, you haven't."

"It was kind of you to invite me for Christmas. But as the time grew near, I just knew I couldn't go. You were only inviting me because you felt sorry for me."

"That's not true," I argued, feeling a warm breath of anger. "The only person feeling sorry for you is you. I asked you because I wanted you to be there."

"You don't even know me. There are things I've done . . ."

Her voice trailed off and she turned her face away. The words spoken, she seemed more lucid than she had since the moment I sat down. It chilled me to hear them.

"Listen," I said. "As soon as you're discharged, I want you to come and stay with us. There's a spare room in the attic. You would be comfortable. Safe."

Already her eyes were closing, like she was locking me out, wanting to be alone again with her troubled thoughts, her guilty secrets.

"Live with us? Isn't that a bit rash?" Caroline said.

"She tried to kill herself. I'm her father —

it's the very least we can do."

She was preparing dinner at the time and I watched as she sliced an eggplant, placing each sliver carefully into a colander and sprinkling it with salt.

"Yes, well," she said quietly. "It's just hard to take in, that's all. A little hard to believe."

"I just think if we can get her back here, provide her with some stability and support, help her get back on her feet again, then it will be better for everyone."

Caroline turned on the tap and rinsed her hands under the water.

"What should we tell the children?" she asked.

"Zoe doesn't want them to know what she did."

"David —"

"Please. She's ashamed."

"But still, are we to lie to them about it?"

A mean thought entered my head: *You've lied to them before. You've lied to all of us.*

"I feel very uneasy about this — all of this," she said, wiping her hands on the towel. "She's clearly unstable and vulnerable, and I'm not sure she's a good influence on Robbie and Holly. I mean, just say she really did try to kill herself — what if she tries to do it again?"

"I don't think that's going to happen."

"But what if it does?"

"You know what? If it were anyone else — the child of a friend of ours, one of Robbie's pals — you'd be flinging wide the doors, laying down the red carpet for them."

She turned away and began hanging the tea towel over the rail of the stove. Her back still to me, I heard her say, "She makes me uneasy."

With her admission, the air between us seemed to deflate, the tension easing.

I went and stood behind her, put my hands on her shoulders and leaned in so the side of my face was close to hers.

"She needs us, love," I said gently. "She has nothing, no one. Only us."

A brief hesitation, and then her hand reached up to cover mine.

I stood in the corridor by the elevators, waiting for Zoe. There was a window looking onto the tops of the trees, the rooftops of Merrion and Ballsbridge. Outside the evening was cold and still. I felt a stirring of nerves in my chest. The sky was a bright blue, so clear I could see as far as Howth Head beyond the bay. Seagulls called out loud and clear. My fingers tapped impatiently on the windowsill.

It was back with me again — that strange

212

sense of déjà-vu — the nervous energy in my body fizzing. Something had changed between us, and even though it felt like I was carrying all the giddy expectancy of a younger man, underneath that lay the solid mass of our bond. The hours I had spent with her at the hospital, holding her hand, listening to her, comforting her, I had felt the bond announcing itself so strongly, it made me wonder how I had ever questioned it.

A door opened and I turned to see her carrying her bag, shoulders slumped forward in her gray hoodie, but she gave a half smile when she saw me and I felt a bloom of hope.

"Hey," she said shyly, and I took the bag from her.

"Plenty of rest, the doctor said," I told her as I pressed the button to call the elevator.

I put my arm about her shoulder. She felt so slight against me, enclosed within my embrace as the elevator doors opened, but I could see our reflections in the mirror and saw that she was smiling, and, for the time being at least, I could also say, she was safe.

# CHAPTER 13
## CAROLINE

That first night, David spent a long time up in her room, his low sonorous tones coming down the narrow stairs as I stood on the landing, looking up at the closed door. I kept thinking of the dark shadows around her eyes and mouth, lending an austere grace to her beauty. The tragic princess. Afterward, when he came back downstairs, he said little of what they had talked about.

"She's calm," was all he said, as if that was his primary concern.

One by one we went to bed.

I lay awake staring at the ceiling, thinking of her in the room above us. I couldn't tell if David was asleep beside me. Perhaps he too was listening for noises overhead, light footsteps across the floorboards, the gentle creaking of the bed as she turned over. My every nerve was alive to the sensation of this stranger in my home.

Sometime before midnight, I heard her

voice, words muffled by their passage through floor and ceiling. She was alone up there and I pictured her sitting on the bed, knees drawn up to her chin, talking on her phone to a friend or a boyfriend, filling them in on the new turn her life had taken. I thought of the room surrounding her — the pitched ceiling under the eaves, the paint fresh and gleaming from the attic conversion completed in the last year. I thought of the striped bedding, the lamp plugged in on the floor, the wall of plastic storage boxes containing some of the children's old toys and clothes that I couldn't bring myself to throw out. Boxes of nostalgia, things that were precious to me, now a part of her domain. I tried to tell myself that this was just a temporary arrangement, a fleeting stay until she had recovered. But as I listened to her voice, the high light note of her laughter coming from up there under the roof, I felt a trickle of doubt. She didn't sound to me like a girl who wanted to end it all. She sounded relaxed, as if she were settling in. "Make yourself at home," I had told her, when really I meant nothing of the sort.

I woke up early on the first morning of the new term and was out of bed, showered, and dressed before anyone else had stirred. David came down sometime afterward, his eyes still puffy, wordlessly fixing a pot of coffee while I sat at the counter, eating toast and making a list on my iPhone.

"Are the kids getting up?" I asked after he had taken his first sip.

"There's movement. Robbie's in the bathroom. Zoe's not going into campus so I don't expect we'll see her until this evening."

It was disconcerting — already he was including her in the collective "kids."

Holly came downstairs, followed by her brother, the volume of noise in the kitchen rising with their presence — the clatter of spoons and bowls, the low-key grumbling — and soon enough it was half past eight and we were gathering in the hall, packing lunches into school bags and pulling on coats.

"Should we check on her?" I asked David as he came downstairs with his bag, taking his cycling helmet from the coat stand.

"She needs to rest, after what she's been through."

The kids were piling out of the door, getting into the car, and David was wheeling his bike down the path. I stood looking up the stairs, feeling uneasy. I didn't like the thought of her being alone in my house. I imagined her tiptoeing down from the attic as soon as we'd driven off, nosing around our bedroom, picking over my things.

I ran up the stairs, making sure my footfall was audible. Knocking sharply on the door, I heard her call out, "Come in," and I pushed the door open.

She was lying on her side, propped up on one elbow, her head resting on her hand, reading *Madame Bovary*.

"Did you sleep well?"

"Yep."

"Well," I said, as she glanced up from her book, a hazy look on her face as if her attention was still with the novel held open with one hand. "I just wanted to let you know that we're going now."

"Right."

She appeared pale and slight, the long sleeves of her nightdress pulled down over her wrists. I hesitated a moment, my eye caught by the coverlet over the bed. It took me a moment to recognize it — a patchwork bedspread, triangles of blue and gray cotton stitched together into geometrical patterns. I had bought it in Thailand years before when I was not long out of college. Zoe must have found it among the storage boxes up here, which meant she had been snooping through our things. It wasn't as if there was anything secret or valuable hidden away up here, but I still felt angry and disheartened. It was another incursion by her into our lives, another presumption on her part that she was entitled to take possession of whatever she found. I considered saying something, but instinct told me it wasn't worth it.

"How're you feeling?" I asked.

She didn't answer, just shrugged, her attention on the book again.

"You know, if ever you want to talk," I began, "about what happened . . . about what led you to . . ."

She looked up sharply.

"I'd be happy to listen," I finished.

"Right," she said, bemused, before she returned to her novel and lazily turned a page.

I backed out the door feeling stung by her dismissal of me. It wasn't that I expected her to accept my offer, but a small show of appreciation would have been nice. It occurred to me that by attempting suicide — if that was what she had done — she had got exactly what she wanted, her foot in the door, which made me doubt whether she had ever intended killing herself at all. By the time I got downstairs, David was already gone, and so I left a key on the hall table, took one last look back up the stairs, and then closed the door behind me.

The rain started that morning and continued all week — heavy, blistering downpours, monsoon-like in their unrelenting ferocity. The air in the hallway was heavy with the odor of damp clothes. Condensation on windows, heavy traffic, leaves clogged in drains pooling with water.

Every day, when we left the house, she was up there in her room. When I came home in the evening, I'd find her curled up on the sofa with her book while eating a carrot, or watching TV with the others. She'd look up briefly when I came through the door, greet me with a wan smile, then return her attention to whatever she was absorbed in at the time. She wasn't hostile, or even cold, but there was a mildness to her, a lack of engagement, that I found maddening. From what I could tell, she had reasonably recovered from her blip at Christmas. There was no evidence of lingering depression, no black moods. She seemed so docile, so willing to fade into the background, that it made me wonder if she had any desire or intention to find an alternative place to live. Not that I mentioned it. Even after she had returned to college, David made it clear that she remained too fragile to live alone.

The month passed in a flurry of storms interspersed with unseasonably warm weather. It was as if the meteorological elements were somehow mirroring the uncertain climate within our home. As the weeks progressed, I felt Zoe's presence solidifying in the house, growing unquestionable. She was making more of an effort to help out around the house and was, I suppose, largely unobtrusive. Tidy and neat, hers was a quiet presence but a presence nonetheless. And when the others were not around — when it was just her and me — she allowed the mask to slip, her polite charm vanishing, replaced by cool remoteness.

The precariousness of our situation was made clear to me one weekday evening — the occasion of our first serious argument about her. We were clearing away the dishes after dinner, David scraping plates into the trash and handing them to Holly, when Zoe stood up from the table and, without a word to any of us, left the room. In her wake, I heard the dull thud of the salad bowl being brought down hard on the countertop.

"Why is she allowed to get out of the dishes?" Holly demanded.

"Until she's well —" David began, but

Holly cut him off.

"There's nothing wrong with her! Why do you keep tiptoeing around her?"

David put down the plate he was holding. From upstairs came the jagged strains of Robbie's cello. He too had been excused from household chores but Holly wasn't interested in that.

"How much longer is she going to be here?" she asked, her whole body stiff with tension.

"Sweetheart," I began, trying to calm her.

"I'm sick of her!" she declared, her voice rising to a screech.

"Holly!" David said sharply, but she was turning from him. Seconds later we heard feet thundering on the stairs, the slam of her bedroom door. We looked at each other.

"Well?" I said.

"What?"

"She has a point."

He turned from me, picked up another plate, and continued scraping, but with a more committed air.

"Can't we talk about this?" I asked. "Holly's not happy."

"Holly's behaving like a spoiled brat."

"I think you're being unfair. This is her home and she's feeling marginalized."

"I'm not saying that Zoe should stay here

indefinitely," he said, putting the plate and knife down. "But it's only a few weeks since she tried to kill herself. I'm not comfortable at the thought of her taking care of herself yet."

"Have you talked to Zoe about how she's feeling now, within herself?"

"A little. I mean, she's doing better but she's still vulnerable. I think she needs our support."

"Shouldn't she be getting professional help?"

"How is she supposed to afford that?"

"What about the university? Haven't they got counselors?"

"I don't think that's the answer."

I could see that I was not going to get anywhere. Turning back to the counter, I began spooning leftovers into a Tupperware container.

"I'll do something with Holly," he said to appease me. "Something to make her feel special."

"Fine." I put the container in the fridge. I could feel David watching me. When I glanced at him, it was obvious there was something else on his mind.

"What is it?" I asked.

"I've been giving some thought to Zoe's college fees," he began. Instantly my defenses rose. "She hasn't said it outright, but it's clear that she hasn't got much money. Gary isn't exactly supportive and these part-time jobs barely pay her rent. I have the impression that it might have been a contributing factor in what led her to what she did on Christmas Day."

"Where are you going with this?" I asked, unable to keep the coldness from my voice.

He was standing opposite me, looking at me squarely. "I want to pay her college fees."

A laugh escaped me, and I could see it startled him.

"With what?" I asked. "A big chunk of your salary goes to pay the mortgage. Have you forgotten the loan we took out to do all this?" I gestured with one hand to take in the new kitchen, the extension with its wall of windows revealing the garden beyond. Despite the bequest from my parents, our house renovation — the renovation of our marriage — had been costly.

"We'll manage," he said, standing his ground.

"What about all the other payments? Car payments, school fees, health insurance, not to mention cello lessons and piano lessons and the other after-school activities? How are you going to make your salary cover all that as well as college fees?"

He began to look shifty.

"Can't you pay for some of that stuff?"

I didn't say anything, just stared.

"Now that you're working, your paycheck could cover the kids' activities and the school fees. Maybe the health insurance too."

I could hardly believe what he was suggesting.

"You want me to pay for Zoe's college fees?"

"I didn't say —"

"That's what it amounts to, though."

"For God's sake. Is it so much to ask that you contribute a little? All these years, I've been shouldering the financial burden. Is it unreasonable to ask you to share the load now?"

Anger shot through every muscle and fiber. It was outrageous. All those years I had worked in our home, raising our children, keeping things running smoothly on the domestic front, leaving him free to pursue his career, all that time it had felt like there had been a pact between us — a mutual appreciation of the other person's endeavors. Now, with the sweep of his words, he was devaluing the years I had put into our family, our home, as if there were some kind of debt I needed to repay him.

His suggestion that I should pay for Zoe's education — and that was what it was, no matter how he tried to dress it up — was like a slap in the face.

"I am not paying for that girl's education," I said emphatically.

"Hang on —"

"No."

I stepped past him quickly, unwilling to spend another second discussing it, and as I went into the hall, I felt it. The slightest movement of air coming from the top of the stairs, the faintest creak of a floorboard overhead. I moved into the middle of the hall and looked up, hoping to catch a glimpse of whoever had been listening.

Perhaps I had imagined it. All the bedroom doors were closed. Robbie's cello was silent. I thought I heard the sounds of laughter drifting down from his room. Still, I couldn't shake the feeling that someone else had overheard our entire conversation in the kitchen.

It seemed to me that David's notion of Zoe slotting easily into our lives was, at best, naive, if not downright clueless. The die was well and truly cast once she moved in, and in the days and weeks that followed I noticed the marked yet differing changes occurring in both my children. Holly became more introspective and moody, slamming doors and frowning behind her glasses, determined to show her disapproval. Robbie, on the other hand, seemed enlivened by Zoe's presence but not in a good way. Instead, he began questioning my authority over small matters, refusing to do household chores, at times openly mocking me in a way he had never done before. I suppose I could chalk it up to adolescence, but there was something about his behavior that suggested he was showing off in front of Zoe. Whenever I raised the issue of our son's behavior with David, he promised to speak to him about it, but beneath his promise I sensed an undercurrent of disbelief. I knew he disregarded my concern, thinking it stemmed from my distrust of Zoe more than my maternal anxiety.

It wasn't long before I got a call from Robbie's school asking me to come down there at once. There had been an incident. An hour later I was sitting opposite the headmistress, Mrs. Campbell, whom I hadn't seen since that business with Aidan, and underneath her stern gaze I felt my humiliation mingling with a niggling sense of annoyance. It was a mistake not to move Robbie to a different school after all that had happened. I knew that now. In the brief pause while I waited for Mrs. Campbell to inform me of my son's misdemeanor, I wondered if David got some kind of satisfaction from this. His petty revenge meted out piecemeal with every parent-teacher meeting stretching through the next three years. Every school play, every sports day, every end-of-year Mass: did he quietly enjoy my humiliation at every occasion?

"I'll be brief," Mrs. Campbell told me.

Ever the professional, she sat behind her desk and filled me in on the campaign of aggression that my son had been waging against his French teacher, Miss Murphy. At first it was small, silly stuff — using the face of his watch, he would reflect sunlight from the window into Miss Murphy's eyes as she faced the class; he made a popping noise every time she finished a sentence; he would hum constantly and then deny it was him. Stupid stuff, the kind of petty misdemeanors that drive every teacher mad but are not enough to warrant serious disciplinary steps. Lately, things had escalated. He had started throwing pens at her whenever her back was turned. When she came into the classroom, someone had drawn her likeness, breasts bared, on the whiteboard, with the caption "Come get it, boys!" in a speech bubble from her mouth. She couldn't prove it had been Robbie, but her suspicions leaned in his direction.

The incident finally prompting her to tell Mrs. Campbell had happened this morning. Having grown exasperated with his constant baiting, she had ordered Robbie to stand up by the whiteboard for the duration of the class, but as she proceeded to give the lesson, he began slowly inching toward her. At first, she didn't notice, until some of the other boys began sniggering and she turned to find him almost upon her. Shouting at him to get back against the wall, she had put a hand to his shoulder to propel him. Instantly Robbie had swiped away her arm and, putting both hands to her chest, he had shoved her roughly back. Miss Murphy, stumbling over the leg of a table, had fallen awkwardly and banged her head against the seat of a chair. She was still in the sick bay, apparently, shaken by the incident.

"It goes without saying," Mrs. Campbell went on, "that a violent assault on a member of staff is absolutely insupportable and must be treated with the utmost seriousness."

"Of course," I said, reeling from all she had told me.

"The most worrying part in this sorry affair is how targeted the attack was," she said. "In every other class Robbie is well behaved. None of the other teachers have any complaints about his behavior."

"I don't understand it," I said honestly. "I have no idea why this has happened, or what he has against this teacher. He's usually such a gentle boy."

Her eyes narrowed, and her voice softened.

"Is everything all right at home? When a student is disruptive in school it's often because of some difficulty he's experiencing at home."

My thoughts veered instantly toward Zoe. But I didn't have the heart to get into it with Mrs. Campbell. Neither one of us mentioned my yearlong absence from the school, my previous indiscretion. I'm sure it must have been on her mind though.

"Everything's fine," I said quickly.

Robbie was suspended for a week.

How strange it had been — going back to the school. Just standing within those stone walls again had touched old memories alive, and I found myself thinking back to that time, as I drove in silence, my son staring sullenly out the window.

If you saw Aidan, the word "handsome" would not come to mind. A tall, thin man, with a longish face and blue eyes, he was affable and self-effacing. His son was in Robbie's class and we were both on the Parents' Committee. It was not love at first sight, but from the start we'd got on. Sometimes, after a committee meeting, a few of us would go for a drink in the pub around the corner. On occasion, it was just the two of us. All we did was talk, but it was such talk! Small things and big things, from school gossip to our own individual parenting concerns. Idle chitchat, that was all, but a constant pleasurable flow of it.

We had been flirting with each other for some time — harmless enough — but on one night, a night where we stayed behind for a third drink after the others had left, it began to grow more serious. He told me his wife was a very neat and organized person — there was never any question of them leaving a trail of clothes along the floor on the way to the bedroom as seen in movies; everything had to be neatly hung up and put away before lovemaking could commence.

"I bet you're not like that," he said, keeping his eyes on me over the lip of his glass.

Outside, he waited while I unlocked my bike from the railings, and when I turned to say good night, he kissed me long and hard on the mouth and I let him. I remember standing in my kitchen a short time later, my hands to my hot cheeks, horrified by what I had done and yet thrilled by it too.

The next day I felt silly and ashamed. I had let things go too far and resolved to stop before it got out of hand. A text from Aidan in the late afternoon and I, foolishly, responded. We began texting every day and soon we were meeting outside of committee nights — for coffee during the day and, when we could swing it, at night. We met in dingy pubs I'd never heard of in rough parts of town. We sat in the back row of art-house movies, necking like teenagers, discreetly fumbling in the dark.

We never actually had sex, although we probably would have, eventually, if we hadn't been caught. And yes, I did feel guilty about it, desperately guilty, but something kept driving me on, refused to let me stop. The seed of anger planted inside me — *She was the love of his life, not me.* Somehow it opened up and grew shoots, tendrils sneaking out to grasp forbidden pleasures. Such a heady time. Between the elation of this illicit romance and the crying fits in the privacy of the bathroom when the children were at school, my husband at work, I would think of what I was doing and grow frightened and depressed.

At the end of the committee meeting one night, while the others were tidying away the coffee cups, Mrs. Campbell made a neat stack of her paperwork and said, "Caroline, Aidan, a word, please?"

She hid it well — I'll give her that much. Throughout the meeting she had behaved as if she were entirely without suspicion that two of her committee members might secretly be fucking. It was only when we went into her office and Aidan closed the door behind us that she addressed us in a tone of icy fury, her eyes bright with disgust.

"I think one of you had better tell me just what is going on."

At first, we feigned ignorance, even hilarity at the suggestion, followed by indignation when she would not be put off.

"You were seen!" she told us, and I felt a twang of fear inside me.

Aidan refused to go gently, challenging her assertions, demanding to know the details behind the allegation — where had we supposedly been seen (Conway's on Parnell Street), when (three nights ago), by whom (she refused to say).

"You have children!" she said with exasperation. "How could you be so reckless with their happiness? So selfish and stupid?"

I couldn't look at him afterward. We both knew it was over.

Still I thought I could keep it secret, hide it from David, from my children.

At the school gates, in the days that followed, I began to notice the nudging and staring, the whispered conversations I was not a party to. Then a phone call from another parent on the committee.

"You've heard the news? Aidan's left. He's taking his son out of the school."

It took a moment for it to sink in, my mind spinning off in all directions.

"What about you?" she asked then.

"Me?"

"Do you still want to be on the committee?"

"What do you mean, Olivia?"

All that time, she had been speaking in her usual brisk manner. Now her voice dropped, taking on a confidential tone.

"I think you know what I mean, Caroline."

Just like that, I knew I would have to tell David.

And when I did tell him later that night, it was like watching a coldness coming over him, like a thin sheet of ice forming over his skin. I had expected anger, indignation, some kind of volatile reaction. Instead he just sat there, his breathing coming heavier as I gave my sorry account, made my shameful confession. Then, in a quiet voice, he had said, as if addressing his words to the table and not to me: "The children must never know."

Robbie refused to speak the whole way home. I tried various methods of coaxing information out of him but he wouldn't answer, and after a while I gave up. The journey took longer than usual, traffic from a rugby match clogging the streets. As the wheels of the car crunched over the gravel in our driveway, I felt exhausted and troubled. Every single book or magazine article I had read about the adolescent male had warned of sudden fits of aggression, still I hadn't believed it. Not my Robbie. Not my gentle boy. Was it arrogance that led me to think that way? The blindness of a mother's love? He had always been softer than other boys, easily hurt. I had worried that he might be the object of bullying. To learn he was the perpetrator of violence had thrown me completely. I turned off the engine.

"Robbie," I began carefully. "I know things have been strange lately. I haven't been around as much now that I'm working again. If I haven't been there for you, then

I'm sorry. Perhaps you feel that I've let you down, but —"

"I don't. I think it's good you have a job."

"Then what is it, love?"

He shook his head, then pressed it back against the headrest, unhappiness filling his face.

"What you did to that teacher. . . . It's so unlike you. What's the matter? Has something happened?"

He didn't answer.

A thought crossed my mind. All those evenings, the two of them up in his room, talking, whispering.

"Does this have something to do with Zoe?"

He shook his head slightly and put a finger to his mouth, biting at the corner of a nail.

"I know you two get on well. But I think it best if you spend less time with her. She's older than you are. These long chats you have in your room — I don't think they're a good idea."

He gave a small, exasperated sigh and shot me a look of disgust.

"Miss Murphy was the one who saw you together — you and Jack's dad. The one who ratted on you."

Something hard caught in my throat, like a cold stone wedged there. The shock of his admission and all the realizations that flowed from it. He knew what I had done. *He knew.* I felt it like a fist around my heart.

"Oh Robbie." I wanted to explain it, to make it better. I knew, though, that nothing would make it better, just as I knew he had lived with the knowledge all this time. David and I had secretly been congratulating ourselves on shielding the children from what I had done, and all the time he'd known.

He opened the car door and clambered out, and I sat there watching him marching to the front door, putting his key in the lock, and then disappearing inside. I thought of all the small triumphs of motherhood — teaching him to read before he started school, recognizing his musical ability before anyone else did, finding the instrument that best suited his temperament, remembering the flush of pride when the librarian remarked on how many books he got through each week for such a small boy. I thought of all these things and felt how flimsy they were, how paltry in the face of the pain I had caused.

It was a few moments before I could get out of the car. Then I locked it, straightened myself, and followed him slowly into the house.

# CHAPTER 14
## DAVID

It happened that around this time, I was invited to speak at a conference hosted by my old stomping ground, Queen's University, Belfast. On the morning I was due to leave, I got up early, before Caroline's alarm went off, and wandered downstairs. It was one of those surprising February mornings when the frost sparkles beneath the hard sunlight, crocuses spearing up through the frozen earth, and you sense the real possibility that spring has arrived. I took my coffee and the notes for my talk and went to sit in the garden on the wooden bench by the back wall.

I read over my notes, but the words kept blurring on the page, my attention pulled elsewhere. It had been years since I had been to Belfast, and while it was nice to receive the invitation, the thought of going back to Queen's University only served to stir up buried memories and awaken old ghosts.

Earlier in the week, I had taken it upon myself to track down the contact details for Zoe's stepfather, Gary. Of course, I could have asked Zoe for his number, but she was so defensive — almost frightened — anytime he was mentioned, that I chose not to. Instead, I went through the university registrar. It was all straightforward enough in the end. A brief phone call suggesting we meet, which he accepted without question, although I noted the surprise in his tone. I told myself that I just wanted to outline for him my plans to become actively involved in her life — paying her tuition fees as well as taking her into my home. I didn't know whether or not to tell him about Zoe's suicide attempt, weighing his need to know versus her desire for privacy. It was still unclear to me what responsibilities toward her Gary felt existed in the wake of Linda's death. I suppose that's why I set up the meeting rather than discussing it all over the phone.

Another question on my mind was whether I ought to tell Zoe about my planned visit. I didn't like going behind her back like this. Part of my intention to see Gary — a big part — was the hope that he might help me get to the bottom of the question that had dogged me since Zoe's arrival: Why hadn't Linda told me? Any time I had tried tackling Zoe on it, she became evasive and withdrawn. I had the impression she didn't know herself.

I was so lost in these thoughts, my notes put to one side, that I didn't notice Robbie until he was almost upon me.

"Mum says you'll miss your train," he remarked, his hands in the pockets of his school trousers. I noticed a new eruption of spots had broken out over his chin. He looked particularly gloomy that morning.

I glanced at my watch. "There's time. Here, sit down for a minute, will you?"

There was room enough for two or three people on the bench, but rather than taking the seat next to me, he chose to perch himself at a distance on the armrest — an awkward solution but one that drove home to me the distance he had been putting between him and the rest of us ever since his school suspension the previous week.

"How's school?" I asked, and he shrugged, not answering.

"Everything all right?" I probed.

"Yeah. Why?"

"You seem tense."

"No, I'm not."

I suppose I might have put his defensiveness down to hormones. But ever since Caroline sheepishly admitted the reason behind Robbie's violent outburst at school, I had worried his withdrawal had deeper roots than teenage disaffection. It upset me that my son had been aware of his mother's wayward behavior, that he had carried the burden of this knowledge in secret for over a year. I had tried talking to him about it, hoping to squirrel out some information over what repercussions he had to deal with — bullying in school? Teasing? A change in any teacher's behavior toward him? But every time I tried to draw him out on the subject, he clammed up. At home, the mood was fraught. He barely spoke to either of us, and even though this incident had served to fire up my anger toward Caroline over what she had done, I felt a duty as a co-parent to rein in Robbie's attitude toward his mother.

"Listen, go easy on your mother while I'm away, will you?"

"Sure," he said with marked disinterest.

"I know you're angry with her, but she's your mother. She loves you. She only wants what's best for you."

He got to his feet and began moving toward the house.

"Robbie."

He turned to me with a withering stare. "How can you stand it?" he demanded. "After what she did?"

"Marriage is complicated," I began to say, but already he was stomping back toward the house, uninterested in my reply.

So that is how he saw me: a cuckold, a worm, spineless and ineffectual.

Back in the house, I put my coffee cup on the draining board, my notes in my bag. Without saying a word to anyone, I took my things and left.

The conference was well attended and lively, a buzz about the university as the lectures attracted students and those outside of academic life who had an interest in the history of the world wars. By coincidence, an old pal of mine from my Queen's University days — Giancarlo — was also attending. He had become something of a star in academic circles in his native Italy, but to me he was the same mischievous, irreverent student I had known twenty years before. On the first night of the conference, we headed out together to revisit some old haunts around Belfast and it was late when I got back to my hotel room, a little the worse for wear. There was a missed call from Caroline, but I chose not to return it. I was still peeved over the conversation with Robbie in the garden that morning, and I guess I blamed Caroline — tracing the roots of his grievance back to her fling.

My lecture took place on the second morning, and it passed off well. Afterward, there was a lunch in the dining hall alongside some of my old professors. I enjoyed their company, and we talked about the passing years, as well as engaging in a lively discussion about the rise of Islamic fundamentalism in the West, so it was with some reluctance that I excused myself and found a taxi outside the main entrance, giving instructions to take me to an address in Holywood, outside the city.

I sat in the back of the cab, staring out at the massive yellow Harland and Wolff cranes, the concrete bridges under which the road passed, the verges becoming green and lush as we left Belfast behind us. I thought of Linda, curious to see how and where she had lived all those years without me, and with whom. It was hard to imagine the Linda I knew — flighty, scornful of formalized commitments, loath to be tethered to anyone or anything — succumbing to marriage, an institution she had roundly derided in the heady days of our love affair.

I felt a little nervous, unsure as to what I wanted to happen at this meeting. What I hoped was to smooth things over, let Gary know that I was on the scene, and that whatever kind of relationship he had with Zoe, the role of father figure he might have played, it was different now.

The taxi stopped at a terrace of houses with pebble-dashed walls and small gardens, facing out onto a green. Some of the gardens were well maintained, while others were strewn with kids' bicycles and plastic slides, garbage cans shoved up alongside cinder-block walls. A group of sullen teenagers were sitting on a wall, staring as the taxi approached. I tried to imagine Zoe sitting there, or playing on the green as a child, cycling her bike along the tarmacadam road that ran alongside the houses.

I paid the fare and stepped out to a house at the end of the terrace, purple and blue hydrangea bushes in the garden, a green Volkswagen Golf in the driveway. I tried to imagine Linda coming home from work every day to this house, pushing a buggy along this footpath, opening the door every morning to take in the milk.

Holywood, I knew, was an affluent town, part of Ulster's gold coast, but there was something down at heel about this street.

Not that there were flags hanging from the lampposts or curbstones painted in the Union Jack. But for all its neatness, there was an impoverishment here. I used to think all of Belfast was too small to contain Linda, let alone this choked suburban street.

I rang the doorbell, and after a moment's wait, a shadow appeared behind the frosted glass. The door opened and I was met by a tall, gaunt man. He was, I guessed, in his early fifties. Wearing brown cords, a black wool-knit cardigan, and horn-rimmed glasses, he reminded me of a geography teacher I might have had at school.

"David," he said, extending his hand to shake mine.

His voice was deep and his handshake was strong. At his request, I followed him inside. He led me through a narrow hallway into a kitchen at the back of the house.

"Coffee?" Gary asked.

"Please."

The kitchen was long and narrow, lined with white cabinets, a butcher-block surface that was almost entirely free of appliances apart from a red Gaggia next to the sink that Gary began fiddling with.

"Please, make yourself at home," he urged, directing me to a light-filled room accessible from the kitchen.

What I had seen of the house so far seemed fairly mundane — even character-less — but stepping into this sunroom, I understood I was now in the heart of the home. Floor-to-ceiling windows gave onto an immaculate garden, and even on this gloomy afternoon, light poured through the skylights in the ceiling onto honey-colored wooden floors. The walls were filled with books and prints, shelves stacked with paperbacks in haphazard arrangement, a reading lamp sitting on top of a neat tower of magazines. There were framed photographs everywhere, photographs of weddings and parties and visits to foreign cities — some with Gary, some of Linda alone, one or two of her among a group of people I didn't recognize. My eyes were drawn to them, searching for her. How strange it was to see this woman with her careful smile, her monochrome clothes, and realize that this was Linda — *my* Linda. It was a shock to see her hair cut short, tamed into a neat bob, still blond but dark at the roots. I suppose she might have also been surprised at how I had aged — the young man with whom she had fallen in love with gray hair, a forehead furrowed with age lines.

I picked up one of the framed photographs from the side table. It was of Linda, standing outside Belfast City Hall in a yellow dress, holding in one hand an umbrella, in the other an oversize hat.

"We thought it was going to rain," Gary said, coming into the room and putting a tray down on the coffee table. "Our wedding day. I insisted we bring an umbrella," he said, smiling. "Linda was holding it up because it hadn't rained."

"When was that?"

"Twelve years ago in March. I'll let you help yourself to milk and sugar."

"Thanks," I said, putting the photograph back where I had found it, but not without wondering where Zoe was when the picture was taken. In my mind's eye I saw a six-year-old girl in a blue dress, hair in braids, new gaps in her teeth showing as she smiled for the camera. But she was not in this picture, nor in any other. As my eyes took in the room, I found there wasn't a trace of her anywhere.

"The last time I saw Linda," I told Gary, as I took my cup and sat in the armchair opposite his, "she was preparing to go to Canada to do her master's."

"Yes, well she did go, but things happened. She dropped out and came home."

Things happened. Pregnancy. Motherhood. I listened for the trace of unspoken accusation in his voice, but there was none.

"She never finished her master's?"

He shook his head, no, before adding: "That's not to say she never studied again, though. Quite the opposite. She was always working away at something. City guilds courses, Open University. Night classes in creative writing or women's studies. One year she decided to learn Italian, another year she took up Mandarin. 'Mandarin?' I said to her. 'Sure, what would you want with that?' I used to tell her she'd be better off learning how to drive, but she wouldn't hear of it."

Something snagged in my brain. "She couldn't drive?"

"No. Preferred to get the bus. Or a taxi when she was feeling flush."

He filled me in on scant details of their life together: she had worked in a bookshop; he taught at a local school, taking a leave of absence when his wife became sick. I thought of Linda and all those night courses, desperately seeking an outlet for her busy intelligence, and heard the wild flapping of wings tossing against a closed window. An exotic bird trapped in a room.

"I was so sorry to learn of her death," I told him. "It seems wrong. She was too young."

He nodded slowly, growing solemn, and neither of us spoke.

"Linda's mother also died in her forties," he said after a minute. "Did you know that?"

"No, I didn't."

"The same type of cancer."

"So it was hereditary?"

A frown line became pronounced on his forehead while he considered that.

"They couldn't say that for sure. And you know, our lifestyle. . . . Well. We weren't exactly health freaks."

I heard the scratch of cigarettes in his voice, thought of Linda smiling mischievously at me over her glass of wine. The air in the room had changed, the sadness within him dragging at me. I had an urge to get out of there and thought it best to get to the point and address the purpose of my visit.

"About Zoe," I began. "I just wanted to let you know that she's living with us now — with my family."

"Right," he said, as if the information didn't weigh too heavily on him.

"Also, I'm going to be paying her tuition fees from now on, just in case you felt any responsibility in that department. I'm happy to step in."

A pucker of confusion around his brow.

"Her fees? But she has money for that."

"No, I don't think so."

"She does," he said firmly. "Linda left Zoe money, specifically to pay for her education. Believe me, I know. I put the check into Zoe's hand myself. Six thousand pounds of it."

I stared at him, unsure of what to believe.

"She failed to mention that, did she?" Gary said drily, reading my confusion.

"She did."

He gave a brief, mirthless laugh. "She has a loose association with the truth, that one."

The way he said it only served as a reminder of all the hints and intimations Zoe had given of this stepfather with whom she didn't get on. Suspicion rolled over in my mind.

"God knows what she's told you about me," he added.

"She said you two never hit it off."

Another laugh, more a quick exhalation of air through his nose.

"That's putting it mildly."

The hardness of his manner faltered a little as he ran a hand over his forehead as if to rub away the tension there. Adopting a softer tone, he said: "It's not all her fault. I suppose I'm partly to blame. It was such bad timing, you see, her coming along when she did, just after Linda's diagnosis."

"Sorry, what do you mean?" I asked, confused by the turn the conversation had taken.

"You asked me about Linda's cancer," he said patiently, "was it hereditary or lifestyle or just pure misfortune? Perhaps all three. But the one thing that keeps me awake at night is the thought of all the hormones she pumped into her body. We couldn't have kids, you see. Unexplained infertility. We did IVF seven times," he went on with a brief shake of his head. "Seven times. All those hormones, all those tests and procedures."

All those disappointments, I thought. I tried to imagine how they managed on their salaries — fertility treatment was not cheap. The house, the estate, it began to make sense to me.

"All those hormone injections she'd had," he said. "I couldn't help but think that it contributed in some way. That's how I felt when the diagnosis came. And when Zoe showed up on the doorstep like that, the child she had given up all those years before, well the timing of it. . . . It felt like a cruel irony."

I stared at him blankly. A buzzing feeling had started in my head, the room seeming to dip and sway around me. There was a radio on in the next room and I wished, irritably, that he would turn it off so that I could think.

"I don't understand," I said. "What do you mean, the child she had given up?"

He scrutinized me again in a way that suggested he was still making up his mind about me.

"Yes. After she was born. You didn't know?"

"No," I said, hardly trusting myself to speak with all the emotions and questions clawing around inside me.

"It was the one real regret of Linda's life," Gary continued. "She never forgave herself for it."

He was talking now about a letter that arrived, indicating the girl's desire to reach out to her natural mother, the subsequent meeting, and how euphoric Linda was afterward, but all I kept thinking about was Zoe, sitting in my car, the orange glow of streetlights outside as she told me about Linda bringing her to UCD — *driving* her there — when she was a girl. *I could tell she had never forgotten you,* she had said, and I had fixed on those words. Was it all lies? Was there truth in anything she had said? Other accounts came back at me: the Greystones cousins, shopping trips to Grafton Street, occasions that my mind had fixated upon imagining the scene had I happened upon them — had I rounded the corner at the Blob that day and spied my Linda and a little blond-haired girl, had I stopped dead on Grafton Street, Linda holding a child's hand, walking toward me saying, "Hello David," the memory of her voice saying my name coming to me in a painful jab. All of it lies.

"At first, she seemed sweet," Gary said of Zoe, his words shaking me from my confusion. "She used to come around here and sit for hours, the two of them talking, swapping stories. In a way, it was a bit like watching a love affair unfolding."

Hard as it was, I tried to imagine it: Linda and Zoe sitting in these chairs, their eyes and voices locked on each other, anxious to make up for all those lost years.

"When Linda suggested that Zoe move in, I wasn't too sure. It all seemed to be happening so fast — and Linda was quite sick, the treatment taking its toll. She loved having Zoe here but was always exhausted afterward, you know? Still, I couldn't object — it was her daughter, after all. Zoe moved in, and it was fine for a while. Then things began to change."

"What things?" I asked, my coffee cooling in my mug.

He crossed his legs, frowned a little, staring not at me but at some spot on the floor, his mind casting back through memory.

"Small things, at first — she'd tell Linda that I'd done something or other to upset her when I hadn't. Making out that I was being cool with her or trying to shut her out — Linda became upset. When she confronted me, I denied it — tried to explain to her that Zoe was imagining it all or worse, making it up. It was ridiculous — the poor woman was in and out of hospital, as thin as a stick, and here we were arguing over silly little lies a teenager had told."

An icy dread flowed through me: had she been doing the very same thing with Caroline and me, playing one against the other, working at pulling us apart?

"I felt like there wasn't much I could do about it," Gary went on, "not without upsetting Linda. So I put it on the back burner, said I'd take things in hand once Linda got the all-clear. But she kept getting sicker, and the situation at home was growing worse. I mean, on the one hand, I felt sorry for Zoe. She was this messed-up kid who just wanted to get to know her mother. On the other hand, I felt she was trying to shut me out so that she could have Linda all to herself."

He leaned forward and returned his coffee cup to the tray.

"Even saying that now makes me feel embarrassed — like I'm jealous of her, this schoolkid." His voice hardened again. "Still, it's difficult to accept what she did. Those last few months with Linda — she poisoned them."

Poisoned them? Was this the same girl whose hand I had held while she lay in a hospital bed, the lifeblood drained from her? What was it she had said to me? *You don't really know me. There are things that I've done. . . .* Did I have any real idea who she was?

After that, the conversation dwindled. I could hardly remember the purpose of my visit, let alone try to question him further. He too grew taciturn, perhaps regretting how much he had admitted, and after thanking him for the coffee, we both stood and he led me to the door.

It was only when I had stepped back outside, and was turning to say good-bye, that I felt the push of the question that was lodged inside me.

"Why did she never tell me?" I asked him. "Linda. About the baby. Why didn't she get in touch?"

He looked beyond me to the green, rough grass covering hillocky ground, bald in places, growing long and clumpy in others.

"Leave sleeping dogs lie," he said, returning his gaze to my face, and I saw that behind the flatness of his features, judgment lay.

Unsatisfied with his answer, but realizing I would get no more out of him, I turned to go.

"Watch yourself," he said after me.

It was a colloquial good-bye I remembered from my Belfast days, one I had heard many times over. And yet when I walked away from him that day, the words remained stuck in my head in a way that felt uncomfortable. Perhaps it was the shock of what I had learned, perhaps it was the cold manner of our parting, but the words themselves and the way he said them kept repeating inside my head over and over: *Watch yourself, watch yourself.* As I raised my hand to hail a taxi, it occurred to me what was so troubling about them. It felt like, far from saying good-bye, they were instead a kind of warning.

# CHAPTER 15
## CAROLINE

David was gone for two nights and for the duration of his absence, we didn't communicate. From the distance of a hundred miles, I could feel him sulking.

There wasn't time to dwell on it. Life was busy with school runs and visits to the nursing home, not to mention work itself. There was a trade fair running all that week, hosted in Citywest Hotel, where our firm had a booth, hoping to attract new business. I was penciled in to attend with a couple of colleagues. It was a frenetic few days, the throng of the crowd ringing in my ears long after I'd left the building, my feet aching from standing for hours. Occasionally, there were lulls in the day, and I would find myself at the booth, my eyes glazing over, thoughts turning inevitably to the uncertain atmosphere at home. I thought about Robbie's sullenness, his trouble at school, and his refusal to discuss it with me afterward; about Holly and her obvious unhappiness at how things had changed. I thought of David and how every conversation between us lately had seemed loaded and dangerous, as if a wrong word spoken would tilt us into argument. I thought of Ellen and how she had cried with confusion during my last visit, begging me to take her away from that place — something I had decided to conceal from David. And all the while Zoe retained her occupancy at the top of our house.

Her presence was constant — at the dinner table, in the evenings when we were watching TV, in the mornings when we were rushing about and she'd sit there calmly eating her yogurt. Even when the house was empty, I could find traces of her recent presence — the bathroom steamy and warm from her shower; a coffee cup cooling on the draining board. Occasionally, I would pass the stairway to the attic and catch the faint scent of cigarettes wafting down. Our home had been invaded by her presence and, despite my unease, I couldn't think how to change it.

"Caroline?"

A voice drew me out of my reverie, the din of the crowd coming back at me suddenly. I turned, my gaze clearing, and as soon as I saw him, the blood came rushing to my cheeks.

"Aidan," I said, as he leaned forward with a half smile and gave me a chaste kiss on the cheek. "This is a surprise."

Over a year had passed since we had seen each other, the last occasion that excruciating meeting in Mrs. Campbell's office. The memory of it flitted through my mind and that alone was enough to stir up feelings of humiliation. We talked for a moment about the trade show, the company I was working for, and then he asked if I wanted to grab a coffee. We were two adults no longer involved with each other. It seemed churlish to say no.

Standing together at a tall table in the hospitality tent, two lattes between us, I told him about my return to work, the pressures and challenges of it as well as the rewards. He filled me in on his recent promotion. It was strange, being there with him, carefully restricting our conversation to safe topics while the commerce continued around us. We had to raise our voices to be heard and lean in to listen, and while we talked I was taking in the changes that had occurred in him. His hair seemed thinner under the bright spotlights, and there were crow's-feet shooting out from the sides of his eyes that

I had not noticed before. He was wearing a suit — his tie was fractionally askew, the jacket a little crumpled beneath the pockets. Small things, but they added up to give the impression of tiredness within him, sadness perhaps, which made me wonder about the health of his marriage.

I inquired how his son was doing; he asked after Robbie. My automatic reply was that Robbie was doing well, but after a moment's hesitation, I added, "There was an incident at the school recently. Some trouble with a teacher."

I explained what had happened, about the intimidation, the bullying, the assault. It was only when I revealed Robbie's motivation that his eyes widened.

"The French teacher? It was her?" Then he grinned and shook his head. "What the hell was she doing in Conway's? It's such a dive!"

"I know!" It felt good to be able to talk like this with the benefit of distance from the event itself.

He was still smiling at me, a note of fond recollection coming into his voice, saying, "When I think about some of the places we used to meet. I mean — the Three Sisters? Jesus! You must have thought I had no class at all."

I laughed and his eyes seemed to flicker over me, the smile dying on his face.

"You have a lovely laugh," he said, more serious now. "I always thought that."

The moment had passed, and I felt the creep of shame again.

"I've missed hearing you laugh," he added.

"How have things been with you?" I asked, uncomfortable beneath the weight of his stare. "With your wife, I mean?"

He rotated his coffee cup a fraction, his weight shifting to his other foot.

"Okay. These things take time, I guess."

I wondered if she had told him about the incident in Ikea. I had a sudden recollection of the ferocity of her shopping cart bashing into mine, her face stripped of everything except the purest anger. I almost said it to him, then changed my mind. Instead, I told him about Zoe.

"A daughter?" he asked, interested. "From another relationship?"

"One that predated our marriage. She's eighteen, almost nineteen."

His eyes opened wider in disbelief, and he exhaled out the side of his mouth.

"That must have been a shock to the system."

It occurred to me that I had not told a single soul of Zoe's existence — not a friend or a family member, not even a colleague. Even though I knew that David had informed his colleagues at work, and the children too had shared the information with their friends, I still could not find it in me to confide in a friend about this seismic change in my family life. It was as though I had been trying to contain it, hoping that it would somehow go away. Talking to Aidan about it was a relief, and once I started, it was hard to stop. He listened carefully, interjecting with questions and opinions of his own.

"Does she look like David?" he asked.

"Not that I can see. A little like his mother, perhaps, but no, not really. She takes after Linda."

"What do the kids make of her?"

"Holly can't stand her. She almost comes out in a rash whenever Zoe's in the room."

"And Robbie?"

"They're closer in age, and they've more in common. I can tell that he likes having her around. It's just . . ."

"Just what?"

"I'm worried about him. He's been acting up lately — and I know he's a teenager and that's what they do. But the way he's been behaving seems out of character. They spend so much time together — Zoe and him. In the evenings, on weekends. Sometimes I find them talking in his room late into the night. I'm worried about the influence she has over him."

"She's living in your home?" he asked incredulously.

"I know."

"Whose idea was that?"

"David's. There was an incident over Christmas. It seems she tried to kill herself —"

"It seems? Do you not believe her?"

"I don't know what to believe, Aidan. She can be two-faced. David thinks it was a cry for help but I can't help thinking it was just a ploy to get into our home. After the overdose, David wanted her to move in with us and I felt I couldn't say no."

"Why not? She's not your responsibility."

"Not mine, perhaps. But David feels responsible. He is her father, after all."

His expression was skeptical.

"Listen, he gave her his DNA, that's all. And in the great big scheme of parenting, that doesn't amount to much. Where's the mother in all this?"

"She's dead."

"Any other family?"

I shook my head. "A stepfather, but he doesn't seem involved."

"So you're left with a cuckoo in your nest."

There was dry humor in those words, but his gaze was serious. I felt that coldness coming over the back of my neck again like some unseen person had just breathed across it.

I picked up the sugar packet next to my cup, turned it over.

"I don't trust her," I said quietly.

"How come?"

"She's always perfectly polite to me, but it feels for David's benefit. There's no real connection between us. It's like she doesn't want it. Every effort I make in that direction just seems to wash over her."

"She's freezing you out."

"That's what it feels like. David thinks she's great. He doesn't see what I see."

There had been incidents over the past few weeks — nothing major, but enough to stir up trouble. Once, returning laundry to her room, my hand had accidentally brushed against her laptop, awakening the screen. At that particular moment, Zoe had walked in. Later, she told David she had caught me snooping through her e-mails. Another time, she had come down to breakfast wearing a blouse that was mine — gray silk, scoop-necked. It been hanging at the back of my closet. I hadn't worn it in months.

"You're wearing my top," I had said, surprise in my voice.

"Am I?"

She had looked down at it, pulling it between fingers and thumbs to examine it in a pantomime way.

"So it is," she replied, laughing. "It must have gotten mixed up with my clothes in the wash. I thought it was mine!"

She was all charm and politeness, David in the background observing. She had offered to run upstairs and change, but somehow that made things worse. I tried to feign a casualness I didn't feel, told her to put it into the wash at the end of the day when she had finished with it. I wasn't as good an actress as she was, and despite my efforts, suspicion leaked into my tone. I couldn't prove it, but I knew she had been going through my things.

I recounted the incident for Aidan, but what I didn't tell him was that when I looked at the gray silk skimming her slender curves, I realized with a pinch of envy that it looked far better on her youthful frame than it did on my older body. I knew that I would never wear it again.

"Have you spoken to David about your

misgivings?" Aidan asked, regaining my attention.

"Any time I do, we just end up arguing."

Sympathy entered the look he was giving me, and when he spoke again, his voice was softer but firm.

"You need to think about what it is you want, Caroline. It's all very well flinging wide the doors and welcoming her in, all very noble, but it shouldn't be at any cost. You're not the girl's mother. Have you thought about what kind of relationship you want to have with her? What you expect from her in return for welcoming her into your family?"

"Not really."

"Take my advice and think it through properly. Work out exactly what you're prepared to live with and what you absolutely cannot accept."

He drained his coffee and returned the cup to the table with an air of finality.

"Work it out and then stand your ground. You can't let this interloper walk all over you with her poor-little-orphan sideshow."

I checked my watch and said I'd better get back to my colleagues.

He came around the table and we hugged awkwardly, each of us feeling the strangeness of contact after all that had passed.

■ ■ ■ ■

It was the final day of the trade show, and once the doors of the great halls closed, I stayed behind with the others, packing up our brochures, free gifts, and posters, folding up the stand, and loading it all into the backs of our cars. By the time I got home, it was after eight. Coming through the front door, I saw David's bags by the stairs and Robbie sitting on the bottom step, his arms folded, his face drawn and anxious.

"What's going on?" I asked.

"In there," he said, nodding in the direction of the kitchen. "Dad and Zoe."

I could hear the rumble of an argument from behind the closed door, the words indistinct. My pulse quickened. What had happened?

"Stay here," I told Robbie, taking off my coat and pushing through the door.

"That's not true! I never meant it like that!" Zoe was saying as I came into the room.

She had her back to me and it was only when she turned to see who was coming through the door that I saw her face was streaked and ruddy with tears. Beyond her, David was leaning back against the countertop, his arms folded, a grave look on his face. He barely acknowledged my presence, continuing the conversation.

"You lied to me. You say you didn't mean it, but you must have known at some point I'd find out."

"Why does it have to matter?" she implored. "What difference does it make? They're not my parents — not really."

"They brought you up."

"So? That doesn't mean they loved me."

"Can someone tell me what's going on?" I asked, startled by what I was witnessing. It was the first time I had seen any sort of confrontation between them. If I'm honest, I felt a small trill of excitement — the whisper of hope that David had finally seen her true colors.

In terse tones, David explained what he had learned of her adoption. He looked tired, almost disheveled, as if he had slept in his clothes, or not slept at all. Although he kept his voice low, I knew he was simmering.

"What about the money?" he asked her.

"There was no money."

"He told me Linda left you six thousand pounds for your education. That he put the check into your hands himself. Are you trying to tell me he didn't?"

"He gave me a check all right, but what he didn't tell you was that it bounced."

"What?"

"There were no funds in the account," she explained. "Linda didn't have any money. Nor did I want any from her. Christ, do you think I gave a damn about the money? All I wanted was her, my own mother, even if it was just for a short while."

He ran a hand over his face, and I couldn't tell if he believed her or not. I, on the other hand, didn't believe a word that came out of her mouth.

"You lied to us," I told her.

"No I didn't!"

"You let us all believe Linda had brought you up," I went on, my voice growing insistent.

She wore a petulant expression and refused to look me in the eye, her body still turned toward David. Somehow, that infuriated me even more.

"Why would you even do such a thing?" I asked. "Deny the existence of people who have cared for you, brought you up, loved you —"

"You don't know what you're talking about. Loved me? That's a joke."

David listened, clearly troubled.

"They never loved me. They thought

adopting me was an act of charity. But they didn't want me for who I was. They're the kind of people who think children are things that exist in storybooks. They expected me to be Anne of Green Gables or Pollyanna, but I'm not fucking like that."

That expletive was a sign that we were getting to her. I saw David blink in surprise — the first time he'd heard a foul word coming out of her honeyed lips. She saw his surprise and when she spoke again, it was in a lowered voice, her shoulders dipping forward fractionally.

"They didn't love me. They treated me more like a servant than a daughter."

"You could have told us all this," David said.

"I know. But I was ashamed."

"Oh please," I said.

"It's true," she insisted, still looking at David. "With my dad . . . things happened. I thought if I told you . . . you wouldn't believe me."

"What things?" David asked, his attention pricked.

She ran her hand over her mouth. Her reluctance and the closed manner of the reveal, I knew where this was going. She didn't say outright that she had been abused, but it was all there in the picking at her cuffs, the summoned tears, allusions to inappropriate behavior after she turned sixteen. It was about this time when she made contact with Linda.

David had his hand over his mouth, his eyes fixed on her, clearly troubled by her account. Did he believe it? The way she told it, all the pausing and hesitation, it seemed rehearsed, every stammered word, every meaningful glance cleverly designed to reel him in. She looked decidedly uncomfortable, but there was something studied about it, deceit at the back of her eyes.

"All my life, I've felt shunted about," she said, her voice small and plaintive, "as if no one really wanted to claim me. Always searching for some way of fitting in, but I never could. Not until I found Linda. Then things began to make sense. We were only just getting to know each other when she died, but I'm so grateful for that time we had. You've no idea how precious it was to me." She bit her upper lip to compose herself, a row of small teeth pressing the color from her mouth. Holding David's gaze she said, "I'm grateful to her for leading me to you. These past few months, getting to know you, getting to know your family — it's meant everything to me."

The way she went to work on him right

there in front of me, it was shameless.

"I know," he said quietly. "And it's not that I don't feel the same way. I just want you to understand that we have to be able to trust you."

He continued to talk about the importance of honesty within a family, but I could see that he was thawing. Her story, thin as it was, had gotten to him. She was nodding as she listened, playing the penitent, bowing her head in remorse, and I felt a lurch of fear. How easily she had crept in among us, her troubling occupancy of the attic room, the nights I lay awake listening to the soft pad of her feet overhead, the murmur of her voice traveling to me through the floorboards. All this time, I had felt her duplicity, the coldness at the heart of her behavior toward me. Just when I thought her deceptions would be revealed, and David would see for himself her untrustworthy nature, I felt the chance getting away from me. Drained by the encounter, he was bringing it to an end — the prodigal daughter, the forgiving father. Panic began to set in.

"Just hang on a minute," I said, coming forward to break up their tableau. "Is that it?"

"What do you mean?" he asked.

"She lied to us about something pretty

serious. What else has she been lying about?"

"I'm right here in the room," Zoe said quietly, which I found a little rich considering how she had refused to make eye contact with me throughout this exchange.

"I'm not happy to have a person I don't trust living in this house."

"Caroline —" A weariness was leaking into David's voice.

"We have to think about the children. What lies have you been telling them?" I demanded of her.

"Nothing!"

"All those hours you and Robbie spend together upstairs — what have you been filling his head with?"

"That's unfair," David interjected.

"Is it? Look at his behavior in school since she moved in. His grades have dropped, notes have come home about him not paying attention in class, not to mention his recent suspension. I'm absolutely dreading his parent-teacher meeting."

"Well, that's hardly Robbie's fault," David replied waspishly.

I stared at him, wounded by this sudden attack. His pointed remark, a reference to my indiscretion, in front of Zoe — I could hardly believe it. I thought I caught the trace of a smirk at the corner of her mouth. In the background, the doorbell rang. None of us made any move to answer it.

"If you want me to leave, I'll leave," she announced, breaking the silence.

"For God's sake," David muttered.

"Just say the word and I'll pack my bags. I'll even drop out of university — that way you won't have to see me at all."

"Don't be so stupid," he said quickly, clearly annoyed at the turn the conversation had taken. "No one wants you to leave."

"*I* want her to leave," I countered.

She glanced at me, then looked at the floor, her shoulders slumping forward again, adopting her vulnerable pose.

"I've tried to be friends with you, Caroline. Why don't you like me?"

I treated that with the disdain it deserved.

"If she's lying to us, what's she been saying to Robbie and Holly? Don't you think we should consider their needs, their safety?"

"Jesus Christ," David snapped, clearly exasperated. "Zoe's their half sister, not a sociopath."

The kitchen door opened and his attention momentarily shifted. She caught my eye and I saw her brow arch just a fraction. Triumph briefly flashed across her face.

"It's Chris," Robbie announced, standing in the doorway, glancing nervously across at Zoe.

"Sorry, is this a bad time?" Chris asked, coming into the kitchen. "We're going for a pint, remember?"

David had his hands to his face, fingertips pressing against closed eyes. Drawing his hands away, he looked tired and defeated.

"Sorry, Chris. I had forgotten."

He made no move to leave, and Chris, detecting the atmosphere in the room, said, "Look, we can do it another time. If you guys have things you need to discuss . . ."

His eyes settled on Zoe as if noticing her for the first time.

"Hi," he said, coming forward and offering his hand, which she shook briefly. "I'm Chris."

"Zoe," she replied, and I could see him taking her in with interest.

"Do you mind if we leave it?" David asked with an air of apology. "I'm just back from Belfast and there's things I need to sort out."

"Don't worry about it," Chris shrugged. "I'm happy enough going for a drink on my own."

"I'll go with you."

We all looked at her in surprise.

"I mean it." Zoe reached for her jacket, which was slung over the back of a kitchen chair. "I could do with a drink."

"Okay, sure," Chris said, surprise tinged with excitement. He stood back to let her pass, then turned and raised his hand in salute before following her out.

Seconds later, we heard Robbie going into the living room, then slamming the door behind him. David and I were alone.

"Does Chris know about Zoe?" I asked, and he shook his head, no.

"Great," I remarked flatly. "God knows what lies she'll tell him."

"Would you just stop that?" David said, exasperated.

"What?"

"I'm so sick of it — this constant negativity toward Zoe, your resentment."

"My —"

"If you actually tried to get to know her, rather than maintaining this suspicion, maybe you wouldn't feel that way."

Now anger rose within me, like a pain, but his back was already turned. He began opening cupboards and the fridge, pulling out bread, cheese, relish, hastily slapping them all together into a sandwich.

"I have every right to be suspicious," I countered. "She's been lying to us —"

"About one thing, that's all. And I can understand her reasons."

"Oh, of course you can."

"Drop the sarcasm, will you? I'm tired and not in the mood. And another thing," he said, moving past me to the kitchen table, bringing his plate down with a hard thud. "I thought it crass the way you said she should leave when she was right there in the room. What got into you? Didn't you see how upset she was?"

My eyes widened. "How upset *she* was?"

"Oh Christ, don't do this now," he said, turning away from me and sitting down at the table.

"Don't do what?"

"Don't make this into a competition between you and her."

*"What?"*

He lifted his palms with an air of surrender. Then he picked up his sandwich and began to eat.

How had things spiraled out of control so quickly? I thought of Chris and Zoe sitting in the warm conviviality of our local pub, sharing a joke over their pints, and felt a twinge of envy. Inside our kitchen, it felt very cold. I could tell from the way David was sitting hunched over his sandwich, a hardened look about him, that I would have to pull back, tread a little softly, if I wanted to persuade him.

"Listen," I began, as I sat opposite him. "One of the girls at work has a place free in the house she shares. All young girls, in their early twenties. It's in Ranelagh, close to UCD. I was thinking Zoe might be interested. What do you reckon?"

"She couldn't afford the rent," he replied, taking another bite.

"Well, we could help out there."

"A few days ago you were losing the plot over my suggestion of paying her college fees. Now you want to stump up for her rent?"

"This was never supposed to be a permanent arrangement, David. It was just a stopgap until she found somewhere new to live. Robbie's going to be doing his Junior Certificate in a few months. He needs to be able to concentrate on his studies. Her presence at home is unsettling for all of us — a distraction."

"Robbie will be fine."

"Really? I'm worried about him."

"You're overreacting. He's fifteen. Teenage boys act up from time to time. And I'll talk to him about his homework, get him to knuckle down a bit."

"Will you?"

He must have heard the doubt enter my voice, for his gaze narrowed, his mouth settling into a grim line.

"I just said that I would, didn't I?"

"You've been so distracted lately. You keep brushing aside Robbie's behavior instead of tackling him about it. I can't help but feel that you've stepped back a bit from him — from Holly too. They need your attention as well, your love."

"Hang on a second. You're the one who's been out until all hours, doing trade shows and what have you, and you're giving *me* a hard time about not being there for the kids?"

"What are you saying?" I asked. "That I shouldn't have gone back to work?"

The swing of the argument took over, each of us drawing on the peculiar accounting involved in parenting, trotting out the hours each of us spent with the kids versus the time we had to ourselves. Revisiting old ground, we criticized each other's parenting styles — I accused him of being too hands-off and then jumping in at the last minute with harsh discipline; he argued that I was too soft on them, too wrapped up in their lives, that I didn't give them the space and freedom to make mistakes and learn from them. The whole thing was exhausting.

"What about her adoptive parents?" I asked.

"What about them?"

"Don't you think we ought to get in touch with them?"

"What for?"

"They're her parents. Do they even know she's living here? I'm sure they must be worried."

He glanced sharply across at me.

"I'm not so sure. Not after what she just told us."

"You didn't believe that story, did you?" I asked, unable to keep the scorn from my voice.

"We have to give her the benefit of the doubt."

"Oh, come on! Seriously, I think we should get in touch with these people . . ."

David finished his sandwich and got up.

"What about Zoe?" I said then, determined not to let him walk out of the room without reaching some kind of agreement.

He put his plate in the dishwasher, then straightened up. "I'll talk to her. Tell her she can stay here until the exams are over."

"That's not until the end of May —"

"It's a natural break, Caroline. End of semester — she'll probably be heading abroad with her friends anyway — she mentioned something about a J-1 Visa for the States. We can just make it clear that when she gets home after the summer, she'll no longer be living here."

There was a degree of sense in what he was suggesting.

"Happy now?" he asked coldly, and without waiting for my answer, he turned and left the room.

The house was empty when I got up the next morning, having waited for the others to leave. The days spent at the trade show had taken an unexpected toll. Peter had given us leave to come in late that morning, and as I lay there watching the time tick by on the digital clock, I felt the passage of dull pain around my body, tenderness at the bridge of my nose a warning sign that I was coming down with a cold. After a while, I got up and stood for a long time under a hot shower, feeling the heat permeating my skin. I thought of David and our argument, which was still unresolved. We had lain in bed alongside each other, not speaking. Sometime after midnight, I had heard the front door open and close, Zoe's light footfall on the stairs. I know he heard it too. The end of May, I thought, mentally tallying the weeks and months that would lead to a time we could finally be rid of her.

After my shower, I felt better. Wrapping my hair in a towel, I went downstairs in my bathrobe to make tea.

Zoe was in the kitchen, her hair pulled back into a ponytail. She stood perfectly still, looking straight at me. My phone was in her hand.

"I'm sorry," she said. "It beeped and I thought it was mine."

It was true that our phones were similar and that we had the same text alert, but still I was annoyed. I moved forward, and she handed it to me. Her bag and coat were on the counter and she picked them up, then said a stiff good-bye.

The door closed. I looked down at the screen and saw the text message that had come through. It was from Aidan and it was open. I read it quickly with a growing sense of alarm.

*When I said I missed your laughter, I should have said that I missed your lips, your lovely mouth, you. You're in my head again, Caroline.*

"Shit," I said out loud.

The front door was open when I stepped into the hall and said her name. She was pulling on her jacket and made no sign of having heard me.

"Zoe," I said again, and grabbed her arm.

She wrenched it away, tripped on the step, and steadied herself against the wall of the porch.

She hurried away from me, her ponytail swinging as she went down the path. Weak sunlight came from overhead, filtered through a canopy of sparse autumn leaves. I held my robe closed with one hand and called out again, but she didn't look back, her step quickening now, as she pulled her jacket tight around her. I thought about her reading that text and something loosened within me. Gazing after her helplessly, I watched as, armed with that new knowledge, she hurried to get away from me, not stopping once until she rounded the corner and was gone.

# CHAPTER 16
## DAVID

It was late that night when Zoe came home. I was sitting at the writing desk in the living room, darkness pressing up against the window, the only light thrown by the small anglepoise lamp onto my notes spread in front of me. The rest of the household was sleeping when I heard the crunch of her footfall on the gravel outside.

I could have stayed where I was, working out my thoughts in preparation for the radio interview I was scheduled to give early the next morning. All week, I had been meaning to prepare for it, but what with my trip to Belfast, the time had gotten away from me, and despite my good intentions to set aside a few hours to get ready, here I was on the eve of the interview with very little done. In hindsight, I often come back to this moment, and wonder had I chosen to remain at my desk, had I not gotten up from my chair and gone outside into the hall, would things have turned out differently? So much of what went wrong in the ensuing days and weeks seemed to stem from that night's events.

The argument we'd had in the kitchen the night before had been on my mind all day. There was a bad taste in my mouth from how we had left things, and I suppose it was for that reason — a desire to smooth things over — that I went out into the hall to see her. She was hanging her coat on the newel post, her back to me, when I said her name and she turned around.

"Christ," I exclaimed.

The left side of her face, from eye socket to cheekbone was swollen and grazed with a dull purple stain of dried blood.

"What happened to you?"

"It's nothing," she said, letting her hair fall over her face.

"Let me see," I replied, stepping toward her.

I reached out to touch her chin, and she allowed her face to be angled toward me, her eyes bright and large in the light's glare.

"I fell. It's not serious."

"That cut is close to your eye."

"It looks worse than it is."

"Who did this to you?" I asked, shocked by the livid wound.

"I told you I fell . . ."

"I know you didn't fall."

Her eyes moved quickly toward the top of the stairs.

"Can we not talk about it here?" she asked. "I don't want the others to hear."

"Come into the kitchen then."

Meekly, she followed me inside and watched as I drew open a freezer drawer, emptying ice cubes from the tray onto a towel.

"Here," I said, gathering it all together. "Put this against your face. It will help bring the swelling down."

She did as I asked, wincing as the cold compress touched her cheek.

"What happened?" I said, my voice softer now that I was getting over my shock.

"I can't tell you," she answered, and then she began to cry.

Gently, I moved her toward the kitchen table and sat next to her, taking her hand in mine, trying to appear calm in the face of her obvious distress.

"Please tell me. Let me help you."

"If I tell you, she might get angry with me again."

"Caroline?" I said, reading between the lines. "Are you saying she did this to you?"

285

I couldn't keep the disbelief from my voice.

Zoe said nothing, just stared down at the tabletop, holding the compress to her face.

While it was no secret that Caroline wasn't happy about Zoe's presence, there was no way she would ever physically attack her. I knew my wife. I understood her boundaries. I couldn't help but think this was some ham-fisted attempt on Zoe's part to get back at Caroline for the things she had said the night before.

"I'm sorry, Zoe, but I find that very hard to accept."

She took the compress away, stared down at the towel, soaked through now, then said in a small voice, "I knew you wouldn't believe me."

"Keep that against your face," I instructed, partially because I was made a little queasy by the wound, the seeping cuts, and partially because I was annoyed at getting drawn into another one of her dramas. The whole thing was exhausting.

"It was my fault," she said in that same quiet voice.

"What do you mean?"

"She didn't mean to do it. She wouldn't have, if I hadn't . . ."

The sentence was left to drift. *Just spit it*

*out,* I thought irritably. My notes, abandoned in the other room, would probably remain unread now. I would just have to wing it at the radio interview in the morning.

I asked her to tell me exactly what had happened.

"I mistook her phone for my own, you see?" she began. "I read one of her text messages by accident. It was private. That's what she said. I tried to tell her that it was a mistake. That I wasn't spying on her or anything like that. But she didn't believe me."

"Go on," I said, listening now.

"Some guy had sent her a text," she said again. "I probably shouldn't tell you . . ."

"Saying what?"

She hesitated, putting the compress to one side, a little crease of a frown appearing between her eyebrows. Her reluctance was apparent, but I was curious now.

"It's okay, Zoe. You can tell me."

"Something about how he missed her. He missed her lovely mouth, or something."

She said the words and my irritation fell away.

It's a funny thing — trust. Trust and love, the foundation stones of a marriage. When I found out about Caroline's little romance, it was like someone had taken a hammer to that block of trust and began pounding at it, causing cracks to run through it like veins. We had spent the past year and a half working to mend those fissures, sealing them up with gestures and promises. I still loved her, still felt grateful that she was my wife. But cracks like those can be hard to fix, and when Zoe said those words — *he missed her lovely mouth* — all at once I was thinking about another man pressing his mouth against my wife's mouth, prizing apart her lips, exploring with his tongue. It was an image I had tortured myself with at the time but had learned to suppress. It was back with me now, and with it suspicion sprang to life. The sealing cement was falling away, revealing the cracks in our trust in all their ugliness.

"I know I shouldn't have read it," she was saying, "but you have to believe me, I would never have read it if I had I known it was her phone."

Keeping my voice carefully neutral, I said, "So what happened next?"

"She was so angry. . . . She snatched the phone back and she pushed me against the wall."

The image snagged in my brain. It didn't seem quite right.

"Are you sure about this, Zoe?"

"I don't think she meant to hurt me. Not really. But, the way I fell, my face kind of hit the wall and I know there's a bruise, and it throbs a bit, but it looks worse than it is . . ."

She started to cry again, and while I was full of conflicting emotions, I couldn't stand seeing her upset like this, her face damaged and sore.

"I'm sorry," I said, even though it was not my fault. My thoughts and feelings were opaque, torn between wanting to believe her and my natural instinct to back away from the hard knowledge of my wife's infidelity.

"It's okay," she said, getting up from the table.

She was going to say good night, but before she did I reached out and held on to her wrist.

"I'll talk to Caroline," I said, feeling her pull away.

"No, please don't. I don't want her thinking I've been telling tales."

"Zoe," I said gently, trying to calm the nervous agitation within her. "She's going to see your face. We need to talk about this — all three of us."

"No, please. Not after last night."

"We have to sort this out. I want you to feel safe here. But Caroline is my wife. This is her home. Whatever has happened . . . we can't just ignore it."

"I need to sleep," she said, twisting her arm from my grasp.

"What will you do?" I asked, suddenly worried that she would pack her bags and leave.

"I don't know," she said, moving toward the door. "Stay out of her way, I guess."

She turned — there was something about her defiance that reminded me sharply and painfully of Linda.

After a while, I switched out the light and went upstairs. In the bathroom, while I brushed my teeth, I turned things over in my mind, wondering whether to believe her or not. I could still remember the swing of doubt inside me when Gary told me of Zoe's adoption — the plunging realization of how she had lied to me. We had moved on from there since, but with this new drama, I felt the nudge of doubt once more. A part of me questioned whether anything Zoe had told me was true.

I finished brushing my teeth, putting my toothbrush back on the shelf above the sink. The children's toothbrushes were in a cup at the edge of the shelf, and I looked at

Zoe's: lilac pink with orange bristles. I thought of the DNA that might have adhered to those bristles and here is where I learned that doubt breeds suspicion. Thinking back to that night in the pub when I swabbed my inner cheek and handed over my sample to her — what proof did I have that it was my sample that was tested? I took the toothbrush and, once back in my bedroom, I slipped it into my jacket pocket, unobserved.

Caroline didn't move as I climbed in next to her, and for a long time I lay there, staring at the outline of her body, her hair spread over the pillow next to mine, with the uneasy feeling that even though she was my wife and the mother of my children, even though I had known her half my life, she was still a stranger to me.

My radio interview was scheduled for eight a.m., which meant leaving the house earlier than normal. As it was, Caroline had a breakfast meeting, so we were all up early — all of us except Zoe.

"Pour me a mug there, will you?" Caroline asked, and I felt a flare of irritation.

I had resolved to talk to her once we were alone, but with Robbie and Holly slumped over their breakfast cereals, conversation was impossible. I had promised to bring Robbie with me to the radio station after he voiced an interest, and now I found myself quietly regretting it. I wanted to spend more time with him, but I had slept badly and my nerves, made worse by my lack of preparation, were getting to me.

I asked Holly to pass me the milk. Both Holly and Robbie looked up.

"You called me Zoe," Holly said in an aggrieved tone like I'd slapped her.

"No I didn't."

"You did, Dad," Robbie said.

"It was a slip of the tongue then," I said, a little crossly. "Could one of you please pass me the milk?"

Holly stood up and left the room.

"Forget it," I snapped, not in the mood for any histrionics. I took my black coffee and left the table, going into the living room where I found my notes, just as I had left them the previous night, spread out on the desk. There was little point going through them now, so I swept them up into an untidy sheaf and began stuffing them into my briefcase.

"Are you all right?"

Caroline had come into the room behind me.

"Fine," I said tersely.

"You seem nervous."

The anger jumped alive inside me. How dare she just swan in here, playing the attentive wife, when only the day before she had been texting an old lover.

"Are you seeing him again?"

"What?" she asked, puzzled.

Not who? Because she knew who I meant. She knew exactly what I was talking about.

"Well, are you?"

Comprehension flickered across her face, and I caught the movement behind her eyes — artifice, deceit, the realization she'd been caught out. I could see her thinking quickly about how to explain it away.

"It's not what you think," she began. "I just bumped into him by accident at the trade show. I had no idea he would be there."

"So? How was it?" I said this in a mean voice, standing straight in front of her, my arms crossed, making a show of outer strength and indignation. Inside, I was trembling.

"David —"

"Did you feel the spark again?" This was a low blow. In one of our earliest arguments post-fling, Caroline had admitted feeling a spark between Aidan and her. I had latched on to it then, using it as a recurring motif in the rows that raged. To bring it up now was like touching alive an old sore. Caroline's eyes briefly flared, but she chose to ignore it.

"Zoe told you," she said flatly. Then, almost to herself, she said, "I knew she would."

I picked up my bag. "Yes, she told me. She also showed me her face."

"Her face?"

"She said you shoved her up against a wall. Her cheek is a mess. I'm surprised she didn't need stitches."

Caroline stood there gaping at me, open-mouthed like a fish.

"I'm going to be late," I said, moving past her to the door.

"I never pushed her," she told me, coming into the hall after me. "I don't know what you mean."

The confusion on her face was annoying. It seemed overly dramatic. Fake.

"Robbie!" I called out. "Let's go."

"David, please. This is serious," Caroline said. "What kind of accusation has she made?"

Robbie was in the hall now, a slice of toast clamped between his teeth as he attempted to put on his jacket and schoolbag simultaneously.

She didn't wish me luck and I didn't kiss her good-bye, didn't say good-bye at all, I just pulled the door shut behind us with force, felt the slam of it reverberating through the air as I hurried down the driveway to the car, where Robbie was already waiting.

The show's producer had sent a brief outline of what the interview would entail and it had all seemed fair-minded and reasonable, and even though I had not prepared as much as I would have liked to, when I took my seat in front of the micro-phone, I felt there was nothing to be con-cerned about. Behind the studio's internal window, I could see Robbie sitting alongside the producer. I gave him a wave and he smiled back gauchely.

The show's host, Des Earley, introduced me to Sean Kelly, a local councilor, who was to give an opposing point of view. I hadn't been informed of this and thought it a bit haphazard and hasty at the time, but in hindsight I see more clearly what it was: a setup, an ambush.

"With the 1916 centenary celebrations fast approaching, figures leaked last week show an astonishing level of government overspend in what many are reading as both a political stunt and a calculated measure to impress the populace in advance of a general election and thereby boost their votes," Earley said for his opening salvo.

Kelly piped up: "Buying votes!"

"As a member of the Expert Advisory Group, Dr. Connolly, can you justify the kind of money that has been earmarked?"

"Well, first of all I would say that those figures are not entirely accurate," I began, "and I couldn't comment on something that isn't official."

"Why not?" Earley wanted to know. "After all, there are many people in this State who think the amounts of money being discussed are eye-watering, and surely it would be better spent on tackling the homelessness crisis or the problems in the health service rather than spending it on commemorating an event that is largely irrelevant today."

"Well, I wouldn't agree that it's irrelevant," I argued. "For many people, the 1916 Proclamation and the circumstances under which it was made . . ."

The words were coming out of my mouth, but they were somehow disconnected from my brain. I had a flash of memory to the night before and the words *lovely mouth* sprang up before me.

"It's all cant, isn't it?" Kelly was saying.

"Why else would the Relatives Association have boycotted the launch of the plan?"

I tried to answer as evenly as I could, but my thoughts were muddled and I muttered something about not putting a price on history.

"You don't think twenty-two million too much to spend on what after all is simply a slap on the back to republican-minded people out there?"

"No, no I don't. . . . It's a chance to re-imagine the future," I stammered.

I was tired, I suppose. Stressed. Here I was, the history expert, and yet I couldn't even get to grips with the events in my own past, couldn't see or understand the history of my own life. A little voice in my head whispered: *You're a fraud.*

"You're just a mouthpiece for government ministers," Kelly sneered.

"You're taking the whole thing out of context," I said. "The purpose of the com-memorations is to —"

"I'm not one of your students, Dr. Con-nolly."

"For Christ's sake, will you let me finish," I said sharply.

"Okay, briefly now before we finish up," Earley interjected, trying to bring the conversation back on track. But Kelly was leaning in, his face reddened with fury.

I hardly heard what he said, some acerbic remark about academics in their ivory towers. I thought about Caroline in Aidan's arms, his mouth on hers. Hers on his. I thought about Zoe's battered face.

"You're talking complete *shite,*" I said. "Is that plain enough for you? You ignoramus."

The words flew out of my mouth. I could almost see them flapping around the studio like birds. Earley went straight to a commercial break, and Kelly sat back, his arms crossed over his chest, a smile of satisfaction breaking out all over his stupid face.

"I can already see the headlines," he remarked.

I took the earphones off and left.

I hurried to my car, Robbie half-running to keep up with me. There was a storm in my brain, fury coursing through my body. If I had come across Kelly there in the parking lot, I'd have decked him, but in truth, it was myself I was furious with. We got into the car, slammed the doors shut, and I let out some of the pressure that had been building in my chest and leaned my head against the steering wheel.

"Are you okay, Dad?"

I closed my eyes. It seemed like everyone

298

lately was asking me if I was okay. And I knew I wasn't. I was trying to hold it together, but inside I was quaking.

"I'm sorry," I said to Robbie. "I wish you hadn't been a witness to that."

"That's okay," he said.

I sat back in my seat. "I shouldn't have lost my temper like that."

"The guy was a creep."

"Still. It was wrong." I pressed my fingers against my eyelids, felt the throb of a nerve at the back of my eye. "Christ, what a disaster."

"Don't worry about it, Dad," he said kindly.

"I don't know what came over me."

"Sometimes that just happens," he said. "Something snaps and you just see red."

I took my fingers away from my eyes.

"There was one time, I thought I was going to lose it, big time," he began, his voice a bit timorous, no doubt finding it strange offering comfort to his father rather than vice versa. "It was at a rugby club disco. I was outside, in the bleachers. And I saw this guy — this guy I knew — and something kind of snapped in me. You see . . ."

He went on, but I wasn't really listening. My nerves were back with me again, anger draining away replaced now with a stomach-churning dread at the thought of all those listeners, what they must have thought. My mind was racing ahead to further media reaction to my outburst, the possible consequences within my academic circle. Which of my colleagues might have heard me? What about members of the interview board, not to mention my students. There was no way to erase my performance from memory. The interview had been broadcast. It had been put into history, and there was no way of expunging it from the record. I had a brief plunge of dread thinking of my mother sitting in her room, the radio on in the background as it always was, having a brief moment of clarity as she listened, appalled.

". . . and the thought that I might have done something like that — it was really scary," Robbie was saying.

"Right," I said, distractedly, slotting the key into the ignition and starting up the car. "Let's get you to school. The last thing you need is to be late after your suspension."

His eyes were on me while I reversed; there was no mistaking his disappointment. He hunched up against the passenger door and looked out the window.

I dropped him at school, neither of us saying another word.

■ ■ ■ ■

As I walked up the stairs to the History Department on the third floor, my phone began ringing. It was Caroline.

"I suppose you heard that," I said, referring to my disastrous radio performance.

Instead she said: "I've just seen Zoe's face."

I trudged up the final few steps and turned down the corridor.

"You can't believe I did that to her? My God . . ."

She sounded slightly hysterical.

"Calm down," I told her. "We'll talk about this later."

"She must have done it to herself," she went on, as if she hadn't heard me. "She must actually have smashed her face into a wall *on purpose.*"

"I can't deal with this now."

"It's frightening," she said. "That she would do something so violent . . . I don't think I can go into the office today. I'm all over the place."

Caroline was normally so together, unflappable. It was disconcerting to hear her sound this agitated, admitting to her own insecurity.

"Please, love," I said, softening my voice, "try and pull yourself together."

I was passing Alan's office, the door open, and I heard him calling my name as he caught sight of me.

"Listen, I have to go," I told her. "I'll call you back shortly."

Before she could stammer a reply, I hung up.

My head was like a jar of bees with what I should have said, what I should not have said scenarios. I knew, entering Alan's office, that he had listened to my interview and now was seeking to reprimand me.

To my surprise, someone else was there, sitting and waiting, it appeared, for me to arrive.

"Niki?" I said.

She sat rigidly, her hands clasped, a little startled, though she must have known I was coming. Alan told me to take a seat.

"Niki came to see me about a matter," he told me, "and rather than me feeding you the information secondhand, I thought you'd like to hear it for yourself."

I could tell Niki was intensely uncomfortable with Alan's maneuvers by the way she shifted in her chair, as if trying to avoid my gaze. It was obvious she did not want to be here. Alan prompted her with a gentle

302

cough as if to say *over to you.*

"I'm withdrawing from the PhD program. I'm sorry."

PhD students have been described to me by Alan as "the holy grail" — the more quality PhD students we "complete," the better it reflects on the institution's reputation and on our chances for funding. Losing Niki was not just a personal defeat, it was an institutional failure.

"But why?" I asked.

"I've been offered a fellowship at Trinity."

"You never said anything about applying elsewhere." It seemed to me that Niki had grown shifty, not meeting my eye.

"I'm sorry, David. I was at a Royal Irish Academy meeting in January that you were supposed to be at. Afterward, I was approached by a professor from Trinity. It's not that I went looking. I've been unhappy for some time, but whenever I wanted to discuss it with you, you seemed too busy or distracted."

I don't think, even with hindsight, that I was too busy or distracted to talk to Niki about her work. To me her argument was self-serving.

"I think you should reconsider, Niki. You've made good progress on your work here. By all means, accept the fellowship but defer. Finish your research here first."

"I'm sorry," she said. "I don't really want to do that."

Alan dropped a sheaf of papers onto his desk as if he were swatting a fly. "Niki says she tried to meet with you, but you didn't make yourself available."

"Well, there was that one time I could not meet you," I said, directing my attention to Niki again, and then to Alan: ". . . I had to cancel, but that was only the one time."

Niki said, her voice gaining a little strength, "There were other times when you were unavailable. And it's not just that — I was hoping to be more included in the research unit, and to play more of a contributing role in the department."

"But that's all to come," I said.

"I just don't feel like I'm getting the support I need," she said in response.

I said by way of my defense, "I'm sorry to hear that, but a good deal of research is self-led independent learning."

"I need regular, rigorous feedback," she said as if she had rehearsed the words.

"Can I ask you to reconsider? We have already made some excellent progress."

"I've made up my mind," she said, avoiding any eye contact with me.

We talked for a few minutes more, but

nothing I said seemed to appease her. Finally, she stood up, and Alan nodded his assent.

She held out a hand and I shook her limp offering with consternation and some annoyance.

"I'm very sorry about this, Alan," I said when she had gone. "Is there no way of persuading her to stay?"

"I tried. I explained the process, how it makes us look." He sat down heavily. "Of course, we will have to carry out an internal investigation."

"Is that really necessary?"

"She was the Vice Chancellor Fellow, for God's sake!" He spread his hands across the desk. "We'll have to form a committee and formally sign off on her release from her research with us."

"I don't know what to say," I said. "I can't believe she didn't come to me before."

"Apparently, she tried."

"I can check my e-mails, but really, I don't think I missed anything."

"It's disappointing," Alan said. "I hope we can make up for her departure in some way."

"We will certainly try," I said in an effort to sound positive.

He appeared distracted, and I took it as

my cue to leave.

"One other thing," he said as I got to my feet. "The radio interview . . ."

"You heard?" I said hopelessly.

"I'm afraid I did. What on earth came over you?"

"I was very tired. I slept badly last night . . ."

My voice petered out, silenced by the weight of concern in his stare.

"The timing couldn't be worse," Alan pointed out.

"I'm truly sorry."

"I will have to speak on your behalf to the dean. I will explain the pressure you are under at home."

I dropped my eyes, uncomfortable at the unspoken assertion that I had allowed problems in my personal life to seep in and pollute the working environment of the department.

"How are things at home, David?" he asked, his tone changing, becoming avuncular. "How is your mother doing?"

I had told him, in one of our informal chats over coffee, how my mother had moved into a nursing home for palliative care. Her decline had become swift and acute.

"She's not so good, Alan. It's only a matter of time now."

"Time is precious. I often think that Time is the commodity that we deal in, as historians. An examination of its passage . . ."

Alan's patter began to sound disinterested, and I lost focus on what he was actually saying. He must have noticed my wavering attention, my despair.

"And your first-year student? How are things there?"

I cleared my throat. "It's a little tricky, to be honest. Not as easy as I'd anticipated."

I thought about Zoe's toothbrush in my pocket, and knew that as soon as I returned to my office I would open up the Internet page of a DNA testing facility, print out a form, and send the damn thing off. Just to be sure, I told myself.

"What about taking a break?"

I protested, but only mildly.

"Take a few days," he said. "Spend them with your mother. With Caroline and the kids. A break will help you get your affairs in order and let matters blow over here."

"What about my lectures? What about my seminars?" I asked.

"Don't worry about any of it. I'll ask John McCormack to cover for you."

Great, I thought as I left his office. McCormack to the rescue.

# CHAPTER 17
## CAROLINE

April started out as a difficult month. After a bruising client meeting one afternoon, in which I presented with incorrect data, Peter called me into his office and informed me that once the maternity leave I was covering was over, my employment with the firm would come to an end.

"It's not just today," he said in response to my craven apology, my pathetic attempts to explain myself. "You've been distracted for a while now — missing appointments, turning up unprepared."

Like an idiot, I began rattling on about another client, a proposal I was putting together, plans I wanted to run past him. I felt like a child, needing him to be pleased with me. He held up his hand.

"I'm very sorry," he said with cold civility. "We have limited resources, and I need someone who is at the top of her game, not distracted by her domestic situation. I'm happy to write you a good reference, but that's the best I can do."

He meant well, but I left his office ungraciously, barely making it to my car before the tears came.

Whatever disappointment I felt had to be put on hold once the news we had been waiting for came. On April 14, a week shy of her seventy-fifth birthday, Ellen passed away. David, who has always had a knack for mentally compartmentalizing, held himself together well in the days before the funeral, making the arrangements, taking calls of condolence, dealing with the nursing home and the undertakers. Even on the day of the funeral itself, he managed to control his emotions, appearing somber but composed, his voice only cracking once during the funeral address.

Up until then, we had managed, somehow, to keep the news of Zoe's existence from our friends and relatives, but with her marked presence at Ellen's funeral — taking her place in the family pew — it was all, suddenly, very public.

"Who's the blonde?" David's cousin asked me. "Robbie's girlfriend?"

"David's daughter," I replied and he blinked in surprise.

It felt to me like I spent the whole day explaining who Zoe was, trying to maintain a breezy air like I was not in the least bothered by her existence. That whole day spent ignoring the stares and the whispered asides, the undercurrent of gossip running beneath the sorrow. If David noticed it too, he didn't say a thing.

Outward displays of grief are not part of David's makeup but in the days that followed he seemed to turn in on himself. He became enervated, his sadness surfacing in a kind of lassitude. He moped about the house, saying little to anyone while the rest of us tiptoed around him, pained to witness his depression.

A week or so later, I suggested we take a hike in the Wicklow hills — all of us. All this hanging around the house in gloomy silence wasn't doing any of us any good. It had been a long time since we had undertaken a family outing, and a trek over muddy terrain in the fresh spring air might be just what David needed to blow away the cobwebs of his depression.

"Why not?" he said.

It was a sharp, clear day, the air crisp with new life pushing up through cold ground. We took the car as far as Tibradden and then got out, lacing up our hiking boots, a brisk breeze whipping at our anoraks as we pulled rucksacks onto our backs. There were five of us that day as Zoe had chosen to come. In the days since Ellen's death, she had seemed calmer, more acquiescent. Her manner had changed — the threat seemed to have left her. Or maybe the change had occurred within me. I was tired of feeling suspicious and angry. I was sick of myself and the constant negativity Zoe inspired. All of a sudden, it didn't matter to me — her insidious presence, her lies, the self-inflicted wounds. She was a silly little girl with her own problems, none of which seemed important after Ellen's death.

We set out, David taking charge of the map, pointing out the route we would take. He went ahead, Holly at his side, while Zoe and Robbie trudged through the mud together. I was happy to take up the rear. It felt good to be silent in the vastness of the Wicklow hills. We splashed through water and trudged through gorse and heather, floundering occasionally in unexpected boggy dips.

"You okay back there?" David called to me.

"I'm great!"

And I was. Seeing him smiling down at me, his face ruddy from all the fresh air, I felt hopeful that the last few months were behind us. My failure at work, the struggle over Zoe, none of it seemed to matter, such was my optimism that day. No harm could come to us in this beautiful place.

After an hour, the climb steepened, and we found ourselves scrambling up a craggy path, slippery with scattered rocks and gravel. Trees grew tall around us — Norwegian spruces, pines — and the shadowy ground was soft with layers of brown needles.

"Will we stop soon?" I called and David pointed to a clearing on one side a little higher up. A space cut into the rock face, shelter from the wind that had whipped up as we made our ascent.

We reached it and set about emptying our backpacks of provisions. My hands and feet were cold. The temperature was lower up here than it had been when we set out.

"What about a campfire?" David asked.

"Is that allowed?" I asked, thinking of gorse fires spreading rapidly over the county.

"Don't be such a wimp," he said, teasing me.

Robbie was eager to help and the two of them set off in search of firewood, with Zoe. Holly clambered up over the hill to explore and I was left alone.

For a while, I just sat there, kneading warmth back into my fingers. The others had disappeared from view. It was very quiet; the rock beneath me felt hard and cold. Clouds scudded across the gray sky, and the outline of the trees along the horizon was jagged and harsh. I wanted the others to come back and break the silence, which seemed vast and watchful like a presence. But no one was there — only the rocks and thicket growing over the windblown hill.

I decided to set off after Holly, up over the hump of gorse, the scrabble of a rutted mud path. It was hard going and I was beginning to sweat under my clothes, my legs tired from the strain of the climb. A copse of trees lay ahead, the ground between thick with nettles and briars. I scaled the perimeter until I rounded the corner and found myself almost at the brink of a sheer drop into a quarry, yellow machinery far below lying idle and unmanned. I peered over the edge, birds wheeling above, and felt my heart pound at the plunging depth. It must have been a drop of thirty feet or more. My fear was chased by indignation — how dangerous! No fencing, no warning signs — if you were to stumble up there in poor light or in a heavy fog, you could easily fall to your death.

I stepped back from the quarry and looked to my left, my eyes caught by the bright colors of Holly's anorak. Her feet were placed almost at the lip of the drop, wind whipping her hair out from her hood as she peered over. She hadn't seen me, her body inclined slightly away from me.

That was when I saw Zoe edging through the periphery of my vision. She seemed to be stepping carefully, stealthily. Her jacket was gray, camouflage against the craggy stones of the quarry. A wave of nausea came up suddenly from my stomach and I opened my mouth to shout a warning, but fear gripped my throat and no sound came out. I watched her creeping up, Holly oblivious to the approaching threat. I watched as she put out a hand, and all the danger in the world seemed to come alive in that moment. Maternal empathy meant that I saw the push before it happened, felt the hands as if they were to my own back, the sickening shove, that terrifying moment as the ground falls away and there's nothing but the air around you and the bone-breaking impact of the ground — no escape. I watched that hand reach out and forced the word up the blind tunnel of my throat: "No!"

Holly turned but I kept my eyes fixed on Zoe's hand as it reached out and gripped

Holly's shoulder — that shot to my heart as I anticipated the fall — and then she pulled her back.

Even now, after everything that has happened, and with all I know, I still look back to that moment with uncertainty. If I hadn't followed Holly up there and shouted out, would Zoe have pushed her? Or was it my feverish imagination, powered and warped by my intense distrust of this girl? But that is the rational thought of hindsight. At that moment, it was pure instinct. I had seen the violence she had done to herself; I had recognized her ruthlessness in getting what she wanted.

Holly stepped back from the edge, came toward me, and I wrapped my arm around her, shooting Zoe a look.

"What?" Zoe shouted after us, because I had already turned away, ushering Holly back down the hill, away from that girl and all the danger she represented. "I was just trying to help her!"

That night, going up the stairs to bed, I passed Holly's door and heard crying. I found her lying in the darkness, hugging a tatty old bunny that had been consigned to the bottom of her closet for the last couple of years. Seeing her clutching it to her chest

— an old talisman against night terrors — set off an alarm bell in my head.

"What is it, sweetheart?" I asked, sitting on the bed next to her, my weight on the mattress drawing her toward me.

"Oh Mum," she said, reaching up and throwing her arms around my neck.

That physical demonstration was so unlike Holly. She was normally self-contained, eschewing large outpourings of affection. I could feel her thin body against me, shaking.

"I was so scared," she whispered, her mouth close to my ear.

I knew she was talking about Zoe and something hardened inside me — a resolve forming.

"It's all right," I told her gently, trying to sound calm and firm. Drawing back so I could look into her eyes, I said, "I would never let anyone hurt you — you know that, don't you?"

"But you're not always there, Mum. You don't see what she's like — the things she says to me . . ."

"What things?"

"When there are other people around, she's all nice and sweet to me, but it's all an act! When we're alone, just the two of us, she's horrible!"

"Why? What does she say to you?"

"She says I'm nothing."

*"What?"*

"That I don't matter. That no one will miss me when I'm not around."

"Holly, that's not true. You know it's not."

"Dad wouldn't notice," she said, her voice dropping a little.

"Of course he would! Your father loves you and Robbie more than anything."

"More than Zoe?" Her eyes, still wet with tears, held mine.

"He has known you your whole life, sweetheart. Since before you were even born. That makes things different. Special."

"It doesn't feel that way," she said. "It feels like *she's* all that matters to him now."

She ran her fingers along the battered ear of her bunny and I remembered a time when she couldn't sleep without him, how well-loved he was, and felt a twinge of sadness that she had outgrown him. Tonight was just a blip. Very soon, that bunny would be consigned to a box in the attic along with the other relics of her childhood, and somehow, I didn't feel ready for that.

"I'll talk to Dad," I told her.

She lay back, turning away from me, but she was not comforted.

"It won't make a difference," she said,

resignation — not reassurance — in her tone.

I think that was when I decided to take matters into my own hands. The danger was alive and living in my house. I couldn't rely on David for help, so I resorted to a deception of my own. Necessary evils were called for.

I bided my time, remaining watchful, until early one morning when Zoe was in the shower, the others downstairs having breakfast, I moved quickly and quietly up the steps to her room, finding her mobile phone lying on her bureau. My heart beating wildly in my chest, I scrolled through her list of contacts before finding what I needed: *Mam Mobile.* I scribbled the number on a Post-it and fled the room before I could be caught, the hiss of the shower jets coming from the bathroom as I hurried downstairs, my pulse beginning to slow.

My motives for meeting Celine Harte were unclear. I wasn't so naive as to think she could solve my problem by whipping her daughter out of my house and dragging her back to Belfast. But I suppose I was seeking evidence of sorts, some confirmation of the fear I felt. Part of me was afraid that I was growing obsessed with the girl and maybe losing perspective. Was I right to suspect her of meaning harm toward my daughter and me? Or was she just a mixed-up kid, meddlesome but benign, who would, with time and support, settle down and find her place within the family? Either way, some poor unfortunate had been landed with Zoe as their kid, and I wanted to meet them to find out what exactly I was dealing with.

We met in Applegreen — a service station on the M1 between Dublin and Newry. Sitting at a plastic table, the coffee cooling, Celine Harte, bundled up in a quilted jacket even though the day was warm, looked at me flatly, her eyes like two inky-black pebbles.

"Why don't you tell me what it is you want?"

Her candor took me aback. The world-weariness of her demeanor gave me the impression that this was not the first time she had been called to such a meeting. I answered with candor of my own.

"It's Zoe," I said. "I want her out of my home."

If she was surprised by that, she didn't show it.

"She has come between me and my husband," I went on. "She has some sort of vendetta against me, like she wants to get rid of me. I'm worried about the influence she's having on my children, my son in particular. I'm afraid she's a threat to my daughter."

Celine took it all in, her expression unchanging, then looked down at her cup, a pale skin forming on the surface of the coffee.

"I'm sorry," I said. "I didn't mean to shock you."

"I'm not shocked." She brought her eyes up to meet mine, tiredness in the heavy lids. "It's what she does."

The dryness of her tone bordered on cynicism. I expected her to go on — it was a shocking thing to say of your own daughter — but rather than qualifying her statements, she just stared at me in stony silence.

"I don't know what to do," I admitted. "Am I imagining it, or does she want to tear us apart?"

"Why don't you tell me what she's done?" she suggested, and I thought I detected a trace of sympathy entering her voice — a softening. Resignation, perhaps, or maybe it was pity.

I told her everything, about Zoe's behavior when alone with me and how markedly different it became when David was around. I told her about the lies, the deceptions, the inflicting of damage on her own face, then blaming me. She listened to it all without betraying any emotion, except when I told her about Zoe's suicide attempt. Briefly, she closed her eyes, and then she was back with me again, having pushed down whatever pain had surfaced at the catalog of trouble Zoe had brought upon my family. I told her everything, except for the part about Holly — the incident at the quarry. For some reason I was reluctant to discuss it — I felt to suggest her daughter was capable of a cold-blooded killing might overstep the mark — and I wanted Celine Harte to share with me what she knew and understood of Zoe. I didn't want to risk her growing defensive.

She finished her coffee, pushed the mug to one side, then leaned her clasped hands on the table in front of her as if she were about to pray. The words she spoke to me then had the rehearsed quality of a prayer, or perhaps a parable, the telling of a story, one that she had told to herself or to others many times over. There was no pleasure in the telling. Rather a kind of bleakness, as if she had learned long ago that, no matter how she told it, the outcome would remain the same.

She began by telling me about a family whom Zoe used to babysit for while she was still at school.

"Every Saturday night, religiously, for over a year. Then it just stopped. I asked her about it, but she said it was nothing, told me to mind my own business. I let it go. But then," she continued, "one afternoon, the mother comes down the road to me all distressed. She tells me that Zoe has been pestering her husband, hanging around his workplace, calling him at all hours of the day and night. The wife had found out about it — she'd looked at his mobile phone, seen the lewd texts Zoe'd been sending him. She showed me some of them — disgusting things — not to mention all the poison written about his wife. Zoe believed this man was in love with her, you see, that he was going to leave his wife for her. The way she got in between them . . ." She leaned forward for emphasis. "She was fourteen years old."

She kept on watching me to see if I took in the significance of that. *Fourteen.*

There were others, she said. A crush on a teacher that had bordered on obsession. The son of a friend, his girlfriend harassed until she complained to the police. The duplicity, the relentless nature of her intent, her

322

consuming passion for one person leading
her to isolate and eliminate anyone who
might stand between her and her prize. On
and on she went. It was depressingly familiar, as if our story had been written for us
long ago and we were merely acting out a
foregone conclusion.

"She wasn't always like that," Celine said,
drawing back now. I could see her account
had drained her. She summoned the energy
to paint a picture for me of a bright little
girl, pale and beautiful, vivacious and
energetic, always dancing and singing, the
center of attention — the center of their
world. As she said it, I thought of my baby
— the baby I might have had — a child who
could have given happiness, fulfillment. And
if I had kept that baby, would David have
gone to Belfast at all? Might there have been
no Linda? No Zoe? A jab of regret came at
me and I took a sip of my cold coffee in a
bid to swallow it away.

Somewhere along the line, Celine told me,
Zoe's childhood energy became restless.
Adolescence came on and spikes appeared
in her personality. The vivacious child
became a cunning and devious teenager.
Unrelenting, refusing to be appeased or
cajoled, her restless energy meant they
could never relax, always jolting from one

crisis to the next.

"The one thing that bothers me," she said, "the one thing I have never been able to understand, is what brought on the change in her? It wasn't always there — I'd have seen it. If I could just know what it was . . ."

She had plucked a packet of sugar from the saucer beneath her mug and was turning it over in her hands, nervous energy overtaking her like a sudden itch.

"Something she told us," I began, carefully because I was on uncertain ground here. "About your husband. She said . . . at least, she implied . . . that something may have happened . . ."

Her hooded eyes opened a little wider, as if in surprise. But she was not surprised. Dismayed, perhaps.

"She told you that story?"

A feeling of shame coming over me as if it were I who had invented the story of abuse.

"You don't know my husband but he's the kindest, gentlest person you could meet. To make those claims about him — it was the worst kind of hurt. Those allegations left him reeling. He was never the same afterward. And the worst part . . ." Here her voice broke for the first time. "The worst part was the cleverness of her lies, the way she worked on me over the course of those few days . . . for just a short while I began to doubt him. I began to question my own husband who wouldn't harm a fly."

She looked down at her hands. She had twisted the packet in two, sugar spilling onto the table.

"My doubts didn't last. But the damage was done."

The air between us seemed to deflate. All the stoicism had gone from her now and I sensed our conversation closing down.

"Did you ever meet Linda?" I asked.

"No. I never wanted to. What would have been the point? And besides," she said, hardness pinching her lips into thin lines, "I knew that once Zoe found her birth mother, all of her attention and love would be transferred from me to her. That I would be discarded. That's how it is with Zoe. Once you've outlasted your use, you become expendable."

Bitter words to speak of your own daughter. I tried to imagine an occasion where I might speak of Holly or Robbie in that way but could not. Celine had grown quiet, and I could see what it had cost her, the lengths to which Zoe had pushed her.

"You still love her," I said, an observation, not a question.

She smiled for the first time, a smile that

325

didn't reach her eyes.

"That's the thing about love," she said. "It doesn't matter if they knock you down, abuse you, push you to the brink. You still love them, don't you? You would forgive them anything."

After that, things deteriorated. I made no secret of my wariness toward Zoe, and she, in turn, maintained an air of injury. Over dinner one evening, she announced that she had found a part-time job as a waitress in a restaurant in town. She was out more than ever now, and I had the feeling she was avoiding me. Her occupancy of the attic continued, but a new coldness had entered her presence. The days and nights went on, as they had before, but something had changed between us, and I came to believe it had as much to do with the day of the hike as anything else. She knew I suspected her of something, though at the time I could not name it, and I certainly did not mention it to her again. But whatever it was, it was foul, and underhand — whether she was, on that day, willing to hurt Holly or simply wanted to plant the notion in my head, it meant we kept our distance from each other. That chill was noticeable, I suppose. Robbie would often ask me where she was when he got home from school, and when I said I did not know, he looked peeved, as if it were my fault that she was not waiting for him.

What she did next, though, I hadn't expected. Even though it was not yet May, the end of semester still weeks away, she moved out.

I had been in Tesco, doing the weekly shop, the evening light fading as I returned home and parked in the driveway. As soon as I stepped inside the hall, I heard raised voices.

Leaving my bags of groceries by the door, I began to climb the stairs toward the attic.

"You can't be serious?" I heard Robbie say, his voice querulous and shrill.

Zoe, sounding more controlled, said, "Please, Robbie. Don't be like this."

"I think it's disgusting."

"Don't be so dramatic —"

"He's old enough to be your dad!"

"So what?"

"That beer belly. How can you let him touch you?"

"What's going on?" I asked.

Robbie stood with his arms folded over his chest, while Zoe turned back to the bed. I saw the open suitcase, clothes flung inside. The drawers of her bureau lay open and empty. She began zipping her laptop into its cover.

"Are you leaving?"

"That's what you want, isn't it?" she replied a little petulantly.

I didn't deny it and she put the laptop into her bag, squashed down the clothes, and zipped up the suitcase.

"Where are you going?" I asked.

When she didn't answer, Robbie spoke up.

"She's moving in with *him.*"

"Who?"

"Tell her," he said to Zoe.

"Tell me what?"

She stood at the other side of the bed, her eyes trained on her bag. There was something shifty in her manner. At last, she straightened up and looked at me, her gaze growing more defensive.

"I'm moving in with Chris."

"Chris?" I asked, momentarily confused, scanning my memory for some recollection of a Chris in her conversation. A new thought broke through, and I said, "You don't mean *our* Chris?"

"It's a joke," Robbie said humorlessly.

"It's not a joke," she countered quickly, her forehead creasing with annoyance. "We care about each other."

"Oh please," he said. "I'm going to throw up."

I couldn't explain it — the feeling of betrayal that arose. The thought of Zoe and Chris together. It was not just shock that I felt, but something with a harder burn: she was creeping into every area of our lives.

"Aren't you going to say anything?" Robbie asked me.

"How long has this been going on?"

She shrugged. "A couple of months."

"The night Chris called over," I murmured. "You both went for a drink." The pieces fitting together in my head. All those nights she hadn't come home, her withdrawal from the household.

"He was really kind to me that night, when I was upset. He made me laugh."

"He's, like, Dad's best friend!"

"So what? He's fun. He understands things."

She lifted the bag from the bed and it occurred to me how young she was — the bag, a monstrous thing, seemed more than she could handle.

"Are you going now? Right this minute?"

"Why?" she asked. "Do you want me to stick around for a long, slow farewell?"

My mind was leaping all over the place. Yes, I wanted her gone, but not like this.

Not to him.

"Have you thought this thing through properly? Don't you have some friend your own age whose couch you can crash on for a while?"

"What do you care?"

"Don't get me wrong. I love Chris dearly. He's a funny, caring man. But he's a lot older than you. And his marriage has only just broken down; his emotions are all over the place."

"So?"

"Aren't there boys in college you'd be more interested in dating? Boys your own age?"

She rolled her eyes, a strand of her hair falling down across her face, which she made no attempt to push back.

"I like Chris. He's fun," she said. I saw the mischief come into her eye, a hard gleam of trouble. "And he's great in bed," she added.

Robbie looked at her in amazement. I rubbed my hand along my brow, the throb of a headache starting in my temples.

"Does David know about this?" I asked.

She shrugged. "I haven't told him."

"I'm not sure this is a good idea. It's a big step."

"I know what I'm doing. It's best for

everyone if I go."

On a rising note of exasperation, I said, "Is this a permanent thing? I mean, are you moving in together or are you just going to stay with him until you get something else sorted?"

"I don't know. I'll see how it goes."

Lowering my voice, I said, "Zoe, please. This is serious. You might get hurt."

"I'll be fine," she said.

All those weeks of her being in the house, the dread that announced itself every time I walked through my front door. All those meals sitting across from her, the careful way she ate, pulling her hair into a twist over one shoulder. Those nights listening for her voice on the phone upstairs, or for the sound of her key turning in the lock. All the time, I had been waiting for her to leave, willing it to happen so that we could be free of her constant presence. Now that it came to it, I got no sense of satisfaction or relief.

"Please just stay until David gets home."

Part of me couldn't quite believe I was saying those words. The corner of her mouth curled up into the slightest of grins.

"Thanks for everything," she said coolly. "You've been so kind — all of you."

The formality of her address — it was like we were right back to that first Sunday lunch. *I hope we can become good friends, Caroline.*

"Help Zoe with her bag," I told Robbie.

"Is that it?" he asked in disbelief.

"I can manage. Really."

"Here." He took the bag from her arms, pounding down the stairs with it. Zoe followed and I closed the door to what had been her room and would now go back to being David's office. When I reached the bottom step, she was already at the door, her bag swung over one shoulder.

There were no embraces, no good-byes. Robbie and I stood together watching her go.

"You could have stopped her," he said quietly. "You blame her for what happened to Holly, on the hike, don't you?"

"Robbie . . ."

"That's why she left. You drove her away."

I looked at him, my son, his face narrowing with contempt, and said to him the same words I would say to his father some hours later when he returned from the office and I gave him the news that she had gone.

"I'm sorry, love. I tried."

He turned from me, disgusted, and soon I was standing alone in the doorway, staring down our road, quiet and empty of traffic, watching for just a moment as if she might change her mind and come running back.

# CHAPTER 18
## DAVID

Caroline and I sat side by side in the darkened auditorium, waiting for the music to start. I have always loved that hush, the rush of nerves and excitement that comes with the dimming of the lights, the last few coughs as people prepare themselves for the performance. But that night, as I sat in the National Concert Hall with my wife, looking up at the orchestra full of youthful expectant faces, I felt no excitement.

The low hum of muted percussion started, the plucking of harp strings, and slowly, elegantly, the gentle rising progression of the melody rose above the droning bass as Debussy's *La Mer* filled the room, little ripples and waves as the string section took over and the brass joined in. I felt Caroline straining beside me to catch a glimpse of Robbie, and there he was, pale-faced up there under the lights, bowing away at his cello. Dimly, I recalled the chords and melodies I had heard him practicing for weeks — how disjointed and odd they had sounded, but now a piece fitting neatly into a puzzle, surrounded by the flow and harmony of the other instruments. I watched him, aware of my paternal pride — his concentration, his seriousness, the way the conductor and the musical score in front of him held his attention. I tried to focus on this fatherly love, hoping it would drown out the shock and indignation I continued to feel forty-eight hours after Caroline had broken the news to me that Zoe had moved in with Chris.

In the past couple of days I had made several efforts to contact Zoe — leaving messages on her phone, texting her, to no avail. I had pointedly not gotten in touch with Chris. He had been at my mother's funeral, and whatever about the time or place, I found it hard to believe that no one had said anything to me about the two of them being an item. I felt the onus was on him to seek me out and offer up some kind of apology for his behavior.

During the intermission, when we streamed out and found our preordered drinks waiting for us, I said to Caroline, "So, when Chris finally does decide to make contact, what do you think he's going to say?"

"I don't know," she said with an air of mild resignation. "I expect he'll say something to appease you."

She sipped from her gin and tonic.

"What sort of explanation could he possibly give?"

We were leaning against a pillar. People were milling past. She shrugged.

"Whatever way you look at it," I said, "he's taking advantage of someone vulnerable."

That caught her attention.

"I'm not sure I'd describe Zoe as vulnerable."

"She's a teenager. Her mother recently died."

Caroline wasn't buying it.

"She's nineteen and pretty savvy, and whether you like it or not, she didn't know Linda all that well."

"That's not the point."

"Well, what is the point?"

"Doesn't it sicken you — the thought of them together?"

"There was fifteen years between my parents."

"That's not the same," I snapped. "When I think of them together, sleeping together . . . Chris of all people! I had no idea he was capable of doing something like this. Doesn't he realize how he's betraying me and our friendship?"

"I doubt very much you are high on his mind when he's in bed with her."

"I suppose not," I said.

"You know, for a second there, you sounded a little jealous," she told me.

"Don't be ridiculous."

I took a large slug of my drink, felt the tonic creeping up the back of my nose.

"Anyway, all of this talk has very little to do with the reason we are here, which is Robbie. I hope he is okay," she said. "He looked nervous."

"It sickens me," I continued. "Right to the pit of my stomach. You know, if he tries to tell me how he's in love, I think I might punch him."

She put her glass down on the wooden ledge with a sudden angry clink.

"Could you please stop," she said in a loud whisper. "I know you are upset about this, but it's all you've talked about for the past two days and now I'm the one who is sick of it!"

The force in her voice silenced me, and for the next few minutes, we stood glancing about at the other audience members, sipping at our drinks. When the bell finally rang to signal the end of the intermission, it was a huge relief. We could escape each other's company and return to our seats.

The Arts Block was quiet at that time of year, the swell of students on campus having fallen after lectures came to an end. The libraries were still busy, but a kind of hush had descended as exams began. I spent a good deal of time in my office, gathering together the papers I had published in the previous twelve months in order to read them before my interview, which had been scheduled for the following week. On this particular day, I was reading through the latest minutes of a student-staff consultative committee when the phone in my office rang. I picked it up and, to my surprise, heard Chris on the other end of the line.

"I'm not going to apologize." The first words out of his mouth, words that might have been defensive and provocative, but he said them with a kind of casual serenity.

"No one's asked you for an apology," I said evenly, putting aside my papers and swiveling my chair so that I faced the window.

"I know you're upset."

"You can't know what I am thinking or

how I feel, so don't pretend to, please."

"It's not something I planned —"

"I'm not even going to get into the age difference thing," I said, with an air of disgust, "because I think you know already how wrong it is, I mean she's a teenager, for Christ's sake —"

"She's a grown-up, David."

"Only barely!"

"You don't give her enough credit. She's very mature and knows her own mind."

"It's you I'm not giving credit to. What the hell are you thinking?"

"I'm thinking that I'm in love with her."

I leaned forward in my chair, as if I'd been punched in the stomach. Through the window, I could see a couple down below in the courtyard. She was sitting on his knee playing with his hair. They were only kids. Love at that age — it retained a sort of innocence. But not this. Not what he was suggesting.

"This isn't love, Chris, it's a midlife crisis."

"It's love," he insisted.

"Answer me this," I said. "Why didn't you tell me? Why did I have to hear it from Caroline that not only were you and Zoe dating but that you'd moved in together? We've known each other for *twenty-six* years, Chris. I would have thought the least you owed me was the decency to tell me to my face."

"You're right," he said, trying to sound reasonable and accommodating. "I should have told you sooner."

"So why didn't you?"

A pause, as if he was trying to find the words. "This might sound crazy, but I was afraid that if I talked about it, then the spell would be broken. The magic gone."

I couldn't believe it. The guy was talking like he was in a Disney movie.

"From the start, I knew she was special. That first evening, the way we talked, the way we seemed to connect, not just on a sexual level but —"

"No, please," I said, cutting him off. "I can't go there, I just can't."

"Okay. I understand that. But the connection we have, the bond, it's so much deeper than anything I've ever experienced before. Even with Susannah —"

"Does she know about this?" I cut in. "Susannah? Have you told her?"

"Not yet."

"Have you thought about how hurt she will be?"

"Susannah has it in for me," he said, sounding peeved.

"She's going to hit the roof when she finds

out," I went on.

"You know what?" he snapped, his tone changing. "Since Susannah and I split up, I've hardly heard from you. Barely a phone call to see if I'm okay. I could have been at home busily killing myself or losing myself in a bottle, and you'd have had no idea."

I shifted in my chair, the truth of what he was saying making me uncomfortable.

"Zoe has been the one person who has taken an interest in my emotional well-being since this whole breakup happened. Not you, not Caroline. You ask me why I didn't tell you earlier? Maybe if you had been more interested in how I was, I might have confided in you."

"You're right," I acceded. "I should have been there for you, and I'm sorry. But I still don't think that's a good enough reason for seducing a young girl who's under my care."

"I wish it hadn't happened like this, but the way we have connected, it feels real. It's not some immature infatuation or a midlife crisis. It feels like this is something" — he struggled to find the right word — "inevitable."

I hated him right then. He seemed so sure of himself. Here he was, one of my oldest friends, trying to conduct a conversation with me in reasonable tones, and all the while he'd been sharing his bed with Zoe. It was too much. I told him I had a meeting, then hung up, dropping the handset petulantly onto the receiver.

Too distracted to continue with my reading, I went instead to the common room for a mid-morning coffee. I should not have been surprised to see McCormack on the couch in the corner — I saw him almost every other day — but I was. He was wearing a formal suit, not the kind of casual garb he normally dressed in for the day-to-day grind of university work. The pinstripes and stiff, ironed tie made him look more like a banker than an academic. I noticed his hair had recently been cut and he was freshly shaved. Engrossed in reading from a thick folder, he did not see me approach.

"McCormack," I said, "you're a little overdressed for the kind of scrutiny you are giving those documents."

He smiled. "Dr. Connolly," he said examining his watch, "aren't you up before me?"

"Up?"

"Interview day . . . I'm just glancing over my presentation."

Two things startled me: interview day, and presentation. Neither made sense to me, but already I was sweating with panic.

"I've chosen not to do a PowerPoint," Mc-

Cormack said. "I hate the damn things."

"What are you talking about? The interviews are next week."

"They changed the date and added that we should present . . . it was all in the letter."

"I never got any letter," I uttered.

"Are you sure? They sent one out, about two weeks ago."

How had this happened? Was it possible that I had received the letter and simply forgotten? Or had Caroline received it and failed to pass it on? My heart rate doubled, and my mind began to race.

"I've already seen two of the other candidates," McCormack said. "Barnes from London, and Gillis from Edinburgh. You're on at twelve. Are you sure you didn't get a letter?"

I looked at my watch. It was eleven thirty. I excused myself and ran back to my office. I rang Alan, but the interviews had already started. I explained what had happened to his secretary, Mrs. Boland, but she insisted the letters had gone out. To my question "How could this have happened?" she was resolute: "The letters went out by registered post. They were all signed for."

I explained to her that I had not signed for anything, then listened to her rustling among paperwork for a minute or two before she identified what she was searching for.

"Here we are," she said, then read out: "Signed for by C. Connolly."

*Caroline.* A warm rush of anger went through me.

"Shall I tell the panel to expect you?" Mrs. Boland asked.

I had little choice but to go ahead.

"Of course," I said. "I'll be right there."

It was too late to dash home for a change of clothes. I was wearing an old shirt, a worn pair of corduroys, and a jacket that had seen better days. So much for first impressions. I combed my hair, took up my papers, and thought about what on earth I would make a presentation on. My mind went blank. I had to run up the two floors to get to the dean's office, and when I walked into the board room out of breath, four serious individuals sat at the large oval-shaped table before me; Alan was the only one smiling. Acting as chair, he welcomed me and asked me to take a seat. I took it and poured myself a glass of water. I drank it right away, parched.

I made an attempt to explain the lost letter, how I had only just then found out the interview was to be that day. Alan was sympathetic while the others looked askance, their eyes taking in my attire. Either way, I opened the interview on the back foot with apologies and excuses. It was not the start I had hoped for.

They asked about my publications, which conferences had I attended recently, would I consider creating a symposium at UCD for combatants and veterans. Alan smiled his encouragement, but the others were tougher. One of the panel asked about enrollment for our graduate programs, possible interdisciplinary degrees that could be developed, and PhD completions.

I gave some platitudes about a personal development program for doctoral students and a mentoring scheme I hoped to initiate. It was bread and butter to me, that is, until the extern asked his next question.

"That's all very good," he said. "But what about the actual retention of your students?"

All I could think of then was Niki. How she had walked out on me. My star student. He must have found out. Alan would have had to divulge the unfortunate fact of her departure and with it the reasons.

When it was time for my presentation, I rehashed the last paper I had written on the relationship between Roger Casement's humanitarian work for the British Crown and his role as an Irish nationalist. Suffice it to say, I did not do the research or the subject matter due justice. The questions were routine, until Professor Mary Sinnott took up the reins. She asked about my doctoral work and brought me back to Belfast. I talked about the Irish Battalion in World War I, the so-called South Irish Horse, how I developed my dissertation into my first book.

"And your media profile, Dr. Connolly — how does it impact on your contribution to university life?" she asked.

I faltered. *This is so unfair,* I thought. I should have had the time to prepare, just like everyone else. The radio interview came back to me in a flush of shame and irritation. The letter of reprimand was no doubt still being drafted. I waffled, and stuttered, but ultimately refocused my efforts. I wanted that professorship after all. I talked about the media's relationship with history through the years — the chasm between ethical reporting and sensational press. A vagrant image of Chris and Zoe together entered my mind. The thought of her living with him. *Sleeping* with him.

"The position of professor is not just another rung on the ladder," the dean said. "It is a position of leadership. We're looking for someone with the necessary charisma and sangfroid not to be rattled in situations of intense or unpredictable pressure."

He could not have disguised his disapproval more thinly. I told him I had learned a great deal about pressure in the previous academic year, and how, all things considered, I was learning to use it to my advantage. But that was not true. *Look at me now,* I thought, *struggling to answer these questions — my life falling apart around me.*

I thought of Linda, her last lecture, her angel of history: "From Paradise a storm is brewing, and this storm has so much violence to it that it catches in the angel's wings and the angel cannot close those wings. The storm grows in intensity, picks up and propels this celestial being into the future."

Alan ended the interview by asking me what history meant to me, what was history?

A line from Ambrose Bierce came to me: *"History is an account, mostly false, of events, mostly unimportant, which are brought about by rulers, mostly knaves, and soldiers, mostly fools."*

I said something else.

At home, I asked Caroline about the letter.

She was adamant she had not received it.

"You might not have noticed actually signing for it," I suggested. "You could have been distracted by something else?"

"I'm telling you, I never signed for it."

"It was your signature," I insisted.

We argued, and she accused me of not believing her, of not trusting her.

But I couldn't let it go, my temper flaring. "Well, what did happen? If you didn't sign for it, who did?"

I asked Robbie and Holly, who both denied any knowledge of the letter.

"It must have been Zoe," Caroline said, and I turned away from her, enraged.

"For God's sake," I muttered. "Everything is her fault, according to you. Why on earth would she sign your name?"

"Because that's what she's like. You know it, and I do too: she's capricious, destructive, cruel."

We argued some more but it was pointless. Whoever's fault it was, the damage had been done.

I waited for an e-mail, a letter, a phone call, but there was nothing.

In the meantime, my mood plummeted. I felt loneliness come over me — as if I had not realized how important my mother's presence in my life had been up until then.

I thought about the afternoons I had spent with her of late, in her room at the nursing home, and how, despite the vacancy in her gaze, I had felt a closeness to her that I could not feel with anyone else. The truth was that I missed her. It was a desperate week, one in which the hope for promotion was not diminished, but, if anything, heightened. As if the professional advancement could somehow counteract the losses I had suffered personally. To say I was unsettled when Alan finally called me into his office is probably something of an understatement.

"I wanted to follow up with you on your interview," he said. "An official communiqué will follow, but I'm sorry to say that this time you have been unsuccessful."

I sat down. The energy seeped out of me. The extra committee work, the substitute teaching, the journalism and research, it all seemed for naught. I couldn't help thinking it had all been a colossal waste of time.

Talking to me like this was a professional courtesy. I realized that. But it had the bitter taste of defeat. I explained to him how surprised I was about the interview date change and how I had not received official notice. He told me rather matter-of-factly that these things happen all the time, that the letter had been sent, and that all of the other candidates had appeared, and besides, he insisted firmly, I had not missed the interview.

I thought again about what could have happened to the letter, Caroline's accusations creeping into my head. Had Zoe signed for it? Then secreted it up to her room, shredding it before she left? Laughing at me. Making a fool out of me yet again. Her cruelty, echoing and adding to how Linda had left me in the dark, all those years ago — some inexplicable disdain having been handed down from one generation to the next.

"David — I realize that it has been a difficult time for you." The line between mentor and manager was sometimes a blurred one with Alan. He invited you into his confidence, but I was never sure whether it was for professional motives or personal altruism. It occurred to me that maybe he did not know the difference. "My condolences again for the passing of your mother."

I thanked him.

"This business with your first-year student, it must be taxing, not to mention distracting."

"It's not entirely pertinent to whether I got the job or not. You know that," I said, noticing the deep grooves of age furrowed on his forehead.

"The panel was very impressed with your interview . . ."

I felt like saying it doesn't matter, I wasn't good enough. No need to sugar-coat the truth.

"It's also beholden to me to tell you that the panel has selected Dr. McCormack for the position of professor."

Anyone but him.

"We realize that you will be disappointed, but for the moment, can I say that your research outputs are strong, teaching and learning is also strong . . ."

"Why didn't I get it?" I asked, despite having a good idea of the answer, playing along with this charade of feedback. "You can be honest with me . . ."

Alan was back at the window. A flock of seagulls swooped by. Behind them, I could see the two red and white Pigeon House chimney stacks at Poolbeg.

"We are relying on anyone hoping to gain the professorial grade to secure a minimum of external funding each year . . ."

"McCormack is bringing in more external funding than I am?"

"In a word: yes. I want this to be an ongoing conversation. We don't have to hash out the whys and wherefores right now . . ."

"How much?"

"David, it's not the time for those kinds of questions, nor the time to disclose actual figures."

"You know, I have been in talks with the Royal Historical Society who are in the process of securing commercial funding . . ."

He turned to me. "How is Caroline? How are the kids?"

He didn't even disguise his desire to sidetrack me. An image of Robbie came into my head, sitting morosely in the backseat of the car on the way home from the Concert Hall. I thought of all the words of praise Caroline and I had spoken to him and how they all seemed to bounce off him, repelled by the negative force of whatever dark mood held him captive.

"They're all good, Alan. Tip-top."

"I'm glad to hear it," he said, sounding utterly unconvinced. "Perhaps you should get away. Take a break."

"I've already taken time off after the radio interview."

"I mean a holiday," Alan said, trying to sound upbeat, the words scraping across his throat in a husky cough. "A proper one. Abroad."

It felt like the department was trying to sideline me, to get me out of the way.

"I'm not sure that's a good idea," I said.

"I have a place in France," Alan said. "A villa on Île de Ré, not far from La Rochelle. Small but comfortable — a winding road that brings you down to a very quaint village. It's a place of tranquility."

"It sounds idyllic, but . . ."

"There's enough room for you to bring the family . . . it's really rather lovely."

"That's very kind of you, really, but I couldn't . . ."

Alan suggested July. "Please," he said, "just consider it."

There was no point in returning to my office, no point even in remaining on campus. As I packed my bag and locked my office, I had the thought that for the first time in my life, the university felt hostile to me. For years I had been stitched up in the cocoon of academic life, blanketed by the security of tenure. But as I walked through the corridors with their tiled floors and characterless cinder-block walls, I felt the hardness of every surface, the smugness of the cliques of academics in their cozy coffee groups. It was like a giant country club that had just refused me membership. What had once seemed a friendly and liberal environment now seemed elitist, unforgiving, archaic.

I had no intentions of going home. The

thought of hanging around an empty house waiting for Caroline to get back so I could give her my bad news filled me with despair. Instead I cycled up the Dublin Mountains to the Blue Light where I sat with a pint of Guinness and gazed out over the city bathed as it was in a great burst of sunshine that had arrived without warning on this May day.

I was exhausted and on edge. It felt like everything was falling apart. The university had rejected me. My wife was barely speaking to me. I had lost the knack of communicating with my children. And there was this girl — a grandchild my mother never got to know — whom, despite my best efforts and good intentions, I had somehow managed to push away.

There was something else causing me disquiet. A couple of weeks previously, in the aftermath of my disastrous radio interview, I had taken it upon myself to arrange another DNA test — this time a clandestine one, a test that neither Zoe nor anyone else connected to me knew about. Putting her toothbrush into a plastic bag and then stuffing it into a padded envelope along with the completed forms and my own specimen, I had sent it off to the lab in something of a petulant outburst. My anger had compelled me to do it — anger and disappointment over her lies, yes, but if I'm honest with myself, it was rage at my own predicament that led me to it. My life that had once seemed so steady and pleasantly predictable had swung out of my control. Elements beyond me were closing in, boxing me off in a way that I found uncomfortable and limiting. I had sent that test off in a mood of indignation, and it was only afterward that I felt ashamed. Going behind her back like that. Questioning her claim when it had already been proven — it seemed grubby and untoward. It felt beneath me.

Still, I had done it, and managed somehow to put it out of my mind. I hadn't really expected the report to contradict the results of the initial paternity test. But when the letter had arrived earlier that week, I had read the results printed in bold capitals with a sinking heart. It was the worst possible outcome. Not one thing or the other. It did not tell me whether I was or was not Zoe's father. Above a blizzard of qualifiers and small print, the words INCONCLUSIVE glared back at me.

Another test would be necessary, the report said. That and a ream of information on why the results had come back as they had. The toothbrush had not been enough, not for definitive confirmation, at least.

I drank another pint and thought about it. It might not mean anything — she might be my flesh and blood. Still, I felt a creep of something close to shame at the memory of how readily I had opened myself to the idea of her, allowing her into my home, tried to make her a part of my family. Perhaps Caroline was right. Perhaps I should have been more circumspect, more hesitant.

I needed to get away. I needed to sort things out and gain some perspective. A holiday abroad was exactly what was required. I finished my pint and freewheeled home to tell Caroline, but as soon as I came into the hallway and rested my bike against the stairs, I knew all was not well. I heard her through the open kitchen door. She was crying.

"What is it?" I asked, and she looked up from where she sat at the counter, a glass of wine in front of her, tissues scattered on the countertop.

The skin around her nose and upper lip was red as if she had been crying for some time. A lurching feeling came over me. *The children,* I thought. She must have seen the panic in my eye; she shook her head and said, "No, it's not that. They're fine."

My heartbeat calmed a little. I approached

her nervously. Whatever it was, I wasn't sure I had the energy for it. Already, I was assailed by the feeling that I was somehow at the root of her misery.

"It's everything else," she said.

Just saying these words seemed to threaten what little composure she had summoned. Trying to cover it up, she took a deep sip of wine.

"I'm forty-one years old," she said quietly, "and on the surface of it, my life is just fine. I'm married with two wonderful children, a comfortable home, friends. So why is it I feel so utterly useless? So completely expendable?"

*Her job,* I thought. Of course: today was her last day. I heard the bitterness in her voice, as if she had been conducting a kind of accounting of her life, looking over her achievements with a critical eye, withdrawing with disgust at what she had seen.

"I don't seem qualified to do anything. It feels like I'm at the mercy of my husband, a kept woman." She enunciated the words in a way that brought home to me the dangerousness of her mood.

"And my husband hardly even speaks to me. Can barely stand to be in the same room with me, in fact."

"That's not true, Caroline."

"Isn't it? I can't even remember the last time we made love."

I took a seat so that we were facing each other. Her expression was flat and unreadable. She took me in as if I were a stranger.

"I haven't a clue what you're thinking anymore."

It was not acrimonious, the way she said it. It was not an accusation. It was said more out of exhaustion than anything else — a last-straw relinquishment, a reluctant capitulation — and despite my earlier thoughts in the same direction, I felt a growing sense of panic. It felt like she had almost surrendered, and it occurred to me that I had not realized that she had been fighting so strongly, or for so long, for herself or for us.

It may not have been the right time, but I told her then about being turned down for the professorship.

"I'm sorry," she said.

I couldn't help thinking that if I had received the letter with the revised date and time, it may have changed the outcome. I hardly needed to say as much to Caroline. It was as if she could read my mind.

"We have to do something, David. She is pulling us apart. Our family, our marriage. You don't actually think I hurt her, pushed her against a wall like she said?"

"No," I answered truthfully.

"She scares me," she said, taking my hands.

"Scares you?"

"All the lies, all the deception. I really feel she is out to destroy us."

I was going to say something about how strong her words were, but I didn't; a part of me agreed with her.

"We have to do something" she said.

"We will." I wanted to reassure her.

I took my wife's hands to my lips and told her everything was going to be okay. I told her about the idea of getting away during the summer. Alan's offer of the villa in France was a chance to not only get away from the disappointments and confusion of life at home but an opportunity to address, without the obstacle of Zoe's presence and probable intervention, all the marital difficulty we had found ourselves in. Caroline seemed genuinely relieved, and over the coming weeks our discussions returned again and again to France, the tickets and travel, the villa itself and what would be, we hoped, a holiday to reconcile our differences, a chance to heal, a holiday to remember.

And all the while we talked about it, I felt, beneath my excitement, the undercurrent of uncertainty. A month had passed since Zoe had left and in that time I had not heard a word from her — not a phone call or a text, let alone a meeting. I began to realize, with a sadness I had to keep hidden, that I had lost her. And whenever the realization crept over me, another thought would surface: *Perhaps she isn't my daughter.* I had kept the inconclusive test results to myself, and, even though I told myself they didn't prove anything, secretly they bothered me. From time to time, I thought about telling Caroline. But as the days slipped toward summer and our holiday grew close, I kept the information to myself, protecting her, or so I believed. Reasoning with myself that it didn't change anything and what harm could it possibly do to keep it from her?

# PART 3

# CHAPTER 19
## CAROLINE

The sun was beginning its splendid descent when we crossed the long stretch of bridge to Île de Ré. We had journeyed overnight by ferry to Cherbourg and spent the day in the car making our way steadily south. By the time we reached the island and found the village of Loix, the air had grown cooler and the sky was starting to pink. The house lay on the outskirts of the village, tucked down a small alleyway too narrow for the car to navigate, so we parked by a square, each of us taking a piece of luggage, and walked the rest of the way.

The villa, like its neighbors, was low and squat, with whitewashed walls, a terra-cotta roof, and olive-green shutters closed over the windows. A six-foot-high perimeter wall masked it from view, but once through the wrought-iron gates, we found ourselves in a pretty courtyard lined with bursts of lavender. A heavy burden of tangled clematis hung low over the front door. The humble exterior masked a warren-like tumble of rooms, and narrow, twisting staircases rose to hidden bedrooms tucked away in the attic. The floors were covered with slate tiles and it was a relief to kick off my shoes and feel the welcome coolness beneath the soles of my hot feet. Robbie and Holly, having dumped their bags at the door, had gone ahead of us, and I could hear the excitement in their voices at each new discovery.

"Mum! Come out here — quick!" I heard Robbie call, and I followed his voice through the now-dark kitchen and living room, out through a set of French windows to a garden at the back with yew and olive trees. A limestone terrace glowed in the half-light. In the midst of it all was a pool — long and narrow, a little wider than a lap pool, the water appearing purple-gray in the dusky light.

"You didn't say there'd be a pool," I said to David, coming to stand next to him.

"I thought I'd surprise you," he replied, looking genuinely pleased. It was the first sign of real delight he'd shown in months.

"I'm going for a swim," Robbie said.

"Isn't it a bit late for that?" I called after him as he hurried back to the house. "Let him," David said. I felt his arm go around my shoulders, drawing me to him. Tentatively, I put mine around his waist. I couldn't remember the last time we had stood together like that.

Holly had taken off her shoes and was sitting at the edge of the pool, her feet dangling down into the cool water. Behind her, the grass grew in long dry clumps, feathery flowers peeking through. I could hear the low hum of nocturnal insects rising around us, and from one of the neighboring houses someone's laughter rang out.

"So what do you think?" David nodded back at the house.

I thought of the cool peace within those rooms. Was he asking if I thought that here was a place where we might reconcile? Within the confines of this island, might we find some kind of healing after the difficult months we had endured? Perhaps it was the relief of arrival after a long journey or the unfamiliarity of his body against mine, but I felt an answering optimism in my heart.

"It's perfect," I told him.

Just then Robbie came running past and launched himself into the air, his hands clutching his knees to his chest. We watched as he plunged into the water, Holly shrieking and turning aside to avoid being splashed. I remember thinking I must freeze this memory in my mind and hold on to it: the beauty of the garden, the coolness of twilight after a long journey, the weight and warmth of my husband's arm around me, and the rocking waters of the pool as my son surfaced, gasping for air, laughing, triumphant.

The first night, we wandered out into the quiet village square and ate outside a bistro while men played boules on the red clay beside the church. By the time we got back to the house it was late and we were all exhausted after the journey. We said our good nights and it was not until the next morning that I had a chance to explore the house properly. David and the kids had gone out to the market to buy some provisions, while I was left alone to wander through the quiet rooms, accustoming myself to the particular sounds and odors they held.

There was a masculine feel to the place — the furniture dark, although comfortable enough. The walls were hung with framed maps of the island and various sepia-tinted photographs — studio portraits of Victorian women with strong jaws and crinolines; mustached men with books lying open on their knees. Indeed, there were books everywhere in the house — stacked in piles behind doors, towers of them leaning against walls. I imagined Alan sitting here alone in the long stretch of the evening, sipping a glass of wine and getting lost in his reading, not noticing the hours ticking by. I was surprised at his gesture of kindness, offering us the use of his holiday home in the wake of David's disappointment.

We hadn't talked much about David's failure to gain the professorship — he was reluctant too to discuss the difficulties in our marriage or the death of his mother — but I knew that it had affected him deeply. It was more than just a professional disappointment. To him it was an indictment of his whole career.

"You'll get another chance," I had told him. "There'll be other opportunities."

"That's just it," he had said, looking at me in a despairing way. "There won't be."

He had always tended toward seriousness, but when we were first married, he would sometimes catch himself in conversation becoming morose or pessimistic and pull the corners of his mouth down into a cartoon face of misery that made me laugh. Just like that, his mood would lift. Somewhere along the way he had lost the knack of finding the humor in things.

As for me, I was still smarting at Peter's parting words: "I need someone who's at the top of her game, not distracted by her domestic situation."

Standing in the darkened living room, running my finger over the gilded titles of those old books, I considered our professional humiliations and the injured pride that went hand in hand with them. I thought about the chasm that had sprung up between David and me over the past six months. I could blame a lot of it on Zoe, but the truth is the first fissure had appeared long before that, back to the first time I'd kissed Aidan, or when I'd stood in a darkened hallway and listened as my husband named another woman as the love of his life. Perhaps it went farther back to the ghost of a baby in my womb. That fissure had been there a long time, but how easily Zoe had caused it to widen and deepen, ripping through our whole family, pushing us apart. I looked around the room and felt the strain of my hope that in this house we might find some solace, a renewal of love. I hoped that here we might find a way back to each other.

The sound of the iron gate jangling on its hinges pulled me back into the present. At once the cloistered atmosphere in the house changed as the others came in, bringing with them the energy of the marketplace, the triumph of their purchases. There was a flurry of activity as bags were emptied, contents spread over the table.

"Hungry?" David asked me, holding up a bag of pastries, the brown paper translucent with grease.

"Famished."

Those first few days, I remember in a haze of lightness, like shrugging off your winter clothes and stepping into the sun. We hired bikes and cycled across the salt flats, along the coastal paths. We went to Saint-Martin-de-Ré and marveled at the wealth of pleasure boats and yachts clustered in the harbor. On our way back to Loix, we discovered an oyster bar with an ocean view and spent a couple of hours there under the shade of parasols, feasting on seafood, David and I getting nicely sozzled on a chilled bottle of Chinon. The village itself hadn't much to offer by way of entertainment — a café by the market, a bistro and a bar on the village square — but it didn't bother us. We were content to spend our days on the beach, our evenings dining on the terrace, reading our books as the sun set.

The kinks and bruises of the past few

months faded a little more with each passing day. The tension that had stiffened David's shoulders dissipated, and he grew relaxed, cheerful, whistling to himself in the mornings as he made coffee, his face animated. Robbie started talking to me again, his exams completed without incident, the trouble at school behind us, as too was the fear I had felt for Holly's security and well-being. The village, and the island, felt small, intimate, safe. The kids were able to wander off on their own, exploring the area on their bikes, while David and I relaxed by the pool or took a stroll down to the seafront.

Toward the end of our first week, David and I were sitting on the terrace eating lunch when his phone buzzed. Shading the screen from the sun with his cupped hand, he said, "A missed call."

"Who from?"

"Zoe."

I reached for my glass.

Since our departure from Ireland, her name hadn't once been mentioned: an unspoken rule among the four of us — a rule that even Robbie adhered to. We needed to get away from her, if only for a short while.

"Are you going to call her back?"

He began pressing keys with his thumb,

then seemed to think better of it.

"No. If it's urgent, she'll try again."

Putting the phone down, he reached for the bottle.

Later, we sat in a companionable silence, reading our books and finishing the wine. The afternoon stretched out long and lazy and there was no sign of the kids returning. I thought about walking down to the harbor, but when I suggested it to David, a slow smile spread across his face.

"I've a better idea," he said.

The house was caught in the white glow of the afternoon sunlight, stillness and quiet filling the rooms. In our bedroom, we undressed with the shyness of new lovers. It had been months since we had made love and we were nervous, despite a long history of intimacy and the loosening of inhibitions brought on by the lunchtime wine. In the quiet hum of the late afternoon, as our bodies came together, I felt an enormous sense of relief. We held each other beneath the sheets, moving toward a new understanding of each other, another layer of meaning added to the complexities of our bond.

We were dressed by the time the kids returned, tiredness making them silent as they slumped in the armchairs, their faces glowing from the sunlight absorbed, Robbie's arms tanned against the white of his T-shirt.

"There are pizzas in the freezer," David told them. "Your mother and I are going out."

We set off hand in hand, still feeling the heat of our afternoon reunion. Something had sparked to life between us, passion rekindled. As we walked through the deserted streets, the noises of domesticity trickled out from open windows — the sounds of saucepans clattering, voices raised in talk. His hand in mine, I basked in the renewed familiarity of it. Warmth from the sun still hovered in the air as we reached the dusty square and took our seats at one of the tables outside the bistro.

I ordered *moules frites* while David had steak, and with a bottle of Sauvignon Blanc in an ice bucket between us, we talked of the village and of Alan's house, speculating as to how he had come to own it. Property on the island was phenomenally expensive — when we had peered through the window of a local estate agent, we had come away reeling. Conversation flowed easily between us. David voiced his opinion that Alan had inherited his house, and this led to a discussion about Ellen, David confiding his sense of loneliness in the wake of her death, the sense that with his parents no longer alive, and no siblings, he had been cast adrift.

"You're not alone," I assured him, and he reached across the table, placing his hand on mine.

"Being away like this," he said, "it's made me wonder whether I should look into taking a sabbatical abroad, maybe take Giancarlo up on his offer to do some research in Sienna."

"Are you serious?"

He shrugged. "Why not? After Mum . . . I need something to clear my head, take a break from UCD for a while."

"What about the kids? What about school?"

"Robbie's got three years left until he finishes — there's time enough before he needs to start thinking about exams and university. Holly's still in primary school. Now might be the perfect time for us to go." He had finished his steak and pushed his plate to one side.

With the wine in my bloodstream and the heat of the sun still in my bones, the idea made me giddy with excitement.

"Won't it take time to organize?"

"I'm sure I could square it with the university. We could be out there by Christmas. And it doesn't have to be for a whole year. Six months would do, don't you think?"

Six months in Italy sounded like a dream.

We leaned toward each other, talking excitedly about what would need to happen — arrangements with the school, perhaps renting out our house. It was all fantasy really, and I think we both knew that. But for just a short while, it was good to imagine that we could unfetter ourselves from those things that held us down.

It was dark in the square as David signaled for the bill. Strings of brightly colored lights reached across the boughs of the plane trees forming the perimeter. A hush had come over the gathered diners.

"What about Zoe?" I asked quietly. Even mentioning her name felt like a gamble. Our afternoon reunion, the flow of conversation between us, the warmth that had returned — it was still tentative.

He looked down at the receipt in his hand, folded it in half, and pushed it into his shirt pocket along with his wallet.

"I think she'll manage."

His voice sounded heavy and I knew that it was not just tiredness. He sat back, casting his eyes upward at the lights looping through the trees.

"I just thought it would be easier. It didn't seem like such a big thing to have her in our lives. Pretty naive, huh?"

I waited for him to go on.

"It's not like having a child you've known from birth. I just don't feel like I'm ever really going to get to know her."

"You've tried hard."

"And I'll continue to try. It's just that . . ."

"What?"

He seemed a little sad in the half-light, a look of defeat coming over him.

"I'm here for her if she needs me, but she has to forge her own path."

Hope bloomed in my heart. Words I had longed to hear.

"This thing with Chris . . ."

"It's a fling. She's nineteen. You have to allow for these things." I didn't say what I really thought: that her relationship with Chris was calculated to get at us.

"I suppose."

"Wait and see. By the time we get home to Dublin, it will probably be over between them."

A chill had entered the air as we stepped away from the square, David's arm around me. Buildings appeared chalky blue in the moonlight. We talked a little of our plans for the next few days. David wanted to visit some of the beaches on the south of the island where bunkers built by the Germans in the Second World War still existed. I had promised Holly a shopping trip to La Rochelle. Tired but content, we returned to the house, closing the gate behind us and crossing the courtyard.

As soon as I opened the front door, I felt a change. The house seemed alive in a different way — the air spiked with a new presence. David behind me, I pushed open the door to the living room and saw Robbie sitting with his arms crossed over his chest, his face dark and unreadable. Movement in the kitchen caught the corner of my eye, but before I could turn to look there, Chris was getting out of the other armchair, his face a mixture of hope and apology.

"What are you doing here?" I asked. He had been crossing the room to greet me, but the abruptness of my question made him stop.

"Caroline, Dave," he said, "I know this is a surprise, calling on you unannounced . . ."

He had a glass of wine, which he was passing from one hand to the other as if unsure of what to do with it. He put it down on the coffee table. Then, straightening up, he addressed us with a smile.

"We wanted to surprise you, didn't we, babe?"

She was almost at my elbow by the time I realized she was there. Wearing a sleeveless short blue dress and orange flip-flops on her lightly tanned feet, I was struck all over again by how slight she was. Without the boots, her winter armor, she seemed even more insubstantial, like a twig that might snap in a brisk breeze.

"It's my fault," she said, the corner of her mouth pulling into a smile, but her eyes were watchful, moving from me to David. "We were in Paris, you see, and I knew you guys were here. Chris said we should ring but I preferred to tell you in person."

She stepped past me toward Chris. I felt David close behind me but couldn't see his face. I was too caught up with these new arrivals. Her new way of dressing made her look younger rather than older. Next to her, Chris was like some trendy uncle. He was sporting new clothes too, clearly aiming for a look that was youthful and flashy. He'd had his hair cut differently — there was a sort of mussed artfulness about it.

"Are you sure it's all right?" Zoe asked, assuming a worried expression. "It's a bit cheeky, I know, turning up out of the blue. It seemed like such a good idea at the time, but then, when we were driving over the bridge, it suddenly felt like a mistake."

"You're welcome here," I told her, thinking of the times before when I had uttered the same hollow statements. Gestures of hospitality, but they were empty of any truth. David said nothing at all.

"You see?" Chris told her, putting his arm around her, smiling with reassurance. "Didn't I tell you it'd be okay?" Then to me: "She worries about everything."

Oh please, I thought. Give me a break.

It was nauseating to watch him clutch her to his side, beaming down at her. How could she stand it? The suffocating benevolence. I had a glimpse of what it was like between them — the way he lavished her with attention, his cloying affection, Zoe enduring it with a patient smile. She looked up at him then and her expression changed, the two of them giggling. There was something shifty about it, as if they were sharing a joke that I wasn't in on.

"What?" I asked. "What's happened?"

They exchanged a look, then Zoe reached for a bag on the table and pulled out a bottle of champagne.

"We brought this," she said, and offered it to me.

I can still remember it, his hand on her

shoulder, her almond-colored skin beneath the reddened tips of his fingers, my eyes traveling the length of her arm to the orange label on the green bottle, the stones in her ring catching the light.

"Oh my God," I said out loud.

I didn't turn to David, not wanting to see the slow shock that was surely coming over his face. Instead, I kept my eyes fixed on her brackish green eyes, gleaming with excitement. Excitement, not nerves, for while Chris was sweating a little under the room's low ceiling, she betrayed no anxiety. I thought again of when I had first met her — how nerveless she had seemed. She held out her hand to us — a queenly gesture — presenting us with her ring as if inviting us to come forward and kiss it.

Robbie shifted on the couch.

"I don't believe it," I said.

"It's true," Chris said, pulling her close to him, the two of them laughing as he kissed the side of her face.

It was only then that I looked at David.

I suppose there is a latent violence in all of us. It lies there in the dark folds inside us, waiting for the conditions outside and beyond us to draw it out into the light. David is a man who goes quiet when enraged, his mood darkening. His anger internalized, he silently broods.

But when I turned to him that night, when I saw him take a step forward, I was sure — for just that brief moment — that there was violence in his mind. It was in his hands, clenched at his sides, in the wild light in his eyes. The room had grown hot, but a coldness passed over my neck and shoulders like a sudden chill breeze. Even now, after all that's happened, that memory refuses to be erased. The weight and coldness of that bottle of champagne in my hand, and the look on David's face as if he wants to kill them. And in that sharp instant, I see that he could.

# Chapter 20
## David

My working life has been the study of days — days and events. The marking of Time. But here's the thing: I have never really felt what it must be like to wake on the morning of one of these historic events, either big or small. I've paused to consider the leaders of the Easter Rising sitting in their cells as dawn broke on the day of their executions, but I've never *felt* it. In the same way I've never experienced the stomach-clenching fear of the trenches in World War I or the sickening shock of a pilot knowing his plane has been hit. I've read about these emotions in the dry pages of books without ever having to experience them myself. Perhaps that is what I have been lacking all along — the peculiar empathy required to truly understand the past.

But I felt it that day — the last day. The portent of something in the air. I felt it from the moment I woke.

It announced itself as a heaviness in the air, like oppressive heat before a storm. Although when I flung wide the shutters, the sky beyond was a brilliant blue, not a cloud in sight. There was a smell like smoke mingled with gasoline — it was distant but I could catch the acrid tinge of it in my nostrils. The bed was empty, Caroline having left it hours before, but I had lain there, trapped within this uneasy heat. Something felt wrong. Sure, I was a little hungover, still fuming from the night before, but this was something else. I am not a superstitious man. I don't believe in signs or foreshadowing, none of that claptrap. But when I consider all that happened that day, and remember how I felt upon waking, it makes me wonder.

I threw on some clothes, my mouth tacky and dry, and stepped into the hallway. It was quiet, heat lurking in the darkened corners of the house, a murmur of unease running through my thoughts like a whispered complaint I could not shake. The door to the kids' bedroom was ajar and I pushed it open, stuck my head inside. Holly's bed was empty, but Robbie was sprawled on his, forearms flung over his head against the pillow.

"Morning, son," I said, and his eyes,

which were open and staring at the ceiling, flicked in my direction.

"Hey."

"Sleep okay?"

"No," he said, pointedly.

This was a reference to his indignation the night before at having to vacate his room and bunk in with his sister in order to provide our unexpected guests with a bed for the night. His reaction when the arrangements were being hastily made had been spluttering and incandescent and his anger still burned albeit at a lesser flame.

"Thanks, Robbie. For giving up your room."

"It's not like I had a choice."

"Well, none of us knew they were coming."

"It's a joke," he said, one that he clearly didn't find funny.

"I agree."

Propping himself up on his elbows, his brow darkening with anger, he went on. "I can't believe she's engaged to that twat! I know he's your friend and all, but come on, Dad, he's ancient!"

I felt some crust lodged in the corner of my eye and wiped it away.

"It's bullshit," he added and I agreed. It was bullshit.

"Can't you talk to them?" he asked. "Make them call it off?"

"I can't make them do anything," I said, laughing a little. There was something child-like and innocent in the way he still thought I had the power to affect that kind of change. I wondered too why he was so upset about it.

I muttered something about needing a coffee and started turning away. Briefly, he called me back. "Happy Birthday, by the way," he said.

July 8 — the day of the birthdays. It was something that marked us out as unique, I always thought, this shared event. What are the odds of a daughter being born on her father's birthday? In the twelve years I had shared the date with Holly, certain traditions had sprung up around it. One of them — perhaps my favorite — was the birthday hug, a long, squeezing clench like a physical acknowledgment of our special bond. With this in mind, I went downstairs in search of her.

As I reached the bottom step, I heard voices in the kitchen and lingered for a moment, listening.

"I think it's ridiculous, Chris, to be honest," I heard Caroline say.

She was clattering around, busying herself with some kitchen task, and I heard the lightness of Chris's laughter above her industry.

"I'm in love! Aren't I allowed behave foolishly?"

"You're in love," she muttered, a little exasperated. "And it's not the age gap that bothers me, you know that, right?"

"What is it then?"

"Have you seen her arms, Chris?"

He made a kind of tutting sound, clearly unimpressed, but Caroline was not to be silenced.

"You know she tried to kill herself at Christmas."

"Yes, I know." His voice dipped. "We've talked about all that. I believe I can help her. I'm good for her —"

"For God's sake, you're only out of a marriage five minutes! Now you want to nose-dive into another one? With *her*?"

"You don't like her," he said with the smugness of his own certainty. "That's what's really the issue."

I heard the dull slap of something flung onto the counter.

"I'm not sure you've really thought about what it is you're taking on." Caroline's tone had changed, caution tempering her forthright words.

Still standing in the narrow hallway, my eye caught a flash of movement beyond the French doors leading onto the patio. I saw the splash of water, an arm raised and then disappearing again, as Holly did her laps of the pool. I could have gone outside, joined her there, turned my back on the low-grade argument rumbling in the kitchen. But I didn't.

Chris was at the table, his iPad in front of him. "Here he is," he said. "The birthday boy," but there was forced jolliness in his tone.

"Happy Birthday, love," Caroline said with warm affection, briefly forgetting her annoyance with Chris as she came and put her hands on my chest, reaching up to kiss me.

"Thanks. Any coffee going?"

"I was going to bring you breakfast in bed."

It was clear she had been to market already, the counters and tabletop littered with her purchases. I picked a croissant from the plate and Caroline poured me a cup while I took a seat opposite Chris. He eyed me warily. My mood the night before, my reaction to his preposterous announcement, made him unsure of me. No doubt he hoped that having slept on it, I'd have mellowed. He hoped wrong.

"So how old are you now? Forty-two, forty-three?"

"Forty-four."

He whistled.

"I don't know why you're so smug. You're only a few weeks shy of it."

"Forty is the new thirty," he declared, determined to be sunny in the face of my terseness.

"Does that make nineteen the new nine?" Caroline asked.

"Touché," he replied, but his smirk seemed to sag a little. I had an urge to lean across the table and slap the stupid grin off his face.

"When are you leaving?" I asked, not caring that it was rude. I wanted him gone, even if that meant Zoe leaving, and I didn't care that he was stung.

"Actually," Caroline said, pausing in her slicing of melon. "There's a bit of a problem."

"What?" Her eyes were fixed on me and I could sense she was reluctant to break the news.

"There's been an accident on the bridge."

"What sort of accident?"

She put down the knife, wiping her hands

on a tea towel.

"An oil tanker crashed into the toll booths early this morning."

*"What?"*

I could hardly believe it, and yet I had smelled the smoke from the moment I woke up, even here at the far side of the island from the bridge.

"They told me when I was at the market. There's a massive fire. No cars can come on or off the island."

"Here," Chris said, offering me his iPad, which was opened on a French news page. "My French is shit but from what I can gather, they've sent in fire brigades from La Rochelle."

I scrolled through the images of smoke billowing from the inferno, the long bridge snaking across to the mainland.

"How the hell did it happen?"

"Who knows?" Caroline said, returning to her task.

"Maybe the brakes failed?" Chris offered. "Or it could be a terrorist attack."

"On Île de Ré? Hardly an obvious target." The notion was absurd.

"Either way," Caroline said, setting the bowl on the table with a sharp clink, "there's no way off the island. Not today. Maybe not for a few days."

She did not sound happy.

"I know it's not ideal," Chris said, coming over all reasonable, "but let's try to make the best of it, hmm?" Caroline cast him a doubtful look but he went on. "Zoe so badly wanted to come here, to tell you our news in person. If you had seen how excited she was, how insistent on sharing this with you. . . . Can't you please try to be happy for us? For her, if not for me?"

He went on a bit about how much we all meant to him and Zoe, but I had no interest in listening to the fairy tale he was peddling.

"What about Susannah?" I asked.

He leaned forward and took a strawberry from the bowl, popped it in his mouth.

"What about her?"

"Does she know about your engagement?"

"I haven't told her yet . . ."

"Chris," Caroline interjected.

"And I'd thank you not to tell her either," he added.

Caroline was nonplussed. "I don't get it," she said. "On the one hand, you're all lovey-dovey, buying rings, making your big announcement, and yet you are trying to hush it up?"

"I want to tell Susannah to her face, not over the phone."

That was a cop-out and we all knew it. I said, "Your divorce could take years to come through. Why couldn't you have waited? Getting engaged while you are still married, it's not right."

Before he could answer, Caroline said, "She's not pregnant, is she?"

It hadn't occurred to me, but now that she said it, it seemed so startling and obvious, I was almost breathless.

Chris stared at her, injury settling on his face.

"No, she's not."

Caroline put a hand to her chest, her relief instantaneous, then reached out to touch his shoulder.

"Sorry. No really, I am sorry — that was crass. I don't know why I said that."

"Is that really what you think? That the only possible reason Zoe and I might want to marry each other is because of an unplanned pregnancy?"

Neither of us said anything. The truth was their relationship confounded us both. For my part, I believed he was in the throes of some kind of midlife crisis. There was something sordid and desperate about the way he had leeched onto Zoe. Caroline's thoughts, when she voiced them, tended toward a darker, more conspiratorial theory.

She believed Zoe was using Chris as part of some game. The words I recall her using were *getting her tentacles into every area of our lives; not even our friends are safe.* I dismissed this theory, but the suspicion remained written all over Caroline's face. If Chris saw it too, he didn't say.

"For years I have been sleepwalking through my life," he told us. "But with Zoe, I can feel the blood rushing through my veins. The divorce might take a while. It's Ireland after all, but once it's done, Zoe has agreed to marry me."

I couldn't listen to any more. Standing up, I announced I was going to find Holly. As I left the kitchen, passing through the hall toward the patio doors, I heard Caroline say in a low voice, "You see how upset he is? You guys being here is the last thing he needs. His mother just died, for God's sake."

I don't know how Chris responded, whether he nodded his head sheepishly or mumbled a reply. All I heard was Caroline's voice, her instructional no-nonsense tone. "As soon as the bridge reopens, both of you need to leave."

It was mid-morning and sunlight was making progress across the back wall of the garden, throwing long shadows from the yew tree onto the terrace below. The pool was half in shade. I stood at one end where Holly's towel was neatly folded and placed on the ground, her glasses sitting on top, and waited for her to finish her lap. She stroked evenly through the water, touching the end and squinting up at me.

"Hey there, Birthday Buddy," I said, smiling down at her.

"Hi, Dad."

She made no move to get out, just stayed there swishing around.

"What's it feel like to be twelve?"

"It's okay," she said, impervious to my attempts at good humor. "Did Mum tell you about the bridge?"

"She did."

"It means we can't go to La Rochelle."

"I know, sweetheart. We'll do something else instead."

"Okay."

Her heart had been set on a day in the city. Caroline had promised to take her shopping and we were going to have lunch, the four of us, in a swanky restaurant. In the wake of Holly's disappointment, she was entitled to have a little sulk.

"Your mum's been to the market. She's bought all manner of things. We're going to have quite the birthday feast."

Taking her glasses from her towel, she put them on and said, "I suppose *she'll* be there."

"I expect she will be," I said gently, "and Chris too." I wanted to be sensitive to her mood but needed to be firm about it too. It wasn't as if I was thrilled at the prospect.

"Mum hates her," Holly said. The words struck me like a physical object.

"That's a bit strong."

"It's true," she said plainly. "I do too."

The blankness of her voice, the way she said the words so tonelessly, with such sincerity — it was chilling.

I didn't say anything, just watched as she put her palms down on the poolside terrace and pulled herself up out of the water. She reached for her towel and began shaking it out while I got over my shock. She was still my little girl. I opened out my arms to her and said, "Birthday hug?"

"I'm all wet, Dad," she told me, turning away so she could dry herself off.

The sun was hitting the water behind her, the shimmering light blinding. I could see her body silhouetted against it and noticed with sad surprise the buds of new breasts beneath her swimsuit. This change in her coupled with her dismissal of my embrace tugged sharply at my emotions, and I felt the shock of imminent tears. This was my first birthday without my mother. Somehow, Holly's coldness and the understanding that she was shutting down the physical affection between us — a natural side effect of adolescence, I knew, but still — these drew my grief out in a new and unexpected way. The light bouncing off the pool made my head hurt. The heaviness I had felt in the air when I first awoke no longer seemed atmospheric. Rather, it had moved inside my head — an inner pressure pushing outward against the boundary of my skull.

Holly went back inside, and I stood there, feeling wobbly, an unbidden thought entering my brain: *What if Linda had told me?* A dangerous thought. It conjured up images of a different life, a different holiday, a different wife — Linda in the kitchen now chopping fruit rather than Caroline. A blond-haired version of Holly going indoors to dry off, a different son lounging upstairs in bed. And Zoe — how differently might she have turned out had her natural parents stayed together? Might she have been less mercurial, more grounded and together? In that scenario, I had no doubt the insides of her arms would be free of scars, and there would be no middle-aged man sharing her bed.

And what about me? How different might I have been? I shied away from the thought, uncomfortable at the gnawing doubt it brought on. I slipped back inside, past the kitchen where Caroline was rinsing out a salad. Her back was to me and I noticed the tension in her shoulders, a tightness that had come on overnight. Holly and Chris had both disappeared, and as I climbed the stairs, I felt the quietness of the house all around me.

The door to the children's bedroom was closed and silent. I had the impression that it was empty. Walking past Chris and Zoe's room, I heard low whispering. At least I thought it was whispering. But as I lingered there I realized that what I was hearing was not language but the fluency of movement. A subdued grappling, the tangle of sliding limbs, a moan so hushed and gentle, I almost had to strain to hear it.

Recoiling from their door, I hurried down the corridor to my bedroom, the heaviness bursting in my head. I closed the shutters and lay on my bed for a long time. But though my body was present in the room, my mind was elsewhere. It was back down the corridor, hiding in a corner, scared and watchful in the darkness as they twisted and writhed together.

# Chapter 21
## Caroline

Because of the fire we couldn't leave. Even though we couldn't see leaping flames or billowing plumes of smoke, as the day progressed and news reports told of a growing inferno, the air above us became infused with the smell of it. Our planned day trip to La Rochelle was canceled. I suggested we take the bikes and cycle along the paths that crisscrossed the salt flats leading to Saint-Martin-de-Ré. There were plenty of shops, mainly of the tourist variety, but still, I was hopeful of finding something to please Holly. It bothered me somewhat when the others pounced on my suggestion, Chris and Zoe making a quick run to the marketplace to rent bikes. But it was part of the weirdness of the day, brought on by the haze of smoke, the heavy heat pressing down on us, that it also didn't matter. Torpor suppressed my fear, making me disinterested. It was just one day, I told myself. We could get through it.

We were sitting around on the beach chairs, waiting for David to come downstairs so we could leave, when Chris said, "So July the eighth. What does that make you, Holly — Cancer or Leo?"

"Cancer," she answered quietly.

The sun was rising high in the sky. I wanted David to hurry up.

"What about you, Robbie?" Chris asked, striving against the collective silence.

Robbie didn't have it in him to be conversational that day. He was sitting at the edge of the pool, his feet dangling in the water. Since the lovers' arrival the night before, he had grown sullen, hardly speaking apart from the odd grudging reply. If either Zoe or Chris was aware of his unhappiness, they hid it well, the two of them perched on the beach chair opposite me, Chris's hand resting on her thigh.

"Robbie's a Leo," I answered.

"Like myself," Chris said, leaning over and bumping his fist against Robbie's shoulder, an awkward gesture. "Not that I believe in any of that astrology stuff."

"I don't know," I said. "There are personality traits common between David and Holly."

"That's because they're father and daughter, not because they have the same star sign."

"What about you, Zoe?"

"I'm Pisces."

"What're they like?" I asked, keeping up the veneer of civility. I already knew what she was like.

"Spiritual, intuitive. The chameleons of the zodiac."

"Chameleons?"

"Yes, we're very adaptable. And our inner lives are important to us. Our secrets and dreams."

Her expression was masked by large sunglasses; she could have been staring at me mockingly or it might have been an empty gaze.

"In other words," said Chris, winking at me, "they have a hard time distinguishing fact from fiction."

"We're watery types too," she continued, ignoring the jibe. "Just like Cancers. Which makes us excellent swimmers."

Robbie shot her a sidelong glance. "You can't be a good swimmer just because of your birthday."

His expression, though guarded, seemed quietly furious.

"Our sign is symbolized by fish," she answered coolly.

"So you're a better swimmer than me just because you're a Pisces?"

She smiled sweetly. "One way to find out."

Instantly, Robbie began rising to the challenge.

"No, Robbie," I said. "We need to go."

He was pulling the T-shirt over his head. Zoe looked on with amusement, although there was something mean about her smile.

"Well?" he demanded. Without waiting, he marched to the far end of the pool.

She rose slowly from the beach chair, removing her sunglasses with a deliberate air and placing them carefully on the table. In a single movement, she reached down for the hem of her dress and pulled it up over her head, revealing a small mint-green bikini with orange laces tied at the back of her neck and below each hip.

"Here she goes!" Chris said, watching as she stepped to the water's edge. It was not pride or amusement I heard in his voice, but an unsteadiness of nerves.

I took in the curve of her hip, the crevice running the length of her spine. Shoulder blades pronounced like wings, she was so thin. Her breasts were small but shapely, neatly cupped by the bikini. Narrow thighs, rounded calves tapering down to narrow ankles, and her skin was smooth and lightly tanned, unblemished apart from a large mole the size of a one-euro coin just above her knee.

I was transfixed by the reveal of her body and held by Robbie's expression as she took her place beside him. Bare-chested, his shoulders wide and square, his waist and legs skinny as a boy's, there was something fierce about him, as if the challenge thrown down was more than just a race. They stood at the lip of the pool, the sparkling water a backdrop to their lithe youthful bodies, and I felt a tug of sadness that I couldn't explain or understand.

Robbie was first to break the water. Harnessing the power in those newly widened shoulders, he charged ahead, Zoe's strokes even and patient as she glided in the wake of all that froth and foam. They reached the end, tipped the side, and turned back. Maybe because the heat had sucked the life from my own limbs, I saw that once the first burst of his energy had been used up, Robbie's body began to flag, his strokes becoming more erratic, while Zoe continued calmly. When he reached the end first, he drew himself up, ready to express his triumph, but as she caught up, she simply tipped the lip of the pool, then swerved in the water, kicking off for another lap. The race was not done yet.

He shouted: "Hey!" then plunged after her, messy strokes like an excited puppy. She had found her groove, strong and steady. She swam with confidence, never looking back to check his progress, her face turning in the water, her mouth an "o" taking in air, clearly in control as she tipped the end and turned back for the final lap.

Reaching the finish, she didn't pause to raise her arms in triumph, nor did she look back. Instead, she pulled herself up out of the pool, wringing out her hair, her face expressionless.

"I won that!" Robbie shouted when he reached the end. Standing in the water, he thrashed the surface with his hands in frustration. "You never said two laps!"

She turned back to the edge of the pool, gazing down at him, towering and imperious. And I watched my son looking up at this girl, the wet bikini gripping her breasts, the outline of two sharp nipples, water dripping from the ends of her hair and between her legs. There was another challenge in the way she stood looking down at him, this one different from the last. Her face was lost from view, but I saw his — the expression changing from outrage to something softer, more secret. He kept looking up at her. I watched as his hand emerged from the water. He was reaching out to clasp her ankle.

I don't know what it was he had in mind, but something within me reared up, seized by a cold revulsion. Don't touch her, I thought. Please don't.

She took a step backward and his hand fell down into the water. Turning from us, she stalked past, toward the house. Robbie launched back into the water, swimming away from us and from his own humiliation. David emerged onto the terrace.

"Everyone ready?" he asked.

Chris ran a hand through his hair, momentarily undecided, before he followed Zoe back into the house.

"What?" David asked, but I didn't answer.

I was thinking about the fire burning away at the other side of the island, making prisoners of us. On the limestone terrace Zoe's dark wet footprints were fading beneath the sun.

We cycled in a row along the narrow white path, through the dead heat. We crossed swamps and marshes, the water glittering through the reeds and grasses. The wetlands, usually straining with life, were unusually quiet, no swish of tails in the water, no sudden flap of wings. As we neared Saint Martin, the smell of smoke changed, became textured with the tang of burning rubber.

We stopped for lunch at the oyster bar and sat with glasses sweating in the heat. It was after midday, but the temperature was still rising. We ate in silence, the food vaguely flavored with smoke. To us, looking out at the haze of blue sea and sky, the horizon appeared shimmery and indistinct. The wine had a soporific effect on the men, and both of them began to voice reluctance to travel any farther, content to sit in uneasy silence gazing at the ocean. Robbie remained locked within the grim confines of his defeat. And so it was that our group split along the gender divide after lunch, as Holly, Zoe, and I mounted our bikes and continued on to Saint Martin.

We pedaled the short distance to the town, locked our bikes at the marina, and set out on foot through the narrow cobbled streets, Holly going ahead, now and then turning back to be sure we were still behind her. The air felt dry, the alleyways quiet. There was a sleepy feeling in the town, as if everyone else were having a siesta while we trudged through shop after shop.

"Look," Zoe said, holding up a black T-shirt, white lettering emblazoned on one side. SWEETNESS, I WAS ONLY JOKING.

"I'm going to get it," she declared, clearly delighted. "I'll wear it anytime Chris and I have an argument."

I couldn't picture them fighting. The way he fawned over her, Zoe's sulkiness — it seemed an uneven match.

Holly, having picked out a few items of clothing, disappeared into the changing rooms while I went outside to wait. Zoe emerged with her purchase in an orange plastic bag, and for a few moments we stood alongside each other on the cobbled street in the shade thrown by the awning overhead.

After all that had happened between us, small talk seemed impossible. She had a way of standing still, her face impassive, as though she were waiting for me to say something, do something, an expectancy that I found troubling. She was twisting the ring on her finger — a trio of diamonds clustered on a white-gold band. It was an old ring, purchased in the Clignancourt markets outside Paris, they had told us, and both the size and the setting of the stones bore the veneer of age. It was not a delicate ring — the diamonds looked heavy on her slender finger — a ring more suited to a woman in her thirties or forties.

It was the first time we had been alone

together since the announcement of their engagement and, I suppose, with the incident at the pool this morning still troubling me, on top of what I already understood of her fickle nature, I couldn't help but wonder whether she was serious about it or whether the marriage proposal and her acceptance were just another move in her elaborate game.

"Have you told your adoptive parents about your engagement yet?" I asked, thinking about Celine Harte, imagining her hooded eyes growing fractionally heavier at the weight of this news.

"No." She let go of her ring and looked around distractedly. "They'll go nuts when they find out."

"Oh?"

"When they hear I'm marrying a divorced man, they'll hit the roof. Not that I care what they think," she added petulantly.

She leaned back against the window, her arms crossed, the plastic bag hanging from her wrist. I had the impression she was affecting nonchalance.

"You never talk about them," I commented.

"There's nothing to talk about." She shrugged and I felt her shutting down that avenue of conversation.

"What about your friends?" I continued. "Have you told any of them about your engagement?"

"Yeah, I've told a few people. Mostly they didn't believe it."

"I don't suppose there are many married students in your class," I remarked.

"Nope, apart from the mature students."

"It'll be something of a talking point, I imagine."

She shrugged. "For a little while, I guess. Until something else comes along."

"How do you think you'll manage it?"

"What do you mean?"

"What about parties, nights out with your friends? Won't it be strange for you, having a husband or a fiancé that you must return home to instead of staying for the parties, the weekends away, all of that? Won't you find it limiting?"

She twisted the ring around her finger. "Not really. Chris is cool — he doesn't believe that marriage needs to tie us to each other."

"Did he say that?"

"Sure."

I thought of how closely he shadowed her, the way his gaze followed her around the room.

"After all he's been through with Susan-

407

nah," she went on, "he wants things with me to be different — more free and relaxed. She was such a headfuck, constantly making demands of him."

"I think that's a little unfair on Susannah."

"I know she's your friend. But she really did give him a hard time."

"I'm not saying that Susannah is a saint, but I wouldn't say that of Chris either. Marriage is complicated. Things go wrong — unexpected things. We all start off full of hopes and ideals, armed with the notion that our relationship, our marriage, is going to be a success. But no one can see into the future. Things come along to test us. Are you ready for all that?"

She pushed her hair over her shoulder.

"Is that how it was for you?" she asked then.

"Yes," I admitted carefully. "When David and I got married, I believed we had faced our big trial. I was young and naive. We both were."

"And now?"

She had put back on her sunglasses so that I could no longer see her eyes. I remembered her in my kitchen with my phone in her hand, having read Aidan's text message. I remembered Holly at the quarry's edge, the hand reaching out to push her. I remembered all those lies Zoe had told about me, the damage she had inflicted on her own face and then blamed on me, the corrosive way she had come between David and me, and with these memories came a pinch of caution. I already knew she was dangerous to me.

"Now things are good," I said.

A thin smile appeared on her face. Perhaps I imagined it, but it seemed to contain a grain of pity, which confused and angered me. Behind her through the window, I could see Holly returning the clothes she had tried on to their racks.

"One thing, Zoe, before Holly comes out, and please don't take offense."

"What?" she asked.

"I hope you're being careful. That you're taking precautions."

She laughed and shook her head, making a deliberate show of her embarrassment.

"Seriously, though. Getting engaged is one thing. Having a baby is quite another."

She ran her finger over her lower lip, the smile still there.

"You don't want to get caught out —"

"Like you, you mean?"

The venom in her voice was unmistakable. It came at me so suddenly, it took a moment to absorb it. Before I could answer, she spoke again, her voice rising with a little tremor in it. "Or were you referring to my mother?"

The coolness of her anger pooled in the air between us.

"Why would you say such a thing?" I asked. Whenever I was alone with her, her iciness announced itself abruptly, slicing through our conversation like a cold blade.

"Any luck?" she asked brightly as Holly joined us on the street.

"No," she answered.

There were other shops that we tried but the offerings were overpriced, largely just souvenirs. Holly became more despondent as the afternoon wore on and eventually declared that she'd had enough.

"We can go to La Rochelle another day," I said. "Once this fire has burned out and we can escape the island."

"Let's just go home, Mum," she said, turning for the harbor and walking back toward the bikes.

We passed through streets of tall buildings with grand apartment blocks, clipped box-woods and lollipop bay trees standing sentry at the doors, all the while the niggle of Zoe's words worming their way inside me.

*Like you, you mean?*

How did she know? Had David told her? It was something we had never discussed with the children — or with anybody. The fact that he might have shared something so intimate with her — a secret so deeply private — felt like the worst kind of betrayal. And if she knew, had she shared her information with Chris? Or with Robbie? This worry brought a new bloom of anger. When was this girl going to leave us? This was our holiday and the days were petering out — how much longer would we have to tolerate her?

We were nearing the harbor, the air drenched with the smell of salt and smoke and gasoline, when my eye was drawn to the draped folds of silk on a mannequin in a window, and I stopped outside a bridal shop.

"What do you think?" I asked Zoe. "Shall we go in?"

I'm not sure what drove me to do it — a niggle of anger pushing me toward meanness. Her reluctance only spurred me on.

"Come on," I said. "It'll be fun."

After the glare of sunlight on the street outside, we had to wait while our eyes became accustomed to the low-key lighting and plush interiors. The shop assistant, a woman I guessed to be my own age in a smart linen suit, pearls at her throat, came forward all smiles and greetings, switching from French to English once she realized we were not natives.

"Ah, but you are so young!" she remarked gaily when we told her that Zoe was the bride.

She drew us farther into the shop where velvet armchairs clustered in the center of the room, a chandelier twinkling overhead.

"Have you anything particular in mind, *chérie*?" she asked.

Zoe chewed her lip, looking around at the rails of dresses, each gown encased in a zipped clear bag.

"Not really."

The first dress she tried on was a lace gown with a slim silhouette and scalloped neckline, the skirts pooling around her bare feet onto the plush gray carpet. The dress dragged her down, her figure appearing curveless within the crusts of lace that clung to it.

"I have something better," Madame suggested.

"I'm not sure about this," Zoe said quietly, but I said, "Oh come on. It'll be fun!"

The hard kernel of anger was pushing me on; I thought, *Let's play my game now.*

I made her try on five dresses in all, and

with each dress, she became increasingly withdrawn.

The last dress was a delicate thing made of white tulle, cinched at the waist by a band of nude pink satin. Beneath the whispery outer layer was a glimpse of the same pink in silk beneath. Dainty lace appliqués adorned the bodice, which closed like a corset low on the back. Behind her a tiny train spread across the floor of the changing room.

*"Parfait!"* Madame declared. "Look at yourself!" she demanded, turning Zoe toward the mirror. "You are beautiful!"

"You really are," Holly agreed, her voice coming out hushed with awe. Or maybe it was envy.

Zoe stood perfectly still, looking down at the reflection of her feet in the mirror, refusing to take in the full length of her body.

"I want to take it off," she said quietly.

"One final touch," Madame insisted, going to the glass cabinet and removing from it a small tiara twinkling with Swarovski crystals. "Just to complete the picture, yes?"

She fixed the crown carefully into Zoe's hair, which fell around her shoulders in a deluge of curls.

"Such hair!" Madame remarked, oblivious to the brittleness of Zoe's mood or the shadowy look crossing her face.

"There!" Madame announced, exultant, standing back to admire her handiwork. "What a proud man your husband will be!"

I could see that Zoe was close to tears. Her cheerfulness over lunch, the sunshine of the day, her delight at her purchase, all of it had vanished. The weight of each dress soaked down through her, crushing any happiness inside. On the floor, tossed to one side by the mirror, lay the orange plastic bag containing her T-shirt, its youthful sensibility forgotten amid these somber dresses and the onerous responsibilities they symbolized. Beautiful as she was, there remained something ridiculous about her, in the same way that her ring was ridiculous — a little girl dressing up in her mother's clothes. She had no intention of going through with the marriage — she never had. I knew it now.

"Get it off me," she said, growing distressed, reaching behind her to claw at the clasps holding the bodice together.

"Careful with that," Madame said, coming alive to Zoe's fragile state and going forward to assist. I just sat there, held back by the coldness of all she had done, her meddling, her manipulation, the memory of it making me cruel.

The clasps undone, Zoe wrenched herself free of the corset, her breasts, small and wide apart, visible for just an instant. The rings of the curtain sang out as she drew them swiftly across the cubicle rail.

Outside, the heat hung above the streets, the houses, down to the white shore, the boats clinking under the sparkling sun. Nearby on the bridge a fire raged. But in that changing room there was cold.

Madame bent down and picked up the corset, fingering it delicately, the look she gave it bordering on distaste as if it had been sullied by the grubbiness of this exchange. There was no sound apart from the weeping in the cubicle and the clink of the glass cabinet as the tiara was returned.

The rest of the dresses were gathered up with alacrity, Madame saying, "I will put these back if you are finished," anxious to be rid of us.

Sometimes, even now when it is all over, I think I can hear her crying like she did that day in the cubicle. Her weeping echoes up from the corridors of the past, making me stop whatever I am doing. And I think of the straightness of her back as she cycled ahead of me that day, along the track, past the oyster bar as the sun dipped toward the horizon. I see her in my mind's eye cycling away from me, moving toward the evening and all that was to come.

# Chapter 22
## David

It began with a change of plan.

Caroline, agitated from the moment she returned, complained that it was too hot to cook.

"Let's go out to eat instead," I suggested.

I was lying in the semidarkness of our bedroom, waiting for the two ibuprofen I had taken to kick in. Caroline was hastily changing out of her clothes made grimy by the bicycle ride in the heat.

"I can't face going back to Saint Martin," she said.

"Did something happen?" I asked. Something was clearly bothering her.

"I'm just hot," she muttered. "That bloody fire. God knows what kind of toxins we're inhaling."

I got up slowly from the bed, felt the heaviness sucking at the inside of my head like a wet cloth.

"Have you got anything else I can take for

a headache?"

She rummaged in her bag before handing me a packet of white tablets. Normally I scoffed at her homeopathic remedies, but my headache had been building all day, blurring my thoughts and making me feel clammy. It had eased after the lunchtime wine but that was wearing off. "I'll ring the bistro in the village. I'm sure they'll have a table free." I slipped the two pills under my tongue, then went downstairs to make the call.

The house was quiet, bar the sounds of shuffling preparation coming from behind closed doors, the others having retreated to their rooms to dress for dinner. Passing Zoe and Chris's room, I heard him say, "What about the little black number?"

Zoe sounded unhappy: "No. I don't think so."

I didn't linger, haunted by what I had overheard of their lovemaking earlier that day. In the kitchen, Caroline's halfhearted start at dinner sat forlorn and abandoned on the table. I took my phone into the quiet of Alan's study, rang the bistro, and booked a table — indoors, because of the smoke — then I lay down on the couch and closed my eyes.

Caroline's remedy, stronger than I had guessed it might be, pulled me under into a troubled sleep. I was caught in the tangle of a strange dream when I heard someone saying "Dad? *Dad!*" in an urgent tone and felt a pulling at my sleeve. Opening my eyes, I saw Holly gazing anxiously at me behind her glasses. In her hand was a piece of paper.

"What is it?" I asked, pulling myself up into a sitting position, a groggy feeling in my head like I was underwater.

"I found this." She held up the piece of paper, watching me with those big worried eyes.

I saw the blue and white insignia of the letterhead and recognized it immediately. Panic began crawling up my throat.

"Hang on."

"It says 'test results inconclusive,' " she read. She pronounced the words carefully, stressing each vowel, making it sound like a verdict of guilt or a fatal diagnosis.

My thoughts teemed with confusion. I was sure I had left the letter back in my desk at the university.

"Robbie and I were playing Scrabble. We needed a page to keep score. Mum said there was paper here on the desk." She pointed to the old mahogany bureau, a sheaf of my documents in a blue folder alongside some journals and books. The letter from the clinic must have been slipped in among them. I had to act quickly, and carefully.

"Listen, sweetheart, it's not what you think."

"It says she's not our sister."

"That's not what it says —"

"It is —"

"No." Her panic was winding me up when I needed to stay calm. "All it says is that the samples they were given proved insufficient to make a match."

"But she might not be our sister," Holly said, stubbornly holding her position.

"Look, love, Zoe is your sister. I know that for sure."

"How do you know?"

"Because there was another test done, and that one proved a positive match between me and Zoe."

"When did that happen?" she asked.

"Ages ago, love. Back before Christmas."

"But this letter is dated last month."

"I know," I said, my voice rising a little. I was in no fit state for this conversation and wished I had destroyed the damn letter. "At the time, I thought it might be an idea to double-check."

"But why?"

"To be honest, I don't know why. It was

more of a whim than anything else. In hindsight, I realize it was foolish of me."

"You mustn't have believed her," Holly stated shrewdly.

"Look, this test means nothing. The important thing is that there is another test that proves beyond doubt that Zoe is your sister."

"Does Mum know about this?" Holly was still holding the letter. I wanted to take it from her, but the way she was clutching it told me she would not relinquish it easily.

"She knows about the test," I said.

"She does? That it was inconclusive?" Holly sounded disbelieving and rightly so. She knew her mother well.

"I know it looks strange, sweetheart," I said, deflecting her question. "I know it's a fright to come across a document like this, but what you've got to understand is that it is only one result."

"But it's inconclusive. She could be any-one."

"It's very common for these tests to come back inconclusive."

"She doesn't feel like my sister," she told me.

Upstairs, I heard a door opening, a voice on the landing.

"Listen, you have to promise me you will

not tell anyone else."

"Why not?"

"You don't have the full facts, Holly. If you'll let me explain . . ."

"But why a secret . . . that doesn't seem right."

"Please stop calling it a secret," I said as calmly as I could. She sounded a little frantic and my own mind was racing. "It's just that this piece of paper is meaningless in the large scale of things."

As if to prove my point, I took the document from her hands and scrunched it into a ball, tossing it into the fireplace. She followed it with her eyes, her brow creasing with thought.

"Now listen. It's really important that we don't upset everyone by bringing this up." I took hold of her shoulders and brushed the hair from her eyes. As reassuringly as I could, I said, "It's not the time or place, okay?"

She continued to gaze at the ball of paper in the grate.

"You and I can sit down later and have a proper chat about it all, I promise." Outside, I could hear Caroline calling to the others.

"It's our birthday, remember?" I said, trying to chivy her out of her mood.

"Fine," she said, turning toward the door,

but I felt her stubbornness and knew that she hadn't given in. My heart was hammering from the encounter.

"We're all set," Caroline said, startling me. I was so lost in my own catapulting thoughts, I hadn't noticed her head peeking around the door. "Are you ready?"

"Sure," I said, flustered but trying to locate my wallet and phone, and put them in my pockets. It was not until we were outside and halfway down the street that I remembered the letter pressed into a ball and left lying in the grate.

On the stroll down to the village square, Holly and Caroline hung back while the rest of us went on ahead. Zoe, wearing a blue dress and makeup, linked my arm as we walked. We talked a little of the day, of the fire and the smoke, but I kept thinking about Holly trailing behind with Caroline. Once or twice I glanced back, but the narrow streets were darker than usual, the shadow of smoke making the air gloomy. I couldn't tell if they were talking, let alone make out the expressions on their faces.

At the bistro, the tables outside were empty. For once, all the diners were cocooned indoors. Our table was at the back, and we made our way through the crowded room. The noise levels were high beneath the stringed bulbs that swung across the ceiling. The scent of garlic sautéed in butter replaced the smell of smoke. At the next table, a group of young men — all ripped jeans and messy hairstyles — were enjoying a raucous meal. They glanced up at us as we took our seats, Zoe and I sitting alongside each other, our backs to the wall, Robbie and Chris opposite.

Things began to go awry when the others arrived. Holly stared at Zoe. "You can't sit there," she said.

Zoe laughed, confused.

"We sit together," Holly went on. "Me and Dad, on our birthday." Her voice was cold.

"Oh." Zoe began to get up. I put a hand to her arm to stop her.

"Stay where you are, Zoe. Hols, why don't you sit here?" I indicated the seat next to me at the top of the table. "That way you'll still be next to me."

A frown came over Holly's face.

"It's not the same," she said quietly.

"Sorry, Zoe," Caroline intervened firmly. "A family tradition, you understand."

"Of course," she said, getting to her feet, a little flustered.

"Here, come sit by me," Chris offered, patting the seat at the bottom of the table, but Caroline had already put her scarf on the back of it.

"Caroline's sitting there," Zoe said in a flat voice, rounding the table to take the seat at the top of the table. One of the guys at the next table glanced over.

Holly sat against me. Despite her small triumph, she did not look pleased.

"How about some champagne?" Chris suggested, seeking to lift the mood.

He ordered a bottle of Veuve Clicquot and I wondered, briefly, whether he was planning to pay for it. Diamond rings, a foreign holiday, eating out — did Susannah know about this? And would she ultimately be footing the bill for Chris's generosity? The champagne, however, was a welcome distraction, all that faffing around with corks and glasses, drawing attention away from Holly's brittle mood, Zoe's obvious hurt.

"Can I have some?" Robbie asked me.

"Go on then. Just this once."

We raised our glasses to the birthdays and turned our attention to the menu. There was some commotion as our orders were given and baskets of bread arrived, a collective hunger voicing itself in the clatter of cutlery. I wish I could say that I became relaxed, that my fear over Holly's new knowledge subsided, that the evening passed off peacefully, but that was not the case. The first signal that Holly was not going to let the matter go came when Zoe presented her half sister with a birthday gift.

"I hope you like it," she said, handing her a small gray box wrapped in a pink diaphanous ribbon, a sprig of dried flowers caught in the bow.

"Oh, thanks," Holly said stiffly.

Inside the box was a bracelet — little shards of colored glass strung together, a delicate thing in shades of lilac and purple.

"I found it in a little shop near the harbor in Saint Martin, when you weren't looking."

An uncomfortable silence stretched across the table. I felt a pinch of annoyance at Holly's rudeness, thought I knew where her behavior was coming from.

"Say thank you," I said in a forceful whisper.

Defiance in her eyes. For the briefest of moments, I wasn't sure what she was going to do.

"Thank you," she said, glancing across at Zoe. "You really shouldn't have gone to the trouble."

"No trouble." Zoe's voice had become small. After a moment, she drained her glass and sat back, casting her gaze around the restaurant. One of the guys at the next table

— the same guy as before — looked over. The incident with the bracelet had disappointed her, I could see. The little box sat forlornly on its side, halfway beneath the breadbasket.

Our food arrived and we began to eat, our conversation naturally turning to the events of the day Holly was born, reliving the details — reinforcing the family mythology, I suppose. Chris, unaware of his fiancée's growing sullenness, her attention drifting to the next table, was an eager listener.

"So tell me," he said to Caroline, "this time twelve years ago, were you screaming your head off in the delivery ward?"

"Not a bit," she answered, shooting Holly a smile. "Easiest birth ever."

"Bollocks."

"I'm telling you, it's true. Robbie, on the other hand, was a complete nightmare."

I kicked him playfully under the table.

"Ha ha," Robbie said. Perhaps it was the champagne, but he seemed to have perked up a little, leaning into the table to be part of the conversation.

"Holly came so quickly," Caroline went on, "I barely made it up onto the bed. I just breathed her out."

Holly stirred with pleasure — she loved hearing this story.

"Tell him about the caul," I said.

"Holly was born with the caul unbroken."

"What's that?" Chris asked.

"It's a membrane that covers the baby's face and head in the womb. It tears during childbirth except in rare instances, and in Holly's case it was unbroken."

"They say it brings luck to the child," I said, putting my arm around Holly's shoulders. "Isn't that right, sweetheart? Or in some countries they believe the child has second sight."

"Do you, Holly?" Chris asked, screwing up his eyes and peering closely at her.

She blushed beneath his scrutiny and shook her head.

"One of the midwives told us that sailors often use a caul as a talisman against drowning," Caroline continued. "She asked us if we wanted to keep it or even sell it."

"Gross!" Robbie cried.

"It was David's birthday and I'd left his present at home, so I turned to him and said, 'There you go, love. That's your present.'"

"Please, Mum. TMI," Robbie said.

"My mother kept my umbilical cord," Chris volunteered, sending Robbie into fresh groans of revulsion. "I found it after she died, this dry, shriveled thing in a box.

It looked a bit like tripe."

I placed my knife and fork on the empty plate and laughed. "Now that is gross," I said. My headache had lifted — the champagne, the wine that followed, the food, it had gone some way to relieving the pressure.

"We kept the hospital bracelets the children wore, didn't we, Caroline?" I said. "Tiny little things — they barely fit around my finger. To think that they were once around your wrist, Robbie, or your ankle, Hols."

Zoe, who had been silent throughout this exchange, brought her empty glass down onto the table with a hard clink.

"Well, no one kept any mementos of my birth." Her smile was brittle and her voice barely controlled. "And whether Linda had a rough time at the birth or if she just *breathed me out,* I'll never know."

"Zoe," I began, "we didn't mean to . . ."

She pushed her chair back. "I'm going outside for a smoke," she announced.

Chris followed her with his eyes, until Caroline asked him to pour the wine. I couldn't shake the feeling that something else was bothering Zoe.

"Is she all right?" I asked Chris.

"She's fine," he said, sounding unsure.

From where I was sitting, with my back to the wall, I could see Zoe through the window outside, leaning against a tree trunk, putting a cigarette between her lips. The guy from the next table was with her — I had not noticed him following her outside — leaning in with his Zippo, her hand cupping the flame as she lit up. I glanced back at Chris. He hadn't noticed.

Our conversation had moved on to our college days by the time she returned, smoothing the folds of her dress against the backs of her thighs, taking her seat.

"You okay, hon?" Chris asked.

Robbie sat between them, making it impossible for any physical displays of affection between the two.

"Fine," she replied, her eyes moving to the guy returning to his friends, tossing his Zippo onto the table and glancing back at her. Chris followed her gaze. His expression darkened.

Caroline had brought with her to the restaurant the birthday cake she had purchased at the market that morning, and once our dinner plates had been cleared away, the waitress carried it out — a delicate cream-filled mille-feuille topped with candles, the lick and sway of tiny flames. We were temporarily the focus of attention in the restaurant, and to the eyes of the other diners we might have appeared celebratory, happy even at the short burst of applause. They had no idea of the tangle of confused allegiances, the discontent crackling in the air between us.

"I sometimes think," Caroline said, puncturing the air with her fork, "that there should be particular flavored cakes for particular occasions. You know, chocolate cake for anniversaries, meringue for birthdays, something fruity for weddings."

I decided she must be a little drunk.

"What sort of cake shall we have for our wedding?" Chris asked Zoe, smiling across Robbie at her.

Zoe put a delicate forkful of cake into her mouth. She had hardly touched her food all night.

"Come on," Chris said, warming to the subject. "What would you like?"

"I don't know," she answered quietly.

"You must have a preference," he persisted. "What's your favorite?"

"I don't have a favorite."

"Chocolate or lemon?"

Putting down her fork, she said sharply, "I don't even like cake."

Without any explanation as to where she

was going, she got up and left the table again.

"Where's she off to now?" Chris asked, crestfallen. He turned in his seat and saw the guy at the next table calmly leaving the restaurant, Zoe turning to say something to him I couldn't discern.

"What the hell's she playing at?" he asked, almost to himself, before he dropped his fork onto the plate with a little clatter and rose from his seat to follow them out onto the square.

"Don't get involved," Caroline warned me, and for a few minutes we sat in an uncomfortable silence, while outside the window Chris remonstrated with Zoe, the guy smoking his cigarette, bemused. I couldn't make out what they were saying, but I could see Zoe's cross face, her body language growing hostile. As I finished my dessert, she pulled the door open and marched back inside, Chris following. He took his seat, smiling at us all, but the redness of his cheeks betrayed his embarrassment. The dude at the next table also returned, remarking something to his friends in French, which set off a rumble of mocking laughter around their table. Chris pulled at his collar. I felt sorry for him.

"Shall we have coffee?" Caroline suggested.

"Perhaps we should just get the bill," I said.

Jealousy is a terrible thing — I know. It's a filthy outcrop of need and insecurity. It eats you up inside, pushes you to do and say reckless things. Chris seemed on the brink of something drastic.

"What are you guys doing the last weekend in August?" he said in an important way, making it sound like an announcement.

"August?" Caroline asked.

"Saturday the twenty-ninth," he went on, leaning forward on the table, knitting his fingers together. "What about it, Zoe?"

"I don't know what you're talking about," she said sulkily, clasping her arms at the elbows and sitting back in her chair.

"An engagement party. Something to make it official. We can invite all our friends." He was smiling at Zoe but there was hardness in his voice, a challenge in his eyes.

Zoe was clearly uncomfortable.

"We're not making anything official," she said, quietly insistent.

"Why not? Isn't that what we agreed? We'd tell Susannah and then have a party."

"You told Susannah?"

"That's what you wanted, isn't it?"

"I thought you were going to wait until we got home."

"Well, I changed my mind." Chris coughed. "She knows."

Zoe leaned forward, her face partially covered by her hands. Her sulky defiance was replaced by shock, the blood draining a little from her face.

"Chris?" she said slowly.

"And," he went on, ignoring the warning tone in her voice, "she's agreed to fast-track the divorce!"

He beamed at the rest of us as if expecting congratulations.

"Fast-track? There's no such thing in Ireland," Caroline said.

Chris smiled. "She's not going to contest it."

The waitress arrived and left the bill in the middle of the table.

"I'm sorry," Zoe said.

"Here." Chris took a credit card from his wallet and tossed it onto the bill. "This is on me."

Caroline and I protested but he wouldn't hear of us chipping in. All the time he was cheerfully punching in the numbers, Zoe sat patiently, biding her time. What was coming was obvious. He was only putting off the inevitable.

"Chris," Zoe said again, trying to hold his attention.

"Shall we go back to the house?" he asked.

"I can't do this," she said.

"Or shall we go somewhere for a digestif?"

More insistent now, she said, "I can't."

I felt Holly shift beside me. All this time, I had been waiting for her to pull the pin on her little grenade. I had not expected the detonation to come from Zoe.

At the next table, the guy stood up, this time openly gesturing to Zoe to join him outside. Chris, seeing this, swung around in his seat and snapped. "She's not going outside for another cigarette, so why don't you just *fuck off?*"

The dude raised his palms and told Chris to chill out in heavily accented English. Evidently, his ardor for Zoe did not extend to violence. He backed away, his friends teasing as he rejoined them, all shrugs and smirks.

"How dare you?" Zoe hissed across the table. Her eyes were lit up — I had never seen her so enraged.

"You're my fiancée," Chris snapped. "I will not be humiliated by your flirting with some creep!"

She was on her feet, twisting the ring on her finger. As soon as he realized what she was doing, he began backing down.

"Now, come on, just wait a minute."

She threw the ring onto the table. It bounced off a saucer, landing on the salver that held the bill.

"You have no claim on me now," she said venomously. Then glancing around at the rest of us, she added, "And you can all go to hell."

She ran from the restaurant, Chris following her.

"Fuck," Robbie said, exhaling the word as if he had been holding his breath.

"What should we do?" Holly asked.

"Leave them to it," Caroline advised. That feeling was back with me — the same feeling that had lingered all day, accompanying the pressure in my head: the sense of something about to happen, something bad.

I told Caroline to follow with the kids while I went on after the others.

What to say of what happened next? When I look back on it now, it is from behind the shelter of raised hands, as if I cannot bear to look on it directly. How I hurried after them through the street, watching as he dragged her by the wrist, tugging at her fiercely, their sparring voices like daubs of paint in the night. To a stranger, he might have appeared like a father dragging his recalcitrant teenager home, not her jilted fiancé. Anger made her lash out verbally, cruelly, calling him a washed-up middle-aged man, a pervert, a predator. I followed without any fully formed notion of how to intervene or whether I even should. It was not until they reached the gate and I saw him slap her — a quick little swat at her mouth to stop the foulness pouring out of it — that I shouted out, "Hey!"

It's a strange thing, living in a world that presents you with violence every day — violence filtered through the screen of your TV or the medium of your newspaper. Film violence, video games, it's there in the cartoons we show our kids. You'd think we'd be inured. But when confronted with it in the flesh, as I was that night, it seemed to rise up as something not frightening but absurd — absurd in how easily it happened, that slap. The simplicity of it and yet it changed everything. Just like the blow I received a few seconds later when I pushed up against his chest — all the reason gone out of him, leaving the blunt instrument of his fist. I didn't even raise a hand in self-defense, I was so amazed by his punch. I think that was the last lucid thought I had before the night unspooled around me. The thought of how easy it was to raise one's fist to a man's face and, in so doing, to take a pop at your own pain.

I was on the ground almost instantly, brought to my knees, pain flooding in to replace thought. One thing shines clear — Chris's words spat at me in the darkness, "Keep her then," he said. "The little bitch."

Hands cupping my face. The warm run of blood from my nose. Someone saying: *Jesus Christ!* The rough edges of cloth pressing against my face, and oh God, the pain. Pressure in my head unbearable now, ready to burst, like just before a sneeze only far, far worse. Vaguely, in the background, *He shouldn't drive. Someone should go after him.* Footsteps. I can hardly see. Asphalt under my feet, moving, stumbling indoors where the lights are too bright and there's something very cold on my face, ice, a new and different pain. *Take it easy,* she says and I try to focus. Concern in her eyes, the liquid softness of them. And I'm back there at the very beginning, to a place I have lost, a place I have longed for, where there's nothing, only time and love and endless possibility. And her, just as she was. *Linda,* I say and I kiss her.

# CHAPTER 23
## CAROLINE

It was so dark that night. Not a star in the sky, the moon disappeared or obliterated behind the cloud of smoke blending into the blackness. As I stood at the side of the road, watching the red taillights of Chris's car in their wild dash away, I fancied I saw a glow coming from over the dark hump of the land — the dying embers of fire on the bridge.

I had tried to keep him with us, for his own safety, not out of any desire to see them reunite. I was glad they were done with each other — one of her tentacles severed — even if the manner of it had been ugly and hard.

"Lying comes to her as easy as breathing," he had told me, bitter tears in his eyes.

He would not be dissuaded and I didn't try.

"There's nowhere for you to go," I had argued, meaning the closed bridge, the island cut off. But his need to put distance between him and her overrode my concerns for his safety. He listened to my pleas and warnings, my quieter regrets — "I wish she had been gentler on you" — then he muttered an apology about David and put the pedal to the floor.

I was staring after his car, exhaust fumes mingling with the night air, when I felt it. Something hard in my pocket. All that commotion in the restaurant, the lovers storming out, David hurrying after them, everyone had forgotten about the ring. I had picked it out of the salver and slipped it into my pocket before going out into the night with the others. Now, I turned it over in my fingers like a worry bead.

The taillights were gone, but the hazy glow remained on the horizon — a dirty orange smear, I imagined it to be the same color as the pocket of hot air inside myself, the sac of heat I had carried within since the day I first heard her name. It wasn't anger, or jealousy, or resentment — those hard, robust emotions pushing outward defiantly. Rather this was something inward-looking, fragile, its membranes delicate; I had to harbor it carefully lest it break. It's a cowering emotion — guilt. It hides in the darkness, quiet for years, not bothering anyone, until something — or someone — comes along and pokes it with a stick, and it swells, its membranes straining to hold it in, pressing up against your insides like another organ. Within me? A womb. For that is where I felt it. A pocket of hot air where a baby had once been.

*Like you, you mean?*

The venom in her words. Her smirk. She knew. She knew. All afternoon and into the evening, I had kept it inside me — the knowledge of his betrayal. I had gone through the motions as I always do — the dutiful wife, the dutiful mother — locking the knowledge of his betrayal away so as not to ruin the evening. But the knowledge had leaked away inside me like alkali seeping from a battery, the corrosion worming down through me, mingling with the pocket of hot air to produce something noxious. As I walked back to the house, I felt the slosh of it inside me, dangerous should it leak. Lethal.

Holly was standing outside, her face caught in the light thrown by the kitchen window.

"Where are the others?" I asked, and she seemed to jump a little, the sharpness of my tone giving her a fright.

"Inside."

It was like entering a different house from

the one we had left a couple of hours before. All that busy energy, the sense of anticipation before a night out, gone, replaced by an uneasy stillness. I found that I was walking softly, as if wary of disturbing someone.

The light was on in the kitchen, illuminating the undressed salad, the vegetables half-peeled and abandoned across the chopping board. Right away, I knew something was wrong. Zoe seemed to have backed into a corner, her hands behind her on the countertop, shoulders a little high and tense.

"What's going on?" I asked. Even from that distance, I could see her contracted pupils — small pinpricks in the green fabric of her eyes.

"Nothing," she said. But it wasn't nothing. I knew it from the way David was leaning against the counter, swaying slightly, as if he hadn't heard or noticed me. His nose was bloodied and, while her pupils had shrunk away to almost nothing, his had dilated. Two black disks fixed on her like a drunk.

"Linda," he said to her, and I just about caught her reaction — that recoil of horror — before my eyes snapped in his direction.

"What did you call her?"

He slumped briefly against the counter, before pushing himself upright. He was still gazing at her in that sluggish way.

I said, louder this time, "David, what did you say?"

My words seemed to hit the middle of his forehead, the way he winced, put his hand to his brow, briefly pinched the skin at the bridge of his nose. When he took his hand away he looked at her again. It was extraordinary the change that came over his face. Confusion cleared, replaced by an expression of naked disappointment. A hurt that went deep. He shook his head to rid himself of it and said, "Nothing."

He was coming back to himself, whatever delirium he experienced trickling away, but the shock of it remained.

"You thought she was Linda."

He looked around for something, then, finding the towel, he picked ice cubes up off the countertop and began filling it with them.

"Didn't you?" I insisted.

"I should go," Zoe said, and started to move past me.

"No," I said firmly. "You'll stay right here until someone tells me what's going on."

"Mum?" I heard Holly say.

"Go to your room." My tone was brusque, my heart beat quickly. I was on the cusp of something — a hard truth.

She turned away leaving the three of us alone. I had no idea where Robbie was, but it wasn't important; nothing was important right then except getting to the nub of the rot, getting to the root of this noxious weed that had sprung up at the center of our lives and was strangling us.

"What happened just now?" I said again.

"Caroline, my face is bleeding, for crying out loud." David was recovering himself but he still sounded groggy.

"The way you were looking at her just now. You were thinking of Linda?"

He took the towel from his nose, examined the blood on it.

"You told Zoe about the termination?" I changed tack.

That caught his attention.

"Didn't you?" My voice trembled with anger.

He put aside the towel. "I didn't think you'd react this way."

"You stupid, heartless . . ."

I stepped forward and he caught my wrists before I could reach him. His grip was strong and all I could do was pluck ineffectually at his shirt.

"Caroline, for God's sake."

I was crying, tears of rage and grief and helplessness. Tears over a decision made many years before. He held my wrists until the fight in me died and he let me twist from his grasp. Leaning against the tabletop, I could feel her eyes on me, but I was so tired of her, exhausted by her constant presence, trying to second-guess her motivation, bracing myself against her manipulation, feeling the waters closing over my head. One thought rose to the surface, a single piece of flotsam: *She must go.*

I told him I'd had enough. Enough of her and the trouble she brewed, enough of him and his wavering loyalty and his lack of trust. Enough of Linda. He blinked as I said her name, a raw nerve touched. I had read it in his lost thoughts; I had felt him summoning her memory like a séance calling back the dead.

"It's her or me."

The hardness of the table pressed up beneath my fingertips. The heavy warmth of the night air came in through the open windows.

"I don't know why, but you've never liked me, Caroline." Zoe's voice came almost as a surprise. What was passing between David and me was so intensely personal, it felt as if there was no one else in the room.

Holly was at my elbow.

"Not now, love," I said. She was handing

me something, and David said "No," with an urgency that made me look.

A scrunched-up piece of paper.

"Holly!" David said.

I started to open it and David said, "I can explain."

*Inconclusive.*

It was dreadful the way David stood there in front of me, his nose bloodied but his face blank of all expression.

"You told me it was positive," I said. "How could you do that?"

"Look, it is positive. There was another test done that came back positive. Christ, you saw it yourself!"

I looked at the letter again, taking it in more completely this time. "But this was done only a few weeks ago. I don't understand."

"I wish I'd never done the bloody thing." David looked exasperated, cornered, running his hands over his face. "It doesn't prove anything."

But it did prove something. It proved he was suspicious.

"You didn't believe me," Zoe's hurt cracking the corners of her voice.

"After the lies you told us about Linda, about your adoption . . ."

"I've tried to be straight with you. I got

447

the test done. I gave you the letter and the results. How could you not believe me?"

"Zoe got the test done?" I said, the realization dawning.

"You didn't want it to be true, did you?" Zoe went on, and oh the anger stirred in me, watching her turning it on, how easily she went to work on him.

"Please," David said, stepping toward Zoe. What was he going to say? That she lied too much to be believed? Or, more likely, how glad he was to know she was his daughter.

But Zoe spoke first. "Linda told me this would happen." I saw him slow and tense at the mention of Linda's name. "Toward the end, when I told Linda I wanted to find you, she warned me not to."

David seemed to be hanging on her words, soaking them up; I listened with insistent skepticism.

"You asked me why Linda never told you about me," Zoe said.

"You said you didn't know."

"Yes," she said, but I could see something moving behind her eyes, some new deception being put in play. "I didn't want to hurt you with the truth."

Linda didn't tell him about the pregnancy or about the birth of her baby because she knew he wouldn't want it, Zoe said. "It broke Linda's heart, but there was no point. Because this had happened to you before and she knew you'd ask her to get rid of it."

Half the things Zoe told us were lies. Even now, sifting back over these memories, I can't be sure of which things were true and which were false. But if David had told Linda, I wondered, *how* had he told her? In what tone was his explanation couched? Heavy with regret? Or with a sigh of relief?

Or did it matter? Zoe would have twisted it, whatever it was. And yet there was something magnetic about her, like you could not pull your eyes away. David hung on her every word, and in that moment I did understand the power she had to hold you in her spell.

"No," he said, "it wasn't like that."

"She thought you wouldn't want her to keep it."

"No," he said again.

It was as if he had forgotten I was in the room. The hurt was instant. *The love of my life.* That utterance held its power to cut and wound. She was a knot in the wood of our marriage, the grain of it forming around her. I was so busy focusing on his admission of love for this woman that I failed to absorb the new truth — the real hurt — in what he was saying. It took a moment for my thoughts to catch up. *He would have kept that baby.* That fact was in his eyes. A deep and bitter regret rose up in me.

He was saying something to Zoe about timing and opportunity, but I was backing away. *Enough; no more,* I wanted to say. I caught the look on her face as I backed away — the narrowing of her eyes and the hard line of her feline grin.

I stumbled against an ancient dresser in the hall, felt the crack of pain against the bone of my ankle, but I didn't stop, not until I was out in the warm dark, the gate jangling in the distance behind me.

Hurrying along the little footpath, away from the lights of the village, I walked quickly, without purpose, toward the welcoming dark of the coast, the gentle hiss of the sea greeting me. The sand running along the crescent of the beach was dark, bluish gray, no moon to cast it in a silver glow. The hulk of an abandoned boat lay rusting on one side, like a beached whale that had long ago given up the will to return home, sinking to inevitable ruin.

There was something inevitable too about the feelings stirring inside me, or so it seemed. The ring in my pocket, the hard roundness of it smooth against my palm.

Feelings of an ending, I was sure of it now. Our marriage, that desiccated thing, was a dead animal we had been dragging about for so long, both of us too cowardly to pronounce its demise. Willing ourselves to look away, to keep things going for the sake of the children. He would leave me once the kids were gone. All that love, the terrible waste of it.

I stood at the shoreline, listening to my breathing, waiting with no clue of what I should do next. Memory stirred uncomfortably. After what had just happened, I was vulnerable, helpless, and I remembered a narrow room with a high ceiling, a milk-white lampshade on a brass chain suspended above us, the shadow of dust gathered in its bowl. I remembered lying beneath it, the two of us, looking up at it, feeling the rise and fall of his head against my chest.

"I'm sorry," he said, drawing away.

It was our first time after I came back. Our first time since the problem had been taken care of.

I needed his touch to make me feel healed. I needed him inside me again as an absolution. But in the darkness of that room, as we tried to find our way back to each other, I had felt a third presence — a watchful eye inside me. Perhaps he felt it too. But when he rolled away from me, his hands going up to cover his face, moaning his apology, I felt ashamed. Contaminated. A failure. The ghost of what I had done watching me, like a fragment of glass mingling with the dust in the lamp above our heads.

I had not returned to that memory in many years. The warm relief of our eventual reconciliation had pushed it down. Two further babies had helped to obliterate it. But stopped dead by the edge of the sea, with the blunt hardness of those old diamonds pressed between my fingers, that memory ripped through me as vital as a new blade of grass spearing the earth.

That long-ago night was a punctuation mark in my life, a pause between the love that had been before and the hard road of our parting. It marked the start of a three-year lacuna and, though I hadn't known it then, from that hole in our history came Zoe.

Out there in the darkness, something moved in the sea. A gurgle of water followed by a faint splash. I didn't move. Inside I had become very still. From a distance a disembodied notion came to me, a shimmering thought. A cancer had taken root in our family, a spreading tumor that needed to be carved out. A reckless thought, but I didn't feel reckless. I felt calm. Surgical, clinical, steady.

# CHAPTER 24
## DAVID

Zoe regarded me coolly. "Aren't you going to go after her?" she asked, picking up her cigarettes and tapping one out of the carton. As she lit up, her demeanor seemed to change. She wasn't upset. Neither did she seem frosty. If anything, she appeared bored. As if the outcome of the disastrous blowup with my wife was dull and inevitable.

"There's no point," I said quietly.

I had said what I should not have said. I could apologize to Caroline, but those words could not be unsaid. Of all the arguments we'd had over the years, all the emotional wounds inflicted, this was perhaps the worst. The one we would not recover from.

Zoe breathed smoke out of the side of her mouth, her eyes narrowing as she watched me.

"You're pretty fucked-up right now,

aren't you?"

"I think you've said enough," I slurred.

On the table, the crumpled letter lay where Caroline had dropped it, ash coloring it gray at the edges. Zoe reached for it, brought the burning tip of her cigarette to one corner. The document started to smolder.

"A second test," I heard her whispering beneath her breath with derision. "I can't believe you did that."

"I wanted to be sure," I explained.

She kept her gaze on the letter, a low flame steadily devouring it. As it neared her fingertips, she dropped the burning remains into the sink. She was acting like a whole new person. Confident, mature, but icy with superiority and disdain. I felt, while she held me with her hard stare, that she resented me. More than that: she disliked me.

"So what now?" she asked. "Shall we do another one?"

At first, I didn't know what she meant, but then I saw where the DNA test results had turned to ash in the sink, and my confusion cleared.

"No, that won't be necessary."

"But how else are you going to be sure?"

I couldn't tell if she was being serious or if it was more of her mockery. I couldn't be sure of anything about her.

"I just don't think . . ."

"To clear up any remaining doubts. Because you must have some little niggling doubts. I mean, I might have faked the first test. Right, David?"

Her voice was high and sharp and I could see how close she was to the brink. All that icy coolness, the bravado of burning the letter — it was a front. Underneath it, she was scared.

I should have told her there were no doubts. I should have declared my firm belief that she was my daughter. But I wavered. Out of nowhere, Gary, her stepfather, had come into my head and, with it, the remembered emotions of the day I had met him — the disorienting shock at the news of her adoption, the crumbling edifice of the truths she had told me — truths I had believed wholeheartedly because I had loved her mother deeply and passionately, and it had seemed, in some fucked-up way, that with Zoe coming to me, I was somehow getting a second chance — a chance to make good my life.

That may have been naive, but it had seemed like a bright and shining hope that only grew opaque and cracked with the knowledge that she had lied. Not once or twice, but continuously with an inconsistency and virtuosity that made it impossible to know what was true and what was not. I didn't know where I was with her. The truth is, I'd been lost from the very beginning.

She saw my hesitation, the doubts announcing themselves in my brief silence, and when I finally spoke up, stammering that there was no need for another DNA test, that I believed I was her father, she gave me a long, measuring look, something angry shoring up behind her eyes.

"You're right not to believe me," she said, her voice soft and dangerous.

"Zoe, it's difficult, okay? I mean, it's not as if you make it easy. This thing you have with Caroline . . ."

She laughed, a bark of bitter amusement.

"God, you're so predictable." The way she said it was loaded with scorn. "You act all solemn and quiet and thoughtful, like you're this deep thinker. But scratch the surface and you're just a frightened little man who will always go running back to his wife."

She wanted to plunge the knife in deeper; she wanted to twist it. Indignation rose within me, but at the back of it came a quieter, more insistent suspicion.

"The letter from the university," I said. "You signed for it."

She was stubbing out her cigarette in the sink among the ashes.

"What are you talking about?"

She was very convincing, but then I knew what a good actress she was. Quietly, I explained what I meant, playing along with her game of ignorance. She was leaning back against the sink, her hands behind her, one fingernail tapping out an impatient rhythm against the cool enamel.

I concluded, "You signed Caroline's name and then hid the letter."

The beat of her fingernail against the sink; I thought of Chris and his parting words to me: *the little bitch.* She had made a fool of him, playing him before dumping him. I thought of Caroline and the wild accusations Zoe had made — the hints of the affair being revived, blaming my wife for the violence she had done to her own face. I thought of Gary and the lies she had spun about him. She had played them all. Why should I be immune? I felt foolish and my anger rose sharply, wild and erratic, like the crazy rhythm of her fingertips inside my head.

Then, it stopped. She became still. In a quiet voice she said, "Yes. All right. I did it."

The breath went out of me. Weakness

came into my legs.

"I signed for it. Then I took it upstairs to my room and burned it. Just like I burned that letter there."

How still she was. Completely unmoved while I was trembling. What had happened to the teenager who had appeared nervously at my office door, picking at her cuffs, frightened half to death at the bomb she was about to drop? Somehow, she had been replaced by this cool, bloodless creature with her dead gaze, her cruel words spoken with velvet softness. And the thing that was most confusing, the thing I couldn't make out, was which one was the real Zoe and which the fake?

"I had worked so hard." The words coming out of me no louder than a whisper, a gasp of helplessness and disbelief.

"I don't care how hard you worked," she said pitilessly.

I blinked, and blinked again, my vision becoming blurred. The headache that had dogged me all day had been made worse by the blow to my face and by the mix of alcohol and pills. It made me doubt my very senses. "But why . . . why would you want to sabotage my chances of promotion, my whole career?"

"You just don't get it, do you?" she said

with bitter amusement, her smile high and tight. "It's what I do. It's what I've always done. Call it the instincts of an orphan."

"But you never were an orphan . . ."

"Excuse me, but I'm not going to be lectured to by a second-rate tutor like you, a cuckold, a failure."

I stepped toward her, and even now I'm not sure what I intended to do — put my hands to her shoulders and urge her to be calm, or hit her, like Chris had done.

Her voice came low and deadly. "What are you planning to do, Daddy? Kiss me again?"

Her words caught me like a glancing blow and I recoiled, horrified by her suggestion, but a deeper horror bubbled up, the knowledge that I had already kissed her. Only a short time before I had pressed my lips against hers in the way of a lover. I may have been confused after having been punched by Chris, I may have thought it was Linda, but I had felt a desire, not imagined but real.

"Perhaps that's why you got the second test done," she said, the sweetness of her tone disguising the poison beneath. She stepped past me, pausing once to glance back from the door. "You never wanted me to be your daughter." She said it so softly, but the pain of it went deep. Nerves raw and touched alive. Her last words to me, before she left the room: "All this time, you've been wishing I was Linda."

*History can bring the dead back to life.*
I have said that year after year to a lecture hall full of first-year students. Something to gain their attention from the outset. I never thought of the expression as misleading. I never thought of it as a lie. I believed in it myself, right up to the moment when she left me alone, weakened, drained, all my beliefs deserting me. I had no faith to cling to, no ideals to hold me up. Inside, I was collapsing, and the only belief I could find was in a bottle.
I drank steadily, unaware of my surroundings, my mind drifting into the past like a boat that had slipped its mooring, falling slowly into a drunken sleep: once again I was back at the cottage in Donegal, with the call of a bird, the woods, and with Linda, a mug of tea cradled in her hands, standing in a shirt of mine reaching halfway down her thighs, lost in thought. When she spoke, her voice was like a splash of color in the room. "Tomorrow," I said to her concerns. "We'll go tomorrow if you want." I kissed her. A long, lingering kiss. Love had

made me careless. Love had made me bold, and a little reckless, but not completely so: I had not told her I loved her, but I did . . .

I kissed her again, felt her hair covering my face, only it was not Linda's hair but Zoe's — the feathery lightness of her curls. I was kissing her, my own daughter, defiling her innocence, revulsion in my throat. In the dream I was trying to turn away, twisting and writhing, her mocking laughter surrounding me, filling me like an oily soup, sucking at my limbs and breath, pulling me in, holding me fast as I tried to escape the coiled chains of DNA entwining us in a never-ending sequence. I gave a shout: "No!" and she laughed again, a laugh that was at once close to my ear and far away. Then a scream: I opened my eyes, staggered to my feet as I might have when woken in the night by my children screaming with night terrors. Stumbling from my bedroom, no recollection of having gone there, I fumbled through the half-light, down the staircase, through the quiet rooms. The granular light of dawn made everything seem gray and empty. Silence hung in the deserted rooms. I began to doubt myself; what I had heard? Something real, or was it something from the depths of nightmare?

The sky beyond the window was streaked

with red. My mouth was desert-dry. I needed water, but instead I went to the window, to see better the fire brightness of the dawn. That was when the words came to me again: *History can bring the dead back to life.* Like a spell or an incantation. Those words were in my head when my eyes settled on the pool and I saw them.

Figures in the water. One standing, the other stretched out like a doll, unmoving. Slowly, as though I were still physically locked inside the dream, I stepped out onto the terrace, felt the coolness of early morning raising hairs on my limbs. I kept my eyes fixed on them as I drew near, unable to make sense of it, the scrambled visuals adding to my confusion. My heart understood it first, my pulse quickening. Caroline leaning over Zoe, holding the girl's face in her hands, kissing her mouth, no, not kissing, but blowing, blowing into her mouth, a dark stain moving through the water.

Then Caroline looked up, the tears streaming down her face. The water swirled about her waist, and her voice rose in a fevered, anguished pitch: "What have you done? Jesus Christ, what have you done?"

Panic gripped me, kept me frozen while Caroline tugged and pulled at the body, dragging it to the ledge, heaving it up onto the cold wet tiles.

Black holes in my memory, her voice reaching me from some far-off place, *"What are you planning to do, Daddy? Kiss me again?"*

What had I done?

The truth remained hidden from me — too much confusion, too much pain.

I walked toward them, knelt down, and gazed into Zoe's face. She lay on the cold hard ground, her gaze fixed far away, into the sky, the crimson flames of the clouds, and the heavens beyond. I thought of the brief moment of joy in the bed of her conception all those years ago in the stone cottage of Donegal. I thought of Linda bearing her birth in stubborn silence. I thought of the nursery rhymes, and skipping ropes, the jigsaw puzzles and books, the parks and cinemas of her childhood, away from Linda and me, her parents. I thought about all the things that made her who she was, the chance and circumstance of her being, and wondered too about all she was not or could not be. I thought of everything she might have done, her plans, the trips, the work, the friends, and the love she may have found.

And then, from my peripheral vision, I saw Robbie. *Go back to bed,* I wanted to tell him. *You should not be a witness to this.* I wanted to kiss him on the forehead and stroke his cheek as if he were a child again. His mother went to him, saying something I couldn't hear, making some demand of him I couldn't discern. *Back to bed, son,* I wanted to say, but he just stood there, staring, already sealing himself off from us. Did I know then what he had done?

All that really comes to me, when my thoughts turn to that moment, is the outline of Zoe's face, pale against the limestone flags. How cold she looked, and how perfect, as if she were the beautiful human plaything of some minor Greek god.

I thought of all the things I did and did not know about her. It amounted in the end to nothing: it amounted to a girl whose green eyes had once flickered but now were glassy and devoid of life.

# PART 4

# CHAPTER 25
## ROBBIE

They come almost every day to get him to talk. Police, social services, his solicitor, counselors from the prison service. Some of them speak to him in English, heavily accented, but he understands what they're saying. Others, whose English is not so good, bring translators, and he can see the look in the translator's eye: *Why on earth won't you talk, you dumbass?* The police and social services are better at concealing their thoughts from him — they have more experience and he can't be the first kid in this facility to clam up with fright. The solicitor just looks bored and a little fed up, like he has better things to do with his time than sit in an interview room with some Irish kid who prefers to say nothing and stay in this detention center indefinitely rather than work on any kind of defense.

His father is the most frequent visitor. Mostly he just talks to Robbie, like he's accepted the silence. He talks about his work, his research — he's using the time on the island to work on a book. He brings news from home. His tone is conversational, cheerful, forced. Sometimes, on days he's finding it tough, when it becomes almost unbearable to see his son in this place wearing his institutional uniform, he will lean over the table and say in an urgent whisper: *Please, son, say something.*

At least he doesn't cry like Robbie's mother did. She would sit across from him, a balled-up tissue in her hands, her eyes and nose red raw from all the crying she had done, begging him, beseeching him to just tell her why? She loved him — she forgave him — he was her son. But please, for the love of God, would he talk to her, just say something.

On and on it went. He watched her within the hermetic seal of his own silence. After what had happened, talking was an impossibility. It was a relief when she went away, back home to Dublin with Holly. He felt the storm in his brain grow quiet.

When they've all gone — his father, the police, the solicitors and social workers — when they've left him to go back to his cell, he feels a sense of relief, a levity almost. He lies on his bunk, closes his eyes. And then it is just the two of them — him and Zoe — locked together in a strange peacefulness.

She was different from how he thought she'd be. Different from him and from Holly. He felt it most when she spoke. Her accent, of course, the strange foreignness of the Northern vowel sounds, and the way her voice went up at the end of each sentence, like a little penciled tick mark on a musical score. When she came for lunch on that first day, it was hard not to stare at her, his *sister,* displacing him now in the role of eldest child. He was taller than her though, stupid to feel proud about it, but he did. Both of them were thin but she was *really* thin. She wore a big floaty sweater so you couldn't tell at first until you noticed her legs, like pipe cleaners coming out of her boots.

He wondered if she had an eating disorder, she was so thin. A girl in the orchestra, a viola player named Claire Waters, had anorexia. Up close, you could see how papery the skin on her face was over the square bone of her jaw. Her skin was kind of hairy too, light blond hair like the hair on her sticklike arms. Robbie sat behind Claire with his cello, so he spent a lot of time staring at the side of her face. She dropped out of orchestra before Easter and someone said she'd been hospitalized. Someone else said they'd seen her and her hair had fallen out — she was almost completely bald on one side of her head.

Zoe's hair was glorious. He'd never use that word out loud to describe it, but privately, that's what he thought. Glorious. The first time he met her, he'd felt this urge to touch it — not that he did. Eventually, a long time after that, he got to put his hand on her hair and he can remember the prickly feeling that shivered over the back of his scalp when he felt his hand sinking into those soft curls.

"What do you think?" Holly had asked him.

It was late in the evening, both of them in his room. Downstairs their mum was tidying up. Dad was dropping Zoe home.

He shrugged. "She seemed okay."

*"Really?"*

He flicked the page of his magazine, said nothing.

"I thought she was a bit full of herself."

He let her talk for a while, zoning out. He was tired. It had been a weird day. The truth was he didn't know if he liked Zoe. Her manner had seemed polite, a little shy perhaps, but at one point she had caught him looking and smiled at him — a different kind of smile than the one she gave the others. He'd seen the spark come into her eye, something conspiratorial about it, mischievous, drawing him in, making an ally of him. But he didn't know if the sum of all these impressions amounted to liking her.

"Want to see my room?" he asked the next Sunday she came over for lunch.

He'd never had a girl up to his room before. Several guys in his class had claimed they'd had sex with girls in their rooms. He wasn't sure he believed them, although maybe one or two. Robbie himself had only kissed three girls — sweaty encounters on the dance floor at Wesley rugby club that never went any further. He'd tried to get off with one of the girls in the orchestra at a party once, but she'd laughed with surprise. She hadn't meant to be unkind, but he'd burned with humiliation anyway.

"Cool!" Zoe had said, when she saw the poster of Thin Lizzy on his wall — Phil Lynott's giant head surrounded by a corona of psychedelic swirls. "You're into his music?"

"*Jailbreak* is like my favorite album ever."

"Put it on," she said, and he scrolled through his iPod while she sat back on his bed, making herself comfortable among his pillows.

They talked about music for a while, and then films. Her taste leaned toward the indie end of the spectrum but she admitted to a weakness for rom-coms.

"You won't tell anyone, will you?" she had said, giving him that conspiratorial smile again. He noticed that her front teeth overlapped slightly.

He made some comment then about a Kate Hudson flick he'd read a review of, and she hooted with laughter.

"You're so funny, Robbie," she'd said. "You crack me up."

He felt himself grinning foolishly. No one ever called him funny, especially not girls.

From then on she came up to his bedroom every Sunday once lunch had been cleared away. Flopping onto his bed with an air of exhaustion, like all the politeness downstairs had been a front but now, up here in his room, she could be herself. The differences he'd been so hung up on at the start now receded, replaced by the familiar. Downstairs, it was prickly with formality, none of them easy — particularly his mother and Holly. But up in his room, just Zoe and him, it was like they'd known each other forever.

When all that stuff blew up in school over

what he'd been doing to Miss Murphy, she was the only one who didn't give him shit. Even Holly had gone all supercilious on him, calling him a delinquent. "You're *eleven*!" he had shouted after her, then slammed the door of his room. It made him so mad, being punished like that. Couldn't any of them understand? Intimidating that teacher, pushing her to the ground, it was an honorable thing! Even his mother, who should have been *grateful,* kept giving him that thin-lipped look of disapproval that he couldn't stand, constantly watching him with anxious eyes. And as for his dad, Robbie thought, don't even get him started! They were so busy with their own jobs, his dad nearly having an aneurism over the professorship and whether or not he'd get it, his mum thinking she was Sheryl Sandberg all of a sudden with her power suits and her appointment diary and her client portfolio. Didn't either of them realize that they were lucky to have such a good kid? Compared to some of the morons and thugs in his year, Robbie was a goddamned saint!

"Why should your mother be grateful for what you did?" Zoe asked in a ruminative kind of way. She was sitting on his bed, listening to a barrage of grievances that he'd stored up over the whole first week of his confinement.

"What?"

He had heard what she'd said, and he knew what she meant, but he wanted to buy himself a few seconds to think. She didn't know about his mum. Could he tell her? Part of him knew that telling her would constitute a betrayal, but he was so angry with his mother right then. *Fuck it,* he thought.

He sat down on the bed opposite her.

"Promise you won't tell?"

Her eyes became alert. He liked the way she was watching him, concentrating while he told her about his mum's affair, about how it was with the father of this other kid in his class, about how the whole school knew about it. That the teacher he'd bullied was the one who'd spilled the beans.

"That's awful!" she said when he was finished. "It must have been so shit for you in school."

He lay back and looked up at the ceiling. He wasn't thinking about the stuff the other kids had said — the taunting and the abuse. He was thinking about the moment he'd stepped toward Miss Murphy, the shot of pure adrenaline rushing through his blood-stream as he put his hands up to her chest, knowing he was going to push her.

"The other kid — Jack — he changed schools. But Mum and Dad left me where I was."

"Why?" She shook her head, not understanding.

Robbie had never told anyone why, but he believed, privately, that it was his father's way of punishing his mother. It was the way he did things, Robbie's dad, how he conducted long, slow, patient campaigns. His mother liked to get things out in the open, have the argument, clear the air, and move on. But there was a quality of patience in his dad, stubbornness. He wasn't going to let her sweep it under the carpet, her infidelity. He'd make her pay for it with three more years of parent-teacher meetings, school plays, sports days, prize-giving ceremonies, end-of-year Masses. He'd make her go to them all. A three-year sentence was her punishment. Robbie knew that his dad loved him. But he also knew that his dad had blind spots and this was one of them. He couldn't see how much it hurt Robbie, using him as a pawn just to get at his mother.

He didn't say this to Zoe, though. He was beginning to regret how much he had already told her.

"They thought it would blow over," he

said instead.

Something in his voice must have sounded forlorn even though he didn't mean it to, because she reached over and took his wrist, giving it a squeeze.

Steadily, they grew closer. In the weeks after she moved in, his life had seemed to re-arrange itself around her, points in the day shifting around the axis of her presence, her company. His mother took him aside and told him that she was concerned about how much time he was spending with Zoe — she worried it was interfering with his study. How to explain to her that the exact opposite was true? His happiness made him not only diligent but benevolent too, pre-pared to think better of everyone. He believed then, as he does now, that those weeks were the happiest of his whole life.

He would have forgiven her anything. Even the lies she had told them about Linda. So what if she had been adopted? He couldn't see why his mum and dad got so worked up about it, and after Zoe had disappeared with that dipshit, Chris, Rob-bie had lain awake in the dark, worrying that they had frightened Zoe away for good.

Sometime after midnight, her step came on the stair. The softest rap on his door and he sat bolt upright.

"Come in," he whispered.

He didn't dare turn on a light. His curtains were open anyway and light thrown by the halogen streetlamp cast the room in an orange glow.

"Do you hate me?" she asked him.

He was out of bed now, on his feet, standing within touching distance of her. Between them, three feet or so of charged air. He felt like every nerve in his body was alive to her, to this, whatever this was.

"I don't care," he told her, his voice clear, not bothering to whisper. "I don't care about any of it."

He realized he was trembling.

"Really?"

"I just don't ever want you to run out on us again."

He said it, and he meant it.

Quickly, she stepped toward him, her arms around his neck, his brain about to explode, flooded with screaming messages from every nerve ending in his body as he felt her against him. Slowly, cautiously, like he hardly dared to do it, he brought his hands up, put them to her back, clasped her to him. Her hair was hanging loose down her back and his hands sank into it. Nerves shivered across his scalp. He lowered his head and felt her hair brush against his nose — the ticklish softness of it. In the back of his mind, a niggling voice whispering: *What does this mean?* The same DNA ran through their bodies. These conflicting sensations — he was at once excited and also at peace.

The atmosphere in the house grew heavy. Not everyone was as easy about Zoe's presence as he was. His mother for one seemed increasingly stressed, although he thought that might have something to do with work. There was tension between his parents — he noticed they were spending less and less time in each other's company. As for Holly, there was no love lost between her and Zoe. That much was obvious.

"She has it in for me," Zoe told him, and this was well before the incident with Holly at the quarry — his mother's hysterical overreaction.

He tried to tell her not to worry, but his mum remained cool and Zoe began spending more and more time out with her friends, and the creep of doubt came back to him, the feeling she was pulling away. He wondered if she had a boyfriend, but anytime he asked she became coy and evasive. Some nights she didn't come home and his mind went reeling in all directions. In school the following day he could hardly concentrate on anything. *She's my sister,* he repeated in his head, like a mantra. His parents didn't seem to notice. They were so wrapped up in their own problems. They were fighting more and more these days — not outright fights, but sniping and sulking. He felt the thinness of his family around him, like at any moment it might snap.

Eventually he found out. And even though he had suspected there was a boyfriend, to discover it was Chris and that she was moving in with him, he felt a wave of revulsion take him, an almost overwhelming urge to grab her by the neck and shake her.

When she left, Robbie had stood at the door watching her go, not speaking to his mum. Afterward, back in his room, he had felt the house around him plunged into sudden quiet, and the anger riled inside him. It wasn't just that it was Chris — although the thought of them being naked together made him want to retch — it was the deceit. That she had kept it from him all along. He felt toyed with, used, like he was something she could amuse herself with from time to time and then discard when she'd grown bored. He imagined her telling Chris about him, about the things she'd told him, the two of them laughing at Robbie's innocence, his foolishness. All those weeks when he'd thought there was something between Zoe and him — a closeness — yet all the time she had been making a mockery of him. He thought of this and felt the rage hum inside him, filling his brain like a swell of music he could not contain. His cello case was lying open on the bed and he slammed it shut, then slammed it again with the flat of his hand. Over and over, he kept hitting it, drawing his hand up over his head, then bringing it down with as much force as he could. The pain shot through his nerves and bones, up through his wrist and into his arm, yet still he kept at it, feeling past the pain, making himself numb to it.

His rage came and went over the next few weeks — sometimes it erupted in spurts of indignation and boiling fury; at other times it was like a slow seeping pool of acid in the pit of his stomach. It was exhausting being angry all the time. It left him mentally and physically drained. He could hardly stay awake at school. His cello seemed heavier than ever and he began to dread having to lug it up the stairs and into the hall for rehearsals. At home, when he was supposed to be studying for his exams, he would instead crawl into bed and try to sleep.

Something had happened to him — he knew that. Something cataclysmic. She had come into their family as if wielding a gorilla bar, wrenching it open, changing its shape to accommodate her. But the shape that it found was skewed — sharp and angular. There were no curved surfaces. He no longer recognized it. He felt that when she had shoved the bar in, looking to gain purchase, it had anchored deep inside him, changing something within.

Chance is everything. A set of circumstances coming together, merging at a particular time. Sometimes, when he is lying awake in his cell at night, Robbie plays the *What If?* game in his mind. What if they had never gone to France? What if Zoe and Chris had not got engaged? He could go farther back and ask: What if he never knew Zoe existed? But that's not interesting to him. She's so deeply embedded in him now, even though she's dead — *especially* because she's dead — that he cannot imagine his life without her in it.

He had been so angry with her — furious — and still, that first night he saw her in Île de Ré, his heart gave out a thump of gratitude. Feelings and thoughts, confused, contradictory — he was outraged by her engagement, flattered by her private words to him that the only reason she had come here was to see him. She had missed him. She couldn't bear to think that he hated her. He listened to it all in sulky silence. It got to him though. He knew the engagement wouldn't last, understood it for what it was: a burst of impetuousness. So like Zoe. It would end, and she would come back to him.

Months have passed, but still he can summon an image of her that day in her bikini standing by the pool, the way the water skimmed down her body in rivulets, the outline of her nipples beneath the wet fabric, another triangular outline of hair between her legs. He believes that is the moment when it started to build inside him. Agitation like a drone in his brain. It kept building and growing and it didn't stop, even after the debacle in the restaurant when Chris left and Zoe stayed. The thing inside him was like a stone that gave off an electronic hum, like a generator, or an electricity pylon. It just would not stop. It frightened him. He didn't understand it, didn't want it, couldn't remember the last time he'd slept through the night. He slipped away from the others, back to the room he shared with Holly. Exhaustion was clawing at him and he nearly cried for want of sleep.

When he crawled into bed that night, the hum was loud in his brain, only this time he recognized the trills and sweeps within it, the swaying movement of waves, the pitter-patter from droplets of sea spray. How many times had he heard this music, how many hours had he spent rehearsing it? Debussy's *La Mer* — a piece of music he had loved — but now he felt infected by it, the score trickling out to occupy every pocket of his brain, soaking it. And yet, it was not quite right — the sound slightly skewed, as if one of the instruments was out of tune, or one of the musicians fractionally out of rhythm. There was no pleasure to the music now, only annoyance and irritation. It scratched around the rim of his thoughts, and he turned over in bed, tried to find a cool spot on the pillow, but the music clung to his brain, the strains of the cello in the third movement like bows scratching across razor wire.

"You know, she's not even our real sister."

Holly's voice skimmed above the pool of his thoughts. He turned and saw her lying on her side, her bed tucked under the window. The jittery third movement was in his head and he tried to silence it as he pulled himself up to a sitting position.

"What?"

"I found out this evening. Dad had a DNA test done."

"Shut up."

"It's true. I saw the letter myself. She's not our sister."

"You're lying. He would have told us."

"He wanted to keep it to himself."

"Why?"

What she said next was too outrageous to believe. Disgusted, he pulled back the covers and left the room.

The house was quiet, empty, no sign of either of his parents. He felt the heat of the day continue to linger within the stillness of the rooms, a smell of burning in the air. The doors to the garden were open and he could see her on the beach chair next to the pool, perched on one edge, her head balanced on one hand. Crazy the hope that bloomed in his heart. Could it be true what Holly had said? If it was true, then it changed everything.

She turned to look as he stepped out onto the terrace. Her phone was in her hand like she'd been texting someone.

"I couldn't sleep," he told her.

"Me either," she said, and gestured for him to sit next to her. "It's so lonely in there, in that bedroom, on my own."

He sat close to her, as close as he dared. It was hot, and he could feel the heat of her thigh next to his. She was smoking and he watched her put the cigarette to her mouth, heard the soft puckering sound of her lips on the filter.

"Have you heard from Chris?" He nodded at her phone, and she answered no.

"It's over," she declared, and he should have felt happy. It was what he wanted, after all. But instead he felt confused, dissatisfied, his brain still reeling from all that Holly had told him. He was so desperately tired and the music kept rising in his brain, then falling back again, little teasing eddies.

"I knew it wouldn't last," she told him. "Nothing ever does."

She sounded deflated, a little forlorn, and he put his arm around her shoulder, felt her bare skin soft beneath his fingertips.

"Some things last," he said quietly, and she turned her face to him.

"You're the only one, Robbie. The only one who understands."

His heart was beating madly in his chest. He felt his courage rise. If it was true what Holly had said, then it would be all right, wouldn't it? Her skin was so soft beneath his touch. Slowly, he ran his fingers down her back.

"What are you doing?" she asked, nerves in her laughter, but she didn't move away, didn't tell him to stop.

He wanted to tell her but didn't dare speak the words. Instead he felt the nubs of her spine beneath his fingertips, the rounded curve of her buttocks on the hard plastic of the lounger.

"Robbie . . ." she said and he heard it all in her voice, the fear at what they were about to do, the undercurrent of excitement. It was like they were embarking on the greatest adventure of their lives and no one could know about it but the two of them. Their little secret. And as he leaned in to kiss her, he imagined he heard something — the rustle of leaves, the low breathing of a third party, someone watching them.

"Don't," he heard her say, but he pressed his mouth against hers anyway, knowing she didn't mean it, recognizing it as a last defense against what they both knew was inevitable.

"Stop," she said, and he felt her hand against his chest, pushing him away.

"What are you doing?" she asked, and he saw the confusion on her brow, realized she was angry.

"I thought . . ."

"You thought what?"

"That you wanted it too."

Her expression was horrified. It left him cold.

He opened his mouth to say something more but her phone buzzed on her lap and she glanced down at it.

"Who's it from?" he asked, not able to help himself, although part of him screamed out to ignore it, to stay in the moment, see where it might take them. Here they were, on the cusp of something amazing, the start of the first true passion in either of their lives, and he had to go and ask about some stupid text message.

"It's Philippe," she said, getting to her feet.

"Who?"

"A guy I met. At the restaurant."

"What does he want?"

"There's a party," she replied, reaching down for her bag, slotting her cigarettes back in.

"You're not going?" he asked.

She didn't answer, just stood up and smoothed down her skirt. She was still angry with him.

"Are you going to fuck him?"

He surprised himself with the sharpness of his words.

She stared down at him.

"I see," she said, frost coming into her tone. "Like that, is it?"

He shrugged, pressed a finger to the corner of his eye.

It didn't matter what she said. He knew she was going off to fuck that guy. He was sure of it, and the sureness of that knowledge made the hum in his head louder, the creaking strains of the string section sawing through his inner ear. And he was tired, so very, very tired. If he could only just sleep. . . .

"What would you know of it anyway," she went on. "You're just a child. What experience have you got?"

"Plenty."

She laughed. "Please, don't bother lying. It's so obvious you're a virgin. You've probably never even been touched by a girl."

"Bullshit. I've had plenty."

"Liar."

"I have."

"Name one."

"Claire Waters," he said — the first name that came into his head. Poor balding anorexic Claire with her viola balanced on her bony little shoulder. Debussy in his head again, the relentless press of the sea.

"And what did Claire Waters do for you?"

she asked, meanness in her voice, taunting him now. "Did she hold your little wiener? Did she take you in her mouth?"

The thought of Claire's spidery fingers gripped around his member made him shivery and nauseous. That and the viciousness in Zoe's voice, made mean by her hurt, fired up the symphony inside him, cymbals crashing in his head. He flung himself back against the headrest of the beach chair, forearms over his face so she couldn't see how much she'd hurt him.

"And as for that pathetic attempt just now."

"Don't," he warned her.

"Coming on to me. Your own sister."

"You're not my sister," he said, petulance trying to cover up his humiliation.

"What?"

"You're not. I know you're not."

He couldn't make her out but he knew, somehow, that she was smiling. When she spoke again, it was in a low whisper, but he felt her voice coming close to him, knew that she was leaning in.

"You thought one little piece of paper could clear the way for you, did you?"

"Shut up."

"All this time, I thought you were being nice to me because you're my brother, but actually, the whole time you've had a crush on me — fantasized about me." She said this in a kind of amazed voice, but there was detachment too, as if it didn't really affect her. It was not shock she was expressing but amusement. Everything was just a joke to her — even his love, delicate and shy, was something to be kicked around with hilarity.

"That's pretty sick," she whispered, leaning forward so that her mouth came close to his ear. "Sick and twisted." Every nerve in his body seemed to sit up in response, a prickling forest of nerve endings swarming his skin. "I think that's even worse than what your dad did to me."

He would never forgive her for this. Never. Whatever she had meant to him before, however much he had loved her, it could never be the same between them again.

Movement behind him. This time he didn't imagine it. A third party. A witness to what he had said, to what he had attempted to do. Zoe looked up.

Suddenly he couldn't bear it. He pressed his arms hard over his face and thought of every sad little sweaty encounter on the dance floor at Wesley, every look of amusement and apology he'd received before the girl turned away and started giggling with her friends. He thought of Melissa Lynch in the orchestra and that time he'd tried to kiss her, heard the surprise in her laughter, her voice in his head saying: "You're the kind of guy girls want as a friend, Robbie. That's the great thing about you. Knowing that we can be friends without things ever getting complicated by sex." Even poor Claire Waters who looked more dead than alive — Robbie knew, in his heart of hearts, that not even she would touch him. Zoe's words were in his head, the way she had looked at him. He knew that she had seen right through him, taken the measure of him. But what he had done — what he had tried to do — that it had been witnessed by someone else brought on an unbearable swelling of shame. The noise rose to a crescendo, all those screaming strings, the screech of brass, and he pushed his fingers deep into his ears. It made no difference. The music was inside his head. No matter what he did, he couldn't block it out.

Did he say her name? He cannot remember. All he remembers is the surprise on her face as she fell backward. The sound her head made as it met the edge of the diving board — a sharp crack like a small pistol going off. Her mouth opening but no sound coming out, nothing, only a gasp of air as she fell backward.

Blood bloomed from the side of her head, spreading out into the waters of the pool. His mother was in the water too, although he has no recollection of her arrival.

He could hear the whines of the violins, the jagged edge of the cellos bowing. How could he still hear them? Why hadn't they been silenced?

Arms went around him, the strong clasp of hands against his back.

"It will be all right," she whispered. "Everything will be all right now."

His father leaned over Zoe, for all the world like he was going to kiss her again. Robbie closed his eyes. Debussy playing in an eternal loop, the waves of the music like the waves of the sea, moving in tides, endlessly back and forth.

# CHAPTER 26
## GIRL UNKNOWN

The evening before Caroline and Holly fly to France, Susannah calls over with a bottle of Margaux — a Christmas present, she says. They sit at the kitchen island and drink it, just the two of them, trying to summon some semblance of festive cheer. There is no Christmas tree, no decorations.

Susannah, the one true friend who has stuck by her, leans on the counter and imparts her news.

"He has a new girlfriend."

Caroline absorbs the information with mild shock. She has not spoken to Chris since Zoe's death, and neither has David, apart from that first terrible phone conversation when they had called to break the news. His reaction, the instant outpouring of grief, was awful. He has not spoken to them since. Caroline reads into his silence the measure of accusation.

"Another infant," Susannah goes on, a

sneer in her voice. "Not quite as young as Zoe but not far off."

They met at a concert, apparently. It seems that, for all the coolness and hostility between Chris and Susannah, there is enough contact between them to keep her up-to-date with his love life.

"I'm glad," Caroline tells her. "At least he's moving on."

Susannah gives her a mild look of pity.

"No, he's not," she says, her voice softening. "He's stuck in the past. This is just his way of hiding from it."

For a while, Caroline had wondered if the shock of Zoe's death might have hurled the two of them back together. But she has learned that people deal with these things differently. Some try to carry on as normal, some cower behind a wall of silence. And some, like Chris, seek to replicate what has been lost, searching out some other young girl with blond hair and a cool feline gaze, a bold meddling streak kept hidden beneath a patina of innocence.

David is waiting for them in the Arrivals Lounge. He sees them come toward him, pulling their luggage behind them. They look tired, as if the journey has taken longer than the two hours of the flight. He goes to greet them and they embrace, all three of them together, a momentary triumvirate before they break apart. To anyone watching, their reunion must seem strange. Clearly, they are family, but despite the emotion of the reunion, there are no smiles. He reaches to take the bags, Caroline turns away and wipes at the corner of her eye, Holly stands with her hands in her pockets looking about her.

It has been four months since he has seen them in the flesh. A whole season has passed. Their corporeal presence is at once startling to him as well as comforting. Holly has grown taller. He is alive to all the changes in her — the new curves, the thinness of her face, grace in the way she carries herself. She catches him looking and he nods toward the exit.

"The car is this way," he tells them.

Sometime toward the end of the summer, they had made the decision to part. It was not named as a separation, more a side effect of the need to protect Holly. Both agreed that it was in her best interest to return home and continue her education as they had planned before all this happened. They wanted, inasmuch as it was possible now, for her to have a normal life. One of them needed to remain behind for Robbie. There was no argument, although that didn't mean there was no guilt. Weighing up the needs of one child over the other. Caroline would return to Dublin with Holly, while David stayed on.

As the car passes over the long meandering bridge back to the island, Caroline feels the tension in her limbs returning. That sick feeling is with her again, panic in her chest. She keeps her eyes trained on the sights outside the window, her hands tightly gripped in her lap. Strange to see those same fields and roads gray now in the dim light of a cold December day. When they had first come to Île de Ré, she had heard it described as a Mediterranean island that had somehow gotten lost in the Atlantic. During the summer months with the glittering turquoise waters surrounding it, and the yellow dust of the roads, geraniums and hollyhocks pouring color over every concrete surface, it was easy to believe that description. Now, with a chill wind whipping over the island from the Atlantic, trees bending to it, a spray of rain on the windshield, Caroline feels like she has come to a different island — hostile, unwelcoming, cold.

As he drives, David tells them about a

heron he has seen on his walks near the house. It is large, he says, estimating its wingspan to be six feet, maybe more. In his conversations at the market, he has discussed this bird, and there are some who have seen it too and believe it to be a great blue heron, very rare in these parts. David wonders aloud if it might have made a nest nearby. Briefly, he scans the horizon, as if looking for the bird in flight.

The villages they pass seem deserted — many of the houses look shut up for the winter, shutters bolted closed, window boxes empty. The little car gathers pace as it bypasses Saint Martin, heading west toward the village of Loix. Caroline doesn't ask David where the car came from — a small white Citroën, several years old by the looks of it. The car is just part of the changed picture. Everything feels different and strange. This car David is driving, his altered appearance — older, roughened, hardy — it serves as a reminder of the life he has carved out for himself during these months he has spent on the island without her. When he drives, it's not with the interest or relaxation of a tourist. He drives hunched forward, intent on getting to his destination. His eyes are fixed on the road, barely glancing past it to the landscapes that surround him.

Caroline takes all this in wordlessly. Four months have passed, punctuated with phone calls, e-mails, Skype. *We are strangers to each other,* she thinks, as the little car shuttles through an intersection, onto a long straight road over the salt flats.

"So, how is he?" Caroline asks.

They are alone in the house. Holly has gone to the village to buy bread, leaving the two of them sitting opposite each other at the kitchen table. It is too cold to sit on the terrace. The swimming pool has been drained. Stray leaves swish and scatter over the flagstones.

"He's the same."

"Has he said anything?"

"No."

"Anything at all?"

"Nothing, Caroline," he says, adding, "I'm sorry." As if it is his fault. In a way, it is.

He watches her taking that in, the way her lips purse, sees her bite down on her inner cheek, then look away. There is something controlled about her now, not like when it first happened and she was overcome with emotion. Fear, anger, bewilderment — he had sat at this very table and watched her sobbing uncontrollably, heard the scraping sound of air wrenched into her lungs, her face ruddy with tears. But that was then. Now, she is composed, and it makes her seem even more distant from him — the sternness of her control over feelings that had once ravaged her. He thinks about reaching across the table for her hand, decides not to.

They sit in silence for a moment, and he thinks of the bedrooms upstairs, his lonely occupancy of this house all these months. It is a relief when the iron gate clangs and they hear Holly stepping into the hall.

Over a lunch of chorizo stew that David has prepared, Holly updates her father as to her progress in school, the subjects she likes, the friends she has made. David asks, tentatively, has there been any trouble over what happened during the summer. He is referring to the brief flurry of media interest in the aftermath of Zoe's death. A couple of tabloids and one of the Sunday papers had shown particular interest in the more prurient details. It didn't help that one of the players in the incident was a journalist, another a lecturer who had made minor waves in the weeks before-hand over some colorful language employed during a radio interview. There was no door stopping or even minor harassment, but both David and Caroline had been fearful of the impact it might have on Holly when she returned to school. There had been a little teasing, and a lot of staring and pointed fingers, but the teachers were vigilant and Holly herself seemed capable of shrugging it off. There is still the fear that it might start up again once the trial begins in a few months' time, but for now they are all grateful for the respite.

A week before she flew to France with Holly, Caroline had come in her front door, picked up the post lying on the mat, and tossed it casually onto the shelf, before taking off her coat. Out of the corner of her eye, she noticed one of the letters slipping off the back of the shelf and sliding down behind the radiator. Getting a closer look, she saw there was a tiny gap between the wall and the lip of the shelf, a small sliver of space just wide enough for a slim envelope to slip through. Finding it impossible to retrieve the fallen letter, Caroline had rooted out David's toolbox and unscrewed the shelf from the wall. The letter was wedged behind the radiator. Unable to reach it with her fingers, she had taken a knife from the kitchen and tried to poke it out. Eventually, it had slipped down onto the floor along with some other post she hadn't known was there. One was a letter from a charity, another a credit card bill, but the last one bore the insignia of the university. Caroline looked at it and felt something drop in her stomach.

Opening it quickly, she scanned the text, dread spreading out to fill the pockets of air inside her. The missing letter. The one she had blamed Zoe for destroying. All that time it had been lying in the darkness. Perhaps Zoe had shoved it down there, but it was unlikely. Caroline knew it was nobody's fault, except perhaps her own.

Even now, back on the island, she isn't sure whether to tell David about the letter or not. What would be the point? So she carries the knowledge around inside her, a small additional burden alongside her guilt.

The juvenile detention center is not far from La Rochelle. The car journey takes a little over an hour. David and Holly spend another hour drinking coffee in a nearby café, looking in some shop windows, before they return to the car to wait. From where he is sitting behind the steering wheel, he can see the doors to the detention center open when Caroline comes out. The wind catches her hair, blowing open the flaps to her coat. She catches the sides and pulls them tight around her, head down, hurrying to the car. From the way she is holding herself, refusing to meet his eye, he can tell that it did not go well. She opens the door on the passenger side, sits, exhaling as she does so, as if she has been holding her breath the whole time she was in there.

"Well?" Holly asks, and Caroline shakes her head to say *No.*

David starts the car, pulls it out onto the main road, tries to imagine the hour spent in that little room, Caroline twisting the tissue in her hands, begging Robbie to talk to her, and all the while he sits still, hands cupping his elbows, keeping his gaze fixed on the windows up above and to the side, his face blank of expression, like the distant beatific gaze of some dead saint.

David drives and Caroline cries. He reaches out and she takes his hand and holds it in her lap.

Caroline blames herself for Robbie's silence. If that snap decision were reversed, undone, or done differently, she might have prevented it. Peculiar the way the body takes over from the mind in a situation like that. She remembers being in the water, holding Zoe in her arms, knowing that the girl was dead and there was nothing that could be done to change it. Caroline can almost see herself standing there, waist-deep in cool water, the strangeness of Zoe's limbs cast in a bluish light and seemingly at broken angles because of the refraction. She can see herself taking it in — the horrifying enormity of it — Robbie standing by the lip of the pool. She hadn't witnessed it — the push, the head cracking against the diving board — and yet it reverberates in her head, the realization of what he has done.

The decision happens in her body more than her head. Quickly, she drags Zoe over to the pool's edge. David is on the terrace now, but he makes no effort to help her, frozen within his own shock. Weighted down with lifelessness and water, it takes every ounce of Caroline's strength to push the body up onto the flagstones, before hauling herself up afterward. Still Robbie stands there. An echo of her own shrieking voice seems to hang in the air. *Jesus Christ, what have you done?* He says nothing. Are the words beginning to jam up inside him already? Swiftly, because there are lights coming on in the other houses, Caroline goes to her son, but she doesn't take him in her arms. She doesn't cradle his face in her hands, tell him it's all right, it will be okay,

505

murmur words of reassurance. She doesn't do anything like that.

"What happened?" she demands, her voice firm but low. She doesn't want the neighbors to hear. "Tell me quickly. What happened?"

He doesn't answer. Doesn't even look at her. His eyes are fixed on the pool beyond, his face bluish in the early morning light. Vaguely, she is aware of David, emerging from his trance. He seems to sleepwalk past toward the dark figure stretched out by the edge of the pool.

A car engine splutters somewhere out on the street. The sky is streaked orange with light. What to do? Call an ambulance? Call the police? For one crazy moment, she considers getting all of them into the car and fleeing the island, getting far away from the body lying stretched upon the terrace. A kind of madness is taking her over and she pulls back from it. She needs to think quickly, to put a story together and have them all agree on it. There isn't much time. The sun is rising now, and in the early morning light, dawn touching the innocence of flowers, the waters of the pool still and quiet, you might never think that a murder had just happened.

Murder. The word is in her head. She

seems to fill up with it. She has been spared the sight of the blow but some shadow of it suggests itself in her imagination. When she had come into the garden, it was the rocking water that she saw — the way Zoe's body lay lifeless, a thread of blood dark beneath the surface, water disturbed.

An accident, she decides. That is the only solution. She slipped and fell backward. A tragic fall.

Afterward, she will think back to these moments again and again — standing by the pool, lost in thought. This is where her deception began. Later, she would lie to police officers, to solicitors, to social workers. But all of the lies came undone in the end, once they got Robbie alone and he picked up a pen and wrote out his confession.

Caroline wonders if she had gone to him then, if she had taken her son in her arms and rocked him to and fro, the way she did when he was a small boy bearing some wound or injury, if she had done that, might she have stopped the sealing up of words inside him? Could she have prevented this burrowing down into a darkened place? In her life, she has known longing, but it is nothing compared to the visceral need she carries around inside her to just hear her son speak. How she misses the sound of his voice — it's an ache that's become lodged in her chest.

It was Holly who went to him. Putting her arms around her older brother, whispering something to him. He kept his arms apart from his sister while she held him, as if afraid of touching her, as if there were blood on his hands. His eyes remained fixed on Zoe. Caroline remembers looking back and seeing the figure of her husband, crouched over the body, his face close to Zoe's, peering at her intently, as if expecting that at any moment she might wake up.

The days pass and begin to form a pattern. They take turns visiting Robbie, in the same way they alternate the cooking. Rain lashes the island, keeping them indoors, and there is something comforting about being holed up with the fire lit, playing Scrabble, reading, talking. Slowly, a form of normality returns, and David feels himself relaxing into the company of his wife and daughter. In the months he was alone in this house he was often troubled by the notion that she was with him still — Zoe. In the hours of the night, when sleep failed to come, his thoughts would turn to her again, remembering how she was on that last day. Sometimes, alone in the house, chopping onions in the kitchen, or perusing one of Alan's books in the study, he thought he could hear the whisper of her voice or the pad of her footstep and he would turn to survey the room, half-expecting to see her standing there, her head to one side, biting down on a mischievous smile that keeps surfacing, as if it has all been an elaborate joke. Zoe, his daughter. He is certain of it now. Samples taken at the autopsy, her DNA clearly matched to his. It is beyond doubt and there is some small comfort to be taken from that.

He grieves for her all the same — a deep, sonorous, primeval grief. She had been in his life for less than a year, and yet his sorrow at her death is so much deeper — it's like she was always there, part of the meat and bones of him.

Some good news. They learn that the judge presiding over Robbie's case has given leave for him to be released temporarily for Christmas. David and Caroline must surrender their passports for the duration, and there are various rules they must abide by. The mood in the house changes, becoming almost celebratory. Caroline is giddy with excitement and channels it into preparations for Christmas, shopping and cooking, readying the house for her son's return. Two days is all they will have with him, but they are grateful for that.

The rain eases off; a chill wind remains. It is the day before Robbie's release. David suggests to Holly that they take the bikes out and cycle toward Saint Martin. He doubts the oyster bar is still open, but he needs to get out into the fresh air, cooped up inside the house for too long. He senses the same claustrophobia in Holly. Caroline's excitement is too large for the small rooms, making them feel cramped, and he has seen the tension in his daughter's face, despite her own gladness at her brother's homecoming. It crosses his mind that all this obvious fuss over Robbie might be making Holly feel that she has become invisible to them.

The bikes feel stiff from lack of use, but still David and Holly are glad to be outdoors, cycling beyond the village, through the fields toward the harbor where they plan to take the coastal path that runs along the northwest of the island. In the summer, these paths are busy with cyclists, tourists with trailers behind their bicycles like chariots, small children peeking out. Today, the path is deserted — David and Holly are the only people present. They reach the harbor, the walls dulled now that the summer sun has deserted them, and continue on over the flooded plains, the reeds growing high around them. They hear the lonely call of an occasional corncrake and pass a flock of geese idling in the water where there had once been a sailing school. The farms look deserted, the ground asleep. In winter the population of the island shrinks considerably. David feels it as they pedal past empty houses, closed shops. The wind is against them, and it is hard work pressing forward. In places the path is narrow with steep drops to the water on either side. A sudden gust makes his heart clench with fright, seeing Holly wobble on her bike. She puts out a foot to steady herself, stops, and turns to look at him.

"Do you want to go back?" he asks and she nods, tiredness etched into her features.

They turn their bikes around and walk back, side by side, the bicycles between them. David wonders whether Robbie might come for a cycle in the days he is home. He can't imagine his son gets much opportunity for exercise — certainly not vigorous outdoor exercise like this. He says as much to Holly and she agrees. Her tone is muted, but David feels his excitement at the prospect of Robbie's imminent return and he talks at length of his plans for those two days — what they might do. Holly listens without offering any opinions of her own.

They are nearing the harbor when a sudden movement in the water catches David's eye. He stops.

"Look," he says to Holly.

They stand together and watch the giant bird rise out of the reeds, its wings spreading as it takes to the air. The great blue heron — the one David has spotted on his walks a couple of times before — he watches it rise, beating hard against the biting wind.

"Look at it," he says in admiration. "Isn't it magnificent?"

For some reason, the bird rising like this, so proudly, makes him think of Zoe. But Holly isn't looking at the heron. She is looking at him, perfectly calm and yet there is flash of alarm in her eye.

"What is it?" he asks.

Still she looks. He realizes her silence, what he had read as tension, is actually something else. He can see that she has been building up to something — that she has been building up to it for months — waiting for the right moment to get him alone to tell him. And now, here they are in this deserted place, nothing around them, only land and water and the vast swath of metallic gray sky.

"I saw you," she says.

Her voice is low, calm. He hears the accusation in it.

"What are you talking about, sweetheart?"

"With her. With Zoe. After Chris left."

Her eyes are dark and unblinking. He feels the hardness of her stare.

"I saw you through the window. You were kissing her."

Something is building inside him, the slow beat of the heron's wings reverberating in his inner ear. He thinks again of the confusion on that night, the struggle within, how Linda came alive for him in that moment. The knowledge of what his daughter has witnessed, brief as it was, fills him with shame. He offers no defense — and the reason he does not is the realization that he is nearing the truth. The hard kernel is within reach.

"I told Robbie," she says. "I told him what I saw. What you did. How disgusting it was."

Her words sear through him.

"Holly . . ."

"I told him. . . ."

"It's not your fault," David says. He thinks of all the months she has carried the knowledge and guilt of what she had done. She seems so self-possessed, standing on the path, holding her bicycle steady at her side while the wind whips her hair around her head. But she is just a child — his child, and the need to protect her is strong.

"What happened to Zoe — what Robbie did — you mustn't blame yourself, sweetheart," he tells her. "You weren't to know what would happen."

He moves to embrace her, but something in the way she stiffens holds him back.

"Holly," he says again, a pleading note entering his voice.

Such pain has come into their home. He cannot bear to think of his daughter witnessing the shameful thing he has done. In the same way he can't bear to think of her shouldering the blame for Zoe's death.

A ghost of a smile passes over her face, a shadow of amusement.

"You don't understand, do you?" she says.

The wind is picking up now, and he has to strain to hear her.

"I did it."

"What?"

"Robbie didn't push her. I did."

His hands are on the handlebars and he feels the cold biting through his skin.

"Holly — sweetheart — it was an accident. Whatever it is you think you've done. . . . You're just a child." An innocent, he wants to say. But the way she is looking at him, the coldness of her expression, the pity in it, he realizes that he is the innocent. How blind he has been.

"I told him about the letter I had found," she says. "I told him she wasn't our sister, and he believed that made it all right, the feelings he had for her. He thought he loved her. He didn't understand how cruel she could be."

"Holly," he says hoarsely, the cold reaching up through his limbs, gripping his heart.

"It was disgusting, wrong. He couldn't see that. She had infected him. In the same way she had infected you."

"No," he says again, but his voice is barely audible. "It was an accident. You couldn't mean to . . ." The denial falters.

"She was just standing there by the edge, the board right behind her. It seemed so easy. So simple. She didn't even see me until the last minute. Didn't even know I was there."

The wind has calmed. On all sides they are surrounded by a flat calm grayness. He stares at her, and the strangest feeling comes over him: this girl, this daughter whom he has known from the moment she was born, this daughter that he has loved, cherished, held close to his heart — he looks at her now as he would a stranger. He realizes that he does not know her at all.

"So simple," Holly says again. "One shove and back she went. She didn't even scream."

"But Robbie . . . he confessed . . ."

This draws her attention and she looks at him sharply, consternation crossing her brow.

"I did it for him. Don't you see?" she says, insistence entering her tone. "The way she used him." Turning her gaze away, she continues in a quieter voice, as if her words are spoken not for David but for herself: "Robbie knows. He knows I did it for him. I put my arms around him and told him that everything would be all right. That we're safe. That nothing else matters."

He cannot think of what to say. Even if he could, speaking is an impossibility, all of it plugged up inside him, held fast by an overwhelming sensation of fear. His whole world is contracting away from him. Everything is strange.

"I know you think I should be sorry," she tells him, "but I'm not."

Coldness goes straight to the marrow of his bones.

"I'm glad she's dead," his daughter tells him. Her eyes narrow and she pulls her bike close. "She had it coming."

With that, she turns from him, his little

516

girl, swings her leg over the saddle, and steps on the pedal, pushing herself away.

He watches her cycling down the path. The words are beating about his head like wings. He looks up to the sky, scanning the horizon as if he might catch sight once more of that majestic bird, its wings spread wide, the proud angle of its head. The sky is empty. The ocean rumbles in the distance — waves beating onto cliffs unseen. Here where the land is flat, and the path twists and turns through marsh, all is quiet. He looks back toward the harbor. Holly has already rounded the bend and disappeared from view. He feels the weight of her words press down upon him, feels the heaviness of a new unwanted knowledge.

The wings of his grief beat in his chest. He thinks again of Linda's Angel of History, how it would like to awaken the dead, to piece together what has been smashed. Above him, the wind stirs. He looks again to catch a glimpse of the bird in flight. But nothing is there. No bird, and no angel. There is only him and the deep silence of the still water.

# ACKNOWLEDGMENTS

This book has been a team effort in many ways, and we are deeply grateful to the following: Kari Stuart and everyone at ICM Partners; Jonathan Lloyd and everyone at Curtis Brown; Barbara Jones and everyone at Henry Holt; Maxine Hitchcock and the team at Penguin UK/Michael Joseph; our dear friend Tana French, for her advice and support; finally, Aoife Perry and Conor Sweeney, whose patience, love, and humor kept us going throughout the writing of this book.

# ABOUT THE AUTHOR

**Karen Perry** is the pen name of the Dublin-based writers Paul Perry and Karen Gillece. PAUL PERRY is the author of a number of critically acclaimed books. A recipient of the Hennessy Award for New Irish Writing, he teaches creative writing at University College Dublin. KAREN GILLECE is the author of four critically acclaimed novels. In 2009 she won the European Union Prize for Literature (Ireland).

The employees of Thorndike Press hope you have enjoyed this Large Print book. All our Thorndike, Wheeler, and Kennebec Large Print titles are designed for easy reading, and all our books are made to last. Other Thorndike Press Large Print books are available at your library, through selected bookstores, or directly from us.

For information about titles, please call:
  (800) 223-1244

or visit our website at:
  gale.com/thorndike

To share your comments, please write:
  Publisher
  Thorndike Press
  10 Water St., Suite 310
  Waterville, ME 04901